Lavish praise for bestselling author
SUSAN JOHNSON

"Johnson uses her fertile imagination to blend a strong heroine, unbridled sex, and . . . history into unadulterated fun."

—*Publishers Weekly*

"Her romances have strong, intelligent heroines, hard, iron-willed men, plenty of sexual tension and sensuality and lots of accurate history. Anyone who can put all that in a book is one of the best!"

—*Romantic Times*

"The author's style is a pleasure to read and the love scenes many and lusty!"

—*Los Angeles Herald Examiner*

"She writes an extremely gripping story . . . with her knowledge of the period and her exquisite sensual scenes, she is an exceptional writer!"

—*Affaire de Coeur*

BANTAM BOOKS BY SUSAN JOHNSON

Pure Sin

Susan Johnson

BANTAM BOOKS
NEW YORK · TORONTO · LONDON · SYDNEY · AUCKLAND

PURE SIN

A Bantam Book / December 1994

ISBN 0-553-29956-5

Published simultaneously in the United States and Canada

Bantam Books are published by Bantam Books, a division of
Bantam Doubleday Dell Publishing Group, Inc. Its
trademark, consisting of the words "Bantam Books" and the
portrayal of a rooster, is Registered in U.S. Patent and
Trademark Office and in other countries. Marca Registrada.
Bantam Books, 1540 Broadway, New York, New York
10036.

PRINTED IN THE UNITED STATES OF AMERICA

OPM   20   19   18   17   16   15   14   13   12   11

Pure

Sin

Chapter One

❦

Virginia City, Montana
April 1867

She met Adam Serre on the night his wife left him.

He walked into Judge Parkman's foyer as she was handing her wrap to a servant, and they nodded and smiled at each other.

"Pleasant weather for April," he said as they approached the bunting-draped entrance to the ballroom together. He smiled again, a casual, transient smile.

"Is the temperature unusual?" Flora glanced up only briefly, intent on adjusting the length of her white kid glove on her upper arm.

Adam shrugged, his broad shoulders barely moving beneath his elegantly cut evening coat. His gaze was on the crowded ballroom visible through the decorated portal, which was patriotically swathed in red, white, and blue in honor of their host's recent appointment to the federal bench. "It's been an early spring," he said, searching for his host in the glittering assemblage. "But, then, the Chinook winds are unpredictable."

Both were curiously unaware of each other. Adam, for whom the previous few hours had been volatile, was still distracted. Flora Bonham, only recently arrived in Vir-

ginia City after a long journey from London, was looking
forward to seeing her father.

They were both late for the judge's celebration party.

But the sudden hush that descended on the ballroom as
they appeared in the doorway had nothing to do with
their tardy arrival.

"He actually came!"

"Good God, he's with a woman!"

"*Who's* the woman?"

An impassioned buzz of astonishment and conjecture
exploded after the first shocked silence, and Lady Flora
Bonham, only child of the noted archaeologist Lord
Haldane, wondered for a moment if she'd left her dress
undone and some immodest portion of her anatomy was
exposed before the expectant throng.

But after a moment of panic she realized all the guests'
gazes were focused not on herself but rather on her companion, and she looked up to discern the cause of such
avid fascination.

The man was incredibly handsome, she noted, with a
splendid classic bone structure and dark, sensual eyes that
held a tempting touch of wildness. But before any further
appraisal flashed through her mind, he bowed to her, a
graceful, fleeting movement, said, "Excuse me," and
walked away.

Almost immediately she caught sight of her father advancing toward her, a warm smile on his face, his arms out
in welcome. Her mouth curved into an answering smile,
and she moved into her father's embrace.

Two minutes had passed.

Perhaps less.

It was the first time she ever saw Adam.

"You look wonderful," George Bonham said as he held
his daughter at arm's length, the brilliant blue of his eyes
taking in Flora's radiant beauty. "Apparently the rough
ride from Fort Benton caused you no harm."

"Really, Papa," she admonished. "After all the outback
country we've lived in, Montana Territory is very civilized.
We had to walk only a dozen times to lighten the stage

through the deepest mud, the river crossings were un-
eventful, and the driver was moderately sober. After a hot
bath at the hotel, I felt perfectly rested."

He grinned at her. "It's good to have you back. Let me
introduce you; I've met most everyone in the last months.
Our host, the judge, is over there," he went on, gesturing.
"Come, now, let me show you off."

But Flora noticed as they joined a group nearby and
greetings were exchanged that the man who'd entered the
ballroom with her continued to elicit extraordinary interest. Every guest seemed alert to his movements as he
crossed the polished expanse of Italian parquet flooring.

No one had expected Adam to appear that night.

And as he strode toward his host, greeting those he
passed with a casual word, a smile, a sketchy bow for old
Mrs. Alworth, whose mouth was half-open in astonishment, a flurry of excited comment swirled through the
room.

"His wife left him today."

"Probably with good reason."

"Rumor has it she ran off with Baron Lacretelle."

"A mutual parting, then. Adam has dozens of lovers."

"He's a cool one to show up tonight as though nothing
untoward has happened in his life," an older man remarked.

"It's his Indian blood," a young lady standing beside
Flora whispered, her gaze traveling down Adam's lean,
muscled form, her voice touched with a piquant excitement. "They never show their feelings."

He looked as though he was showing his feelings now,
Flora reflected, watching the animated conversation between their host and the man who was attracting so much
attention. The bronze-skinned man smiled often as he
conversed, and then he suddenly laughed. She felt an odd,
immediate reaction to his pleasure, as though his cheer
was beguiling even from a distance.

"Who is he?" Flora asked, struck by his presence.

The young lady answered without taking her eyes from

the handsome long-haired man. "Adam Serre, Comte de Chastellux. A half-breed," she softly added, his exotic bloodlines clearly of interest to her. "He's even *more* available, now that his wife has left him."

"Available?" Did she mean marriage? Never sure of female insinuation, since her own conversation tended to be direct, she made a polite inquiry.

"You *know* . . . ," the pretty blond declared, turning to wink at Flora. "Just look at him." And her sigh was one of many—surreptitious and overt—that followed in the wake of Adam's progress that evening.

Flora was introduced to him much later, after dinner, after a string quartet had begun playing for those who wished to dance. When Judge Parkman said, "Adam, I'd like you to meet George Bonham's daughter. Flora Bonham, Adam Serre," she found herself uncharacteristically discomposed by the stark immediacy of his presence. And her voice when she spoke was briefly touched with a small tremor.

"How do you do, Mr. Serre?" Her gaze rose to meet his, and her breath caught in her throat for a moment. His beauty at close range struck her powerfully, as if she were imperiled by such flagrant handsomeness.

"I'm doing well, thank you," he said, his smile open and natural, the buzz of gossip that evening concerning his marriage apparently not affecting him. "Is this your first visit to Montana?"

"Yes," she replied, her composure restored. He seemed unaware of his good looks. "Montana's very much like the grasslands of Manchuria. Beautiful, filled with sky, rimmed with distant mountains."

The earl's daughter was quite spectacular, Adam thought with a connoisseur's eye, her mass of auburn hair so lush and rich and heavy, it almost seemed alive, her face dominated by enormous dark eyes, her skin golden, sun kissed, from so much time out of doors. He knew of her travels with her father; George Bonham had visited several of the Absarokee camps in the past months. "And good horse country too," he replied, "like the steppes of Asia. Did you see Lake Baikal?"

"Have you been there?" Animation instantly infused her voice.

"Many years ago."

"When?"

He thought for a moment. "I'd just finished university, so it must have been 1859."

"No!"

"When were you there?" He found the excitement in her eyes intriguing.

"June."

"We set up camp on the west shore near Krestovka. Don't tell me you were in the village and we missed you."

"We were a few miles away at Listvyanka."

They both smiled like long-lost friends. "Would you care for some champagne?" Adam asked. "And then tell me what you liked most about Listvyanka. The church, the countess Armechev, or the ponies?"

They agreed the church was a veritable jewel of provincial architecture. It was natural the artistic countess would have appealed more to a young man susceptible to female beauty than to a seventeen-year-old girl obsessed with horses. And the native ponies elicited a lengthy discussion on Asian bloodstock. They found in the course of the evening that they'd both been to Istanbul, the Holy Land, newly opened Japan, the upper reaches of the Sahara, Petersburg in the season. But always at different times.

"A shame we didn't ever meet," Adam said with a seductive smile, his responses automatic with beautiful women. "Good conversation is rare."

She didn't suppose most women were interested exclusively in his conversation, Flora thought, as she took in the full splendor of his dark beauty and power. Even lounging in a chair, his legs casually crossed at the ankles, he presented an irresistible image of brute strength. And she'd heard enough rumor in the course of the evening to understand he enjoyed women—nonconversationally. "As rare as marital fidelity, no doubt."

His brows rose fractionally. "No one's had the nerve to so bluntly allude to my marriage. Are you speaking of Isolde's or my infidelities?" His grin was boyish.

"Papa says you're French."

"Does that give me motive or excuse? And I'm only half-French, as you no doubt know, so I may have less excuse than Isolde. She apparently prefers Baron Lacretelle's properties in Paris and Nice to my dwelling here."

"No heartbroken melancholy?"

He laughed. "Obviously you haven't met Isolde."

"Why did you marry, then?"

He gazed at her for a moment over the rim of the goblet he'd raised to his lips. "You can't be that naive," he softly said, then quickly drained the glass.

"Forgive me. I'm sure it's none of my business."

"I'm sure it's not." The warmth had gone from his voice and his eyes. Remembering the reason he'd married Isolde always brought a sense of chafing anger.

"I haven't felt so gauche in years," Flora said, her voice almost a whisper.

His black eyes held hers, their vital energy almost mesmerizing; then his look went shuttered and his grin reappeared. "How could you know, darling? About the idiosyncrasies of my marriage. Tell me now about your first sight of Hagia Sophia."

"It was early in the morning," she began, relieved he'd so graciously overlooked her faux pas. "The sun had just begun to appear over the crest of the—"

"Come dance with me," Adam abruptly said, leaning forward in his chair. "This waltz is a favorite of mine," he went on, as though they hadn't been discussing something completely different. Reaching over, he took her hands in his. "And I've been wanting to"—his hesitation was minute as he discarded the inappropriate verb—"hold you." He grinned. "You see how blandly circumspect my choice of words is." Rising, he gently pulled her to her feet. "Considering the newest scandal in my life, I'm on my best behavior tonight."

"But, then, scandals don't bother me." She was standing very close to him, her hands still twined in his.

His fine mouth, only inches away, was graced with a genial smile and touched with a small heated playfulness. "I thought they might not."

"When one travels as I do, one becomes inured to other people's notions of nicety." Her bare shoulder lifted briefly, ruffling the limpid lace on her décolletage. He noticed both the pale satin of her skin and the tantalizing swell of her bosom beneath the delicate lace. "If I worried about scandal," she murmured with a small smile, "I'd never set foot outside England."

"And you do."

"Oh, yes," she whispered. And for a moment both were speaking of something quite different.

"You're not helping," he said very low. "I've sworn off women for the moment."

"To let your wounds heal?"

"Nothing so poetical." His quirked grin reminded her of a teasing young boy. "I'm reassessing my priorities."

"Did I arrive in Virginia City too late, then?"

"Too late?" One dark brow arched infinitesimally.

"To take advantage of your former priorities."

He took a deep breath because he was already perversely aware of the closeness of her heated body, of the heady fragrance of her skin. "You're a bold young lady, Miss Bonham."

"I'm twenty-six years old, Mr. Serre, and independent."

"I'm not sure after marriage to Isolde that I'm interested in any more willful aristocratic ladies."

"Perhaps I could change your mind."

He thoughtfully gazed down at her, and then the faintest smile lifted the graceful curve of his mouth. "Perhaps you could."

"How kind of you," Flora softly replied in teasing rejoinder.

"Believe me, kindness is the last thing on my mind at the moment, but people are beginning to stare. It wouldn't do to besmirch your reputation on your first

night in Virginia City. And I like this waltz, so allow me
the honor of your first dance in Montana." He was avoiding temptation as he swung her out onto the floor, cutting
short a conversation that had turned too provocative.

But he found dancing with the alluring Miss Bonham
only heightened his sensational response to her, and everyone in the room noticed as well. A palpable heat ema-
nated from the beautiful couple twirling across the floor,
and people turned to watch as they passed.

She wore violet tulle, elaborately ornamented with
moss-green ribbon and ivory lace, a dazzling counterpoint
to her pale skin and auburn tresses and to the severe black
of Adam's evening clothes. The diaphanous froth of her
gown and her lush femininity were a counterpoint as well
to Adam's harsh masculinity. And later as they danced,
when a silky tendril of Flora's hair fell loose from the
diamond pins holding her coiffure in place, Adam bent his
head and lightly blew it aside. At his intimate, audacious
gesture, simultaneous indrawn breaths from scores of
wide-eyed guests seemed to vibrate through the room.

And molten heat flared through Flora's senses.

Even as she shut her eyes against the exquisite sensation
of his warm breath on her neck, she felt his arm tighten
around her waist, as if he too were susceptible to urgent
desire. And she understood suddenly why women pursued
him. Beyond his obvious beauty he offered a wild, reckless
excitement; oblivious to exacting decorum and every
watchful eye, he did as he pleased. Heedless, rash, direct.
And she felt him hard against her stomach.

She was far too beautiful, too impetuously unconstrained, and even as he moved against her in the dance,
his arousal pressed into her yielding body, he struggled to
retain a pragmatic grip on reality. Only short hours ago
he'd vowed to give wide berth to pampered patrician
women. But she's not precisely pampered, his libido
pointed out, allowing him the rationalization he craved.
She's lived in tents in far corners of the world most of her
life. There. It's all right, his heated voice of unreason said.
And as his erection swelled, he found himself surveying

possible discreet exits from the room. "Can you leave?" he bluntly asked, deliberately omitting the familiar seductive words. He didn't wish to be so aroused by her. His irrational, heated desire disturbed him; he would prefer she refuse.

"For a short time," she said as bluntly as he.

His surprise showed.

"If it will ease your discomfort," Flora softly said, her dark eyes touched with violet squarely meeting his, "*I* could seduce *you.*"

"Do you do this often, then?" His voice was cool, but his grip tightened at her waist.

"Never." The brush of her thighs against his as they turned in graceful slow loops around the floor seemed patent contradiction.

"Should I be honored?" A certain insolence colored his words.

"If you wish," she tranquilly said. "I prefer the concept of mutual pleasure."

His reaction to her last two words was immediate. She could feel it. "Could I interest you in a view of Judge Parkman's new garden?" Adam brusquely queried, turning them toward the terrace doorway.

"It depends on the view."

His head snapped around from a swift survey of an exit route, and he found her smiling up at him.

"I'm serious," she said, but a teasing impudence gleamed from her eyes.

"I'll see what I can do," he gruffly declared. "Do you need a wrap?" A nearly forgotten politesse.

"How chivalrous," she said with a smile, "but I think we're both comfortably warm. It must be the dancing."

"Or *uncomfortably* warm," he muttered, gazing down at her with heated black eyes. "And dancing has nothing to do with it." They'd reached the border of the dance floor, and with an edginess Flora found equally tantalizing and disturbing, he wordlessly guided them around two potted palms to the terrace door, pushed it open, and pulled her outside.

He stood on the flagstones, his hand firmly gripping hers, scrutinizing the garden that was almost bare of flowers this early in the spring; the foliage of hedge and bower consisted only of half-formed leaves. A decision apparently made, Adam turned toward the back of the stone mansion, moving less swiftly so Flora could keep up. Then, leaving the terrace, he walked across the carefully raked gravel of the back drive into the dusky entrance to the carriage house. With the large double doors open, the spring moonlight illuminated the front third of the interior, which Adam carefully noted before moving farther back into the shadows.

He seemed to know where he was going, for he strode surefooted to a landau set against the wall, abruptly swept her into his arms, and deposited her in a tumble of violet tulle on the wide satin-upholstered seat.

"Should we put the top up?" Flora murmured, stripping off one long kidskin glove as Adam unlatched the lacquered door and stepped into the open carriage.

He shook his head. He'd selected the landau for its roominess and open top; he'd made love in enough closed carriages to know the merits of space. "Will your father look for you?" he asked as he seated himself beside her and slid into a comfortable sprawl.

"Not since I turned eighteen and came into my own fortune." Her smile was pale in the dim light.

"You're very unusual," he softly said, gazing at her.

"You are too. You must know that." She was unbuttoning her second glove at the wrist.

"One's constantly reminded," he dryly said, stretching his arms above his head, then relaxing again. "Acting Governor Meagher and his drunken volunteers are currently dividing their time between Con Owen's Saloon and their inebriated pursuit of Indians." He shifted his posture slightly. Restless, he was questioning the wisdom of his libido-driven actions. "My clan is trying to stay out of their way."

"You sound resigned."

"Armed and alert, actually. It's safer."

"Are you in Virginia City often?"

He shook his head again. "I prefer my ranch, but Judge Parkman's a friend." He sighed. "And of course Isolde was added reason."

"Has she truly gone off with the baron?" Flora's voice was hesitant as she slid the second glove free.

He didn't answer for several moments, and Flora thought she'd overstepped politeness again. Then he laughed, a warm, intimate sound in the darkness. "I certainly hope so." He turned to her and, raising his hand, touched her cheek lightly with the back of his fingers. "This is a mistake. You shouldn't be here. I shouldn't be here. Our garden promenade wasn't a sensible idea. We should go back inside."

"We should." Her voice was hushed, her mouth only inches away as she let her gloves slip through her fingers to the carriage floor.

He drew in a deep breath of restraint. "Lord, you're tempting. . . ." Her skin glowed in the shrouded moonlight. Her shoulders, unsheathed arms, the swell of her breasts above the low neckline of her gown, seduced the eye; the opulent jasmine scent of her perfume enticed his senses.

"Kiss me," she whispered, because she couldn't help herself any more than he.

"No." But he didn't move.

"Then I'll kiss you."

He could feel her breath light on his lips and hard, insistent desire pounding in his brain. "How much time do we have?" he softly said, capitulating.

"You know better than I." Her words held a hushed double entendre.

"It's not going to be enough time." He felt like staying with her, in her, over her, possessing her for limitless hours—a startling, unique sensation he consciously ignored. "You're not sixteen now. . . ." Wary, guarded, it was a masculine question. And his last, he knew, regardless of her answer.

If she responded, he didn't hear, because her hands

were suddenly on his face, drawing him closer, and when her lips touched his, he was already unbuttoning his trousers.

He moved her under him swiftly, pushing her voluminous skirt and petticoats aside, his mouth hard on hers, the sharp-set urgency of his need astonishingly matched by hers. She tried to help him unbutton his trouser buttons, but he said a harsh "No," against her lips, impatiently brushing her hands aside as impediments to his haste. When his erection was free, he entered her immediately because he couldn't wait a second longer, and then he moved her upward on the cushioned seat, half lifting her, half driving her higher by sheer force of penetration. She cried out, breathy, wild, impaled, and she fiercely clung to him as exquisite sensation quivered through every nerve and receptor, deep inside her and in her brain and fingertips and on the hot surface of her skin.

In the darkness of the carriage house, the elegant landau rocked and swayed, only the sounds of lovemaking and squeaking springs audible as Adam Serre indulged his partner's wanton desire and his own turbulent lust. He whispered softly to her in his mother's language, astonishing words he'd never said to a woman before. And she kissed him hungrily, as if she were greedy for the taste as well as the feel of him.

There was no explanation for the ravenous need she incited in him, no previous guidelines in his memory to measure such overwhelming desire. But he knew he didn't want it to end, these sensations that were inexplicably acute, intense. As if a fever possessed him. Don't stop, his mind recklessly ordered—never stop. . . . The rhythm of his lower body echoed the unbridled litany reverberating through his brain. His breathing was harsh, his eyes shut against the ecstasy bombarding his nerves as he drove into her voluptuous body, submerged himself in her flesh until they both trembled desperately on the brink. And sensational moments later, he'd slowly withdraw only to plunge in again and then again with heedless, unrestrained fury.

Flora met him eagerly with her own fierce arousal. She should have known when she first saw his eyes that he was capable of this wildness. And she sighed with pleasure and kissed him and purred in contentment. After their initial frenzy had abated, he partially undressed her, unlacing, unhooking, untying so her full breasts gleamed pale under his hands, so he could taste their sweetness. "It's my turn," she said after a languorous time, climbing on top of him, reaching for a diamond stud on his shirt front. And when she'd divested him of those garments in her way, he found her small hands inventive, and ultimately her mouth when her warm tongue licked a sensational path downward.

Like adolescents they were frantic in their intoxication, insensate to the vulnerability of their locale, focused on the lavish joys of arousal. They made love in numerous and varied positions, versatile, imaginative, playful. And much later when Adam rolled Flora over on the seat and began to mount her from behind, she looked up over her naked shoulder and, faint from another recent climax, whispered, "You needn't . . . be . . . so selfless."

Already plunging into her sleek passage, he buried himself inside her before he said on a suffocated breath, "I'm not doing it for you." And holding her waist firmly between his large hands, he drove in deeper.

She moaned, her soft cry trailing away in a breathless, heated sigh.

Neither seemed to breathe for a lengthy interval, too intent on registering the minute degrees of pleasure inundating their senses. But their mutual pleasure eventually came to an end, because Adam hadn't completely abandoned caution even in the extremity of passion. And they'd been absent too long. So as Flora began peaking once again, he allowed himself release at last, forcing her wider, penetrating so deeply, she whimpered in heated response, and he joined her in tumultuous orgasm, pouring into her in shuddering ecstasy.

Only the rasping rhythm of Adam's breath filled the silence, for neither was capable of speech. And then Flora gently touched his sweat-sheened forehead—a small, possessive gesture as he lay above her. "You're remarkable . . . ," she murmured. Sublime contentment drummed through her senses. "I think I'm going to like Montana." She felt him suddenly tense under her hands and softly added, "Don't be alarmed. That was a thank-you, no more."

She could hear rather than see his grin in the shadowed interior. "Consider it my distinct pleasure, ma'am. I'd forgotten how friendly the English could be."

"I'm half-American too."

Ah, he thought, that was the extraordinary heat. And charming frankness. But despite a powerful temptation to stay comfortably submerged inside her delicious warmth, Adam recognized the ticking away of their last secret moments. He kissed her lightly, then said with genuine regret, "We have to go back in." And easing himself off, he sat up and began buttoning his shirt. "You probably need my handkerchief," he courteously offered, reaching into his pocket to pull out the plain linen square.

"How sweet," Flora whispered, drowsy from the sustained violence of their passion, reclining still, disinclined to move, her body throbbing in small, blissful pulsations. 'But why don't I use one of these dozens of petticoats I'm wearing instead?" She stretched languidly. "Later, though . . . ," she murmured. "When I have more energy . . ."

"Now, *bia*," he softly contradicted, the Absarokee endearment uttered in a husky whisper. "We don't have time for you to revive." His evening clothes were speedily restored to order—a specialty honed to perfection during years of casual seduction. Equally adept at undoing ladies' petticoats, he managed to untangle Flora from one petticoat, lifting her easily to expedite the procedure. But when he began to wipe away the residue of their lovemaking, issues of time suddenly lost their urgency. Contemplation of her silky thighs and enticing bottom, the enchanting promise she offered in her languid pose was almost more than he could endure. Shutting his eyes briefly against his fierce urges, he drew in a sharp breath, said, "Sorry," on an explosive exhalation, then kissed her gently and set her carefully on the seat opposite him. "Stay there now. This isn't worth a scandal in your life." But when he caught a glimpse of her shameless, alluring smile, he laughed at her coquettish impudence. "I really wish I could," he added with a grin, "but trust me on this one."

Beneath the teasing and lassitude, Flora understood his dilemma. "Maybe later," she softly said, and began arranging her gown into some semblance of propriety.

Ten minutes later, their clothing composed, they approached the terrace door. The spring night was cool enough to keep the other guests inside; no one else had chosen to brave the chill temperature. Stopping at a secluded corner, Adam checked Flora's appearance one last time. Patting a ribbon in place, tucking a stray curl behind her ear, he smiled at her like a fond father. "Now, stay by my side, and no one will dare say anything to you."

"Are you dangerous?"

"Not to you." His voice had changed. She hadn't heard that warding-off tone before.

"Would you harm someone over this?" It was a sudden, curious thought.

"Your father, you mean? No." His voice had returned to its normal nonchalance.

"But you might injure someone else? Surely our time together was harmless."

"Of course it was. Don't worry. We shouldn't have any problems. No one ever challenges me directly." That warding-off voice again.

"Why?" Her question was automatic; she already knew the answer just looking at him.

He paused, wondering how to respond to a woman he barely knew. Complex reasons impelled his enemies, not the least of which was his Absarokee blood. But his adversaries rarely confronted him face-to-face and never without a small army at their back. "It's not easily explained," he simply replied.

"Have you killed people?" Her brows had unintention-
ally drawn together in a faint scowl.

"It doesn't really matter, right now." His smile was remarkably bland. This wasn't the time to analyze their disparate worlds. "All we have to do *now*, darling," he softly
said, "is walk in, ignore everyone staring at us, and see
that your father is assuaged."

"Papa will be fine," she quietly said, sure of her father's
unconditional support.

"You can do no wrong?"

"Something like that."

"He may not so easily excuse me."

"He excuses all my friends."

It turned out Adam Serre was right about his authority.
Although numerous glances took note of their entrance,
of Flora's tousled hair and the occasional crushed bow on
her gown, their leisurely passage across the ballroom went
unobstructed. No one spoke to them.

"I'm impressed," Flora whispered as another guest
smiled at them in acknowledgment of Adam's nod. She
grinned. "And you're not even armed."

"*Now* I'm not armed," he quietly said. "Everyone understands the distinction." He didn't smile back. And she
wondered at the reputation of a man who could intimidate
so effortlessly.

"Could you take any woman from this room with equal
impunity?"

He glanced down at her, not with surprise but with
sudden recognition, as if his thoughts had been elsewhere.
"I don't coerce women."

"That's not what I meant."

"Yes, then." Spare, unornamented words, softly uttered. "Are you sure your father won't be upset?" he
added as if the incongruous subjects shared some common
sentiment.

He was genuinely concerned, Flora thought, fascinated
by his complexity, or maybe simply distracted.

"Perhaps you could intimidate him too," she teased, allowing him the distraction.

A faint smile appeared on his handsome face. "I'll leave that to you, *bia*. You're fierce enough for both of us."

She found herself blushing.

"I'm not complaining," he said, amused at her embarrassment. "Believe me."

"I don't have any complaints either, Monsieur le Comte," she lightly replied.

"I don't use my title here. But thank you." He touched her fingers lightly as they lay on his arm. "Thank you for everything."

When they found George Bonham in the billiard room, their conversation had nothing to do with their disappearance from the party, but rather with the earl's plans to purchase horses from Adam. After some discussion of diverse schedules, arrangements were made to meet at Adam's ranch in two weeks.

Adam left Judge Parkman's home very soon afterward. He found it impossible to socialize with equanimity, the extraordinary sensations he'd experienced in the carriage house difficult to disregard. He found he no longer cared to smile and talk of trivialities. Troubled by his singular reaction to Flora Bonham, he wished to escape her presence and his disturbing feelings.

Perhaps the contentious style of Isolde's departure today had taken its toll on his emotions, he thought, exiting the mansion with relief, or maybe he was responding with his normal weariness to fashionable society. Perhaps he simply missed his home and daughter. The only thing he was certain of was that he wished to leave Virginia City immediately, tonight. And forget Flora Bonham. After his wretched experience with marriage, his interest in women was purely physical, and Flora Bonham, despite her fascinating conversation and captivating sensuality, didn't fall into the category of transient pleasures. Unmarried women like Flora generally expected more than an amorous interlude. Or if they didn't, their fathers generally did.

And he wasn't inclined to be anyone's gentleman suitor.

But he found himself bothered on the long ride home by her statement that her father excused all her friends.

What exactly did that mean?

How many men had there been?

Was she as sensational with all her "friends"?

He shook away the heated anger and the damnable longing, forcing the nagging question aside when it slipped past his defenses. He didn't need her, he reminded himself. He didn't want her. He didn't want any women after so recently delivering himself from a miserable marriage. And now he had all the time in the world to forget her.

Chapter Two

~❧~

In the following days Flora found Adam Serre much on her mind. Despite the bustle and activity of packing for their journey to the Absarokee[1] villages, evocative memories of the night at Judge Parkman's keenly affected her concentration. Normally so efficient that her father had long ago relinquished the organization of their expeditions to her, she found herself duplicating lists, forgetting simple tasks, conducting interviews for needed staff with a curious disregard for replies. All because she would suddenly see Adam's smile in her mind, or remember the feel of his hard body or the sensation of his warm mouth on hers, and any continuity of thought would abruptly cease.

On more than one occasion her father remarked on her unusual abstraction.

"There's just so much to do, Papa," she would evasively reply, forcing her mind back from heated memory, aware of the true reason for her preoccupation. Equally aware that such ardent infatuation was a novelty in her life. She'd never been so intensely attracted to a man. As a beautiful woman familiar with male adulation, she'd long ago acquired the habit of casually dealing with lovesick suitors, earning herself the sobriquet Serene Venus within London's elite society. Her affairs of the heart were conducted with playful nonchalance, detached from excessive feeling—unlike her current tempestuous emotions apropos the hot-blooded Comte de Chastellux. With him an overwhelming, irrepressible lust impelled her. She smiled, thinking how appropriate the word in conjunction with a man so skilled, so spectacular in stamina, so reckless that he made love in dangerous proximity to a houseful of guests. Her smile widened as she sat at the small *bonheur-du-jour* in her sitting room, the lists before her forgotten.

She was looking forward to summer on the Yellowstone.

In the days since Adam had returned to his ranch, he took unalloyed pleasure in the tranquillity of life without Isolde. Always a devoted father, he and his daughter Lucie became inseparable. She rode with him when he surveyed the horses in the summer pastures or observed the training runs of the thoroughbreds. Perched on his lap or shoulders, she kept him company at the daily meetings with his men and household staff. With the carte blanche of a favored child, she added her voice to the scheduling discussions, her interruptions politely accepted by her father, his replies always calculated to bring forth a happy three-year-old smile.

From Adam's first day back from Virginia City, Cook's menu had been adjusted to cater to a child's palate, and dinner was served again unfashionably early so Lucie could join her father. After dinner, in lieu of the former de rigueur period of the last few weeks in the drawing room, when a sulky or querulous Isolde had presided over the tea table, Adam and Lucie went directly to the nursery and played together until Lucie's bedtime.

No one had seen Adam so happy in ages.

Like the old days before his marriage, everyone close to him observed.

But beneath the surface a private distraction compromised this life of unruffled well-being, for persistent visions of Flora Bonham continued to tantalize him. He found himself dreaming of her at night, the scenes invariably those of unrestrained passion, and he'd taken to rid-

ing out after Lucie fell asleep, avoiding his bed and the
searing images. The cold night air helped, and the wide,
quiet expanse of moonlit countryside. He felt free from all
impediments in the untrammeled, limitless land, one with
nature under the star-studded sky, absolved from intem-
perate desire. And later in the foothills on the northern
boundary of his holdings where he always rested his
horse, he'd gaze down on the darkened plain with a satisfying sense of accomplishment. He could see for miles, all
the rolling country lush with green grass, enough for his
herds, for those of his clan, enough to see the horses
through the winter. After years of hard work, his ranch
was thriving, becoming profitable, his racehorses were acquiring a reputation on the racetracks here and in Europe,
and if the persistent greed of the cattlemen pressing the
borders of his property didn't develop into an all-out war,
he could build a contented, peaceful life here for Lucie
and himself.

Always more cool-headed after the hard ride, his rest-
lessness and hunger for the earl's daughter having dissipated, he was able to dismiss the intoxicating dreams as
impractical illusions. Flora Bonham was just a hotter-
than-hell female, lush, voluptuous, sensual—but best forgotten. He didn't need any complications in his life.

With travel uncertain due to flooding spring rivers,
George Bonham had allowed ample time for the trip
north to Adam's ranch. But the weather had cooperated—
so much so, that not only did the earl's party arrive without mishap or delay—they arrived one day early at the
ranch on the Musselshell.

Only to find their host absent.

He was out tracking some horses stolen from his eastern herd, they were told by his housekeeper as a full reti-
nue of staff came out to greet them. But Adam was
scheduled to return for his meeting with the earl, Mrs.
O'Brien explained in a lilting Irish brogue, and in the
meantime, she finished with a beaming smile and a bobbing curtsy, they were entirely welcome.

Adam's home was handsomely situated against low
foothills covered with dark pines. One of the many
streams flowing into the Musselshell ran through the
grassy meadow in front of the house. Orchards had been
planted to the west, the chartreuse tracery of new leaves
like feathery down from a distance. The mansion, built of
native stone, was vast in dimension; the exterior sprawling
with terraces and verandas; the roof, moss-covered slate,
verdant green in the cool shadow of the pines; the whole
framed by two spiral-staired turrets reminiscent of Blois.
A solid French château in the wilds of Montana.

They met Lucie soon after their arrival, when she
pulled her reluctant nursemaid into the drawing room
where Flora and her father were having tea. "I'm Lucie,"
she informed them with a smile, standing just inside the
doorway, her large dark eyes surveying them with childish
candor. "This is Baby DeeDee," she added, lifting up the
porcelain-faced doll she held by its golden hair. She spoke
English with a faint French accent. "Papa's gone," she
declared with an emphatic shake of her shiny black ring-
lets.

The young maid, obviously embarrassed by her
charge's intrusion, tried to pull her from the room, but
Lucie shook her hand free. Breaking away, she ran across
the broad expanse of pastel carpet in a flurry of yellow
muslin, came to a skidding stop before the tea table,
pointed at a strawberry crème cake with a chubby hand,
and said, "I'd like that, please."

Flora handed her the cake without hesitation, instantly
sealing their friendship, and when she went on to ask the
young girl to join them for tea, Lucie's sudden smile reminded her of a similar quirked grin.

Lucie had her father's eyes too, very dark, heavily
lashed, riveting in their beauty, and his same directness of
speech. Sitting very straight on a Louis Quinze chair upholstered in coral satin, her short legs barely reaching the
perimeter of the cushioned seat, beaded moccasins incongruously peeking out from under her dainty muslin skirt,
she proceeded to entertain them with a child's-eye view of

ranch life in Montana Territory while she systematically
demolished the tray of sweets. Her vocabulary was precocious for her age, though Flora quickly realized a surfeit
of personal staff no doubt accounted for her language
skills. The drawing-room doorway had quickly filled with
hovering nursemaids.

"I'm almost four," she said when asked her age, holding
up the proper number of fingers. "How old are you?" she
inquired pointing a whipped-cream-covered finger at
Flora and her father. When she heard their ages, she
thought for a moment before declaring, "I think Bellemere and Maman are like that. But Maman went to
France to live with Bellemere. She hates the dirt, Papa
said. And we don't have pav-ed streets," she went on, pronouncing the word with two syllables. "I like my pony
Birdie, and I've never seen a pav-ed street. Have you?"

"The city I live in has many paved streets, but I like the
country too," Flora replied. "What color is your pony?"

"She's a paint. My cousin Raven taughted me to ride.
Do you want to see her? Birdie likes cookies." Grabbing a
handful of cookies, she'd already begun sliding off her
chair.

George Bonham politely declined the invitation, preferring a peaceful brandy and a cigar after their long ride,
so Flora went alone with her small guide. Lucie brought
Flora up to the nursery first—because she needed her riding boots, she said with the seriousness of a well-learned
injunction—and after exchanging her moccasins for boots,
she proceeded to introduce Flora to all her nursemaids—
who were hovering now in a different locale; her favorite
toys merited introductions as well. She was enchanting
like her father, Flora thought, charming with ease as she
took Flora in tow, and, beginning with Birdie, gave her a
grand tour of the ranch, the countryside, and the spacious
house.

The progression of the tour was informal, dictated by
Lucie's schedule and fancy, and in the process of looking
for Lucie's misplaced riding quirt the next day, Flora

found herself standing in the doorway of Adam's bedroom.

A sudden heat raced through her senses, uncontrollable, heedless of circumstance, and she wondered at her loss of restraint. It was only an empty room, she told herself, an austere chamber with hardly any indication of the man who inhabited it. But she felt the hot sensation regardless of the monkish atmosphere, as if Adam were standing before her, reaching out to touch her.

Lucie was chattering at her side, tugging at her hand to guide her within. And as Flora stepped over the threshold into the room, she was struck by his fragrance. It pervaded the large chamber, subtle, seductive; his skin and hair smelled like this—of pine and mountain sage, with undertones of bergamot.

"See," Lucie was saying, and Flora shook away the overpowering weight of fragrant memory. "That's me."

A small pastel portrait on a gold easel held a place of honor on a bedside table, and an exquisite rendition of Adam's daughter smiled up at her. The polished wood surface was otherwise bare, as was the matching table on the opposite side of the oversize mahogany bed. Her gaze dwelled for a moment on the plain white seersucker coverlet crisply tucked under the pillows and around the mattress, the corners almost military in their preciseness, and she found herself jealously wondering how Isolde looked against such pristine purity. She'd seen Isolde's room yesterday when Lucie had brought her in to show off the shiny green eyes on the gilded swans decorating her mother's bed; Flora had taken note of the fashionable Winterhalter portrait over the mantel of a delicate woman with flaxen hair and a sultan's ransom in diamonds adorning her bosom. Adam had married a very beautiful woman.

Isolde's rooms were ornamented lavishly in swathed silk and gold tassels, gilded stucco work shimmering on the woodwork, the walls richly covered in rose damask. The suite was filled with pillow-strewn furniture upholstered in pale silks, expensive porcelains and bric-a-brac in lavish array adorned every tabletop, small gold-framed paintings of bucolic landscapes covered the walls. The scene was reminiscent of a stage set, a rococo palace. Or an expensive bordello.

In sharp contrast to such drama, Adam's room held only a glass-fronted bureau, a small desk, a leather sofa before the fireplace, a Feraghan carpet in subdued shades of navy and wine, the massive bed. A utilitarian room stripped of personality—or perhaps devoutly personal.

If compatibility was measured in decorating tastes, Flora thought, she wondered that Adam and his wife had survived marriage for so long.

"Come see Papa's knives," Lucie coaxed, interrupting Flora's jaundiced speculation, already moving toward the dressing-room door. And moments later, when Lucie threw open the doors of one of the built-in armoires lining two walls of the narrow room, Adam Serre stood revealed. Arranged on shelves or hanging from brass hooks inside the double doors, a colorful array of decorated sheaths held dozens of knives. Bone-handled, bronze-handled, large, small, plain, and embellished—a lethal collection of exquisite Indian craftsmanship.

"How spectacular," Flora declared, struck powerfully by the latent force, each weapon potently functional. This wasn't a glass-cased museum display.

"These are pretty too," Lucie went on, moving to the next cabinet. "Maman says they're barbaric, but Papa and I like them." Two more doors opened as she released the latch, and before Flora's fascinated gaze appeared a stunning display of fringed, beaded, fur-draped leather clothing. Lavishly decorated moccasins lined the floor of the armoire. The hanging garments were constructed of pale, almost white leather or buttery yellow skins soft as heavy silk, ornamented with ermine tails, wolf tails, liquid leather fringe, embellished with elaborate beaded designs on shirtsleeves, shoulders, sweeping down the length of fringed leggings. Obviously Adam Serre was proud of his Absarokee heritage.

"They're very lovely," Flora said, her voice subdued

before such magnificence. She understood the lengthy,
skilled process necessary to produce clothing of this quality.

"This is Papa's special spirit sign," Lucie declared,
pointing at the stylized portrayal of a wolf repeated within
a fretwork border decorating a shirtfront. "And here too,"
she added, pulling out a sleeve with a beaded medallion of
a wolf head in black on red. "His people call him Tsé-
ditsirá-tsi." She spoke the words with the quiet sibilance
of the Absarokee language. "It means 'Dangerous Wolf.'
Although Papa is ever so nice, even if Maman doesn't
think so." She sighed a curiously grown-up sigh for a
child so young. "Maman always screamed at Papa. Even
though she told me it was unladylike to raise your voice,
she screamed a lot. Papa said she was un-sym-pa-the-tic"
—Lucie struggled slightly with the long word, an obvious
new addition to her three-year-old vocabulary—"to the
outdoors. And I'm glad she didn't ask me to go with her
to Paris, because I like Montana the best."

The artless disclosures left Flora feeling like a voyeur in
a very personal relationship, and for a moment she wasn't
sure how to respond. Although shamefully, she felt an
ungracious elation at being reminded that Adam and his
wife weren't deeply in love. "I'm so glad you enjoy Montana," she said, opting for a neutral reply. "My father and
I think the country is beautiful. And now we should see if
we can find your quirt," Flora suggested, deliberately
changing the topic, "so we can take Birdie out for a ride.
She's going to wonder what happened to us."

"I'll use one of Papa's," Lucie said with the kind of
decisiveness Flora was recognizing as a Serre trait. "And
I'll show you the lodges where Papa's cousins live when
they're at the ranch."

As evening approached, Mrs. O'Brien entered the drawing room where Flora and her father were playing a simple card game with Lucie. "I'm afraid Adam's not
returned yet," she said, apologizing for Adam's continued
absence, "and dinner won't wait. He'll be here tonight,

though," she firmly added, opening the doors into the dining room. "If he said Tuesday, he means Tuesday. Now, there's huckleberry pie for dessert, Lucie," she went on, gazing at the little girl swinging her feet over the edge of an embroidered chair, "but you have to eat some vegetables first. You like new peas, and Cook made a small Cornish pasty for you."

"I always eat my vegetables, Mrs. O," Lucie cheerfully said, looking angelic in pink organza.

"Humpf . . . or that dog at your feet does," the housekeeper muttered, glancing at the large otter hound sprawled at the foot of Lucie's chair.

"Caesar only likes meat."

"He likes anything eatable, raw or cooked, but eat the peas at least before your dessert," Mrs. O'Brien said with a small sigh, giving up the struggle.

"I'll remind Lucie to eat her vegetables, Mrs. O," Flora interjected, on a familiar footing with the housekeeper after visiting in the kitchen with Lucie several times in the last two days. "And I'll see that Caesar stays under the table during the meal."

"Thank you, Miss Flora," the housekeeper said with a grateful smile. "It's a pleasure to have a real lady in the house. Now, Lucie, you mind Miss Flora. And we have a fine claret for you, my lord," she added, turning her smile on George Bonham. "From Adam's special stock. Come, now, dinner is informal now that she—well . . . on the count's orders," she quickly altered, "so please eat while the food is still warm." And bustling like a mother hen, she saw them into the dining room.

Dinner was an extravagant affair, decidedly not informal in terms of variety and elegance but casually served, with Lucie and the servants gossiping throughout the meal. The young girl was obviously everyone's pet, though treated in a curiously adult way. Without playmates her own age, Flora thought, it was natural the staff should take the place of friends for Lucie. And during dinner Flora heard a number of anecdotes in which Adam figured prominently, so by meal's end she knew several more revealing fragments of a decidedly remarkable man.

He cooked, Flora heard. He made a perfect Lady Baltimore cake—an American recipe, apparently—no one surpassed his wild grape jam, and his biscuits were of unequaled lightness—for which skilled hands were a requisite, everyone agreed. That didn't surprise her, she decided, recalling the sensitive touch of his hands. And he played the piano. Which accounted for the well-used look of the Bosendorfer in the drawing room and the disorganized stack of music on its top. He had an unrivaled reputation for training horses in the Absarokee style, where horse and rider were friends rather than adversaries. He played a vicious game of croquet, dressed a baby doll with finesse, and could shoot the eye out of a fly at fifty yards. Before long Flora realized that not only was Lucie adored by the staff, but her father was as well. She wasn't surprised. He had an extraordinary appeal.

After Lucie was seen off to the nursery to prepare for bedtime, Flora and her father relaxed on the veranda. Rocking gently in deep-seated wicker rocking chairs cushioned and sculpted to offer maximum comfort, they enjoyed Adam's best cognac and a spectacular twilight sky. Although the sun had set, a warm golden haze still lightened the horizon, bathing the plains to the east in a tawny glow. A palpable peace as unclouded as the gilded landscape enveloped the shadowed veranda.

"Are you happy?" the earl softly asked.

"Very much," Flora replied, her head resting against the chair back, her eyes half-shut.

"I worry, you know."

Flora's eyes opened, and she turned her head slightly so that her gaze rested on her father seated on the other side of the table separating them. "You needn't worry, Papa. I'm vastly content."

"You probably should be in London with your friends, not out in the wilds again with me."

"You're my dearest friend and I *like* the wilds. Don't bring up those old conventional arguments again. I find society so much less interesting than our studies. You've spent your life researching Blumenbach's theory of the biological equality of all peoples and given me the opportunity to observe and document cultures all over the world. It's exciting, Papa, and enlightening, and so much more fascinating than devoting my life to finding a husband, as every society miss is programmed to do."

"You might care to marry someday, though," George Bonham said. "And for that you need society."

"And how would a fox-hunting gentleman fit into our travel schedule? You know their entire existence revolves around the hunt seasons, race seasons, Cowes, Mayfair, Scotland in the fall . . ." Her voice trailed off. "I *like* the freedom of our life," Flora added with firm conviction.

"If your mother had lived . . . perhaps she could have better explained about the necessity—"

"For what Papa?" Flora interposed. "Propriety? Fashionable custom? You told me yourself Mama ran off with you the day after she met you." Flora smiled. "She'd approve of my life, as you well know. Didn't she always accompany you abroad? Wasn't I born on a freighter off the China coast? My disregard for rules can probably be traced to Mama's emancipated inclinations."

"She *was* a darling," the earl fondly recalled.

"And you never found another quite like her in all the ladies who have so ardently pursued you over the years." At fifty-six the earl was still a handsome man. Tall, lean, tanned from years out of doors, his sun-streaked sandy hair only lightly touched with gray at the temples, he'd always attracted female interest.

"No," he quietly replied. "Your mother was very special."

They'd had this conversation, or a variation of it, often over the years, her father's concern for her happiness a constant. And each time she'd reassured him, genuinely content with her peripatetic life.

"If I ever find someone I care about in that unique way, Papa, I'll marry him, but since I can't have children, there's no pressing reason to marry someone simply to be married."

"Perhaps the doctors are wrong."

"A dozen of them in countries as far afield as Greece and Turkey? I doubt it. The virulent fever in Alexandria that summer nearly killed me. I'm fortunate to be alive."

"Amen to that." The earl still shuddered at how close he'd come to losing his sixteen-year-old daughter that steamy July. She'd hovered near death for almost a week, and only the skill of the Greek and Arab doctors had saved her.

"And consider, Papa, the cast of suitors in my life. They're all well-bred and charming but hardly impassioned or interesting enough to touch my heart."

"Not even the Comte de Chastellux?" her father queried with a faint smile. "Your walk in the garden at Judge Parkman's caused some comment."

She found herself blushing. "I'm old enough to do as I please, Papa," she softly remonstrated, "regardless of strangers' comments."

"I've no argument, darling," he quietly reassured her. "Your independence is as important to me as it is to you. And if your mama were alive, she'd have you quoting all her favorite female authors on gender equality. I was just wondering if Adam Serre might have touched your heart a bit more than the London blades."

She didn't answer for a moment, trying to understand herself precisely why he attracted her so. The obvious physical reasons didn't account for the intense degree of his allure. "I think he may have touched some emotion . . . ," she slowly declared, "although I'm not sure what or why." Her smile shone for a moment in the lavender twilight. "He's unutterably handsome, you have to agree."

"All your suitors are handsome," her father said.

"He's not a suitor."

"Perhaps that's the attraction," the earl suggested, his tone cautionary. "His reputation is thoroughly wild."

"Papa, surely not that tone from you, when Auntie Sarah says your rakish ways were what attracted Mama."

Lord Haldane grinned. "Ummm," he teasingly murmured. "Is it too late to caution you to prudence?"

"Years too late, I'm afraid," Flora answered with a wide smile. "And you know as well as I do that my fortune protects me."

"As it did your mother. Which is precisely why she saw that you had control of it."

"Dear Mama knew the merits of the title 'heiress.' So any or all of Virginia City may gossip till doomsday while I do as I wish."

"As long as you're happy, darling, I'm content."

"Then rest easy, Papa. My life is perfection."

They spoke then of more mundane matters, discussing the number of horses they planned to purchase from Adam, debating whether to send some back to England for the hunt season.

"Adam's jumper bloodstock reminds me of the German hunters out of Schleswig-Holstein," George Bonham remarked. "Their quality is superb."

"I like that huge bay best. Lucie tells me she can go over a six-foot jump without breathing hard." Flora smiled. "For a three-year-old, Lucie's amazingly knowledgeable about horses."

"Not so amazing considering her father's primary interest. He's been seriously breeding horses for almost ten years, I'm told." Lifting his glass, the earl pointed at a rising dust cloud on the horizon. Shimmering in the remnants of the sunset, the filmy haze expanded, drifting westward. "Someone's riding fast in this direction," George Bonham said, emptying his glass before setting it aside. He rose to gain a better view.

"A large party, from the amount of dust they're kicking up." Flora's gaze was trained on the approaching riders.

As they watched, the moving pale vapor slowly drew near until mounted men could be distinguished from riderless horses against the yellow sky, and as they advanced closer, it became possible to distinguish their Indian regalia. Twenty-some riders were galloping toward the ranch, leading several strings of horses in their wake, the staccato rhythm of hoofs audible now.

The party didn't slow as it rode up the long hill to the gate, its progress a steady, pounding flow over the last rise, like an inexorable pulsing stream. Flora stood up in a reflexive startle reaction at the excessive speed of the advancing horsemen, gauging the diminishing distance between herself and the thundering mounts.

Their leader rode full out toward the green lawn bordering the terrace as if he'd misjudged the distance and the position of the small group of servants assembling where the lawn met the gravel drive.

"He's going to ride over those servants!" Flora exclaimed in a suppressed whisper.

But the lead warrior painted fearsomely in black and green hauled his horse to a plunging stop with breathless precision just short of the motionless group of servants, his men following him in perfect drill. And when the dust settled, with a small shock of recognition, Flora distinguished Adam beneath the dark, spectral war paint. Laughing in the midst of his men, he was exchanging genial congratulations with them and jovially greeting his servants as though war parties were no more than a casual country ride.

His fierce image of war precluded such a prosaic activity, however, Flora thought, gazing at his forbidding appearance. His powerful body was nude above his leggings and fully painted, his face and form vivid with alternate areas of black and green, accented by red stripes across his forehead and nose, by red hash marks descending symmetrically down his chest and arms. His long hair swirled loose on his shoulders as he turned to talk to one man and then another, his smile starkly white against the black paint on his face. A rifle and bandoliers slung over his bare chest and back gave evidence of the seriousness of the raiding party. This wasn't the charming Comte de Chastellux she'd met in Virginia City.

In the animated flurry of the celebrating troop one warrior first noticed Flora standing on the shadowed veranda —her pale gown and fair skin luminous in the darkening gloom. His arrested glance drew attention, and as others in turn regarded the ethereal sight, a gradual silence descended over the bantering camaraderie, like ripples moving across the surface of a pond.

Engrossed in conversation, Adam didn't notice the growing quiet until a companion called his attention to the visitors. When he saw her, his smile instantly vanished. What was she doing here? He was expecting the earl, not Flora. As he gazed at her across the deepening twilight, despite the shock of her appearance, lurid possibilities immediately raced through his mind—graphic, carnal images—all as swiftly discarded; he was a practical man. But he struggled against the adrenaline of combat still pumping through his veins, the high-strung excitement of a successful raid impelling an incautious energy that pressed the bounds of reason.

And she was here.

After nights of erotic dreams and suppressed desire, she stood in virginal white on his veranda—so close he could touch her. Taking a restraining breath, he handed his reins to the man beside him, slid from his horse, and moved toward his guests.

"Forgive the raucous entry," he said as he neared the terrace, his moccasined feet silent on the grass, "but it's always good to be home. And forgive me for not being here when you arrived, but we had to ride halfway to the Canadian border before we found our horses." He looked at George Bonham as he spoke, his impulses too uncertain, his return to the niceties of etiquette still too recent to risk a sustained appraisal of Flora at close range. Absarokee culture would allow him to take her away without constraints. He found the sudden adjustment difficult.

"Those are prime horses," the earl said. "I would have gone after them too. No need to apologize. We've received every hospitality." In his wide travels he'd seen men in war regalia before. Adam's appearance gave him no pause. "Your daughter served as a very gracious host-ess," he finished.

"You've met Lucie, then." Adam's smile was that of a fond father.

"She's a darling child," Flora said, her voice oddly hushed. The sight of Adam's powerful body covered with war paint and the accoutrements of combat overwhelmed her despite her cosmopolitan background, despite her familiarity with native cultures. Perhaps the sight of blood-stains on his leggings or the fact that the bandoliers crossed on his chest were almost empty of shells struck her with the grim reality of his mission.

He gazed at her briefly, his dark eyes shrouded by black paint, shuttered against his audacious feelings as well. "Thank you," he quietly said. "She's the joy of my life." Then, glancing around at the melee of men and mounts on the gravel drive, he added, "If you'll excuse me for a brief time, I'll see to my friends and let Lucie know I've returned. Then I'll meet you in the drawing room in . . . say half an hour. You'll be more comfortable inside with the sun down."

He hadn't intended the last comment to sound so per-sonal, but somehow it did, as if he were intimately con-cerned with the cool air on Flora's skin.

"Don't worry about entertaining us," the earl inter-jected. "Flora and I are perfectly capable of seeing to our-selves. If you'd prefer waiting till morning . . . please do."

"No," Adam countered. "I'll be down shortly." He shouldn't, of course; he should never come within a mile of Flora Bonham. But she looked particularly beautiful in white silk and pearls—and he was more familiar with do-ing what he pleased than with what he should. "Depend-ing on Lucie's plans," he added with a grin, and bowing faintly, he took his leave.

He wore pink shell earrings, Flora noticed as his hair swung away when he straightened from his bow, the deli-cate shells a striking contrast to his intense masculinity, to the war paint and weapons.

She felt an overpowering urge to touch them.

But the earrings were gone when Adam arrived in the drawing room some time later, though faint traces of black paint subtly shadowed his eyes. He wore an open-neck shirt of carmine wool, leather trousers, and moccasins; his hair was damp from his bath, pulled back, and tied at the nape of his neck, giving him the clean, scrubbed look of a schoolboy. But when he sank into one of Isolde's pastel chairs, his harsh masculinity the antithesis of the delicate rococo design, any impression of schoolboy innocence vanished. "Lucie's enjoyed your company immensely," he said, smiling. "Thank you for giving her so much attention."

"Our pleasure," the earl graciously replied. "She reminds me of Flora at that age. We were in Venice once when—"

"Don't begin one of those embarrassing stories now, Papa . . . ," Flora warned lightly. "I'm sure no one's interested."

"I expect you were a handful," Adam said, more interested than he wished to be in the beautiful Lady Flora.

"I was simply curious as a child. Like Lucie. In fact, we spent some time today in your library perusing the Montana maps, checking possible directions you may have taken. She's been waiting for your return since morning."

"It shouldn't have taken us so long." Adam rubbed his forehead briefly with his palm and then reached out for the liquor decanter on the table beside his chair.

"You look tired," Flora said, surprised to hear herself sound like a wife.

Adam looked up swiftly as he poured his drink, the tenor of her voice not sounding wifely to him but bewitchingly intimate. "There's not much time to sleep on the trail," he replied, schooling his voice to a mild neutrality, forcing his thoughts away from contemplation of intimacy with Flora Bonham. "And we've been traveling for three days," he added. Lifting the glass to his mouth, he drank a long draught of bourbon, feeling suddenly as if he needed fortification.

"Did the Blackfeet take your horses?" George Bonham inquired.

Adam nodded. "They're consistent marauders of our herds, but they decided to abandon the horses when we overtook them." He made it sound casual and benign, unlike the running skirmish contested over thirty miles of rough terrain. "Have you had a chance to look at our stud?" he inquired, not wishing to discuss the raid; white women invariably asked questions he didn't care to answer.

"I think we've seen it all," the earl answered. "You've built an impressive operation here. The question is," he went on, "which of your beauties we can come to an agreement on. Flora particularly likes the big bay jumper."

She hunts, then, Adam thought, adding another fragment to his picture of the intriguing Miss Bonham.

"And Papa thinks he might be able to give the Earl of Huntley a run for his money at Ascot with that sleek black racer you have. Harry won last year and Papa is out for revenge."

"We've clocked that black at one forty-six for a mile," Adam said. "He's damned fast."

"Lucie told us," Flora's father said. "She knows most of the racers' times."

"That's because she handles the stopwatch at the trials," Adam explained, as if it were normal for three-year-olds to understand stopwatches. "You're not thinking of Ascot this year, are you? Arrangements for shipping the horse would be tight."

"No. We'll be here in the Yellowstone valley most of the summer. Provided the clans don't become annoyed with my constant inquiries and scrutiny."

Adam shrugged. "I think you'll find the majority of Absarokee cooperative. Our culture has a long tradition of contact with whites."

"With your own history a case in point," the earl remarked with a smile.

"Exactly. My father was here with Prince Maximilian in

the early 1830's.[2] But he wasn't the first by any means. The smaller population of the Absarokee in relation to the large tribes surrounding them has always made it prudent for them to attempt an amiable relationship with the whites and government.[3] A matter of necessity, though neither can be trusted when it comes to land. Against the possibility of future treaty negotiations, my father saw that he had title to this area by act of Congress. Not that I don't have to convince intruders on occasion that this entire valley is mine," he added.

"The new cattlemen, no doubt," George Bonham noted.

"The new cattlemen," Adam agreed with a minute sigh. "They see this Indian land as free range, regardless that the treaty last year to bring roads up the Yellowstone was never ratified, and this country is all within the limits of Absarokee tribal lands."[4]

"Do they see you as an Indian as well?" Flora asked. "Forgive me if it's inappropriate to ask, but you seem very comfortable with your heritage."

"It always helps to have money in this world," Adam replied without any evidence of discomfort at her query. "And a title's not to be discounted for its value in fashionable society, which," he noted with a grin, "we have in Montana, too, as you witnessed in the elite assemblage of notable people at Judge Parkman's." He was smiling broadly now. "So the color of my skin and the length of my hair count for much less than my wealth and the quarterings on my family crest."

"How unusual," Flora sardonically noted. Having a broad cultural understanding, she viewed the pretensions of society with well-founded cynicism and privately considered that Adam's reputation with a gun may have been added reason for the tolerant viewpoint of Virginia City's fashionable that night at Judge Parkman's.

"Are you an advocate of the simple life, then?" he insolently inquired, taking in her couturier gown and jewels, her languid pose, the glass of champagne in her hand.

"Often I am," she softly replied, responding to his tone

and his jaundiced gaze. "I expect you knew how to use a fish fork from a young age and didn't refuse your inheritance, either. It doesn't make me like all the rest."

"Are we going to have a discussion on democracy?" the earl inquired, amusement in his eyes. "At least you both had American mothers, which should better qualify you to argue the topic."

"Really, Papa," Flora remonstrated cordially. "No one's arguing. It's too fine a night to disagree. Would you like another cognac?"

"No, I still have my journal entries to write." The earl set his empty glass down. "So if you'll excuse me, I'll find my way upstairs. I'll see you in the morning," he said to Adam. "And don't stay up too late, Flora," he reminded her, his admonition a fatherly platitude of long standing.

"I won't, Papa."

As her father walked from the room, Adam said, "Do you tend to stay up late?"

"Occasionally."

"And sleep late too, no doubt." Like his wife, he thought, and every other aristocratic lady.

"No, I don't. Do you?"

"No. There's too much to do each day, and Lucie gets up early."

"I noticed. We went riding this morning. She's an accomplished rider."

"Her cousin's a good teacher."

"She said that."

"We're fortunate to have so many of my relatives near."

"Lucie took me to the lodges down by the river."

"Yes, she told me."

An awkward silence fell as both struggled to converse casually when both were remembering their last passionate encounter.

"I—"

"I'm—"

"You first," Adam said, his voice very quiet.

Flora swallowed before speaking, thinking she'd not felt

so awkward since adolescence. "I'm sorry if I make you uncomfortable."

"I didn't expect you."

"Obviously."

"Forgive me."

"Is there someone else? I don't wish to intrude."

"Someone else?"

"A woman you're involved with."

He debated for a moment—a facile lie would solve his dilemma. "No," he said.

"It's just I, then, who makes you uncomfortable."

"No," he softly murmured, "it's not that simple, and you know it."

Flora gazed briefly at the golden liquid in her glass before her eyes met his again. "You're tired," she sympathetically noted, "and I'm being bothersome."

"No I'm not and"—he sighed—"you're not."

"You're very candid."

"I don't think so."

She leaned back against the cushions and looked at him for a contemplative moment. "Wary, then."

His brows raised fractionally. "Probably."

"Should I wait for you to ask? I don't know if I can."

"Lord, Flora . . ." He shut his eyes for a moment. "Don't say that."

"I'm sorry, I should be more circumspect."

He grinned suddenly as flagrant impulse flashed into his mind. "Circumspect sex?" His gaze was roguishly appraising. "That should be interesting."

She grinned back. "We could try, though I'm not sure you're capable of it."

"Nor you. Lord, I need some help here."

"Perhaps—"

"No. Don't move. I'm trying to deal with this rationally. Do you know I've dreamed of you every night since Virginia City? And it's bothering the hell out of me."

"How romantic."

He glared at her teasing smile.

"It doesn't have to alter your life," she said.

"It?"

"Sex with me. Is that clear enough? I'm not looking for a husband."

"I think I've heard that before."

"Too many times?"

"*One* time too many, for certain."

"But I'm not like her."

"I know. And that's the dilemma."

"It doesn't have to be a dilemma."

He sighed and slid lower in his chair, his leather-clad legs stretched out before him, the glass of bourbon in his hands resting just under his chin. "How long are you staying?" he quietly asked.

"Here? Not long. In the Yellowstone—all summer. After that I'm sailing for the Yucatán."

"For?"

"I'm meeting friends for an expedition to Tikal. I'm not inclined to impose on your life, Adam."

"I'm not certain I'm interested in a woman who fills my dreams. Lucie and I have just regained a modicum of peace in the last weeks. Forgive me for my bluntness."

"It's just sex, Adam. Don't be so alarmed."

He gazed at her, beautiful as a Titian Venus on his gilded settee, all voluptuous womanhood and soft skin and gleaming auburn hair. "You could be offering me tea," he softly murmured.

"I could be but I'm not," she answered as softly, rising from the small sofa and placing her glass of champagne on a lacquered end table.

He didn't shift from his lounging posture as she walked toward him, until she stood inches from his beaded moccasins. Then his dark gaze leisurely traveled up her body, and when it reached her eyes, he said, hushed and low, "I think I'm losing this battle."

"It looks like it to me," she whispered, her glance drifting downward until it rested on the obvious bulge in his doeskin leggings.

"Shut the door." His voice was no more than a murmur.

Her eyes lifted to his. "And if I don't?" The product of privilege, she took orders poorly—no matter how softly put.

"Suit yourself," he quietly said. Setting his glass aside, he pulled himself upright, leaned forward, took her skirt in his hands, and began lifting the heavy silk.

She twitched her skirt away, pique added to the warm heat of her arousal, umbrage in her voice. "This is too public."

"Are you saying no?" he insolently inquired, looking up at her from under the dark fringe of his lashes for a moment before he sprawled back in his chair.

"Are you?" she countered, her own insolence matching his, her gaze flickering briefly to his erection, the length blatant beneath the soft stretched leather.

His smile appeared, full of grace and charm. "We could *both* shut the door."

She smiled back, mollified by his concession. "Or use your bedroom or mine."

He seemed to consider. "Or neutral territory."

She moved so swiftly, he almost didn't catch her when she fell into his lap. Gazing up into his startled eyes, she whispered, her mouth only inches from his, her arms twined around his neck, "Would a bed be possible in this neutral territory?"

She felt like heaven in his arms, silky warm and scented, her soft bottom settled in his lap adding inches to his arousal. With distance he could resist Flora Bonham, but in proximity she was irresistible. "Any of dozens," he murmured, bending his head to kiss her. "Or all of dozens," he added in a heated whisper. "If you prefer a marathon."

"Ummmm . . ." Her hands slid up to pull his head down, and just before their lips touched, she whispered, "Show me. . . ."

Chapter Three

∽❧∾

He carried her up the servants' stairs to avoid the hazardous possibility of meeting her father in the main corridors, the whisper of her crinolined skirts swishing against the wainscoting in the narrow staircase; the dim light defining the stark modeling of his face in grisaille; tempestuous desire warming their blood. In order to navigate the sharp turns, he adjusted her position in his arms in a smooth stirring of powerful muscles, his smile closer now and the scent of his hair fragrant in her nostrils. He stopped to kiss her on the second landing, a compelling, deep, heated kiss that left them both breathless.

"Hurry," Flora murmured on a deep inhalation. "Please . . ."

He looked down at her, his dark eyes muted velvet in the shadows, her urgency matched by his. "Wait," he whispered, the word hot with promise. "We're almost there." He moved quickly then, taking the stairs in great strides, glancing down the lamplit corridor as he reached the second floor, looking for the nearest empty room.

They were inside in seconds, the door abruptly kicked shut, and in seconds more he made his way in the darkness to the bed, placed her on the silk comforter, and followed her down. She lifted her own skirts, so frantic was her need, while he ripped open the tie on his leggings,

and in only breath-held moments more he was deep inside
her. They blazed hot with two weeks of pent-up desire,
and their first time that night was an incoherent memory,
so ravenous was their passion, so overwhelming their hunger. Panting afterward, they wondered how pleasure
could be so fleeting.

"My . . . apologies," Adam breathlessly murmured as
he lay over her, his heart beating like a drum.

"No need . . . ," Flora replied on a suffocated breath.
"Believe me. . . ."

He tried to smile in reply, but he didn't have the necessary energy. Later he did when his body had cooled and
his brain was capable of more than one thought, when
he'd lit the bedside lamp and they lay side by side on the
rumpled blue comforter. "Lie to me if I'm wrong," he
said with a grin, propped on one elbow beside her, still
fully clothed, his finger tracing a lazy pattern over her
collarbone, "but isn't this combination—you and me," he
added in unnecessary explanation, "more intense than—
say—other . . . experiences?" It was the understatement
of his life.

"Why would I lie?" Flora replied with a teasing smile,
gazing up at him in tumbled disarray, her gown and petticoats pushed up in crushed folds, her bare thighs above
her silk stockings rosy pink, matching the glow on her
face.

"I retract the phrase." His finger drifted downward
over the swell of her breast. "Tell me," he murmured.

"Yes," she whispered, moving his hand slightly to one
side so his fingertips brushed her nipple through the silk
of her gown. "Yes, ummm . . . definitely, yes."

"I almost rode to Virginia City one night to see you,"
he whispered, lazily circling the rising bud of her nipple.

"I wish you had."

"I wanted to feel your legs wrapped around me. . . ."

"But it wasn't worth a ten-hour ride." Her smile was
mischievous.

"It turned out to be a three-hour ride," he said. "I was

able to bring my libido under control by the ford at Pine Creek."

"A shame," she theatrically pouted. "When I was in decline."

"For lack of sex?"

"For lack of *your* sex."

His fingers closed firmly on her nipple. "Whom did you sleep with?"

"You're jealous."

"I don't get jealous," he answered, the pressure of his fingers easing. His familiar drawl had returned. "Who was it?"

"It's none of your business. Whom did *you* carnally entertain these last two weeks?"

"Is it a contest?" Withdrawing his hand, he studied her, a new cynicism in his eyes.

"Not with me." Her dark brows rose archly. "You're remembering your wife."

"And you're different?"

"I didn't even kiss a man in the last fortnight because I wanted only you. Is that plain enough? I'm not much good at subterfuge."

"Pardon me if I don't believe you after our fascinating introduction at Judge Parkman's."

"Whether you believe me or not doesn't concern me, but I'm going to fuck you to *death* tonight," she softly whispered, "because two weeks is a long wait."

He suddenly smiled. "I love a plain-speaking woman."

"Provided she's talking about sex?"

His grin widened. "Provided she's talking about sex with me."

"And I'd adore you, Adam Serre, even more intensely than I already do, if you'd substitute performance for talk."

"Impatient libertine."

Rolling over on top of him, she kissed him lightly. "Very impatient," she murmured, placing her palms on his chest and pushing herself upright so she straddled his legs. "And seeing how you seem to be . . . um, ready," she breathed, tugging her petticoats out of the way with a tantalizing movement of her hips and bottom, "why don't we"—rising slightly on her knees, she guided his rigid erection to her pulsing labia and softly finished—"be libertine together . . ."

He shut his eyes as she lowered herself, the sensation momentarily heart stopping, and when he opened his eyes, his erection ensconced deep inside her, he said in a low, heated growl, "Maybe I'll fuck *you* to death first. . . ."

"Starting now, I hope, Monsieur le Comte," Flora murmured, coquettish demand beneath the velvety resonance.

His hands came up leisurely and grasped her waist, but his grip was hard and possessive, and his dark eyes were touched with a flash of temper. "You like to give orders." His grip tightened at her waist.

"Sometimes. Do you mind?" Her violet eyes were teasing and unintimidated, her hands resting lightly on his shoulders.

He shrugged so she felt the small ripple of his muscles under her palms. "It depends," he carefully said.

"On?" She moved her hips slightly so they both felt the slippery friction, the acute throbbing response.

"On what the orders are," he answered with a seductive smile, his temper dispelled by carnal diversion.

"You're accommodating, then," she whispered, his powerful shoulder muscles bunching under her hands.

He lifted her as if she were weightless, sliding her up his rigid length. "To a point," he murmured, intent on gauging distance.

"Will I know . . . when that point is reached?" she asked in a breathy hush, tantalized by the exquisite gliding ascent.

He held her suspended on the pulsing tip of his penis for a provocative moment. "You'll know," he whispered, exerting a gradual pressure downward with his hands so she was slowly filled with his hardness again, deeply penetrated, stretched. Then he arched his back and drove upward that small sensational distance more.

She cried out in a fierce heated whimper at the irrepressible rush of pleasure. And when the flaring intensity had partially diminished and her lashes half lifted to let the world in again, he softly said, "Hello . . ." He smiled then, self-confident, assured, a man skilled at pleasing women. "And now we have to take your gown off, sweet *bia,*" he murmured, sliding his fingertips over the silk-covered stays at her waist. "It's in my way."

"Only my gown?" It was a sultry courtesan voice, heated and low, and those violet eyes gazing down at him were wanton, audacious in their challenge.

He chuckled at her unabashed sensuality. "We'll begin with that," he softly replied, "and go on from there. We've plenty of time. It's a long night. . . ."

The breakfast room was awash with sunshine, Lucie's bright chatter sunny like the warm spring day outside. The small table held a steaming array of food on crested china and gleaming silver: scones; porridge; bacon; ham; poached eggs; buttered toast; colorful jams. A small bouquet of lavender-blue iris in a celadon vase graced the center of the table, the arrangement suitably low so conversation wasn't impeded. Adam and Flora, seated opposite each other at the round table, exchanged discreet smiles over the delicate blooms. Neither had slept more than an hour, their senses languid in the aftermath of a night of heated passion, tantalized by their nearness, hot desire a tangible presence to the initiated.

"Can we ride to see the baby foxes?" Lucie inquired, stirring Chantilly cream into her hot chocolate so briskly it splashed over the rim of the cup.

"After your lessons," Adam replied, ignoring the widening chocolate stains on the linen cloth, a silver spoon with a dollop of cream in his hand. "Do you want more?"

"After my *morning* lessons?" Lucie stopped stirring in her excitement.

"Right after," Adam answered. Assuming her nonreply to his question meant no, he placed the sweet mound of cream in his own chocolate. "Tell Miss McLeod she can come along if she wishes."

"Cloudy doesn't like to ride horses."

"But she likes baby foxes. She told me." Reaching over, he began cutting the ham on his daughter's plate.

"Maybe she can ride old Charlie."

"Is Charlie the big chestnut?" Flora asked, thinking no man deserved to look that good in the morning after a near sleepless night. He appeared fresh, alert, his hair still damp from the bath, his white linen shirt crisply ironed, unbuttoned at the neck, the dark vest he wore over it a handsome Irish wool tweed. An ornate gold charm dangled from the watch pocket—an elegant touch, as if a valet had dressed him.

Lucie's curls bobbed in affirmation. " 'Member," she said through a mouthful of ham. "Charlie was the one who liked apples."

Adam's gaze met Flora's fleetingly over Lucie's head, a swift, private look, explicit with torrid memory. "Tell Miss McLeod she can have the padded Mongolian saddle," he said, his attention returning to his daughter, his neutral tone distinct from his obsessive thoughts.

"Cloudy's too fat," Lucie explained to Flora and the earl, "so she always rides in a carriage if she can, but the foxes' den is up in the hills and the baby kits are ever so cute and fuzzy, which is why Cloudy will probably change her mind just this once and try old Charlie."

Adam allowed himself to watch Flora as Lucie spoke to her, his observation ostensibly benign. He thought her ravishing even dressed simply in a tan silk blouse and twill skirt. Or nothing at all, his inner voice noted in pleasurable memory. She was astonishingly beautiful with her coppery hair pulled back in a sleek chignon, although the bright morning light accented the faint lavender shadows under her eyes, causing him a slight twinge of guilt. He'd have to allow her more sleep tonight.

"Papa, could you put *two* Mongolian saddles on Charlie?"

Forcing his mind back to the immediacy of his daughter's query, Adam said, "Why don't I check with Montoya in the stables? He knows what Charlie likes. Now, do you want strawberry jam on your scone?" he asked, the prosaic routines of the breakfast table so at odds with the lust so prominent in his mind.

"Can we have a picnic too?"

He smiled. "Why not?"

Lucie clapped her hands perilously close to the full chocolate cup, but her father didn't flinch. "I want lemon pie and sugar cookies and those little white puffy things with nuts inside."

"Perhaps we should see what others want," he suggested, not certain a three-year-old's favorite foods held universal appeal. "Why don't you check with Lady Flora and Lord Haldane?" Adam said, his dark gaze resting on Flora.

She immediately looked away, dropping her gaze from such vivid, hot-blooded allure. It felt as though he'd touched her intimately or kissed her in full sight of everyone, so uncontrollable was the heated sensation. It took her a fraction of a second to find her voice. "What do you think, Father?" she asked, needing time to compose her emotions. "Do you have any preferences?"

"If you include a flask of brandy for me, I'm content," George Bonham pleasantly replied. "And those white puffy things sound intriguing," he added, smiling at Lucie. "Are they really good?"

Adam's bronzed hand dwarfed the silver knife he held to spread jam on his daughter's scone, Flora noticed, drawn to the powerful image, to the subtle flex of his muscles and the rhythm of his movements. Heedless of her father's voice, she remembered instead the delicacy of Adam's touch the night before.

"They melt in your mouth, Georgie," Lucie replied, addressing the earl familiarly after the last two days of easy friendship. "They taste like candy and cookies mixed together. You'll like them immensely," she went on, "but make sure you take some before Cloudy reaches them, because she likes them the very best and she can eat hundreds and hundreds."

"I'll race her for the basket." The earl leaned back in his chair, his coffee cup in his hand, his smile for the little girl across the table from him. She reminded him of Flora as a child; she had the same captivating charm and lucid assessment of the world. Pure and genuine and guileless.

"You'll win, Georgie, because Cloudy can't run at *all*. And I'll run with you if Cloudy doesn't holler at me for being unladylike. Papa, do I have to be ladylike on a picnic?"

Adam didn't hear the question, occupied as he was with wondering if he could spirit Flora away during the day somehow, somewhere.

Flora could feel her nipples grow taut against the fine linen of her chemise and an insistent ache throb between her legs. All because Adam Serre was too perilously close. She squirmed on the padded blue-and-white upholstery of her chair. How was she possibly going to wait until nightfall to feel him inside her again? As confident as he, she didn't question her tempting allure.

"Papa! Listen!"

"Whatever you want, poppet," Adam vaguely replied, absorbed by carnal thoughts, hoping he wasn't agreeing to anything outrageous.

"Yahoo! *Thanks*, Papa. Now I'm going to go and tell Cloudy she can't scold me because you said it's all right." She slid from her chair. "You have to come up to the schoolroom, Papa, and tell Cloudy about Charlie. She won't believe me."

"I will, when I come to fetch you."

"Our picnic's going to be *fun*! Flora and Georgie, you'll just *love* it!"

The grown-ups smiled at one another as Lucie raced from the room.

"I can't guarantee an expedition to match that fervor," Adam said with a grin.

"She has enormous vitality," Flora said. Like her father, she thought, recalling the pleasures of the previous night. "And a real appreciation for the outdoors."

"*Luckily*," Adam declared with feeling. "If she took after her mother, she wouldn't be very content here."

"This wilderness would be too distant and remote for many of *my* friends too," Flora noted, feeling as if she owed Isolde a certain indulgence after having so profligately made love to her husband all night.

Adam shook his head briefly, his expression shuttered. "Isolde never stayed here long. She spent the season in Paris and generally visited friends in London for the English season. We saw her only for short periods during the year." He pushed his plate away and leaned back in his chair, as if memories of his wife had quelled his appetite.

"I think I may have met her at a country-house party at the Darcys'," the earl interjected, blasé about society marriages, and much else, after fifty-some years of viewing the foibles of mankind. "Is she a Deauville Haubigon?"

Adam nodded. "And her mother's family prides themselves on their ducal blood and Leoville vineyards."

"Yes, I remember. She spoke of the vineyards. I don't think you were there, Flora. It was when you were in Italy visiting Adele."

Flora suddenly wished she'd been at the Darcys' to meet the woman Adam had married. As if she could know him better or differently or more completely if she knew his wife. She was curious, too, about the beautiful blond pictured over the mantel in the pink silk boudoir. How did she speak and laugh and move? Was she seductive like her husband? Was she cool? Did she wear diamonds often? And then, on a less charitable level, a more primitive impulse drove her, enigmatic but powerful—perhaps she wished to experience a perverse triumph over the woman whose husband had kept her awake all night.

"I may meet her some other time," she said, opting for the safety of bland politesse.

"Not likely," Adam bluntly retorted, "unless Baron

Lacretelle tires of her. You wouldn't get along anyway," he added with gruff displeasure.

Thin-skinned at the tangled state of her emotions, Flora responded more forcefully to his brusque rebuff than she should have. "I can get along with *anyone*."

"So can I," he coolly replied, a masculine arrogance to his pronouncement. "But I know Isolde."

"Maybe you're wrong. Perhaps we could be friends," Flora sweetly retorted, absurdly irritated by his certainty and—considering their short acquaintance—at his husbandly tone.

"You're not the right gender to be a friend of Isolde's."

His abrupt, dismissive delivery rankled. Flora didn't tolerate authoritarian men. After years of serious research she'd established herself as a recognized scholar in her field. She'd cut her eyeteeth on the Aegean explorations of Ludwig Ross and had first been recognized at the precocious age of seventeen when her paper on *The Lampstand from Phylakopi*, defining the distinctive design elements of an early Aegean civilization not yet discovered, had been read before the Royal Society. So Adam Serre could run his large valley like a local god, but he didn't control her. "Under the circumstances," she replied with a small testiness, "forgive me if I question your complete understanding of your wife."

"Don't be ridiculous." He glared at her from under his dark brows.

"Must everyone agree with you?" An arch retort, female and heated.

"This is stupid," Adam snapped.

The conversation had turned disastrously personal.

"Could I suggest a truce?" Flora's father cordially interjected. "You two sound like squabbling siblings."

Adam smiled instantly, his scowl erased. "Forgive me," he apologized, his manner conciliatory. "And excuse my temper." His mouth quirked into a grin. "Isolde always has a predictable affect on me."

How smooth he is, Flora thought. How hatefully smooth.

"Now, then," he graciously went on, "why don't we go out to the stables and see if you can decide on some horses?" His offer was pleasantly put, his voice undemonstrative again, unruffled.

She wanted to hit him and wipe that well-bred smile from his face. And mar that unruffled calm. With inexplicable, hot-tempered resentment, she also wished him to pay for Isolde's presence in his life.

Chapter Four

❦

The stables were built of the same cream sandstone as the house, the style reminiscent of lavish royal studs in size and amenities. Each stall had running water piped in from a reservoir in the foothills, the half walls were of imported mahogany, the large stalls so immaculate Flora wondered what ratio of grooms to horses was necessary to maintain such cleanliness. This was the third day she'd visited the stables, and each time it appeared as though fresh hay had been newly spread in the stalls, the horses had been recently brushed, the stone floors between the rows of polished wooden compartments had been freshly washed. And if she had been less peeved with the owner of the pristine establishment, she might have posed her questions and assuaged her curiosity.

As it was, she followed the lengthy tour of available horses principally as an observer, speaking only when necessary, keeping her answers brief but courteous, smiling at her host with politeness but not sincerity, wishing on more than one occasion that it were possible to land a solid kick where it would do the charming Comte de Chastellux the most good.

In this temperate fashion she helped her father decide on several horses—hunters, racers, riding stock. George Bonham's impassioned enthusiasm more than made up for his daughter's less effusive response; in fact, in the grip of his delight in Adam's stellar bloodstock, the earl appeared unaware of Flora's muted feelings.

"By God, you've prime mounts, Adam," he declared as they stood before one of the larger stalls, admiring a three-year-old thoroughbred stallion. "No wonder your colors are taking so many prize purses of late. What's the price on this beauty? Harry Aston would fall to defeat with a goer of this quality running for me."

"Sorry, George, but this youngster's a special favorite of mine. He's not for sale."

"For the right price everything's for sale," the earl said with a smile for his host. "Come, now, name it."

Adam shook his head. "I can't. Magnus is going to win the Grand Prix for me next summer at Longchamps."

He raced in France too, then, not only in America, Flora thought, wondering how he dealt with his wife when he met her at the races. Did they nod at each other when they passed, or did he snap at her too? Or was he simply a consummate liar and they enjoyed a marriage of convenience—convenient to both their licentious libidos?

"You'll be up against Devonshire's Whirlwind at Longchamps," the earl pointed out. "Freddie's bound to run him again after taking a first there last season."

"I'd suggest putting a large bet on Devonshire's horse to *place* next year, then, and you'll profit. Because *Magnus* is going to win."

"From the sound of it," George Bonham said with regret, "there's no room for negotiation. I don't suppose you have a brother to this horse hidden away somewhere," he added.

"I've his half brother," Adam offered, "who has definite promise, though he's still fairly young. Would you like to see him? He's across the stable yard in the other wing."

"Is he for sale?" And at Adam's nod the earl said, "Lead the way."

The dark bay was a beauty: powerful, long-legged, sleek —and within minutes the men had agreed on a price. At

Adam's suggestion a groom readied the horse for a trial run so the earl could see the thoroughbred's speed.

Lord Haldane helped with the tack, his excitement obvious as he kept up a running commentary on the bay's glorious attributes and the possibility of future revenge on the Earl of Huntley.

It was an old rivalry, sportive rather than serious, but it pleased Flora to see her father's exhilaration.

"Are you coming, dear?" the earl queried as the groom set the last buckle in place. He patted the bay's glossy neck. "Let's see what this splendid creature can do."

"I've a lady's mount perfect for Hyde Park," Adam interjected. "I thought I'd show her to Lady Flora. We'll meet you at the track later."

"Come on, then, Tom," the earl promptly declared, hardly listening to the complete explanation, eager to see the horse run. "Does he really do a mile in one forty-six?" And without a backward glance George Bonham and the groom led the thoroughbred away, both men deeply engrossed in a discussion of timed runs.

Adam and Flora watched the two men disappear through the distant doorway into the bright morning sunlight. It was cool in the shadowed stable . . . and quiet. So the sound of their breathing seemed magnified.

"I don't have a horse to show you," Adam softly said, sliding a gentle brushing fingertip over a tendril that had loosened from Flora's chignon. "Although maybe you knew that."

"Of course I didn't," she retorted, not sure in the chaos of her mind whether she was perjuring herself or not. "And don't!" she added, slapping his hand away, still ruffled from their scene at breakfast. She glared at him. "I think I'm angry with you."

"I *know* I'm angry with you," he bluntly said.

"Really," she said in soft rebuke. "It's hard to tell." She cast a significant glance at the fingers he was rubbing.

He slowly exhaled, deeply frustrated by his unsatisfied libido, by Flora's tempting lure, by his stinging fingers. "I don't appreciate senseless challenges about my wife," he said, ill-tempered and querulous. "Especially," he added, his voice taking on a cool clarity, "after a sleepless night."

"Did I keep you awake?" Flora queried, gibing and overgracious, "or was it you who wouldn't let *me* sleep?" she sweetly asked.

"Don't start," Adam growled.

"My, we're touchy. But regardless of the reasons for your fatigue," she retorted, sarcasm rich in her voice, "*I* don't appreciate snappish orders from you. Just because we spent the night together doesn't give you authority over my life. Before, during, and after sex," she precisely enunciated, "I make my *own* decisions, and if I wish to meet your wife someday, I will."

"Whether I like it or not." A suppressed fury vibrated beneath the curt words.

"Yes."

Utter silence surrounded them, a kind of palpable anger strumming in the air.

The distant wing was less busy, the few horses housed in the facility resting after their morning workouts, the light from the low windows diffused by the immense space and high arched ceiling.

"You may rule your household and small empire here with an iron fist," Flora enunciated into the crisp silence, half turning to leave, "but you don't rule me."

Moving with blurring speed, Adam's hand clamped hard on her wrist. "Maybe I can," he murmured, drawing her back.

She wasn't sure if the gleam in his eyes was mischief or anger or some innocuous reflection of light from the windows. Was he entertaining himself, or was he truly provoked? But she answered without amusement, for she'd lived too long an independent woman. "*Some* people," she pronounced with regal imperiousness, her body taut with affront, "won't allow you to have carte blanche with their life, Mr. Serre."

"Meaning you," he said.

"Yes. Now kindly release me."

"We seem to be at an impasse." He still retained his hold on her wrist, though his grip had loosened.

"I don't think so, Monsieur le Comte, because I'm going to walk away."

"We're not in a London drawing room, darling," he softly drawled. "It's a different world out here. Maybe you *can't* walk away." But he released her wrist as if to say: "Try."

She stood very straight in her mannish blouse and plain skirt, her spine stiffly erect, her eyes lifted to his direct with challenge. "I'm not so easily intimidated, Adam, by your reputation for violence and your royal prerogatives in this valley. For God's sake, do you think me just out of the schoolroom?"

"On the contrary, darling," Adam said, smiling faintly, amusement suddenly vivid in his eyes, "what I like about you is your frank and unconstrained worldliness. Which makes everything so much more interesting—"

"And less predictable," she returned with a small, heated vehemence. "Keep that in mind."

"That too." He said it pleasantly, as though they were discussing dance cards instead of imperious principles. Then his gaze drifted away, surveyed the great length of the stable wing, the open doorway, and when his eyes met hers again, he said, as if oblivious to their prior conversation, "It seems we're quite alone."

"Not for long, I'm sure," she briskly said, a sureness to her voice. "Father should return soon."

Adam shook his head. "The track's across the river."

"It doesn't matter. I'm not some timid ingenue, Adam, who's uncertain how to deal with you." But her attention had been drawn to the fluid dark silk of his hair as it swung over the starched collar of his shirt. Imprudent memory recalled its sleek texture and fragrance.

"Lucie should be in the schoolroom for another hour or so."

"I fail to understand," Flora declared, an uncharacteristic primness infusing her voice—when she perfectly well understood, when she could already feel the rising heat flowing through her body, when such salacious intent sent a shiver of longing down her spine.

"I should be more direct, then," Adam murmured, taking a step toward her.

"I won't allow this." She moved a step backward, determined to resist his casual arrogance.

"Revelation has overcome you?"

"Damn you, Adam. As if your lust can be concealed."

"Or yours," he softly whispered, looking down at her trembling hands. "Even if you won't admit it," he added in a husky undertone, advancing another step, gently forcing her back against the polished mahogany wall. "I felt your desire across the breakfast table," he whispered, lowering his head so their eyes were almost level, "and I saw it in your eyes. I can smell lust in the scent of your body, and I can't wait until tonight." His hands came up to rest palm down on either side of her head.

"And if I say no, now and tonight . . ." Her voice was hushed.

"You can't." His smile was wicked.

"Maybe I can . . ."

"Maybe you're wrong." Leaning into her, he pinned her to the wall with the hard length of his body, his arousal rigid against her belly.

He didn't kiss her—deliberately—wanting to force her to acknowledge the utter truth of her need. Of their need. Without his customary effortless seduction or charming words. Needing her to acknowledge her desire as a sop to his chafing frustration.

"Please!" She attempted to move against the solid weight of his body.

"Are you asking me?" Adam whispered, his breath warm on her mouth.

"Oh, God . . . Adam, please . . ." But her voice had dropped to a breathy sigh, and her taut posture had altered, yielded.

"We'll try it standing up the first time . . . ," he murmured, moving one of his hands, beginning to lift the heavy twill of her skirt. "And then . . . after that . . .

you might like to see the hayloft . . ." His words were
promises of pleasure, low, heated, intense with suppressed
urgency. "Or do you want me to stop?" His hand paused,
the crush of her skirt and petticoat at midthigh. "Look at
me," he softly ordered.

Her dark lashes slowly lifted. Driven by burning desire,
she could no more control their ascent than she could
arrest the sweet aching heat coiling deep inside her.

"That's a good girl," Adam murmured, his smile knowing. "Now, answer me."

"You're hateful." Her eyes were hot with longing.

"And you're obstinate," he whispered, a fiery passion of
discord burning in the darkness of his eyes. "Say it."

"I won't."

He moved, swift and sure, purposeful, wrenching up
her skirt, forcing her thighs apart with a thrusting hand,
sliding his fingers solidly into her pulsing cleft in a plunging assault so deep, she gasped at the shocking invasion.
And a moment later she groaned as an answering molten
rapture flooded her senses. "*Now* tell me," he gently said,
subtly caressing the hot, slick tissue. "Tell me you want
me as much as I want you."

Silence engulfed them once again, a hushed quiet muti-
nous with suppressed, feverish need. He held her rebel-
lious body immobile between himself and the solid wall,
his fingers buried inside her, drenched with the opalescent
fluid of her desire.

"Damn you," she murmured on a suffocated moan, her
head thrown back, her spine arched against the rutting
fire burning through her senses. Adam's deft fingers
moved inside her, an answering flare of unutterable pleasure spiked upward, and she cried out in a long, low,
keening scream.

"Would you like something better?" Adam murmured
as her soft cry subsided. "Something more . . . substantial?"

"Must I say it?" A whisper, hardly audible.

He smiled. "It's not so difficult . . ." He knew exactly

how to touch her, how deep, how slow, how hard; he knew precisely where she lost control.

And for long breathless moments she was oblivious to all but exquisite, delirious sensation. When she slowly opened her eyes again, she said in a low, heated whisper, her gaze orchid-black with longing, "I want you, Adam Serre . . . and I hate you for making me do this," she went on in an almost soundless murmur. "And I hate myself for needing you so desperately, and if I don't feel you inside me now, this instant," she finished in a trembling rush, "I'm going to die. . . ."

He grinned—a warm, singularly personal smile that was quite capable, she didn't doubt, of luring an angel to earth. "A simple yes would have been enough," he said, slipping his fingers free.

"I want you inside me *now*," she purred, rubbing against the mahogany half wall like a cat in heat.

"You want satisfaction?" His mouth was almost touching hers, his long dark hair brushing her shoulders as he leaned close.

"Ummm . . ." She reached for his belt, feeling for the odd serpentine clasp on the gold buckle.

"And speed apparently," he teased.

"Initially," she murmured, rising on her toes the scant distance to brush his smiling lips with hers. "After that, I'll let you know."

"I already know what you like."

"*Some* of what I like," she breathed, her smile seductive.

"Jesus, Flora," he muttered, perturbed by her flaunting prerogative, resentful of her amorous past, of the pleasures she'd given and received. "You can be irritating."

"Among other things . . ." She ran her hand over the prominent bulge in his trousers. "But, then, you're more interested," she murmured, her voice husky and low, "in other things . . . at the moment, aren't you?"

"You need a damned whipping," he gruffly declared, stopping her insolence with a hard, bruising kiss. And he didn't relinquish her mouth as he finished unbuckling his belt and unbuttoning his trousers, his mouth crushing hers, nor as he lifted her skirt, nor when he bent his knees slightly to ease himself inside her. He tasted her sudden cry of pleasure as he drove upward. And they both felt it. Untrammeled rapture, pure and sharp—white-hot, extreme, like a frontal attack on their senses.

He held her pinned hard against the wall like a sacrifice to carnal pleasure, wondering in the indefensible, selfish tumult of his brain whether he could keep her permanently captive for his pleasure.

The enormous power of his body engulfed her, aroused and tantalized and lured, and she wanted him with an all-inclusive hedonistic delight. "Adam . . . sweet Adam," she whispered, his mouth leaving hers momentarily as he adjusted her hips to absorb the solid rocking of his lower body. She wanted to hear and taste the sound of his name on her tongue, as if paganlike, the words would make his spirit hers. So she could keep him beyond the transient peaking pleasure in some endless cycle of gratification.

He kissed her again, responding to his name . . . knowing she wanted something more from him, feeling as though he too wished to give her more. Forcing himself deeper, he held himself hard inside her, a kind of unknown violence impelling him as if his savage penetration somehow appeased the turmoil in his brain. He never experienced this ferocious intensity with other women; he always played at love with expertise and charm, but never with feeling. And now furious emotion pervaded his mind, or perhaps, he cynically thought, only the screaming clamor of raw, convulsive nerve endings. But whatever the cause, his feelings were profound.

"Can we . . . stay here . . . forever . . ." Flora sighed, almost delirious from the explosive pleasure . . . intent on prolonging the sumptuous gliding sensations . . . totally absorbed in the intoxicating flux and flow.

"Here?" Adam whispered, moving deep inside her so she whimpered—acute overload assaulting her quivering senses, "or here," he added in a throaty growl, lifting her under the arms so her feet completely left the ground, so his legs had better leverage.

"Hey, boss!"

The man's sharp voice cut through the filmy light and dappled shadows of the stable wing, and for a moment Adam Serre stood arrested as his head swiveled toward the door.

A second spun away as he focused on the man; then he shouted, "I'm busy!" And resumed his engrossing rhythm.

Flora tensed in his arms, the glowing pink of her skin modified to the deeper rose of embarrassment. "Oh, Lord . . . Adam!"

"He's gone," Adam whispered, bending his head to kiss her soft mouth in reassurance. "No one else will come," he soothed, Matthew's shocked expression burned into his retinas.

"He saw us!" Flora's whisper was breathy with horror.

"I don't care if all Montana watches us," he answered on a suffocated breath, shifting her weight so he could penetrate deeper, peaking rapture so near, an entire world of voyeurs wouldn't have stopped him. "Just *this* matters, *bia*," he added, withdrawing slightly so she quickly clutched at his shoulders to draw him back. "And *this*," he murmured, sliding in again, confident with her nails biting into his shoulders he once again had her attention, "and *this* . . . ," he went on, the rhythm of his lower body matching the melodic litany of his words. "Hold on, now. . . ."

"As if I'd let you go . . . ," she purred, the shocking interruption banished from her thoughts, her body a receptacle for pure sensation, Adam Serre possessing the awesome potential of a dissolute satyr.

She was his most engaging houseguest to date, Adam decided, although he was accomplished enough in the world of amour to acknowledge that she might retain the title for the foreseeable future.

In his memory of hot-blooded females, Flora Bonham was unique.

Their climax was lavish.

·   ·   ·

Afterward—after the visions had cleared and the phantom music had muted in their ears—he carried her farther back into the shadows and took her up the narrow stairway to the hayloft. Lowering her into the sweet-smelling hay, he followed her down, kissing her tenderly to waken her from the drowsy insensibility of release. "You squander your body like a prodigal," he whispered.

"It's only you . . . you have some sorcery . . . ," she faintly murmured, weak from the unbridled excess of her orgasm.

"Or the Montana air . . . ," he softly said, settling in a comfortable sprawl beside her, his smile more gentle than ribald, his recuperative powers more potent.

"They should mention the air, then, in the advertisements. . . ." Flora's voice was still weak, her lashes half-lowered, her attempt at a smile ending in a languorous sigh.

"Would such copy attract you?"

"If your engraved portrait graced it," she playfully noted, her gaze drifting over his lounging form. He had a magnetic beauty not entirely the consequence of the stark perfection of his features. Imbued with a dark primeval power beneath the rumpled white shirt and opened vest, the polished boots and tailored trousers molding his long, muscled legs, he projected a curious serenity, or perhaps an assurance. She found that self-confident authority compelling. Even now, in repose, he exuded the privileged air of an exotic princeling, assured of his place in the world.

"I'm glad I went to Judge Parkman's," he abruptly said, sensible of his vast content.

"You didn't mind my assertiveness."

"*Au contraire.*" He reached over to straighten the collar on her blouse, then smiled down on her. "I'm very grateful."

"Am I disheveled?" It was a female question.

"You look luscious."

"Good enough—

"—to eat? Definitely."

"Where do you get your energy?" She could hardly move, her senses still languid, blunted by surfeit.

He shrugged. "I was born with it."

A flaring jealousy raced through her brain at the visions of Adam Serre dispensing his passionate vitality. "I don't care to hear about it," she coolly said.

"What are we talking about here?" A small crease had formed between his dark brows.

Conscious of her discourtesy and his perplexed expression, she quickly said, "Forgive me. A slip of the tongue." And she stretched in a slow, luxurious movement, as if she could physically shake off the disagreeable covetousness she felt toward Adam Serre.

Had she known, the Comte de Chastellux was understanding covetousness for the first time in his life with a mild sense of unease. And watching her move, voluptuous, feline, sensuous as a perfectly trained houri, enhanced his discomfort level. His scowl deepened.

"Don't pout, darling." She smiled up at him flirtatiously. "I promise to be more prudent in my choice of words. I may even mind your orders once or twice." She blew him a conciliatory kiss.

How many times had she cajoled a man into a better humor? he suddenly wondered. How many times had she smiled like that in bed? How many men had seen her pose in such lush display—tousled, flushed from passion, her skirt raised above her knees, her open thighs inescapable carnal invitation?

"Are you thinking of beating me?" she teased, his expression curiously reproving.

"It's a thought." His voice was subdued.

"Ummm . . . you look devilishly wicked when you say that, Monsieur le Comte. Will I like it?"

He forcibly banished the galling visions, reminding himself that Flora Bonham was only a temporary diversion, and when he abruptly smiled at her, she saw the same fascinating wildness in his eyes she'd first observed in Virginia City. "I think I can guarantee a certain gratification," he drawled.

"How nice," she dulcetly said, delight in her gaze, and she began unbuttoning her blouse.

He stopped her fingers with a staying hand. "I don't want you to do that."

Her fine brows rose in query.

"*I'll* undress you." Her scent surrounded him, hothouse rose and ambergris—precious, costly, redolent of harems.

She smiled. "And then *I'll* undress you."

He should have casually said yes, and with anyone else he would have, but complex and incomprehensible reasons restrained him. She was too self-reliant and direct—neither trait at issue had he not considered to whom she'd offered the same unfettered choices. So he only said, "Later," in a neutral tone, knowing she would soon be beyond sense and sensibility. Knowing there, at least, she would be pliant to his will.

For a flashing moment he wondered why he required submission from the beautiful Lady Flora when making love had always been a pleasant game. But the contentious thought dissolved when the lady in question, warm and soft and willing, pulled his head down for a kiss.

He left her briefly to fetch a clean blanket in the tack room, his mission executed with speed and dispatch.

And when he returned, she sweetly said, "A true gentleman."

"Only a practical man," he replied, spreading the blanket on the billowing hay. "Your father might feel inclined to call me out should you appear raked with scratches."

"The voice of experience?" She couldn't disguise the coolness in her voice although she tried, although she knew she would make love to him regardless of his answer.

"I've never been here before," he honestly replied, his smile all roguish charm. "At least for this. Is that the right answer?"

"Perfectly." She gave him high points for gallantry as she kicked off her low boots. "I'm not usually so moody," she admitted with a moue of self-reproach, "and I abhor myself for carping. You'd think I was your wife."

"You haven't even qualified for the reserve team in that regard," he said, charmed by Flora's need for atonement. "Isolde's in a different league—a different solar system," he added in reconsideration."

"In contrast, you're saying, I'm sugar sweet."

"A veritable candy plum." And reaching over, he gathered her into his arms and deposited her on her back in the middle of the forest-green wool of his racing colors. "Now tell me about your childhood, or your favorite book, or the best dig you've ever been on, and I'll see if I can get these ridiculously small buttons undone."

"I was born in Yorkshire," she facetiously began, finding Adam's struggle to manipulate the tiny pearl buttons a charming sight, "and my first governess fled after a week because I threw my chocolate at her when she scolded me for not sitting up straight, and she said she didn't have to put up with a little hooligan no matter how much Papa paid."

He looked up from his task with a grin. "You haven't changed."

"I'm still adorable."

"Ummm . . ." He was concentrating again, sitting cross-legged like a tailor beside her, his long, slender fingers moving more swiftly now that he'd established a rhythm.

She touched his sleeve and he looked up, his dark gaze holding hers, both acutely aware of their indiscreet attraction. "You're enormously strong," she said, stroking the muscled length of his bicep, remembering how he lifted her as if she were weightless.

"I'll show you in a minute," he promised, sliding her blouse from her shoulders, slipping the sleeves over her hands, noting the absence of a corset before placing the garment on the border of the blanket.

"How long will it be before Father returns?" She found it difficult to speak in a normal voice with his cryptic promise to demonstrate his strength, with his fingers untying the ribbons of her chemise, with the golden sunshine warm on her naked shoulders.

"I told the groom to take his time. An hour—maybe more."

"So you knew!"

He looked up at her burst of words. "Didn't you? I found your message pretty clear across the breakfast table."

She met his cool regard with her own direct stare for a moment, and then she smiled at him with an artless innocence. "Did it mention what I wanted?"

"Not everything." His gaze drifted downward to her breasts—magnificent and thrusting, asking to be kissed. "I'm improvising."

"And doing an admirable job," she sensibly agreed, purring as his fingers slid over the plump roundness of one breast. Leisurely, his palm slipped under it, testing its weight as if gauging its ripeness. Then he gently released it, watching with a connoisseur's eyes the satiny flesh quiver and tremble. Her nipple sprang to life, sharp and hard, and he bent his head to lick the peaked crest with a gentle, gliding tongue, ministering to the susceptible pap as he slipped her chemise from her arms. Her blissful sigh warmed his cheek as he leaned over, raising her slightly so he could draw the chemise from beneath her. Placing it beside the silk blouse, he unbuttoned her skirt, slipped it down over her hips, then untied her petticoat with deft skill. He said pleasantly, "Venetian lace," as he lifted her hips to slide it free and didn't notice Flora's sudden displeasure until she said, "Your areas of expertise annoy me."

Dropping her petticoat beside the other clothing, he turned back to the nude splendor of Flora Bonham on his racing green, her white silk stockings and pink lace garters the only wanton ornament to her image of bursting opulence. "You're very prickly, *bia*," he said with a small sigh, although the counterpart of her volatile temperament was a decided asset in bed. "I sincerely wish I hadn't mentioned it. Should I say my mother collects Venetian lace?"

"No." Thin-skinned discontent.

"Should I lie?"

"No." Although she was restive now under her conflicting urges.

"I don't have an answer, then, unless you're very understanding."

As she lay under his gaze, floundering in the intricate maze of her emotions, she thought how curious the divergent sensations. Despite her resentment she was overwhelmed with need, despite chafing logic; she wanted only to feel his hard, muscled body covering hers. She could protest all the women he'd known, but she wanted him in the same critical way. "Lie to me," she said.

"I distinctly recall that lace from the museum at Chantilly," he dissembled, quixotic and unabashed. "Does that please you?"

She nodded, impudence in her gaze.

"And do I please you?" His voice was low, almost diffident.

And she thought him excessively modest for a man of wealth and power, for a man who drew attention when he walked into a room, for a man who held records in the boudoir. "You please me too much."

"It's never too much." He made the statement sound like a heated promise.

"Soon I'm going to have to wake up from this abandoned state," she said with a shameless, seductive grin, "and reclaim my psyche."

"Not *too* soon, I hope," he said with a smile, moving closer, seating himself beside her. "Why don't we finish what we started?"

"Are we running out of time?" Lying beside him on the soft hay offered a kind of rare, exotic pleasure, as if they'd known each other as children or were isolated from the modish conventions of their world.

Reaching out, he ran a light fingertip down her arm. "Stay as long as you want. I'm very good at excuses."

"So I needn't feel rushed."

"Take your time. . . ." His fingers trailed over her rib cage; they were warmer than her skin, his body temperature degrees hotter, the pads of his fingers slightly rough like a working man's—a curiosity she didn't doubt in French noblemen.

She lay her hand on his for a moment, the size of his dwarfing hers, and then she moved his bronzed fingers downward while he watched with calm, dark eyes—over her stomach to the coppery damp curls between her legs.

"You've had intercourse," he quietly said. "Look." And he slid his finger down through the silken curls, down the translucent runnels of sperm on her inner thigh.

Her hips moved at his soft command, at the heated feel of his fingertips spreading the sticky fluid over her skin, and instead of looking down, she gazed at him and softly said, "A man forced me to have sex with him."

His brows rose in brief surprise, and then he smiled. "And you resisted?" he softly queried, following the traces of moisture upward again, to their reservoir.

"I tried." Her lashes had drifted low, and she saw him through their lacy shield, the familiar pulsing deep in the pit of her stomach beginning.

"I don't know if I should believe you." A small chastisement infused his voice. "You obviously had sex with the man." His lean dark fingers gently parted her pouty pink labia, slowly stretching the entrance. "I see sperm everywhere."

"I didn't have any choice. He was too strong. He held me against the wall, pushed my skirt up, and forced himself inside me." Her voice turned husky. "He was so large."

"But not too large to fit . . . here. . . ." With infinite care he slid three fingers into her sticky sweet passage, very slowly, so she'd feel the lingering penetration. "Was he large like this?" he asked when his fingers were completely submerged.

"Larger . . ."

With some difficulty he added a fourth finger, gently expanding the entrance until it had stretched sufficiently to allow access. "Like that?" he murmured, stroking the distended tissue surrounding his knuckles.

"I think so," she answered in a stifled, breathy murmur,

the throbbing in her vagina pounding in her brain and toes and shuddering nerve endings.

"But you don't remember precisely." Adam's erection was rock hard, and it took enormous self-control to keep his voice level.

"Everything was . . . very . . . heated."

"Did you like it?" In just such a tone might a church elder catechize a transgressor.

"I can't say," she replied, flustered and nervous.

"Are you embarrassed?" That same cool voice.

"Yes . . . oh, yes."

"Because sex is illicit?"

She nodded, her eyes tightly shut.

"If no one saw you, you needn't worry."

"But a man came in." That small horror in her voice he'd heard at the time. "I was mortified."

"But no one can see you now. And I promise the man who saw you will tell no one. How does this feel, Lady Flora?" His fingers were moving inside her with more ease now, her intense arousal lubricating the passage, his gliding motion effortless.

"Extremely . . . pleasant, Monsieur le Comte." And she sighed in blissful rapture.

"You can open your eyes. There's no one else here."

"But *you* can see me." Hesitant, delicately put, like a young lady of purity.

"I find you delectable. And I'm not scandalized by your behavior. Open your eyes so you can see the fierce lust I'm feeling. Look at me," he ordered, his tone suddenly exacting.

Her eyes opened—burning iridescent amethyst.

And he more amiably said, "Look at this. Do you want it inside you?" He measured the stretched fabric over his arousal with a gliding fingertip.

She took a deep breath. "I shouldn't. . . ."

"But you want to," he said, his voice like velvet, "I can tell. Here . . . come here," he murmured, drawing her hand to his erection. "Touch me."

"I couldn't." She resisted the pressure of his grip, her hand trembling with the effort.

"I'll help you," he softly offered, sliding his fingers free from her slick vagina.

"No, please!" she pleaded, suddenly bereft of the exquisite manipulation.

"Hush, sweet," Adam soothed, touching the peony tips of her nipples with a brushing caress, her dampness on his fingers, cool. "You're going to like this better," he whispered, forcing her palm hard against his arousal. "It goes in deeper."

With her gaze focused on his erection, she whispered, "What must I do?"

He smiled at her capitulation. "Unbutton my trousers," he softly said, leaning back on his elbows.

"Must I?"

"If you want to feel me inside you," he pleasantly said.

She sat up then as if suddenly resolved and reached over, her small fingers struggling with the concealed placket, the sturdy twill fabric of his riding pants stiff and unyielding.

"You aren't very proficient at this."

"I'm sorry." She looked up at him, guileless and proper. "I've never done this before."

"You'll get better with more practice," he assured her. "Here," he said, shifting his position to help, easing the fabric aside, "put your fingers around the button like this now and then slide it free."

Of course he was an expert at unbuttoning his trousers, Flora thought, hot temper flooding her mind. Fractious, temperamental whenever she was reminded of his legendary reputation with women, perhaps grudgingly resentful of her own intense attraction, she went motionless and in a different voice—a cool, pragmatic voice—said, "Why am I doing this?"

"Because it amuses me," Adam murmured, "and it makes you hotter than hell. What did I do now?"

His unperturbed tranquillity affronted her. How often had he played the game? How many times before had he

casually responded to a heated encounter? Why was she
drawn to him so powerfully when no man before had ever
stirred such feverish desire? "It doesn't matter," she dis-
claimed, taking exception to his far-flung fame and her
own ardent response, as if the word "button" had suddenly triggered a caviling list of enigmatic offenses.

"Tell me." His tone was soft, cajoling, untouched by
temper.

How soothing his voice, she thought, as though she
needed petting. Could she as equably repress all emotion?
Had she not always in the past? Had she not earned her
sobriquet Serene Venus for just that accomplishment? "If
you must know," she said, her voice smooth as silk, "your
reputation for vice and indiscriminate debauch frustrates
me."

"What makes you think it's indiscriminate? And your
eager lust annoys me too, if you wish to argue libertine
propensities." He was surprised it bothered him. He was
even more surprised to hear himself admit it. He generally
preferred worldly women.

A dilemma of sybaritic equity, then, Flora drolly mused,
and she found herself suddenly smiling. "Does this hap-
pen to you often?"

"This, you mean?" He grinned at her nakedness.

"Debating principle in the midst of lust, Monsieur le
Comte," she countered with an impudent lift of one brow.
"The extent of your libidinous repute is well-known and
not in question."

His smile was delectable; she could almost taste the
sweetness on her lips.

"I see," he softly whispered. "And no, of course not.
You're the absolute first where the subject of debate has—
er—intervened. Should we compare the nuances of our
frustration and annoyance, or would you rather . . . um
. . . deal with them in a more gratifying way?"

"Don't you talk with women?"

"Always," he glibly lied. "Do you with your lovers?"

It stopped her for a moment. She didn't or hadn't; none
had sufficiently interested her beyond the pursuit of pas-

sion. Could it be Adam Serre's attraction wasn't exclusively physical? "Yes, certainly," she replied, as capable as he of artful response.

"We still have forty minutes," he softly said, glancing at the small timepiece he'd slipped from his vest pocket. "What would you like to talk about?"

It was as though his quiet words stroked her skin, her senses, her libido. How could he so blatantly exude sexuality in a few innocuous words? How could his tone so perversely be suggesting something quite different?

"Only forty minutes?" she breathed, a tremor of susceptibility quivering in her voice.

"More if you need it," he murmured, understanding her answer, beginning to unbuckle his belt.

She watched with heated anticipation while he slipped the buttons free, a throbbing lust dominating her senses, her appetite for him heedless of the profligacies in his past, her body seemingly immune to carnal scruple.

Then, leaning back on his elbows, he quietly said, "Why don't you take it out?"

And when she obeyed, when her fingers first closed around the hard shaft, he sucked in his breath and groaned. He was enormous, she thought, and hard—as if he'd not recently climaxed.

His erection lay arched against his belly, against the rumpled tails of his shirt still haphazardly tucked into the loosened waistband of his trousers, the swollen tip visibly pulsing, the distended veins throbbing with the rhythm of his heartbeat.

Flora's breathing had altered in the past moments as she gazed at his splendid proportions.

"Touch it," he murmured. "Take it between your hands."

"It's very large," Flora whispered, beyond denial of her vaunting need, wet with desire, tantalized by the engorged size. She took the rigid length in both hands, running her palms up the warm, velvety skin; then, circling it with her fingers, she exerted pressure, gliding downward to the stem, stretching it until the shiny throbbing crest flared high. Lowering her head, she heard Adam's soft moan when the flourishing tip first touched her mouth, and another when it slid over her wet lips and her tongue glided down its length, and his deep sigh of pleasure when the crown came to rest against the back of her throat. His hands came up to cup her head, to hold her while the agonizing rapture flooded his senses.

Moments later he pushed his fingers through her hair, sparking static, destroying what was left of her chignon, hurtling pins into the hay and onto the blanket in a cascading shower. Then, wrapping the waves of her hair around his knuckles with swift, abrupt sureness, he measured the rise and fall of her head, setting the rhythm, eyes shut, his head thrown back so the muscles of his throat were cast in relief, his breathing a harsh, raspy staccato as the feverish delirium peaked.

It was almost too late when he forced her head away and he lay panting for breathless seconds, wondering where she'd learned such incredible technique.

"And now it's my turn."

Flora's provocative words breached with volatile impact his tempestuous preoccupation, and it took an incoherent moment to deal with the sentiment. A second passed, then two before his gaze assessed her. "You seldom wait to be asked, do you?"

She was balanced on her knees with her palms resting on her thighs, her tumbled hair framing her face, lying in disarray on her shoulders, her lips glistening, incarnadined, the mouth of a fellatrice. "Not usually," she said, knowing what she'd done to him, knowing he was as eager as she for consummation.

"Then be my guest," he insolently said, lightly holding his stiff, gleaming penis upright. "I know you're familiar with the drill."

"Would you prefer a postponement?" Flora queried, her insolence matching his.

"Come here."

"Are you asking me now?" Her smile was shamelessly cheeky. "I wouldn't want to broach any carnal etiquette."

"I'm telling you."

"I'd rather be asked."

"I'm asking, then."

"Politely."

"Would you please bring your sweet body here, Lady Flora?"

"Where?"

"Right here," he said in a repressed murmur, his gaze moving from her to the relevant portion of his anatomy. "Please."

Her smile held the sunny glow of triumph.

But she'd no more than lowered herself down on his blatant erection, when he rolled over, taking her with him, and proceeded to ravage her undocile body.

They mated as if they were out to annihilate each other, consumed by their ravenous passions and greedy lust—in turn possessive and bewitched, seduced and overwhelmed, enraptured and devoured, first he on top and then she, moving from position to heated position, until they lay at last in the shipwreck of orgasmic release, breathless, sweat-sheened, shaken to their core.

Both experienced, they recognized the rare mystery of the bond that joined them.

And they smiled at each other like secret conspirators.

"I think I need a nap," Flora lazily murmured, so drowsy her eyelids felt weighted. The fragrance of the hay perfumed the air, the illumination from the clerestory windows suffused the loft in a delicate golden glow, the narcotic of the sun's warmth drifted through her senses.

"I'll carry you to your room," Adam softly said, brushing away a damp lock of hair from her temple.

"No, I'll walk . . . in just a minute or two . . . but—"

"Not right now," he helpfully finished with an understanding smile. Flora Bonham was less accustomed to his profligate life, perhaps less familiar with sleepless nights. In the end he found enough scattered hairpins to roughly restore her coiffeur, remarking with a grin as he smoothed her hair into place with his fingers, "I'm going to have to begin carrying a comb until you leave Montana. Anytime I'm within a mile of you, I'm like an out-of-control adolescent."

"And I'm more than grateful . . . ," Flora softly said, her smile so tempting he quickly gauged their remaining time against the risk of exposure. But cautioning himself to prudence, he began dressing her instead. Swift moments later he lifted her into his arms and made his way to the stairway. "This is getting to be a habit," he teased, moving across the stable yard toward the house, "my dressing you and making you presentable. Luckily as a father I've experience dressing little girls."

"And big girls too, no doubt." But she said it facetiously, not in anger.

"Only one big girl," he softly corrected.

"There are times I adore your facile charm," she murmured with a smile.

"While I find you adorable and remarkably facile in any number of charming ways," he whispered.

"Good," she cheerfully retorted, "then I don't have to feel guilty about having you carry me when I'm perfectly capable of walking. Although I suppose I really should walk," she went on, glancing at the narrowing distance to the house. "Everyone will see and wonder and gossip . . ."

"Do I detect a certain lack of conviction?" Adam noted with a perceptive smile.

"It *is* embarrassing."

His heavy brows rose fractionally as he gazed down at her. "But not *too* embarrassing."

She blushed. "If you weren't so insatiable, I wouldn't be so tired."

"I accept full responsibility," he gallantly said, rather than debating varying degrees of insatiability. "Will two hours of sleep help?"

"Heaven on earth," she pronounced with fervor.

"In that case I'll postpone the picnic until afternoon."

"Are you sure?" A touch of anxiety echoed in her voice.

"I'll explain—*something* to Lucie," he said with a grin. "Something acceptable to a three-year-old. And it wouldn't do to have Cloudy see you so completely worn out. She wouldn't approve."

"Of what?" Flora's voice had taken on an acerbity; she categorically disliked censure.

"She wouldn't approve of my lack of hospitality to a guest. And I'd suffer the consequences."

Flora laughed. "You're afraid of her."

He grinned like a small boy caught out in a prank. "Let's just say I'm suitably impressed with the power of her punch. Additionally, she's an important, stable influence in Lucie's life, which I greatly appreciate. Now, put on your best swooning pose, because I see Mrs. O. and two servants peering at us from the entrance porch."

"Why did I swoon?" Flora whispered, as if the servants could hear across the gravel drive.

"The heat."

"Adam, it's seventy degrees."

"Something you ate?"

"And put an onus on the cook's breakfast?"

"Good God," he muttered in exasperation, "since when do I have to offer explanations to my staff?"

"How very French."

"What's that supposed to mean?" He cast her a searching glance.

"Everyone knows of their arrogance."

"Perhaps they have reason to be arrogant," he roguishly replied. "Shut your eyes, we're almost there. I'll take care of everything. . . ."

Flora's lashes fell as if weighted with a bloat of hippopotami, gladly relinquishing the role of savior to Adam.

"She twisted her ankle in the stable and fainted away," Adam briskly declared as he ascended the shallow bank of stairs leading to the porch.

"Oh, dear, I'll fetch the doctor," Mrs. O'Brien exclaimed, moving toward Adam with a solicitous expression on her round face. "The poor dear. Is it swollen? Do you think it's broken?"

"It's only a minor injury, Mrs. O. I'll send for the doctor later if necessary. These society ladies faint at the smallest discomfort. They're always needing to be rescued"—he repressed a yelp as Flora pinched his arm—"from some disaster," he finished through gritted teeth.

"Not sweet Lady Flora," the housekeeper declared, defending her favorite houseguest.

"*Especially* Lady Flora," Adam muttered under his breath as he swept by them.

"You've got nerve," Flora scolded him as they entered the empty foyer, glaring at Adam through the lace of her lashes. "As if I'm in need of your rescue."

"Who's carrying whom?" he pointedly whispered, as he started up the stairs.

"You needn't sound so smug. It's all your fault anyway that I'm so tired."

"Right, and elephants fly," he snorted, his long strides taking them to the second floor so swiftly she marveled at his strength. "I'll remind you tonight when you're, shall we say—anxious," he softly said, "exactly who's at fault."

"You presume too much, Mr. Serre," she said with the coy accents of a fashionable lady. "I may not be interested in seeing you tonight."

He didn't answer, his concentration focused on remembering the location of her room. "There," he softly said, recognizing Flora's bedchamber from the numerous rooms they'd occupied last night. "And it's not presumption, darling," he quietly murmured, gazing down at her. "It's deductive reasoning. You can't last more than a few hours"—his voice dropped a half octave—"without it."

"I *certainly* can. Your ego is monumental, Mr. Serre."

"Not as monumental as your delectable libido, Miss Bonham," he cheerfully noted, in great charity with the world after an uninterrupted hour of carnal relations with the delicious Lady Flora. Shifting her to one arm, he reached for the doorknob, unlatched the door, kicked it open, and walked inside the sun-filled room.

"My libido is none of your concern," she said with that female dialectic that overlooked pertinent facts such as their mutually gratifying regard for libidos in the hour past. "And I can survive perfectly well without you," she coolly finished, annoyed at what she viewed as masculine conceit.

"Fine," he casually replied, walking over to the bed. "We'll play billiards tonight instead. Or you can entertain us at the piano." He placed her on the bed, pulled off her boots, unfolded a comforter, and covered her, tucking it neatly under her chin. Kissing her lightly on the forehead, he smiled as he stood upright. "I haven't heard you play. Can you manage Chopin?"

"No."

"A shame." He was walking over to the windows. "Do you play billiards?" He began pulling the yellow brocade drapes closed.

"Extremely well."

He turned from his task to gaze at her briefly. "For money?"

"Of course."

He grinned. "Well, then, the evening won't be completely wasted." He stood in the half shadows, framed by the swathed and draped brocade, tall, handsome as sin, a bronzed half-blood with dark, sensual eyes, a hard warrior's body, devastating charm, and a luxurious sense of pleasure.

"Although I *could* change my mind," Flora murmured, gazing at his tantalizing image, her eyes heavy with sleep.

"Plan on it." His voice was scarcely a whisper, the sound too low to be heard in the bed across the room.

He remained motionless for some time, gazing at her in slumber, wondering how he'd become so obsessed. Her heavy hair lay in shimmering auburn on the lace-trimmed pillow, her face had the look of a Madonna in repose— although she had that sultry sensuality of a Bouguereau Madonna. Her lips, slightly parted in sleep, were bee-stung ripe and luscious, the color of mountain cherries, her dark lashes shadowed her flushed cheeks. The soft, plump breasts he'd suckled and caressed only minutes before, rose and fell in opulent mounds under the white silk coverlet, and his eyes drifted lower to the valley between her thighs, to the sweet delight that drew him like Circe's song. But her beauty alone wasn't responsible for the magnitude of his attraction, because beautiful women had been a constant in his life since adolescence. She was more than an exquisite woman; Flora Bonham exuded a rare vitality and a more rare capacity to see beyond the vanities of society. Gifted with a sharp intelligence, she was also playful, challenging, inquisitive, unreservedly candid—at times embarrassingly direct. She was also the first woman he'd met who was his equal in bed—wild, inventive, provocative . . . lush as a Persian odalisque.

Like an addiction, she could make one forget duty, reason, the clear-sighted vision of sensible goals.

She was frankly perilous to his peace of mind.

And she'd become an inexplicable fire in his blood.

Chapter Five

⤜❦⤛

The picnic was the kind of perfection one encounters only on rare occasions in life. The weather was warm and sunny, so the mother vixen Lucie had alluded to had brought her kits out of their den to play, and for the better part of an hour the party from Adam's ranch was enthralled by their gamboling play. The picnic group was downwind from the foxes and distant enough so the humans could whisper and not be heard; Lucie particularly was prone to loud, sibilant exclamations of astonishment. Even Mrs. McLeod, who was not called Cloudy to her face, was heard to utter a restrained "Heavenly days!" or two when the babies rolled themselves into furry balls and tumbled down the hill in sport.

Mrs. McLeod had managed the journey uphill on Charlie without mishap, but it had taken both men to help her down from her saddle. At which point she'd dusted off her black bombazine skirt and said, "Did my chair get packed?"

She was now ensconced in a folding campaign chair like an oriental potentate with a bonnet, her several double chins bobbing as she directed the disposition of the picnic like a born general.

"Le Comte," she said, with the harsh pronunciation of her native glen, even the ladies' finishing school in Edinburgh not successful in smoothing her consonants. "Did you think to bring the telescope? I see some kind of animal down the ridge there. . . .

"Lucie, offer the earl some of the queen's meringues. . . .

"Lady Flora, do sit down on that cozy blanket and help yourself to some of the smoked-salmon sandwiches."

Adam had handed her the telescope with dispatch, and for some moments, so intent was she on the landscape beyond the lens, the stream of orders ceased.

"I've missed you," Adam quietly told Flora as he returned to the plaid blanket spread on the ground, reaching past her for his flask of cognac tucked away in the bottom of the picnic basket.

Blushing at the intimacy in his tone, she quickly glanced to see if anyone had taken notice. But Lucie and her father were working on the assembly of a small wooden boat the earl had carved while they were watching the kits play, and Mrs. McLeod was momentarily content surveying the mountainside.

"No one's looking," he whispered, uncorking the silver container. "I'm the soul of discretion. Would you like some?" he offered, tipping the engraved flask in her direction.

She nervously shook her head, not as blasé as Adam, who was the least likely soul of discretion she'd ever known.

"It'll help you relax," he said with a warm smile, offering her the flask again. "You're nervous."

"I'm happy nervous." Flora politely took a sip. She was in marvelous good spirits, fully rested after her nap, intensely conscious of Adam's presence and of his solicitous charm. She glanced over to Cloudy. "But she reminds me of my short-lived governess. Nerves from childhood."

"Cloudy's harmless."

"In what way?" The woman had the look of an overfed drill sergeant.

"She overlooks my peccadilloes and sincerely loves Lucie."

"Which is enough."

"More than enough. Loving Lucie would be enough."

And she realized suddenly that beneath the impudence and air of casual disregard, he'd experienced his own kind of heartache. "You're very lucky to have Lucie," she said.

"I know. Even with Isolde as the maximum price."

Flora didn't remember her own mother, for she'd died when Flora was very young, and she'd never known life with two parents. But she knew that to have an uncaring mother like Isolde must be painful.

"Now, if she just won't come back," Adam went on with a grin, "in the words of a popular song, 'Life would be grand.' "

"Where did you find her?"

His face went dead for a moment, and a muscle clenched high over his cheekbone, the black rush of memory etched on his liver.

"I mean Mrs. McLeod," Flora quickly interjected, the intense bitterness of his expression alarming.

The malevolence instantly disappeared, and he seemed to breathe again. "I found Mrs. McLeod at Fort Benton, standing at the end of the gangplank after disembarking from the last steamer of the season at nine-thirty in the morning on October eighteenth, four years ago."

"A very specific memory, apparently."

"She saved my life," he solemnly said. "I remember the absolute minute." And he did, because he'd just come out from Carson's Saloon that morning, where he'd spent the night, drinking, gambling, and taking his turn with the ladies upstairs. He was miserably hung over, he was miserably married to Isolde; he'd come north to meet the nursemaid supposedly sent from St. Louis to take care of their expected child, and the woman wasn't aboard. There wouldn't be another steamer up the Missouri until spring, and the thought of Isolde touching his child was enough to give him nightmares. Not that she'd consider the possibility, but he'd feel safer with someone—preferably someone large and menacing—in charge of the nursery.

All Isolde had done in the short months they'd been

married was complain: of the heat, of the cold, of the dust, of the wind, of the lack of courtiers nearby, of Adam's propensity for drink—a recent tendency since his marriage—of the inconvenience of her pregnancy. Which he considered eminently more of an inconvenience for him, since he'd been forced to marry her as his father's last dying wish.

Not that he didn't assume responsibility for his child, but the circumstances of its conception had always given him pause, and the word "scheming" on that particular occasion had always struck him as appropriate.

"And you've been together ever since," Flora politely noted as the silence lengthened.

Brought back to the more enjoyable present by the sound of Flora's voice, Adam said, "Cloudy turned out to be perfect. Her prospective employer hadn't come to fetch her, so she became *our* Cloudy by default."

"She reminds me of the queen."

"A considerably larger version, though," he asserted with a grin. "I have to use utmost diplomacy since she outweighs me by several score pounds."

"*You're* diplomatic? I thought your propensities tended toward the autocratic." But she said it with a devastating smile that heated his blood.

"And you *like* it," he murmured, gazing at her with a shamelessly brazen look.

"I don't." But she was blushing, and she felt the small pulsing between her legs as if he only need look at her like that and she opened for him.

"Then I'll have to think of something different tonight, something you *do* like."

Her nipples stiffened at his soft, husky words, at the promise of pleasure, at the memory of their heated play in the stable hayloft. "You have to stop. . . ."

"I'd like to lay you down right now, over there, behind that outcropping. You couldn't make any noise, or the others would hear you; you'd have to take me inside you without a sound; you couldn't even breathe hard, or they'd wonder what we were doing, and when you climaxed, I'd let you scream into my mouth. And afterward you'd feel my sperm slippery on your legs under your skirt when we returned to the picnic, and I'd know it was there too when you drank your lukewarm lemonade and ate your salmon sandwiches. . . ."

He'd moved to block her body from the others, although everyone was intent on the boat construction, but if they glanced over, he didn't want them to observe the pink blush on Flora's face or notice her agitated breathing, or the tips of her nipples pressing through the fine linen of her pristine white blouse.

"I'd rather not play billiards too long tonight if you don't mind," he murmured, touching one protruding nipple with a light, brushing fingertip. "I'd like to show you my bed."

"I'm obsessed with you," Flora whispered, holding her hands tightly clasped in her lap to still her trembling.

"After one game, then, I'll say good night . . . and wait for you upstairs."

At dinner that night as the fish course was being served, Adam was handed a message by one of the servant girls.

"Excuse me," he briefly said after scanning the note and, rising from the table, he left the room.

He returned in only a few minutes with a guest in tow, a tall young half-blood like himself, so close in physical resemblance, his kinship with Adam was obvious.

"I'd like you to meet my brother," Adam said, using the Absarokee term of kinship for his cousin.[5] "Lady Flora Bonham, Lord Haldane, James Du Gard."

"Forgive me for intruding," the man said with a bow, a trace of a French accent in his words, "and for my appearance, but Adam insisted." He was dressed in the hybrid fashion of the frontier in a combination of leather and cloth, his fringed leggings and moccasins topped with a tunic shirt and vest.

"By all means join us," George Bonham said. "We're not formal. You've had a long ride from the looks of it."

"He's up from Virginia City," Adam said. "Here, sit down, Esh-ca-ca-mah-hoo," he went on, calling him by his Absarokee name, "Standing Lance." Pulling a chair out, he signaled for a servant. "Would you like wine, bourbon? Or perhaps coffee." He knew his cousin was fatigued after hours on the trail.

"Coffee's fine."

"James tells me that Meagher has received official authorization from General Sherman for his militia. Now that the acting governor can issue government vouchers to the local merchants, his citizen army will be moving beyond the confines of the local saloons."

"Does it affect your clan this far north?" the earl inquired, aware that distance was a distinct advantage in the wilderness.

"Since Bozeman was recently killed and the Lakota are causing trouble as far west as the Musselshell, Meagher has any number of excuses to lead his vigilantes just about anywhere. And unfortunately, he now has the vouchers to finance his operations."

"His men have been promised plunder in addition to wages," his cousin added. "They have permission to keep 'all the property they capture from the Indians,' were Meagher's words."

"How dangerous will they be to your valley?" Flora asked.

"We can protect ourselves," Adam quietly said. "They may not bother us." His words held a curious threat despite his soft tone. "James assures me my land claim is secure, and I trust his expertise. He's my legal adviser."

"Thank your father instead for having the foresight to guarantee title through Congress."

"Papa understood the value of land," Adam said with a grim smile. "A family's estates are improved by marriage and maintained by sound fiscal responsibility, he always said."

"A shame Isolde had those vineyards he wanted," his cousin said with a grin.

"A shame that his health was so precarious," Adam murmured. "And that you weren't finished with your studies at the Sorbonne. You might have been able to find me a less confining way to acquire that land."

"You're forgetting his marked interest in Isolde's ducal bloodlines."

"Or more aptly *belle-mère*'s interest in ducal bloodlines. *Papa* chose to marry for love. Tell me what you know of the telegraph from General Sherman," Adam went on, disliking the discussion of his personal life. "And what of the talk of reapportionment? Has anyone given a date for the new elections?"

And through the remaining courses conversation was exclusively political. Two forts, one at the forks of the Musselshell and the other near the big bend of the Yellowstone, were scheduled to be operating soon to supply Meagher's citizen army. Governor Green Clay Smith was still in Washington pursuing the interests of the territory from the comforts of civilization while Acting Governor Thomas Meagher was in the process of living up to his reputation as a former Civil War general in the Irish Brigade.

When dessert was served, Adam excused himself to say good night to Lucie. She'd gone up to the nursery early, tired after their journey into the mountains.

"Have you been here long?" James asked the Bonhams, having intercepted a small glance between his cousin and the dazzling Lady Flora that suggested an intimacy beyond that of casual guest.

"Three days," the earl replied. "We came north to buy some of Adam's bloodstock."

"And Papa is enormously pleased with his purchases," Flora added with a smile. "Tell him, Papa, about the mile time Aleppo ran this morning."

"You're sorry you and Adam missed them, I'll wager, now that you heard how fast he ran."

"What was the time?" James inquired, taking note of the sudden blush coloring Lady Flora's cheeks, aware of his cousin's interest in beautiful women, recalling suddenly the gossip from Aurora Parkman and others in Virginia City concerning Adam and Flora's temporary disappearance from her husband's party.

"Damned if he can't run the mile in one forty-six. Sweetest goer I've seen since Argonaut took the Gold Stakes at Ascot in sixty."

"Are you shipping him back to England, then?"

"Eventually."

"Will you be in the territory long?"

"I'm not exactly sure," the earl replied, waving away the servant with the cordials. "It depends on the time necessary to assemble my specimens."

"And whether Papa wears out his welcome with the Absarokee," Flora added with a gracious smile. "He's studying the culture and bringing back fauna and flora for the collection at Göttingen and for Professor Prichard in London."

"Do you assist your father?"

"More likely the other way around," the earl proudly declared. "Flora was the youngest person to have a paper presented to the Royal Society."

"Congratulations, Lady Flora," James politely said. "You expect to study us for some time, then."

"Only Papa will. I've a commitment in Yucatán this fall. An expedition is being mounted to study Tikal."

He should have suspected, he thought. Adam was careful to amuse himself only with women who would make no permanent demands on him. "You amaze me, Lady Flora. Most English ladies wouldn't venture past the fashionable boundaries of Mayfair."

"Flora isn't 'most English ladies,' " her father said with obvious pride. "She can probably ride and shoot as well as you and hold her own with a desert sheikh or a Tartar cossack."

"Papa, you're embarrassing me. I'm quite commonplace. I simply like to travel."

"Commonplace" was not a word he would choose to

describe Flora Bonham, James reflected. She reminded him powerfully of any number of depictions of Venus; she had the same overwhelming sensuality. Her flesh above the low décolletage of her gown glowed with a palpable lushness, her violet eyes held a mysterious heat, the heavy mass of her hair, rich with golden highlights lured the touch. And her mouth, full-lipped, provocative, tantalized with an intense eroticism.

He hoped she'd leave for the Yucatán soon, because with the volatile state of territorial affairs, he needed Adam's full attention in the coming months.

He said as much to Adam later when they'd retired to the library after the billiard game and they were seated before the windows facing the mountains. The stars were brilliant in the night sky, the moon a sliver over the rugged peaks. "You must be deeply enamored," James said. "You let her win."

Adam shrugged. "I almost didn't have to let her win. She's damned good. Did you see the seven-bank shot she made? The last time I saw one was in Paris a couple of years ago when Duvall won against Francois. She's very accomplished."

"In a variety of ways, from the barely concealed lust I observed this evening."

Adam grinned. "She's quite astonishing."

"When is she leaving?" James's voice held a certain grimness.

"In a day or so."

"And then I'll have your attention again?"

"You always have my attention, Esh-ca-ca-mah-hoo," Adam said.

"Will you leave her tonight?"

"If I have to. Are you asking me?"

"We have to make plans to avoid Meagher's volunteers or defend ourselves against them, as well as deal with the Lakota who will be in camp soon looking for allies in their war. And I have to leave early in the morning for the summer camp."

"I'll see you before you go."

"After she falls asleep."

Adam nodded.

"She's waiting for you now, so go," James kindly said. "I can find my room without you."

Chapter Six

※ॐ※

She was there when he walked over the threshold into his room, seated fully clothed in the middle of his bed.

"I didn't know how long you'd be with James. I didn't know whether someone would come in, a servant or chambermaid. My heart's pounding like a hammer."

He softly shut the door. "I gave orders to be left alone tonight."

She exhaled in relief and fell back on his pillows in a playful sprawl. Then, abruptly rolling over on her side, she lounged in a sweep of pale flesh and crushed azure silk. "You think of everything, don't you, Mr. Serre?" Her smile warmed the room.

"We try," he replied with an answering grin. His gaze swung to the ebony-and-ormolu clock on the mantel. "It's early. What would you like to do?"

"Are there choices?"

"Always."

"First I'd like to dance with you."

"Here?"

She nodded. The thought had come to her earlier in the day when someone at the picnic had mentioned the Tuileries, and she'd suddenly wanted to be with Adam in Paris before the eyes of his family and friends. It was a dangerous premise, completely out of character.

"You'll have to sing."

"Or you."

His brows rose as he leaned against the door. "You're asking a lot."

"Will you?"

"I'll try." And he turned the key in the lock.

When he moved toward her across the large chamber, she felt the now familiar excitement at the sight of him. He was elegant tonight in a black frock coat and embroidered vest, the dramatic sleek length of his hair a primeval flourish to his fashionable attire. And when he stood at the bedside with his hand out in invitation, she saw the same untamed sensibility in his eyes.

"I believe this dance is mine, Lady Flora," he softly said.

Their fingers touched, and then her hand rested in his and they smiled at each other like lovers—shared jubilation, shared pleasure, shared intimacies forever coded in their memories.

He swung her up into his arms, impelled by the same unbridled emotions that had postponed his conversation with James—his need to touch and hold her, his hunger for the warmth of her body. And she flung her arms around his neck and held him fiercely tight as if she knew beneath the hot passion and desire, the immediacy of his body close to hers, the inexorable passage of time ticked away the minutes of their happiness.

He stood motionless, holding her for an inexpressible moment of pungent pleasure overlaid suddenly by a swamping sense of melancholy.

"Remember this," Flora whispered, her eyes filling with tears, feeling as though she were losing him already, the sensation so powerful she touched his cheek to reaffirm his presence.

He silently nodded, turning his head to brush her fingers with his lips.

"May of sixty-seven," Flora murmured, his breath warm on her fingers.

"I won't forget. The Little People are crying over my shoulder."[6]

"James is taking you away."

"Not tonight."

"But soon."

He sighed, knowing how limited their time. "It depends . . . on the activities in Virginia City."

"You could be hurt."

He shook his head. "My medicine guards me." His soft voice seemed to enfold her as if his own spirit had the power to comfort. "Now sing to me," he quietly said, placing her gently on her feet. "And we'll dance together this spring night in May."

And he joined her in the chorus of the song, his low voice almost a caress, the words of the love song poignant, as they sang of eternal pledges. He held her close, the rhythm of their movements languid in the lamplit bedchamber, their footsteps a whisper on the plush handloomed carpet.

"When were you at the Tuileries?" he softly queried, as if he knew her mind, as if they might have passed each other in the same ballroom.

"Twice last year . . . during the season."

He shook his head because he'd been guarding his herds last winter when the Lakota were ranging west beyond their normal boundaries.

"And the year before in the spring."

"When?" He wanted to have been in Paris then.

She smiled. "In April during the first race meets."

"And you saw Dongen win the Royal Cup," he murmured, a smile in his words.

"Your horse?" She suddenly stopped and looked up at him so she could see his eyes, so she could see the answering pleasure she was feeling.

"My horse," he softly agreed, pulling her closer, his smile elemental happiness. "And the Tuileries were perfumed with mignonette that evening."

"I remember the night, and now I know why."

"Our spirits met," he whispered.

• • •

They made love that night with uncommon tenderness, as if their bodies and minds, their susceptible emotions, were spun-glass fragile, as if the melancholy that overcame them at times muted their previous covetous hungers, as if they were alone together in a collapsing world.

"How do you feel?" Flora softly asked very late that night as Adam lay over her, momentarily sated, resting on his elbows, his eyes in shadow. She gently touched one of the pink shells suspended from his ears.

"Favored by the gods, *bia.*"

"Or luck."

His head tipped slightly to one side, and he gazed at her in mild query. "No mystical perceptions?"

"Why do you wear these so often?" she said instead, indicating his earring with a tapping finger, her pragmatism too well developed for myth.

"They were a gift from my mother when I was born. They protect me from harm. They're very strong medicine," he softly added.

The demons came back then, his words recalling all the talk of militias and citizen armies, of plunder and defensive forts over the dinner table. "Will there be killing?" Flora fearfully asked, the calm warmth of his body on hers the antithesis of warfare and death.

"I'll see that you have an escort. You needn't worry."

"And they want to kill only Indians, anyway. . . ."

"It's mostly whiskey talk and political expediency. It shouldn't last long," he soothed.

"I'm afraid you'll be hurt."

"I won't be. Hush, now. Kiss me." And he followed his words with satisfying action.

Adam entered James's room at dawn. Softly closing the door, he ran his fingers swiftly through his ruffled hair before moving toward the bed.

"You look tired," his cousin said, raising himself up into a seated position, "and damned disheveled," he added, casting a look at Adam's hastily thrown-on clothes. "I've been watching the horizon lighten," he meaningfully commented, hooking his arms behind his head and leaning back against the pillows.

"Sorry," Adam apologized, dropping heavily into an upholstered chair near the bed. "She just fell asleep."

"Flora Bonham seems different. You seem different." James's gaze narrowed slightly. "And so soon after Isolde. I'm surprised."

"Not as surprised as I," Adam retorted in a low rasp.

"You met her at Judge Parkman's, I hear."

Adam slouched lower in the chair and gazed at his cousin from under his dark brows. "From whom did you hear that?"

"Aurora Parkman, among others. The gossip is rife. In your inimitable fashion you neglected several of the normal conventions of etiquette that evening. Maybe you two shouldn't have come back into the ballroom"—he paused significantly—"afterward."

"I'm not sure it was my idea to leave in the first place," Adam said with a small reminiscent smile. "It's possible *she* asked me."

"And you never say no."

"I may have thought about it."

"But not for long, apparently."

"She was undressing at the time, making it damned hard to seriously consider refusing."

"What if someone had come in? Her father, for instance."

Adam shrugged. "They didn't. What's the point?"

"The point is I can't have you in love right now. The situation is too grave."

Adam's dark gaze met his cousin's with a penetrating intensity. "Let me calm you, then. This isn't love."

"I'm relieved," James said with a grin. "Such devotion is unusual for you. Allow me my confusion when I see you openingly adoring."

"You must be losing your eyesight," Adam quietly replied. "Is Sherman marching north?" he interjected, the subject of his lovelife abruptly curtailed. "Do we have federal troops to contend with as well as Meagher's volunteer army?"

"No to both questions," his cousin replied, understanding conversation pertaining to Flora Bonham was at an end. "But Sherman's aide, Major Lewis, is on his way to Virginia City to determine the extent of the Indian danger."

"So we spend the summer avoiding Meagher's political ambitions and hope for an early winter to drive the militia back home."

"Something like that. Unfortunately, the two forts they're constructing are extremely close."

"And talk of gold on the Yellowstone may be of more interest to the volunteers than war with the Indians," Adam noted. "Since last year's treaty negotiations to open up this land remain unratified—an added excuse to overrun the area would be advantageous."

"Don't forget the railroads' interest in the coal here."

"Nor sundry cattlemen's keen desire to graze their stock north of the Yellowstone. Damned Storham and his bunch are pressing our borders already." Adam's voice had taken on a heated irritation.

"I'll be picking up the additional weapons you ordered in Fort Benton after I stop at the summer camp with news of Sherman's telegram."

"I'll meet you in Fort Benton. In what—four days?"

"Will you still be alive in four days?" James sardonically inquired, surveying Adam's fatigued sprawl.

"In case I'm not," Adam replied with a grin, "you inherit my best horses."

James laughed. "A dilemma of conscience, then."

Adam heaved himself to his feet and stretched with a great sigh. "I'm going to sleep now for a few hours. I'll see you in Fort Benton on Thursday."

In the following days Adam's interest, his thoughts and fanciful whims, centered on Flora Bonham. He cleared his schedule of all normal activities, turning over the daily operation of the ranch to Montoya. Beyond the necessary commitments of a courteous host to the earl, and the fatherly duties that Lucie required, Adam devoted himself to unremitting sex with Flora.

Time was limited. They both understood. And they plotted and contrived like impassioned lovers to spend every possible minute together. They snatched kisses in shadowed corners, behind hastily closed doors; they stole away for heated rendezvous in the midst of the daily bustle; they met by contrived accident in secluded niches and leafy bowers, in the hushed sanctuary of vacant rooms; they spent blissfully uninterrupted hours of the night together, waking each morning with a small ruinous feeling of despair . . . for another day was gone.

On Wednesday morning, in the shrouded dark of predawn, Adam turned his head on the pillow and watched the door to the balcony open. Faint light from the waning moon outlined the form slipping through the doorway, and as the curtain fell back into place over the closed door, he murmured, "*Xatsi-sa*," meaning "Quiet."

Easing his arm from under Flora's head with infinite care, Adam slid away from the warmth of her body, and glancing down to make certain she was asleep, he gingerly rose from the bed. Motioning the warrior standing in the shadows toward his dressing room, he followed and, quietly shutting the door behind them, spoke rapidly in Absarokee.

"How close are they? And from what direction?" The danger had to be imminent if his people had sent this wolf, meaning scout, for him.

"They moved across the Crane Nest River yesterday from the southwest," White Otter replied.

"How many?" Adam strode toward the wardrobes, the paneled room dimly lit by a small kerosene lamp that had been burning every night since James had left.

"Fifty men."

"Weapons? Supplies?" Swiftly opening a door, he snatched a pair of leggings from the shelf.

"Sharpses, Winchesters. A munitions wagon leaving deep tracks."

"We'll move the village into the south valley today. They won't find it if we stay far enough ahead of them," he said, belting the waistband closed. "Is the camp alerted?" He reached for an elkskin shirt.

White Otter nodded. "Everything should be packed for moving by the time we return. They were taking the lodges down when I left."

Adam's head slid through the beaded neckline. "Have Montoya bring up two ponies, and I'll meet you in the stables in five minutes."

"Esh-ca-ca-mah-hoo says you found a new yellow-eyes," White Otter said, a quirked smile creasing his bronzed cheek. "And more trouble. Will she let you go?"

"I won't ask her," Adam said with a grin, pulling out a pair of beaded moccasins.

"A sensible man," the tall Absarokee softly said. "Do you want your war pony?"

"Yes," Adam replied, sliding his feet into the soft leather.

Short moments later, his knife sheath strapped to his leg, his Winchester slung across his back, Adam stood beside the bed to take his farewell. Flora slept with her hand under her cheek like a young child, the gentle rise and fall of her breathing peaceful, serene. When he bent to gently kiss her cheek, she stirred in her sleep, and he stood motionless and quiet until her breathing had lapsed back into the rhythm of slumber. "Pleasant dreams, *bia*," he whispered. He stood for a moment more gazing at her, memories of the past days flooding his mind, and then he softly sighed. "*Kamba-k 'úewimà-tsiky*," he murmured, telling her "I must go." He'd stayed too long already, with the militia tracking down his clan. And they'd both understood from the first that their time together was brief.

It was over.

He turned and strode from the room.

·   ·   ·

When Adam entered the nursery, he woke up Cloudy first. She came to with a start when Adam touched her shoulder, but she quickly recognized his native gear and, struggling her bulk into a seated position, briskly said, "The militia must be close."

"Close enough to move the summer camp out of their way. White Otter's here and I came to say good-bye to Lucie."

"Do you know when you'll return?" She automatically straightened her nightcap and tucked in errant wisps of her sandy-colored hair, her notions of nicety a constant in her life, even when attired in a rumpled nightgown.

"As soon as I can. Take care of Lucie for me."

"As if you need tell me," she said with a small sniff, "since I've been with Lucie from the day she was born. More likely I should be telling you to take care of yourself with the bloody militia riding up and down looking to shoot anyone remotely resembling an Indian. Like the heathen Sassenach in forty-five when they massacred my great-grannie's clan and nigh on every other Highland family."

"I'm always careful, Mrs. McLeod," Adam said with a smile. "And we're well armed."

"Superior firepower will win the day, my uncle Roddie always said, and he should know, with customs men on his trail most of his life. But I see you shifting politely on those beautiful moccasins, so go and wake Lucie and be gone. Except one last thing," she added in a staccato rush. "Will the Bonhams be staying on? Lucie's monstrous fond of them both." A note of compassion underlay her normal resolute delivery.

Adam hesitated for a second, not absolutely sure of the Bonhams' plans, not sure he wasn't above going back into his bedroom and saying, "Don't leave," to Flora. Not certain, either, of Cloudy's intent. "You might suggest they stay on for a time if you think Lucie would like it. My return depends very much on circumstance."

"Put a bullet in one of those 'circumstances' for me, and God go with you."

Adam grinned. "I'm surprised your Methodist God's so bloodthirsty."

"Presbyterian, my lord, and he's not above smiting those of evil intent now and again."

Lucie gazed at her father from a drowsy half sleep when he picked her up and held her in his arms, and she sleepily murmured with that open acceptance of children, "Bring me back my own cradle-board for Baby DeeDee." Familiar with her father's occasional abrupt departures, she took no alarm from his nocturnal appearance.

"I promise. Now, you help take care of Cloudy while I'm gone."

"And Georgie and Flora too. Can I give them tea in the drawing room?"

"I'll tell Mrs. O. you're to be hostess when I'm gone," he said, smiling at his daughter.

"Hurry back, Papa, because you promised to take us swimming in the river pool and you never did and Flora and Georgie are just dying to see it." Her child's agenda ignored volunteer militia and their evil intent.

A comfort to her father. "I'll ride back as soon as I can. Now, give your Papa a kiss."

After Adam and White Otter had crossed the boundaries of his ranch, after they'd discussed all the necessary details of escorting the camp to safety, hours later when they were still riding north, Adam found his mind dwelling on unbidden vignettes of Flora Bonham in his river pool— the images so vivid, so potent, he shook his head once in an attempt to dispel them. But his subconscious wasn't so easily deterred, and Flora in the dappled sunlight of the willow groves, lushly nude as she rose from the sparkling water, smiling, opening her arms to him in welcome—any number of variations on the theme—moved through the internal landscapes of his mind.

It occurred to him only moments before they crossed the river to the dismantled camp that Flora might be pregnant—the strange, unsanctioned thought forcing it-

self into his consciousness with eleventh-hour impact. As
if it could be no longer repressed.

Normally, the women he took pleasure with were experienced and as disinclined as he to deal with any consequences of their heated passion. But Flora had made no
use of the customary precautions, he suddenly recalled,
while his libido had never cooled sufficiently to consider
possible ramifications.

Which he did now with a keen, stabbing shock.

As his pony splashed through the shallows, throwing up
water, his mind grappled with the notion of Flora Bonham pregnant with his child. Outside of Isolde, he'd never
dealt with the phenomenon. And with Isolde the news had
been presented with permanent shackles attached. Curiously, he found the possibility of Flora having his child
. . . agreeable.

Welcoming shouts broke into his reverie as their
mounts forded the deep water in the center of the river,
children called out greetings from the opposite bank,
women waved and hallooed, some young bucks rode into
the water to meet them, the dogs yelped in a steady, overriding din.

"Welcome, Tsé-ditsirá-tsi," a young warrior cheerfully
said, swinging his mount around to ride beside Adam.
"We're ready to fight at your side."

"If we have to," Adam replied with a smile. "And then
we'll see how Meagher stands against a well-armed war
party. Is Esh-ca-ca-mah-hoo still here?" And felicitous
speculation of Flora Bonham and babies was replaced in
his thoughts by the more pressing demands of survival.

Chapter Seven

❧

Adam had left a hastily scrawled note addressed to the earl on the table in the morning room. And at breakfast, before Lucie came down to join them, Flora's father said, "Adam left last night for the summer camp. Here," he went on, handing the crested paper across the table. "He says good-bye to you too."

Flora had known when she woke to an empty bed that James had called Adam away, but the flow of black words on the cream stationery finalized his leaving. He was truly gone from her life.

> *My apologies for leaving so precipitously, but I'm needed in my village. If I can be of any further assistance in your studies, please call on me. My best regards to you and Lady Flora.*
>
> *Au revoir,*
> *Adam*

She hadn't expected anything more, but the impersonal words reminded her of the reality of their disparate lives. Adam Serre was riding out to ward off a threatened attack on his village, while she and her father were only transient visitors on this northern plain, foreign observers of a rare and vanishing world. Adam understood the ephemeral nature of their visit, and there had been nothing more he could say beyond the prescribed courtesies.

"It was only a matter of time once James came," she casually replied, handing back the note. "We'd already heard the rumblings about the militia raids in Virginia City, and your horse buying *is* completed. I'm ready to leave whenever you are." It was amazing, she thought, how one learned to disguise all feeling—an encomium perhaps to the education acquired in the brittle milieu of fashionable society.

"I'm going to leave the racers behind until I'm ready to ship them home," her father declared, pouring himself more coffee. "Otherwise everything's in order to continue our journey. Adam's arranged for us to visit Four Chiefs's village."

"I can pack in an hour," Flora said with a spurious calm. She felt suddenly cut adrift—a novel sensation for a young woman who prided herself on the mobility of her life.

Mrs. McLeod entered the morning parlor at that moment, bringing Lucie down for breakfast, and, standing beside her small charge as they reached the table, she formally said in mannered accents, "Lady Lucie would be vastly pleased if you would extend your visit during her father's absence."

A reprieve! Flora's ungovernable emotions crowed, neither logic nor rationale a consideration in her instant response. Nor that it was a reprieve from, to, or for what didn't bear contemplation. She could possibly stay and that was enough. That she might see Adam again was an overwhelming expectation of hope. She understood such unrestrained excitement couldn't be publicly expressed, so she smiled at Lucie, swung her gaze to her father, and serenely said, "I think it's a capital idea. What do you think, Papa?"

"We *could* stay on for a short time, Lucie," the earl answered with a genial smile for the expectant young child. "But your father might be gone for some time. In

that case we would have to go on with our plans to visit
the other clans."

"When Papa woke me up to say good-bye last night, he
said he would be back as soon as he could," Lucie said
with firm, absolute conviction. "He's never gone very
long. And," she went on with a new excitement in her
voice, "Papa said I could be his hostess when he's not
here. I can serve tea and everything—he was going to tell
Mrs. O. before he left and he did, and I can—and won't it
be fun?"

Adam had said good-bye to Lucie but not to her, Flora
sadly thought. And she suddenly wished for a portion of
that affection.

"If you're going to be hostess," the earl cheerfully said,
interrupting Flora's winsome musing, "we must certainly
stay. Will you have strawberry cakes for tea?"

"If you want them, Georgie, we'll have Cook make lots
and lots. Then let's go to the track after breakfast?"

"Your lessons first, Lady Lucie," Cloudy reminded her.

But between Lucie's morning and afternoon lessons,
they went to the track. And later in the day they rode to
the river pool with Tom as escort and admired the sylvan
setting. A curve in the river slowed the water flow, the
eddies over time having carved out a deep backwater pool
framed by willows. The tranquil setting, the tall, waving
grasses bordering the rim of the pool, the weeping willows like lacy curtains shading the water, the melodic
birdsong alive on the air, and flitting, colorful butterflies
dancing in the sunlight rendered an idyllic picture of a
prairie paradise.

"I'll race you to the water," Lucie exclaimed, jumping
down from her pony with the finesse of a skilled rider.
And she flew through the tall grass with screams of delight.

The adults followed pell-mell, and while Lucie waded
and splashed in the water, the rest of the party lazed in the
sun-warmed grass. It was a pastoral scene of great beauty
and peace, and had Adam been present, Flora wistfully
thought, the afternoon would have been perfection.

Flora rocked Lucie to sleep that night, although to an almost four-year-old resisting sleep, it was instead a time of conversation before bedtime. They told each other stories and exchanged favorite nursery rhymes and songs. Lucie was fluent in French, English, Absarokee, and the Dublin patois of Mrs. O., so her repertoire of music was a blend of cultures, her accent flawless with the perfect ear of childhood.

She was warm and soft in Flora's arms, her small body cuddled close, the sensation of contentment beyond Flora's previous experience. That she was an irresistible child nurtured Flora's curious sense of happiness; that she was Adam's child fostered feelings of unalloyed bliss. And for the first time in her life, Flora regretted not being able to have children. She'd never considered it a deprivation before. But, then, she'd never held Adam's daughter before, nor realized she could miss someone so. A sense of irreclaimable loss crept into the fullness of her joy.

"You should stay with us," Lucie said, her eyes gazing up at Flora, miniature versions of her father's, the fluffy cloud of her lavender-scented nightgown pale in the half shadows of the room.

"I'd like that," Flora replied, as honest as the little girl in her arms, "but we have to continue our studies."

"Papa could have the clans come here, and you wouldn't have to travel anywhere."

"I think your Papa has a busy enough life without having to take care of our schedule too."

"He'd do it because he likes you. I can tell. Papa hardly ever has company; he doesn't have time, he says. But he laughs with you and smiles a lot and he's happy when you're here. So you should stay."

How tempting the offer in the quiet of the nursery with Lucie in her arms and Adam's spirit lingering in the twilight of the room. "Perhaps we'll come back to visit," Flora kindly declared, not wishing to distress the young child.

"You *must* come back," Lucie insisted, "and stay a long, *long* time. Even Cloudy likes you," she went on, her sunny smile artless, "and she doesn't like very many people. Only Papa and me and maybe some of the servants who 'know their places,' she says. Cloudy disapproves of Papa in shirtsleeves at dinner and the servants chatting with us and any number of other things she calls proper rules," Lucie rattled on. "Did you know a lady can't go to a play except in a black or blue dress? Although Maman knew all the proper rules, and Cloudy didn't like her at all. But, then, Maman didn't like Cloudy *either*, so they were even there. I heard Papa tell Maman in the sternest voice one time long ago that Cloudy stayed while he still had breath in him. I think that means till the very last."

Flora forced back a smile at Lucie's explanation and said in a voice schooled to neutrality, "I think you're right."

"Cloudy says you're an independent woman," Lucie continued in her open, guileless narrative, "and she thinks it's just grand that you had a paper read somewhere in England to a bunch of old men, and more women should be educated like you, she says. She's going to teach me Greek and Latin too and ever so many subjects that she says only gentlemen get a chance to study. Papa says she has free rein. I think she likes that, and she's a good teacher too because I can already read, and Papa says lots of almost four-year-olds can't."

"You're very lucky to have Cloudy. My Papa let me learn all kinds of things other little girls didn't get the chance to know too. I was raised out on the frontier like you, although the countries were always different."

"Papa said I can go with him this year when he travels, if I want. Cloudy doesn't like to travel, but I'm old enough now not to need a nanny, so I'm going to go. Papa races his horses everywhere. Maybe we'll see you in Paris."

"That would be fun. And you must come to visit me in London sometime too."

"We will," Lucie adamantly replied, with the confidence of a favored child. "And we'll watch Aleppo race on your tracks."

· · ·

It was past midnight when the small Absarokee camp made their way into the isolated mountain valley. Travel had been slow at first through the river bottoms, but no trail was left to trace their journey, the rushing water obliterating any evidence of their passage. When the band finally came ashore miles downstream, scouts destroyed any evidence of their passage over the river bluffs.

Despite the hour, the camp was bustling with activity, everyone helping to erect the lodges. And before long, enough dwellings were standing to shelter everyone from the cool mountain night. Small fires burned inside the lodges, food was being prepared, children put to sleep, the events of the journey discussed with a general sense of satisfaction.

A recent buffalo hunt had filled the larders; the clan could remain comfortably in this valley until the militia were driven back into the towns for the winter. No one but the young bloods wished to fight the volunteer army. Since the white men had come pouring into their lands four years ago with the discovery of gold, only the most obtuse or militant considered combat a solution to their problem.

The Crow were a small tribe, their population no more than four thousand if both divisions of Mountain and River Crow were totaled. As long ago as 1825 their leaders had understood the need to survive with the white man. Today was simply another passage in the long journey of survival.

Adam, James, and White Otter rested around the fire in Adam's lodge. The others had gone back to their own lodges some time ago, and only the young men who'd grown up together as brothers remained. They'd eaten and smoked and argued the various possibilities of Meagher's route; they'd retold stories from their youth and laughed at their escapades. Their voices had taken on a husky lassitude as the night had passed, their weariness visible.

But their journey was safely done.

The clan was out of harm's way.

A sense of satisfaction overlay even the inevitable problems of the future.

The door flap lifted and a woman entered, carrying a bowl of small cakes. "If you're not going to sleep, I thought you might like some hazelnut cakes." Spring Lily smiled at the men.

"I *should* be sleeping," James said, taking one of the small fried cakes from the bowl. "And if you'll excuse me now, I'll do just that."

"I'll join you," White Otter said. "I didn't realize how late it was." He cast a knowing look at Adam.

Within seconds only Adam and Spring Lily remained.

"My friends aren't very subtle," Adam said with a smile.

"Maybe I'm not either," Spring Lily said, placing the bowl down.

"You never were." Adam grinned. "But I can fend you off. I've had lots of practice." He lounged against his willow backrest, wearing only his leggings and moccasins, his weapons put aside.

"But White Otter says your wife's gone now."

"You're still my brother's wife.[7] His memory touches me."

"What of the yellow-eyes woman at your ranch?"

"She wasn't staying long. You're a member of my family. I'd feel an obligation I couldn't honor."

"You already care for me and your brother's children. I wouldn't be demanding. You need a woman, Tsé-ditsirá-tsi. You slept with me when we were young, before I married your brother. I know I can make you happy."

"We were all without cares in those days," Adam softly said, remembering the days before the gold discoveries. "It's not the same now." In his youth Adam had taken part in the amorous play between the young warriors and pretty girls, but with his marriage he could no longer honorably offer himself as a prospective suitor to a young maid. Since then he'd resisted numerous seductive overtures, unwilling to father a child he couldn't properly raise. In the elastic clan structure of multiple relationships, his child wouldn't have suffered, but he would have felt an obligation he couldn't properly sustain. His time was no longer exclusively spent with his mother's clan as it once had been in his youth.

"I don't expect you to stay in camp, Tsé-ditsirá-tsi. Just let me give you pleasure."

"Tell me of my brother's children. Give me *that* pleasure. And don't tempt me with what I can't have."

"What you won't have, you stubborn man. I could attack you. I'm very strong."

Adam laughed. "Tonight you might be. I'm tired."

"Because of the yellow-eyes woman. James said you hadn't slept in days because she wouldn't let you go."

"James talks too much," Adam said with a small sigh. But he wondered at the tantalizing lure of Flora Bonham that he would set aside everything in his life for the sweet taste of her.

"He speaks the truth, Tsé-ditsirá-tsi. Tell me her name."

"She's gone."

"Forever?" she quietly asked, having seen his eyes when he uttered the two words. "How will you live?"

A small silence descended in the firelit lodge. "As I always have, Lily," he said at last. "With my daughter and my clan."

"Are you rid of your countess?"

"I hope so," he said with a small grimace. "And you ask too many questions for a man with no sleep. Go and care for your children now, and bother me tomorrow when I'm rested."

"I intend to, Tsé-ditsirá-tsi. Until you tell me yes."

"Just what I need," Adam said with a roguish smile. "A woman with a mission."

"My determination will help you keep your fine edge," she replied with a smile. "Expect the children and me for breakfast."

He groaned and then broke into a wide smile. "Are you cooking?"

"As if I'd let my children eat your cooking. And afterward you can help Bear Cub with his riding."

"Anything else?" he sardonically inquired.

"You can comb my hair," she sweetly said.

"Not likely," Adam answered with a pleasant smile. "Get someone else to comb your hair."

"I thought I'd try."

"I'm still awake enough for clear thinking."

"Did you comb the yellow-eyes's hair?"

He hadn't, he thought with regret. It was a sign of great affection for a woman in the Absarokee culture when her lover combed her hair. "No," he softly said.

"She wounded your heart, Tsé-ditsirá-tsi."

He slowly shook his head. "Nothing so serious, Lily. She was only a short-lived fire in my blood."

But her memory stayed with him that night after Spring Lily left, and he dreamed of violet eyes and a courtesan's mouth and a smile that made his heart sing. And he wondered what she was doing when he woke from his dreams with a start. Deliberately forcing away the unwanted memories, he methodically began a mental checklist of the scouting parties necessary to guard the camp—where they had to be posted, their range, the number of men. He wouldn't allow himself to dream of Flora Bonham. But he was gratified when the lodge walls slowly took on the translucent sheen of sunrise. Throwing aside his fur robe, he raised the door flap to the morning light and gazed out over the peaceful camp. Dew sparkled in the sunlight, the scent of juniper perfumed the air, the sky was clear blue—promising a warm day. Everyone was safe, the mountain valley secure against attack. A child giggled in a nearby lodge, bringing an answering smile to his lips.

To preserve his clan, his land, was the reality of his life, his support, his cause, his duty.

He had no time for dreams.

Chapter Eight

❦

Flora and her father stayed at the ranch for three more days before they moved on to Four Chiefs's village. Joining their entourage at their base camp near the mouth of the White River, they traveled east for two days over the grassy plains bordering the Yellowstone. With the familiarity of long practice, Flora and her father's secretary, Douglas Holmes, began transcribing notes on the native fauna and flora into the large leather-covered ledgers. Alan McDonald, the expedition's artist, was busy at work capturing the landscape in pale watercolor washes while the earl's valet, Henry, saw to the comfort of their journey. They paused occasionally to add to the collection of plant life or to allow Alan the time he needed to capture a particular scene in more detail. Both Douglas and Alan had traveled with them for years; the delegation of tasks was accomplished with ease. Plants were carefully wrapped to preserve them and placed in compartmented boxes; local birds and animals were studied, described, sketched; weather was noted at various times of the day— temperature, wind direction, cloud formations. Everyone knew, after decades of traveling the globe, what was needed to record their journeys.

Once they arrived in Four Chiefs's village, Flora began interviewing the women, documenting their roles, their daily routines, their leisure activities, learning the rudiments of the language through an interpreter so she could ask simple questions. She had an ear for languages, nurtured by her travels, and she took pleasure in learning the soft-spoken Absarokee. Interested in the native foods, she helped with the cooking and tried her hand at curing hides; she learned to play the gambling games enjoyed by the women and marveled at the skill needed to create the beautiful decorative beadwork and leatherwork. In the households with multiple wives, she studied the shared domestic activities, the interaction between members of the family, the diverse forms of address.

She interviewed two women warriors with positions of stature in the community, their exploits in battle honored with the same pride as those of the men. And she spoke with a berdache, a man who'd chosen to live life like a woman. He dressed like a woman, participating in the female activities of the village, his decision to adopt the role of a woman fully accepted by the clan. Flora conversed with the medicine women, who were as highly revered as their male counterparts, and she heard with wonder the stories of women chiefs among the Absarokee. Not the stuff of legends either, she discovered, for Red Plume had participated in the councils of the clan only a few years earlier.

Many stories featuring Adam emerged over the weeks she spent at Four Chiefs's village. He had great medicine, she was told; his war parties were always successful—not many warriors could paint as many coup stripes on their horses. Tsé-ditsirá-tsi brought good luck on his raids and added many Lakota, Blackfoot, and Cheyenne horses to their herds. He was wise in the councils too, his advice on dealing with the yellow-eyes sensible. When the women mentioned Tsé-ditsirá-tsi, they all expressed pleasure in knowing his wife had gone away with another man.

"He'll sleep with us again," they said with smiles and laughing eyes. "And play the flute at night for his lovers the way he used to."

Flora didn't doubt he would. Adam Serre wouldn't go

long without a woman. She always found it difficult to maintain the casual detachment of a researcher when they gossiped about him. He'd been much in demand before his marriage, the women affirmed with giggles and knowing glances; he'd pleased a great number of them. They were hoping he would come to the summer gathering of the clans so they could flirt with him, dance with him, seduce him.

The egalitarian sexual freedom of the Absarokee evidenced a culture of unusual parity. Gender roles appeared equal in many areas: marriage was a mutual decision; divorce was simple, an identical procedure for both; either sex had the prerogative to take a lover; children were shared and nurtured by both parents and by a large extended family. Conjugal love was revered; most marriages were monogamous and permanent, but no prejudice was attached to those that weren't.

As the days passed, she found it easier to consider Adam with equanimity. His name didn't evoke that sudden heated rush of memory any longer; she could recall the tempestuous days at his ranch with a moderately philosophic spirit. They had shared a wildly passionate encounter, and like a feverish tempest, it was quickly over. Adam's life didn't turn on impetuous passion, nor did hers. There was no need to magnify or overcolor the incident. They were adults with adult concerns. And their lives went on.

Flora found the systematic routines of her research brought a kind of peace. The process of interviewing, transcribing notes, collating stories, myths, songs, was familiar, a personal continuum in a world of change, like a melody from childhood that conjured up happy times. Vitally interested in documenting the history of a culture without written records, she derived a satisfying sense of achievement from her work.

Her father was immersed in the complex structure of the military societies, the training of warriors, the protocol of buffalo hunts and raiding parties, the intricate procedures in the Absarokee training of race horses, buffalo ponies, war ponies. The days flew by, and then the weeks, until in the middle of June Four Chiefs moved camp to pastures farther north.

When the camp passed within two days' ride of Helena, Flora and her father took the opportunity to travel into town and replenish their supplies.

Since moving their clan into the mountains, Adam and James had divided their time between the camp and Adam's ranch. Three of Adam's best racers were being groomed for the races at Saratoga, the cycle of planting had begun, new orchards were being planted, the perpetual improvements to the stables required attention. And constant patrols had to guard the mountain camp and the boundaries of Adam's property.

After the militia moved from their camp near Moon Creek, and there was less risk of meeting them, Adam and James rode north to Fort Benton to collect the Winchesters they'd ordered. Choosing a circuitous route, distant from the mountain camp, they arrived in the river town two days after a recruiter for Meagher's volunteers had set up shop in one of the local saloons.

That night, as they gambled with Judge Husmer and the sheriff in Bristol's Saloon, the topic of conversation centered on the acting governor and his problematic militia. With the recent redistricting, supported by Meagher to control the power of the dissenting federal judges who had declared the last two legislative sessions invalid, Judge Husmer had been relocated to the outlying Fort Benton area. Because judges' salaries depended on the number of cases they tried, banishment to the sparsely populated hinterlands had resulted in a drastic decline in his income. Husmer was furious. Every Republican in Montana was furious at having their political maneuver of voiding the legislative sessions outmaneuvered. And while the majority of the population was Democrat, enough influential men had been appointed by the Republican administration to make a serious and dangerous opposition party.

"Damn his scurvy hide," the judge fumed, discarding

an excellent card in his distraught state of mind. "If he thinks I'm going to starve up here in this outland river town, the Acting One," he said with sneering emphasis, "had better get himself a *real good* bodyguard."

Picking up the queen of spades and adding it to his other queens, Adam calmly said, "I hear Meagher's planning a junket up this way next week."

"Upstart prick!" the judge exploded. "We should extradite him back to England so they can fulfill sentence on him. I can't think of a better man to be hanged, drawn, and quartered."[8]

"When next week?" the sheriff softly asked, his salary paid by a group of local businessmen bitterly opposed to the acting governor.

"Saturday or Sunday," James said, before putting the glass he was holding to his mouth.

"Berger mentioned it at the north-pass stage station," Adam casually added.

"That should be plenty of time," the judge declared with unguarded ambition, "to plan a reception for the acting governor."

"Four queens and three threes," Adam said, placing his cards on the table. "Sorry to take your money again."

"Hell no, don't feel bad," the judge magnanimously replied, waving his cigar in a flutter of dismissal, a cheerful smile on his rotund face. "This has turned out to be a helluva good evening."

"Are you thinking that Montana's volunteer militia might be without a leader soon?" James murmured as he and Adam were walking toward their hotel later that night.

"It's a distinct possibility," Adam calmly replied. "I just thought I'd give the malcontents an extra day or so to organize. They would have heard soon, anyway. Meagher travels with fanfare."

"A leaderless militia would ease the pressure on our people."

"That's what I was thinking."

"Are you planning on taking a hand in it?"

Adam shook his head. "We're going to be a good distance away by next week. Preferably at some social function attended by numerous people who can attest to our presence. It never hurts to be prudent."

"Since when have you been prudent?"

"Since I heard Meagher was going to be in Fort Benton next weekend. Why don't we accept Harold Fisk's invitation to his ball in Helena? I think it's scheduled for Saturday."

"Certainly Fisk is suitably rabid in his denunciations of Meagher to offer an ironclad alibi. And his wife presents an elaborate table," James added with a smile. "But we'll have to set out for the camp tomorrow if we want to deliver the Winchesters and travel to Helena by Saturday."

"We'll leave at first light," Adam said.

Chapter Nine

⚜

Adam and James walked into the elegant walnut-paneled bar of the Planters House Hotel, their throats parched from their long ride, their boots dust covered, their eyes straining to adjust to the sudden dimness. Moving toward the oasis of the ornate marble bar, they ordered drinks and were leaning comfortably against the pale polished stone, their gazes resting on the painting of a reclining nude customary above every bar with pretensions to gentlemanly style, when someone shouted, "Adam, Adam Serre!"

Adam turned, searching the shadowed interior with a narrowed glance.

"Over here," a familiar voice urged.

Adam recognized the accent before he actually saw the Earl of Haldane and, picking up his drink, walked toward him, followed by James.

"You're a long way from Sun Creek," Adam said with a smile as he approached the red velvet banquette against the wall.

"You're no little way yourself from the ranch. What brings you to Helena?"

"My question exactly," Adam replied with a grin as he sank into a fringed velvet chair. "We're here for a short visit."

"We've been in town replenishing our supplies. Four Chiefs moved his herds north last week."

"How has your research been going?" James asked.

"Extremely well. What are you drinking? Cognac? Bourbon?" George Bonham signaled for a waiter.

Over several bourbon and branch waters, the three men went on to discuss their various activities of the past weeks. In the course of the next half hour, Flora's name wasn't mentioned, although she was prominent in Adam's thoughts with the earl seated opposite him. Was she here in Helena? he wondered. Or had she stayed behind in camp? Did she look the same? he mused, as if they'd been parted for years. Had she thought of him during their separation?

But when the earl suggested they come up to his hotel suite to look at some of Alan's watercolor drawings, Adam found himself momentarily indecisive. If she was there . . . He wasn't sure. Despite a sharp-set desire, more prudent counsel warned him off.

His hesitation generated a small pause.

"Perhaps you'd like to come up later," the earl politely suggested. "After you've settled into your own rooms."

James glanced at Adam, sensitive to his struggle of conscience.

As the silence lengthened, James opened his mouth to speak, intent on offering some plausible excuse.

"Why not now?" Adam softly said into the cigar-scented air, and, smiling briefly at his cousin, he lifted his glass to his mouth and drained the liquor.

She wasn't there when they entered the ornate sitting room. No evidence of her presence was apparent. He looked—his gaze swiftly surveying the room decorated in striped silks and ponderous furniture. But he smelled her scent, like a wolf recognizing his mate, and Adam glanced at the two closed doors in the east wall, wondering which was hers.

Would she appear over one of those thresholds? Would

he inhale her rose perfume at close range? Or was she being entertained this afternoon by another man?

The subsequent image hit him like a blow, and with effort he focused on the conversation directed at him.

"Alan did spectacular work on the drawings of Absarokee garb," the earl was saying as he motioned them across the room toward a large table spread with leather folios. "I can't thank you enough, Adam, for introducing me to Four Chiefs. His recall is almost complete, and he recaptures the mood and atmosphere of the days past with scrupulous detail."

"He was already an old man when my father first met him in the thirties," Adam replied. "Father spoke of his phenomenal memory too. I'm pleased he's been of help to you."

"He mentioned your father," the earl said, untying the strings on the folio covers. "Four Chiefs said the duke had been generous with his gifts to the River Crow."

"Papa lived with mother's clan for almost two years before they returned to France. He always remembered those days as the happiest times of his life."

"I don't doubt it," the earl said with feeling, his own pleasures found far afield from London society. "See what you think now of Alan's drawings. To my mind he captures the colors and textures perfectly."

They were standing at the picture-strewn table when Flora walked in on the arm of Governor Green Clay Smith's nephew. A tall young Kentuckian who'd just made his fortune in the Lucky Blue Grass Mine north of Helena, he was smiling down at Flora as they entered the room.

She suddenly laughed at something he said, the sound an enchanting trill of delight. Then she spoke inaudibly, in a rush, half turning toward him, the roses on her bonnet trembling when she laughed again, so she wasn't aware of their visitors.

Ellis Green playfully touched her uplifted chin with a brushing fingertip. "Now you keep that up, Lady Flora, and I'll forget my gentlemanly manners," he said in his soft Kentucky drawl. "A man can only take so much teasing."

Some men didn't take any, Adam thought, reacting with hot-tempered exception to the dalliance, instantly wanting to carry her away and still her flirtatious laughter with a hard, scorching kiss.

With her left arm still entwined through Ellis's arm, Flora swung away from her escort in a coquettish sweep of green pongee and white guipure lace. Then she saw Adam, and her gliding movement abruptly checked midturn.

A second of hushed expectancy descended on the large parlor of the suite.

Ellis Green, reacting to Flora's fingers cutting into his arm, took note of the earl's guests.

Adam shifted on the soles of his riding boots, restraining his impulse to move only with enormous effort.

James touched his cousin's arm in warning.

The earl, less personally involved, spoke first. "Ellis, come and meet my friends. They're in town from their ranch on the Musselshell. Flora, you remember Adam and James."

"Yes, of course," she managed to reply in a near-normal voice. Her fingers relaxed, then slid away from Ellis's arm.

The two men were dressed for riding, Ellis Green reflected, the dust of the trail still evident on their boots and clothing. And even if he hadn't known the Musselshell was Crow land, their looks proclaimed their heritage. Half-bloods, he thought, even without the clue of their beaded leather shirts; gradations in skin color were easily distinguished by a man from a border state.

Oblivious to everyone else, Adam watched Flora as she moved forward, the skirt of her silk walking dress gently swaying.

Ellis observed Adam's intense regard and realized he had a rival for Lady Flora.

The man and Flora obviously knew each other. On the other hand, he decided, the nail marks in his arm suggested Flora viewed the half-blood with less than blissful joy. The Kentuckian smiled as he reached the three men, because good manners were second nature to a man from a family of career politicians. "Ellis Green, here. It's a mighty fine pleasure to meet you," he said, putting out his hand.

"James Du Gard," James responded, stepping forward to take his hand.

"Adam Serre," Adam quietly said, shaking Ellis's hand with barely perceptible reluctance.

"You have the Aspen River valley in Indian country," Ellis said, recognizing the name. "You're the French count."

"And you're the governor's nephew," Adam softly replied. Although he'd never met Ellis before, everyone had heard of the Blue Grass Lode. "Are you expecting the governor back from Washington this year?"

"As a matter of fact, he's on his way back now."

Adam's eyes met James's for a fraction of a second, the news of special interest for them, with Meagher's visit to Fort Benton imminent. "I'm sure everyone will be pleased at his return," Adam said, his sudden smile casual, polite, the minute aggression vanished from his stance. "How have you been, Lady Flora?" he smoothly queried, turning his urbane gaze on her. "Your father tells me your studies have progressed well. We were just admiring Alan's watercolors." His mood had abruptly altered; Governor Smith's return was propitious should Meagher meet with an accident. Additionally, Smith was committed to amicable relations with the Indians, a remarkable posture for a politician, a rarity in a political appointee.

"I'm fine, thank you," Flora said, responding with a prickly testiness to Adam's maddening suaveness. "Our days in camp have been productive."

He suddenly felt as though he were in control of his emotions again, as though he could deal with Flora Bonham in a reasonable way. There was no rationale to explain the abrupt volte-face; he only experienced a kind of liberating elation. "I'm pleased to hear it," he replied. "Guipure lace becomes you," he added with a grin.

"You haven't changed," she softly said, annoyed by his insolent allusion to lace and their intimacy in the hayloft.

"Was I expected to?"

"I have no expectations with you, Mr. Serre."

"How reassuring."

"It pleases me to reassure you," she sweetly said, placing her gloved fingers lightly on Ellis's hand as it rested atop his walking stick.

"And it pleases me to see that you haven't lost your flare for flirtation." But Adam's voice had changed, the silky insouciance tempered by a flinty coldness.

"Will you be staying long?"

"Long enough," Adam bluntly said.

"Is he annoying you?" Ellis interjected, certain now the conversation wasn't teasing repartee.

"Probably," Adam softly declared, challenge in his voice.

"No," Flora snapped. "I'm not annoyed," she added in a tone of intense annoyance.

"They do this," the earl said with a sigh, recalling similar contretemps during their stay at the ranch. "So I'll step in as referee."

"And I as well," James interposed, pulling at Adam's arm.

"Forgive me, Lady Flora," Adam said, shaking James's hand away. "It was my fault entirely." He smiled. "I've been out in the wilderness too long."

"He has," James softly agreed, amazed at Adam's loss of control.

"You're forgiven," she said with the precise degree of sweetness intended to provoke.

"Flora!" her father ordered.

"I'm sorry." Her eyes were veiled behind her lashes as she looked up at Adam, her expression shuttered. "Perhaps it's the heat," she said in a theatrical wisp of a voice, turning to her father. "If you'll excuse me, I'll go lie down." She smiled up at Ellis last and then walked away.

"Humpf," her father muttered, bewildered at his daughter's melodrama. "She can outlast me on the trail."

"She's probably not used to her corset," Adam casually remarked, taking note of the door she entered. "Damned uncomfortable, I'd say."

"I hardly think it's a subject of concern to you," Ellis said with decided affront.

"Don't get chivalrous, Green," Adam calmly said. "It was an observation, no more."

"I'll thank you to keep such observations to yourself."

"Are you her keeper?"

"I'd gladly defend her."

"Nonsense," George Bonham interjected. "Flora can defend herself probably better than any of us. Have you seen her skill with a pistol?"

"I haven't, sir, but she strikes me as an amazing lady."

"She's amazing, all right," Adam softly murmured.

"I beg your pardon?" Ellis' pale-blue eyes had narrowed.

"I've seen her shoot," Adam replied with unruffled tranquillity. "She *is* amazing. She tried my new Winchester 1866 at the ranch," he added, his dark gaze swinging to the earl, "and emptied the chamber into a three-inch circle on the target in ten seconds."

"You're the same one who drove Ned Storham off his grazing lands, aren't you?" Ellis said with sudden revelation in his voice. The new Winchesters were still rare on the northern plains.

"Off *my* grazing lands," Adam corrected.

"That Indian land is open grazing land."

"No, it isn't."

"It always has been."

"No, it hasn't. I've title to it."

"Not after the treaty is ratified."

"The treaty isn't ratified, and even if it were, those lands are excluded. They're mine."

"That's not what Ned Storham says."

"He's wrong. I already told him so."

"He doesn't agree."

"Then he's welcome to try to use it," Adam said very softly. They'd driven Ned Storham and his crew off his land early that spring in a violent confrontation. A dozen of Storham's men had been wounded, his herd stampeded and forced south of the Yellowstone. Ned might have been talking big in town, but he'd not attempted another drive north since then.

"What the hell, there's enough land out here for everyone," Ellis jovially said with a politician's tact and smile.

"That's the way I look at it. They can stay out of my territory," Adam replied with a matching smile.

"Montana's larger than England," the earl said. "You'd think there'd be sufficient land for everyone."

"And there certainly is, sir," Ellis congenially agreed. "Will I be seeing you at the Fisks' tonight? Flora tells me you haven't decided yet whether you're attending. Molly puts on the finest spread of food west of the Mississippi, if that's any inducement."

"It's really up to Flora," the earl replied. "I don't know how she's feeling."

"I'll wish her a speedy recovery, sir, so I might see y'all tonight," he cordially said. "If you'll excuse me now," he added with a dip of his head, "I've an appointment." With his interest chiefly in Flora, he took his leave.

"James and I will be in the card room if you decide to attend the Fisks' ball tonight," Adam said after Ellis left. "Sit in on a game. Harold always plays for high stakes."

"A more tempting incentive than the banker's menu," George Bonham waggishly remarked. "Flora might be interested. She likes high stakes."

"If she's not indisposed," Adam reminded him with a faint smile.

"If she's still talking to me, you mean. I haven't chastised her in years. You do get her back up, Adam," the earl noted, "damned if you don't."

"I'll be on my best behavior, sir, should you join our game tonight," Adam promised, his voice suddenly boyish.

"I'll see that he is," James added with a custodial gleam in his eye.

"Fifty guineas to raise?" the earl said.

"Why not say five hundred dollars gold? Specie is almost nonexistent out here."

"You're on."

Adam smiled. "I look forward to the evening."

Chapter Ten

꧁◦꧂

Shortly after Adam and James left, the earl knocked on Flora's door. Entering at her invitation, he found her standing at the window. "Am I forgiven?" he asked, moving toward her across the sunlit room.

Flora released the lace curtain she was holding, letting the sheer fabric drop back into place. "Adam didn't go to his room. He and James walked across the street to Ballantine's Saloon." Turning away from the window toward her father, she added, "There's nothing to forgive. It was my fault. I shouldn't have acted like a petulant child."

"Everyone seemed a bit tense," her father replied, sitting down on a rose velvet settee, his gaze taking in his daughter's contemplative expression. "Are you feeling better now?"

"Adam Serre seems to bring out my temper."

"And you his. Could it be lover's jealousy?" he gently inquired. "I think Ellis bothered him."

"With no reason," Flora said, dropping into a matching chair in a flurry of silk pongee. "He's only a diversion."

"Adam can't know that, and it's obvious Ellis would like to become more important in your life."

"Papa, really." She cast her father a searching look. "Could you see me as a political wife? I'd offend the wrong person within the week. And consider how dull life would be with Ellis Green. He thinks ladies are soft, sweet-smelling, mindless objects of flirtation. He said he thought it very *brave* of me to live in Four Chiefs's village with only you, Alan, and Douglas as protection. Brave to live in a placid summer village? What would he think of the Ajjer Tuareg chief on our Saharan journey who threatened to abduct me at Ghat?"

"Or the Chinese pirates who were persuaded to let us go only after you gave them your black pearls and intimidated them thoroughly with General Chen Ping's letter of free passage," her father added. "So are you brave enough," he teased, "to go to the Fisks' party tonight? Adam will be there."

"Should I be fainthearted?" Her smile was amused.

"Preferably just not in the mood for a scene, darling," he replied with a grin.

"It depends on what *he* says first. *I* can be infinitely polite."

"Those inflections sound as though I'm to be chaperon again," he said in a resigned fatherly intonation bereft of censure.

"I promise to be well behaved," Flora pleasantly declared. "If he is," she significantly added.

"Did I say there's going to be high-stakes gambling?"

"Why didn't you mention that first, and we could have avoided all the futile speculation about Adam? I adore high stakes."

"I was curious, I suppose."

"About?" she gently queried.

"Adam Serre . . . your feelings."

A small silence ensued. "I admit he attracts me," she said at last. "But he intrigues a great many other women as well."

"And you don't like the competition?"

"His casualness, I think, bothers me. I'm more familiar with fawning men."

"But you disdain fawning men."

"Of course." She smiled. "Must I be reasonable about this?"

Her father gazed at her, his expression amiable. "Not with me," he genially replied, comfortable with her frank response. "We're invited for dinner first, if you wish."

"I'm resisting the thought of Ellis through eight courses."

"Why don't we just attend the ball, then?"

Her eyes lit up. "And try our hand at the gambling."

"They haven't seen you play yet, have they?"

She stretched leisurely, her smile delicious. "No. It should be fun."

"You're drinking more than usual," James remarked, comfortably disposed on a wine velvet sofa in their suite, his feet up, his arms crossed behind his head. Dressed for the evening festivities, he was patiently waiting to leave for the Fisks' ball.

Adam didn't pause in his pouring, nor did he turn around until the large tumbler was full. "Is that a question or a statement?" He lifted his glass to his cousin in impudent salute.

"Whichever you prefer."

"Neither appeals to me," Adam nonchalantly murmured as he moved a short distance and dropped into an overstuffed chair dripping with the fashionable ubiquitous silk fringe. "You're not my keeper. I don't have one."

"If you continue at that pace," James replied, eyeing the tall glass of bourbon, "you might need one."

"For?"

"For your own health."

"I'm capable of taking care of myself." Clipped, curt, delivered with a cool basilisk stare. Then, lifting his glass, Adam poured half the liquor down his throat.

"She really agitates you."

"She?" An intentional obtuseness.

"The flirtatious Lady Flora, of course."

"Is this going to be some purposeful lecture?" Adam idly stroked the pattern on the crystal glass, his dark gaze on James.

"Do you think you need one?"

"I *know* I don't need one. And certainly not from you. As I recall, you couldn't make up your mind last winter which of two ladies to sleep with in some vaguely permanent arrangement, until Rosalie Chantee came down over the Canadian border with her businessman father, and you spent the rest of the winter holed up at his trading post spending a fortune on trinkets for her. You were saying?"

"Perhaps I'm saying you won't be able to make the same *business* arrangement for the daughter of an earl," James replied, undeterred by Adam's pointed reproach. "So you might want to consider a less brusque approach than yours this afternoon in George's suite. I thought I might be playing second in a duel for a moment. I've never seen you so rude to a woman."

"Are we through now?" Adam insolently drawled, gazing at his cousin with a mild lift of his brows.

"You won't listen."

"I heard you." Adam's voice softened; his friendship with James was of long standing and could not be treated callously. "Consider your duty completed."

"You thought you could walk away as you always have, didn't you?"

"I did walk away."

"You haven't slept with another woman since Flora Bonham."

"I've been busy. And since when have you kept records?"

"Lady Flora looks as though she may have found someone new to enliven her leisure."

"Ellis Green? I don't think so." He'd felt the same precipitous attraction when they'd met again; he'd seen the heat in her eyes too.

"So what are you going to do about it other than drink yourself into a dangerous mood? Have you considered just asking her?"

"Why don't I send her a note?" Adam replied with mocking sarcasm. "Would you be interested in fucking me, Lady Flora? I have some free time this evening." He quickly drained his glass.

"Isolde's warped your perceptions. You never used to be so damned calculating. What's wrong with sincerity? Flora Bonham doesn't look to me as though she's a simpering maiden. She's familiar with suitors, she's bright, independent, apparently very select in her choice of husbands, or she'd have one by now. And you're not even available. She understands."

"Don't mention Isolde," Adam grimly said. "She warped the last five years of my life and probably my future as well. Also," he went on with a grimace of a smile, "I think you're putting altogether too much trust in female reasonableness. Flora damn near bit my head off this afternoon, if you recall."

"While you were being charmingly insolent. Even I knew you weren't alluding to lace when you mentioned guipure."

"Merde, you're full of advice tonight," Adam grumbled. "I need another drink if you're intent on overhauling my character."

"Don't drink *too* much," James chided, his smile sunny as a summer day, "or you'll not be able to please her as well."

"I thought you didn't like her," Adam moodily challenged, the empty glass balanced on his chest as he lounged in the brocaded chair. "I thought she was taking too much of my attention," he softly added. "I thought you wanted me totally committed to our clan."

"You haven't smiled much since Flora left. And the militia might be disbanded soon, so I won't need your undivided attention. Now that I think about it, what time is it?"

Pulling out his watch from his white satin waistcoat pocket, Adam perceptively said, "It's nine o'clock in Fort Benton. Meagher probably rode into town this morning. By now he should be roaring drunk."

"Or suitably welcomed by his enemies."[9]

Adam twirled his empty glass between his palms, his

smile broadening. "On second thought, maybe I don't need another drink, after all."

Adam Serre was more cheerful than he'd been in weeks as he entered Harold and Molly Fisk's grand mansion on the hill. He greeted his hosts with cordiality, complimented Helena's premier banker for talking him into buying the latest issue of railroad stock, which had doubled in price the month before, praised Molly's Pingat gown and her floral arrangements towering above the receiving line, agreed with them both that Montana needed its governor back home, and in general exuded bountiful good spirits.

His convivial humor even survived the sight of Flora in the arms of Ellis Green on the dance floor; he barely broke stride in his journey past the ballroom to the card room at the back of the house. She had the right to dance with anyone she wished, he reminded himself.

"Did you see her?" James asked, keeping pace with Adam's long stride down the carpeted hall.

"I saw her. White tulle over white silk satin, tulip embroidery, a very pricey Worth gown," Adam brusquely declared. "Empress Eugénie had a similar gown at the Tuileries last spring."

"Are you drunk?" James had never heard that clipped curtness.

"You wouldn't allow me, if you recall. I'm unfortunately dead sober." Dammit, she could dance with the smiling, smooth-as-bear-grease Ellis Green all night if she wished, his voice of reason resentfully acknowledged.

"What are you going to do?"

"Play cards."

"I mean about her."

"Play cards."

"You don't know what you're going to do."

Adam gave his cousin an ill-tempered glare. "I'm trying to keep my options legal," he growled.

Flora danced with a great many men besides Ellis that evening, for she'd been besieged by partners immediately after she'd arrived and with a gracious courtesy had agreed to several of the most ardent requests for a waltz. But she'd kept one eye on the time, and later, when Ellis took his turn again, she suggested they go into the card room to play poker.

"Poker?" he incredulously asked, gazing down at her upturned face as if she'd asked for a slice of the moon. "It's not usual for ladies to sit in on the poker games. Wouldn't you rather play whist?"

"No," she sweetly said. "I'd much rather play poker. Papa said the games are exciting."

Ellis cleared his throat before replying, his handsome face marred by a faint frown. "The poker games might be a bit *too* exciting for you, my dear. The stakes are high."

"How wonderful," Flora exclaimed. "Do let's go in."

"Would your father approve?" he sternly inquired.

"I have my own money, Ellis. He doesn't have to approve." Her voice held the smallest hint of exasperation.

"I see." Flora's status as heiress to her mother's inheritance was common knowledge. And Yankee shipping fortunes had reached fantastic heights during the Civil War. "Regardless of your independence," he persisted, "if your father knew, I'm sure he wouldn't like you to risk such a large amount of your money."

"But that's why it's *my* money, Ellis, so I can do with it as I wish," Flora carefully enunciated as if his understanding were defective. "I want to play." She abruptly stopped dancing.

"If you insist, Lady Flora," he rather stiffly declared. "But I warn you, it's most irregular. And Harold dislikes ladies in his games."

"Harold seemed so sweet," Flora theatrically cooed, ignoring Ellis's added effort to dissuade her, immune to his Southern notions of female nicety. "Why don't we find out if he'll let little ol' me play a hand or so?"

George Bonham had joined Adam earlier in the evening, but it was near midnight when Flora walked into the card room with Ellis Green and, on reaching the poker table, said with a dazzling smile for the players at large, "Would you mind if I sat in on the next hand?"

Harold Fisk, who decried women players, stumbled over himself finding a comfortable chair for Flora. She smiled up at him as she seated herself in a froth of white tulle and embroidered scarlet tulips, touched his chin lightly with her folded fan, and offered him a beguiling look of helplessness. "I'm looking forward to playing with you, Mr. Fisk. I hear you're one of the best."

A clear score for the lady, Adam dryly thought. Harold Fisk had forgotten he was married by the time she'd finished talking.

"What are we playing?" Flora sweetly inquired, her violet gaze sweeping around the table with guileless innocence. Slipping her ivory-and-lace fan off her wrist, she placed it on the table and minutely adjusted the fluff of tulle on her upper arm—a sensuous, personal gesture guaranteed to draw every man's eyes. Her superb shoulders and arms gleamed in the lamplight. Her breasts rose in luscious splendor above the low neckline of her gown, the satiny flesh framed in frothy ribboned tulle like lush presents to the eye.

"Whatever game you prefer, my lady," Harold quickly replied, trying not to stare at her luminous, half-naked breasts.

"Hmmm." She looked over to Ellis, who had pulled up a chair behind her. "Do you have any suggestions?"

"Why not simple draw? It won't be too complicated."

"Would that be all right with everyone?" She'd infused her voice with a small-girl breathiness that had every man at the table leaning forward in fascination.

Well, almost every man. Adam lounged back in his chair, his dark eyes cool, while Lord Haldane considered he'd be lucky to break even now that Flora had taken her place at the table. She'd surpassed him in skill as a gamester long before she'd given up her schoolgirl braids.

Flora played an abstemious game for the first three hands, losing a little money, only seeing the bet, never raising, taking measure of the individual players, learning their style of play. When Ellis leaned forward to give her advice on occasion, she always thanked him prettily and played the cards he'd suggested. When she asked for a glass of champagne, several of the men who were crowded round the table to watch the game jumped to oblige her.

She drank down two of the many glasses that appeared at her elbow and then, with a small, quirked smile one could misconstrue as tipsy if one wished, said, "I'm feeling particularly lucky tonight. I think I might bet slightly more this time." With a feigned casualness she placed her cards facedown on the table so Ellis could no longer see them.

She raised the already substantial bet by threefold, looked round the table with a wide-eyed innocence at the shock appearing on the faces of some of her opponents, and winsomely inquired of those rich merchants of Helena registering degrees of astonishment, "Is that too much?"

"Of course not, my dear," Harold Fisk quickly retorted. "But we wouldn't want you to lose too heavily."

"Oh, Papa doesn't mind how I spend my money, do you, darling?" she sweetly said, her opulent eyes lucid and clear as they met her father's.

"I don't mind at all, dear," the earl tolerantly replied, "but my hand won't qualify for this rich a round. I'm out."

Faced with the option of losing a large sum of money to a flirtatious beauty, two other players also folded.

"I'll stay," Harold Fisk gruffly said, "and raise you five thousand more." His hand merited a run for the stakes, anyway; he had a full house.

"I'll raise you ten thousand more," Adam quietly said, pushing his chips toward the pile in the center of the table.

"I'm afraid I don't have that much in front of me. Could I have some paper?" Flora asked.

Ellis leaned forward and whispered at length into her ear while she gave every appearance of listening. And then she whispered back, her brief reply leaving the young Kentuckian purse-lipped.

Seconds later a pen, ink, and paper appeared on a silver tray, and Flora wrote a few short words, folded the paper in two, and said, "I'll see you and raise twenty thousand more." She was holding a four, all aces. She could be beat only with a royal flush.

A small gasp went up around the table.

"I fold," Harold swiftly declared, understanding one rarely bluffed for that amount of money.

"Twenty thousand," Adam softly murmured, glancing at his chips, assessing their value. Then, reaching for the writing instruments, he inscribed swiftly, the pen scratching across the slip of paper. "I'll see that and raise you five thousand."

A low murmur of shock trembled in the air as many of those observing considered the lady had taken on more than was judicious. Ellis leaned forward despite his pursed lips, intent on averting disaster.

Their whispered conversation was inaudible, his words only a low rumble, her sibilant murmur accompanied by arched brows, a faint smile, and a small brushing-away movement of her hand. After which Ellis abruptly rose from his chair, his expression resentful, and shouldering his way through the crowd of spectators, stalked away.

"Lovers' quarrel?" Adam silkily inquired.

"It seems so," Flora pleasantly replied, not inclined to rise to the query in his tone. "Just a small misunderstanding," she dulcetly added. "I'll see your bet and raise you ten thousand," she mildly went on, writing a chit for the balance and placing it on the pile.

"I'll see your ten," Adam calmly replied, adding his chit to the bet, "and call."

Flora laid her cards on the table in a slow sweeping motion, the four aces bright-colored on the green baize.

"That's too good for my hand," Adam blandly declared, burying his cards in the deck.

The smile she cast him held an irritating triumph. "Thank you, Mr. Serre, for such a profitable evening."

"And thank *you* for the entertainment," he replied with an urbane smile. She was beautiful, graceful, aristocratic. And wholly sensual.

"You're very welcome," she said, sweeping the chips toward her. "Cards can be entertaining."

"That too of course," he softly said.

She looked up, her gaze suspicious. "Would you care to share your mystifying inference, Mr. Serre?"

"Not at the moment," he tranquilly replied, surveying the standing crowd surrounding the table, "but I was wondering if you'd care to play another hand, Lady Flora, say, for fifty thousand this time?"

Sitting back in her chair, she cast him a searching look. "That's a sizable amount. Do you feel your luck has changed?"

He shrugged and smiled. "Or yours, perhaps. You can't always win."

"But I usually do."

He rather thought she did after watching her expert play, but then again, so did he. "Well?" he succinctly queried, his lounging pose, his bland gaze, the insolent curve of his smile bold with challenge.

She looked to no one for confirmation or advice but returned his unruffled gaze and said, "Why not?"

Adam scanned the players seated round the table. "Is anyone else interested?" The expressions of blankness and demur greeting him needed no further interpretation. His eyes met Flora's. "We seem to be alone."

His voice held a curious intimacy in the midst of the hovering crowd, reminding Flora of the first time they'd met at a similar social gathering. "It appears so," she said, sweeping over the rows of spectators with a swift glance. "Figuratively speaking," she added in a hushed undertone.

Adam quelled the urge to respond to her intimation, when he restlessly wished to lift her over the table and carry her away through the pressing throng. "You've been practicing on Ellis," he smoothly said instead, curbing his rash impulses, the pitch of his voice low, like hers, so their conversation remained private.

"I don't need practice," she coolly murmured, reacting to his suave insolence. "Are we going to play, Mr. Serre, or discuss your views on women?"

"Why don't we play?" He pronounced the verb with a delicate inference.

Flora smiled. "Are you asking, Mr. Serre?"

"Do I have to?"

"It depends on my schedule."

"Are you heavily booked?" A small heat infused his voice.

"I'd have to check," she nonchalantly replied, beginning to unbutton her glove, determined to resist such casual intent. "But right now I'm interested in winning some of your money," she added in a conversational tone. "Could we have a new deck of cards?"

"Keep me in mind when you arrange your schedule," Adam murmured.

"You're on the list and I've a very good memory." She smiled at him over her gloved fingertips. "Now, are we playing or are we going to continue debating in this extremely public venue?"

"Your servant, mademoiselle." And then in a normal tone of voice he queried his host, "Could we have a fresh pack of cards for the lady and some markers?"

As they waited for a servant to bring over new cards and markers, Flora finished unbuttoning her gloves. Sliding the soft white kid down her arms, she tugged her fingers loose, then pulled the delicate leather free. Her movements were slow, leisurely, unmarred by any show of nerves, and every man, watching with rapt attention, admired the languorous unveiling of her satiny flesh.

Watching with an equally approving gaze, Adam wondered how often she'd used that maneuver to advantage while playing cards. There wasn't a man who was concentrating on the game. "You won't be too cold now?" Adam said with a faint smile.

Her glance met his in brief understanding, but her

voice when she spoke was as mild as his. "I find it easier to deal without gloves."

Since only two were playing, one of them would have to deal.

The new cards arrived; Harold unwrapped the deck and dealt a card faceup to each of them.

Adam had a jack.

Flora a deuce.

Low-card deals.

Picking up the deck, Flora shuffled with facile ease, the cards a blur of color in her hands, and everyone watching realized no little skill was needed to gain that degree of proficiency.

When she'd finished, she handed the deck to Adam. Every player had the right to shuffle, and for fifty thousand dollars she was sure he would.

The pack seemed to disappear for a moment in his large palm, and then the cards slid to the tips of his fingers and he fanned them in a ruffled, glossy flux, flipped them over with a fingertip, racked them together with his other hand, and slid them back. Lapsed time, five seconds.

Since the dealer shuffles last, Flora briskly snapped the cards together in a pliant flutter, evened the edges, and set the deck in the middle of the table for Adam to cut. Then she dealt them five cards.

Looking briefly at his cards, Adam put them facedown on the table. "No cards," he said without expression, and slid the fifty-thousand ante forward.

"None for me," Flora agreed, and a buzz of speculation burst from the massed viewers. Could they both be bluffing? With fifty thousand on the table? Or was it possible they could have been dealt hands worth that kind of money? "I'll see that," Flora declared, oblivious to whispered comment around her, pleased with her cards, looking forward to winning more of Adam's money. She held a full house, three kings and two aces. Her very good hand and the taste of victory inspired a mad, self-indulgent impulse. "Would you be interested in a small side bet?" she softly queried, her violet eyes touched with a capricious audacity.

"Of course." No hesitation, an adventuresome glint in his dark eyes.

Flora pulled a slip of paper from the silver salver, dipped the pen into the crystal inkwell, and wrote briefly. Folding the paper, she handed it to him.

He read: *My room for twenty-four hours. Winner's rules.*

The thought of being locked away with the lush Lady Flora almost brought a smile to his face, and if a hundred thousand hadn't been riding on his cards, he would have given in to his urge. Reaching for the paper and pen, his face impassive, he murmured, "I'll see that and raise the side bet." He swiftly scrawled: *My room for forty-eight hours. No rules.*

He pushed the folded slip of paper across the green baize tabletop.

When Flora read his words, a small heat raced through her blood—no rules, two days of untrammeled sex . . . an enticing fantasy. "Do you always raise?" Flora queried, no hint of her feelings in her voice.

"Only when it's worth my while," Adam said as calmly.

She placed her cards down one at a time, a formidable array of colorful face cards. "I'll call," she asserted, sweet victory within grasp.

"I've two pairs."

"Not enough, Mr. Serre, I'm sorry." Her smile was luxurious with satisfaction. "You owe me now." And she reached for the pile of chips.

But as he laid his cards down, a suppressed murmur rippled through the ranks of spectators.

She looked up.

Two matching pair—four deuces—were strung out in a neat row on the far side of the table. "You lose," Adam gently said, leaning forward, covering her hands with his, arresting her actions, the chips she'd been gathering tumbling into disarray. "Room twenty-eight," he said very, very softly so that his voice wouldn't carry. "Anytime tonight will be fine."

"I can't," she whispered in shocked accents.

His brows rose and his hands over hers tightened their grip.

"I mean tonight . . . ," she stammered. "I don't know . . ."

"I'm sure you'll think of something," he said with a smile. Releasing her hands, he leaned back in his chair and in a conversational tone added, "I appreciate the opportunity to play with someone of your competence, Lady Flora."

"It was interesting, Mr. Serre," she neutrally replied.

"Perhaps we could schedule a rematch soon," he proposed, his message plain.

"As *soon* as possible, Monsieur le Comte," she replied with a small heated emphasis that wasn't completely due to nettled pique at his insistence.

"I hope you don't keep me waiting too long," he smoothly murmured, sliding the four deuces together and slipping them into his pocket.

"I'll see what I can arrange."

He stood, then, as though he had a demanding engagement to meet and bowed to Flora with fluid grace. "Until we meet again, my lady," he gallantly said, taller than the other men surrounding him, more handsome than a dozen of them together, dark, predacious power in evening dress. Nodding to the other players, he said to his host, "I'll pick up my winnings later," and walked away, the mass of onlookers falling back before him with that awe displayed toward those of extraordinary good fortune.

Although Flora was in that rarefied company as well. She'd won $120,000 tonight. And provided she could arrange her schedule, the prospect of forty-eight hours with Adam Serre held gratifying promise.

Her hands were trembling slightly as she gathered her chips, anticipation fluttering through her senses. Adam Serre had a special gift with women, a virtuoso talent in giving pleasure and a libido capable of sustaining his unbridled desires.

Incongruously, an image formed in her mind—from a

long-ago history text—of relays of runners bringing mountain snows great distances to Rome for an emperor's precious Persian ices. Adam Serre reminded her of that rarity.

A man superb enough for an empress's pleasure.

So beautiful, he would tempt the vestal virgins themselves.

With a brute primeval force beneath his charming grace and civility.

And hers for forty-eight extravagant hours . . .

A similar heated musing ran through Adam's mind as he strode down the lengthy hallway, the crimson brocaded walls and spurious ancestor portraits flashing by his peripheral vision.

Flora Bonham was his prize—a tantalizing bonus for his four deuces.

He took his leave of his hostess in the supper room, pleading an early-morning appointment when she coaxed him to stay.

"But you promised to dance with Henrietta tonight, and she'll be wretched if you don't."

How could he refuse such shameless pressure with Molly's niece Henrietta seated at her side?

"Forgive me, Miss Henrietta," Adam politely said, his smile effortless after years of accommodating pursuing women, "but the stakes went high at our table, and I forgot the time. Would you care to dance?"

"I would most dearly love to, Adam." Her moue instantly altered, and her gloating smile reminded him of a spoiled young lady given the bauble she'd been crying for.

Dutifully offering her his arm as he had a thousand times before at a thousand other balls, he led Miss Henrietta Fisk into the ballroom under the beaming gaze of his hostess.

"I missed you tonight," the young girl said. "But Auntie said Uncle Harold always lures all the good-looking men off to his card room. I'm glad you came back."

She spoke with a proprietary air that set off familiar warning signals in Adam's brain.

"The high stakes attract a large crowd," he blandly said, not responding to her personal comments. Molly's niece had inappropriately declared her love for him last month, and he was treading cautiously. Sweet virgins with love in their eyes had always made him uncomfortable. He prayed the waltz would be brief.

A few moments later with a sigh and longing in her large blue eyes, young Henrietta said, "You dance divinely, Adam." And she leaned into his body.

He moved into a turn to ease her away, concerned with appearances even if she wasn't. Henrietta was much too romantically inclined, and he wondered at times, when Molly or Harold threw her into his path, whether his marital status was incidental to their plans. Divorce in Montana Territory was swift and simple. "You're an excellent dancer yourself," he replied in what he hoped was an avuncular tone. "Did you learn in Chicago?"

"Oh, yes, my finishing school had the dearest dance master who knew positively every new fashionable step. Where did *you* learn to dance so divinely?"

At a brothel in Paris when he was fifteen, Adam thought with fond memory. Therese had been sixteen, a sweet peasant girl from Provence, and they'd spent a week exploring each other's bodies, haunting the all-night dance halls, and practicing with Spanish guitars—flamenco dancers all the rage in Paris that year. "My dance master was an old Venetian my father hired on an Italian tour. Very staid and dull," Adam said in measured half truth.

"How truly divine. I've been abroad only once, but Mama will take me now that I'm old enough to be presented at court. Mrs. McKnight has promised Mama to introduce us to a baroness who will sponsor me."

Adam glanced at the clock wreathed in white roses above the door. Almost one-thirty. How much longer was this waltz going to continue? "You'll enjoy Napoleon's court. It's more lively than Victoria's. And you'll meet

many other Americans." The emperor allowed entreé to
the nouveau riche like Henrietta's American meat-pack-
ing family, causing the ancient régime who boycotted the
upstart emperor to sniffingly refer to his court as *couleur
de théâtre.*

"Oh, you know just *everything!*" she enthused with a
toothy smile, glowing eyes, and a toss of her chestnut
curls.

In relation to a young maiden from Chicago, he no
doubt did, Adam sardonically thought. But in lieu of the
tactless comment that came to mind, Adam mildly said,
"I'm a bit older than you. I've seen more."

"And ladies just *adore* older men," Henrietta purred.
"Especially handsome, *experienced* men," she added with a
tittering giggle.

Oh, Lord. He didn't train virgins. "Your mama
wouldn't agree," he quickly asserted.

"But Auntie Molly thinks you're *divine.*"

She might also think his fortune—a portion of which
was in her husband's bank—was divine, Adam more cynically reflected. "Your aunt and I are good friends," he
said, moving away once again from her ample bosom
pressed against his embroidered waistcoat.

"Could *we* be good friends?" She gazed up at him with
wide-eyed candor.

"I'm afraid I'm going to be leaving Helena in the morning," he replied, avoiding her question, adjusting his hand
at her waist so he could ease away slightly. "I was here
only briefly for business."

"Are you going back to your ranch?"

"Eventually," he evaded.

"Uncle Harold said he'd take me out to see your house
sometime during my holiday this summer. I'm just *dying*
to see it. Auntie says it's so elegant that royalty could live
there even though it's out in the mountains. *Do* let Uncle
know when you'll be home so we can come out to visit.
We'll have *so* much fun."

Adam had left the card room precipitously because he
wished to be back in his room before Flora arrived. He

didn't question whether she'd come, but simply when. And in his current highly frustrated frame of mind, if the orchestra didn't stop playing soon, and if Henrietta didn't stop babbling soon, he couldn't guarantee his civility. "When I know my plans," he equivocated, gazing over her head at the orchestra—surely they had to finish soon —"I'll let your uncle know." And the waltz came to an end in a flourish of violins as if through mental telepathy he had pointedly commanded them to stop.

Adam bowed over Henrietta's hand.

"Oh, dear, must you go?" she wailed, clutching his fingers.

"I'm afraid James is waiting for me," he politely parried, surveying the crowded ballroom for his hostess or some other duenna. "Ah—there's Molly," Adam declared with muted relief. "Allow me to escort you to your aunt."

He was outside the Fisks' Italianate mansion two expeditious minutes later. Swooping down the entrance steps in a flying descent, he felt like a schoolboy let out of a dreary classroom. As he pushed open the elaborate wrought-iron gate seconds later, he murmured, "Freedom," with a profound sigh.

"You did look extremely pained on the dance floor," James said, chuckling, his long stride matching his cousin's as they moved down the street.

"I was damned near ready to hit someone during that interminable dance. But you needn't leave with me if you prefer staying."

"I wasn't at the Fisks' for the company."

"Nor I. God, callow young ladies are a bore."

"Molly looks to me as though she's seriously matchmaking. And Isolde's trail is hardly cold."

"Molly was matchmaking already two months ago. Apparently expeditious divorces are socially acceptable on the frontier."

"Are you *divorcing* Isolde?"

"I don't have any plans. I just want her out of my life.

And I'm definitely not in the market for another wife, regardless of Molly's plans."

"So you prefer not being single again."

"With earnest young ladies like Henrietta around, it's a temporary excuse at least. The chit's irritatingly aggressive."

"Speaking of aggressive women, what was Lady Flora's side bet?"

Adam turned to his cousin with a grin. "You misunderstand. Aggression's the wrong word for Flora Bonham. She's pure temptation."

"Every man in that card room would agree; they all wanted her side bet."

"They'd have to go through me first. She's mine." An uncustomary assertion of ownership from a man who had always viewed women casually.

"Really?" James's eyebrows rose. "Is this serious?"

"It is for two days. The lady's exclusive time is mine for forty-eight hours, per her side bet and my raise."

"So you won't be leaving Helena tomorrow."

Adam cast him a sidelong glance, a faint smile creasing his cheek. "Not likely."

"Do I detect a smile after these many long weeks?"

"She has that effect on a man, doesn't she?" Adam said with a broad grin. "I have a feeling I'll be smiling a lot in the next two days. By the way, you'll have to move to another suite tonight."

"The hotel's full."

"Well, I'm sure Harold can find a bed for you at his house," Adam said with a facetious lift of his brows.

"Spare me. I had to listen to Henrietta's *divine* chatter during my duty dance too. She must get bonus points every time she utters the word. I think I'll just head out of town tonight." He glanced at his cousin. "Should I explain to Spring Lily that you're busy for a few days demonstrating the finer points of Absarokee culture to the British?"

Adam turned his head, his gaze on James for a moment. "*Not* if you value your life," he softly said.

"She's buying love potions to change your mind, you know," James retorted, his smile sportive.

Adam groaned. "Lord, I think of her as a sister."

"Unfortunately," James cheerfully declared, "she doesn't view you in the same familial light."

"She'll have to," Adam muttered, "because I'm not marrying anyone ever again."

"Do I detect a misanthropic view of marriage?" James playfully inquired.

"Five years with Isolde, however irregular her sojourns in our conjugal home, is as high a price as I'm paying for marriage. Never again," he emphatically declared. "Never."

"Think of poor Henrietta's afflicted heart and those dozens of other women who were hoping to land you now that Isolde appears to have deserted the territory."

"Actually, I'm thinking of my own *unafflicted* life now that she's gone. I'm damned pleased. And with Flora about to entertain me for two days, pleasure has taken on a whole new meaning."

Walking through the clamorous center of town, the men passed by the hurdy-gurdy dance halls and saloons blaring music through their opened doors into the summer night. The street running down the gulch was crowded with miners celebrating their latest gold finds, spending their gold dust for female company, gambling, and drink.

As they wove their way through the raucous crowds, they approached the Planters House, its lanterns on the colonnades casting a golden glow over the pale stone facade and white-columned veranda. Taking the shallow steps in a bound, Adam passed through the double doors with a brief nod to the doorman, crossed the floral carpet in the lobby in rapid strides, and mounted the broad balustraded stairs three at a time.

"What if she doesn't come?" James said, slightly breathless after their swift ascent.

"She'll come," Adam succinctly replied as they moved down the lighted corridor.

"So sure?"

Adam nodded, reaching for the key in his jacket pocket, his room only three doors away. "She's missed me," he softly said with a smile.

"And you've missed her."

Adam's head swiveled toward his cousin, and he stared at James for a moment. "Do you think so?"

"I've never seen you run for a woman."

Adam shoved the key into the lock. "She's damned good," he murmured, pushing the door open.

"She must be."

"Can you pack and be out soon?" Adam asked, tossing the key on a table.

James's eyes widened, astonished at Adam so noticeably bestirring himself for a woman, fascinated at the transformation in the man he'd known all his life. "You're hooked, my dear cousin," he murmured.

"Maybe," Adam cheerfully admitted. "But just for two days, Esh-ca-ca-mah-hoo," he added with a grin, loosening the crisp white tie at his throat. "Just for two days . . ."

Chapter Eleven

The lamplit suite was quiet. James had left long ago. Still in his evening clothes, Adam was lounging in the brocaded chair, his eyes shut, waiting. But he wasn't sleeping. Far from it—a moody, restless energy animated him, his thoughts filled with Flora's image . . . with memories and expectation. How long had it been since he'd touched her? he mused. Two weeks? Three? More, he decided, running over the sequence of time; it had been over a month now . . . a very long time. His fingers closed over the pleated whorls on the upholstered chair arms, his knuckles white under the pressure. And then he consciously relaxed; she'd be here soon. He glanced at the clock on the mantel. Two-thirty.

It was shortly after three when Adam heard the knock on the door. He came to his feet in a smooth uncoiling of muscle and moved toward the door.

Before he reached it, the rapping repeated itself in a brisk tattoo, and when he opened the door, Flora quickly slipped inside. "Do you know how many people are still in the corridors at three in the morning?" she hastily murmured, dropping her small canvas valise in a thud at his feet. "Too damned many," she answered herself, expelling a small sigh of relief at having reached safety undetected. She smiled up at him then, as though remembering her manners. "I should have made *you* devise a plan for my disappearance," she added with the warm smile he'd seen in his memory countless times since he'd slipped away from her sleeping form weeks ago.

"You obviously came up with one," he replied with a faint smile, taking in her riding garb and valise.

"By the merest chance, no thanks to you," she retorted, although her voice was amused rather than resentful. "I saw James in the lobby when Papa and I came back from the Fisks'."

"He's leaving for camp."

"And *I'm* ostensibly leaving with him. He was very cordial to my hastily contrived plan. Papa didn't question the story, and I'll meet Papa at Four Chiefs's camp in a few days. James even came up to our suite and waited while I packed. He's *very* nice."

"Just so long as he's not *too* nice."

Flora's violet eyes sparked with mischief. "I love your jealousy."

"You delude yourself," Adam murmured, his expression amused.

"Perhaps I could still catch James," she sweetly asserted.

Moving with infinite speed, Adam kicked the valise aside, swept her into his arms, and holding her close, said very softly, "You can try . . ."

"Ummm . . . are you going to make it worth my while to stay?"

"Definitely."

"Such assurance, my lord."

"You've been on my mind . . . since I left the ranch. And I've been waiting for you tonight now for"—he flicked a glance at the clock—"an hour and seventeen minutes. . . ."

"Did you put that time to good use?"

"I think so." His smile was very close, seductive.

"You were always so *excellent* without planning," she said, her breath warm on his chin, "I tremble at the prospect of a thorough plan."

"Hardly thorough yet," Adam replied, bending his head to kiss the tip of her nose, "with forty-eight hours to consider."

"Forty-eight hours . . . ," she whispered. "How blissful. We've never been together for more than a single night at a time. I'm enormously happy I lost the bet."

"Not as happy as I," he murmured, his dark eyes heated. "Now, let's get you out of these clothes. The riding you'll be doing here won't require any."

Carrying her into the bedroom, he seated her on the edge of the bed and began to unbutton the blouse she wore with her black riding skirt. After three buttons slid free, the bodice gaped open, revealing a glimpse of her lush breasts peaking out from beneath the turquoise silk.

"James saw you like this?" he softly said. "Without a chemise or corset?" A nuance of censure infused his voice.

"I'm sorry," she appeased, sensitive to the challenge in his expression. "I was in a hurry. And when I changed from my ballgown, it took so long to remove all the layers of petticoats and underclothes, I redressed in the simplest possible way."

"You can see your nipples through the blouse." He pressed the fine material against her breast, prominently outlining her nipple.

"I didn't mean to be provocative," she soothed, the delicate pressure of the silk on her nipple sending a heated tremor spiraling downward. "I'm sure"—she took a small breath as the warmth settled between her legs—"no one noticed."

"Perhaps," he murmured, thin-skinned and frowning, quickly rebuttoning the front. "Stay here now," he directed, placing his hands on her shoulders for a moment to underscore his command. "And when I'm seated over there," he went on with a nod of his head toward the windows, "walk toward me."

Releasing his hold, he moved across the room and settled in an ornate armchair, his dark gaze narrowed on her in critical scrutiny.

Sitting on the edge of the large four-poster bed, her

feet not touching the floor, her hands resting on the cut-velvet coverlet, Flora felt a small disquietude, not certain how to deal with Adam's remonstrances when her consciousness was eclipsed by desire. The flush of arousal pinked her cheeks, colored her pale throat, where it slipped down the vee of her blouse, burned unsated in her blood.

Even dressed in a simple unornamented skirt and blouse, Flora exuded a lavish sensuality, Adam resentfully thought, struggling with his unruly jealousy. Even seated in utter stillness, her ripe form seemed ready to burst from the stifling constraints of her clothing like some opulent fertility symbol. More disturbing, though, to his condemnatory mood was the flush on her cheeks—the color of revel and dissipation—and her flattering willingness, wholly indiscreet and enchanting, as he well knew. And, damn her, she was so *easily* aroused. Could he somehow blame *her* for his savage resentment, for his suspicions and doubt? Could he censure the luxury of her womanhood for its replete abundance? Could he more pertinently subdue his brute impulses and his need to tame her?

A second passed, then two, and he lifted his hand to motion her forward. "Come," he said.

He could not.

She slipped off the bed, obeying his curt command for heated, complex reasons that had to do with their extended separation, Adam Serre's flagrant virility, and her own passionate lust. But as she walked toward him, the length of the large bedroom seemed endless—an infinity of Axminster carpet under his frowning scrutiny. With every step she felt her breasts sway under the fine silk, the level of tension rising with each conspicuous swing.

"It's obvious you're naked and bouncing under that blouse." His voice was gruff with displeasure.

"I didn't wear it intentionally." She stopped a short distance from him, trying to gauge the extent of his moodiness.

"James must have been pleased." A glowering rebuff, replete with unspoken stricture.

"He didn't mention it." Her voice was reasonable.

He seemed not to have heard her as he shrugged out of his jacket, taking the time to remove the four deuces from his pocket before tossing the coat across a nearby table. Leaning back in the chair, he idly held the cards between the index and middle finger of his right hand and, lifting them slightly in her direction, said, "Have you played this particular game before—giving yourself away at the poker table? Or knowing you, perhaps it's a naive question."

"I've never understood your sense of possession." She refused to give him the satisfaction of the truth. He didn't own her past. That he was the only recipient of such a wager was none of his business.

He tossed the cards onto the table with a small sigh. "That makes two of us. Forgive the tantrum. I respond to you"—he shrugged away his unease—"with a curious barbarism." He smiled suddenly, a seductive smile of enormous charm and appeal. "But as long as you're standing there . . ." He settled back in the green velvet chair, stretched his legs out in a comfortable sprawl, and gazed at her from under the heavy dark fringe of his lashes. "Why not undress for me?"

She responded to his enticing smile with a mischievous lift of her brows. "If you promise not to scowl."

"A deal," he replied with a grin. "Is that better?"

"Infinitely," she answered, her own smile luscious. "Now, pay attention, Monsieur le Comte," she huskily murmured, and kicking off her low boots, she reached for the top button on her blouse.

Adam laughed. "As if any man with a heartbeat could look away."

"I'll consider that a compliment," she said, her voice playful, her fingers deftly loosening the second button.

"By all means. Did I mention I find outspoken females with auburn hair and a penchant for Absarokee culture particularly enticing?"

"Good," she sportively replied, slipping another button

loose, "because you've always been a special favorite of mine." She realized immediately she'd uttered the words he was going to take issue with, so as his expression darkened, she offered him a coquettish, mitigating smile and hastily added, "You promised not to scowl."

Shifting slightly lower on his spine, his eyes bold, ravishing her with a studied nonchalance, he leisurely crossed his legs. "You're absolutely right," he said with soft deliberation. "I'm to be on my best behavior."

"Can you do it?"

He smiled at the unintentional double entendre. "I'll certainly try. You can grade me," he impudently added, "at the end of the forty-eight hours. . . ."

"And you usually score well, I assume," she replied with a matching impertinence, her fingers sliding the last button free. "How nice for me. . . ." She tugged the blouse out of the skirt waistband, slid it from her shoulders and down her arms. As the turquoise silk slipped over her fingers and fell in a shimmering puddle on the dark carpet, she softly murmured, "Do you like what you see?"

She was bare to the waist, her breasts immense, provocative. Like a pale Earth Goddess, bounty to all men. But his alone tonight, Adam thought with a strange, intoxicating violence, and tomorrow, and another day and night as well. He flexed his fingers, the impulse to sink them into her great cushiony breasts powerful. "Touch your nipples," he lazily said, his voice trenchant in its authority despite its dulcet tone.

A thrill blazed through her at the dispassionate command, the quiet words like a fiat. Her nipples were already gorged, her body feverish for his touch, his compelling charge tantalizing in its authority. When she gripped her nipples even the first slight pressure assaulted her senses, searing her susceptible nerve endings, and her eyes shut as she absorbed the melting heat.

"Look at me." He spoke in a low rasp, the sound dragged from deep within his throat. "Now."

It took her a moment to respond, to return to the cooler environs of reality.

And when her heated eyes met his seconds later, he murmured, "Welcome back. If you recall, I'm your—er—current assignment for the next forty-eight hours. And I'd like you to do something more to entertain me now. I want you to squeeze your nipples so I can see them swell and grow thick and long." His voice turned to velvet. "Do you mind?"

He knew the answer, of course. He could see her jewel-hard nipples; he knew how she needed him. "Answer me," he softly commanded.

"I don't mind," she whispered, forcing her attention back to his sprawled form, her thoughts drifting away so easily with her body so heated. "Tell me what you want."

"Squeeze them hard," he pleasantly said. "So you feel it in your cunt."

Her eyes widened at the coarse word, at his blunt emphasis.

He smiled up at her. "Squeeze them so hard *I* can feel it in your cunt," he softly added.

"I shouldn't," she said in a small indrawn breath.

"But we both know you will because you want to feel me inside you and"—he paused long enough to make sure he had her attention—"you don't have a choice."

She touched the tips tentatively.

"Not enough," he casually said, lying back in his chair. "Remember I won you for two days. You must do it correctly."

Taking a firmer grip with a minute petulance he hadn't seen before, she softly said, "Fuck you."

"In due time," he lazily drawled. "If you're *very* good."

"I hate you."

"I don't think so."

"I could leave."

"Really?" His dark brows rose faintly.

"You can't make me stay," she persisted. But she hadn't moved her fingers from her nipples.

He noticed. "Of course I can make you stay," he calmly replied. "I can do anything I want with you. Now, come, sweetheart," he softly coaxed, "you know it feels sublime."

"You're rude." A sinfully delicious pout.

"While you're the hottest piece I've ever seen, my dear lady Flora," he silkily murmured. "And if you recall—the wager was on your initiative."

"I can change my mind." Her violet eyes were hot with resentment and another more tempting fire.

"It's too late," he tranquilly replied. "Word of honor et cetera, et cetera. So you must do as I say."

She glared at him and he smiled back.

She shifted her stance and he pointedly glanced at the clock.

But under his watchful eye, she at last succumbed to the pressure of his command and her own traitorous libido and squeezed her nipple properly, to which he pleasantly said, "That's much better." As if he knew the workings of her body, her nipples instantly changed, elongated, hardened, the tips tingling with such exquisite sensitivity, and she felt an unnerving helplessness before the sudden surge of desire inundating her body. Pressing her thighs together, she tightened her fingers of her own accord on the hard crests, to sustain the profound throbbing that seemed to beat through her body without respect for her outrage.

"Are you getting wet?" Adam murmured.

It took a moment for her to speak, her voice husky, touched with a curiously seductive temper. "I've been wet, Mr. Serre . . . since I first saw you at the gaming table."

He grinned. "You should have told me."

"You should have known." She took a small breath to steady herself against the sustained pulsing between her legs.

"I did," he quietly confessed. "I smelled your heated scent." His voice dropped in volume. "Like now. Show me how wet you are. And maybe I can help you."

She lifted her skirt because she desperately wanted him and because she realized too she would have him only if she was obedient to his wishes.

With the black skirt drawn aside he could see the auburn patch of hair was darker as it slipped between her thighs, glistening with the aromatic dew of her arousal. Unmoving, his voice neutral as if he were ordering dinner, he said, "Reach inside with your finger. I want to see if you're ready for me."

Holding her skirt in a crush at her waist with one hand, dark folds of gabardine framing her pale legs and belly and silky curls in erotic display, she complied, slipping her fingers deep inside. Her fingers moved, her hips swayed minutely in response, her breasts swung in counterpoint, like delectable fruit hanging from a tree, and hot pleasure bombarded her brain.

Adam's gaze focused on her hand, stimulated and incited her as if the wanton drama of masturbating before him was a salacious performance with a critical audience of one. And his approval was paramount to her urgent need.

"Bring some of that over here," Adam said after a time, his voice low, heated. "Show me your fingers."

She dutifully obliged, the melting friction of her fingers as she moved toward him registered in her half-lidded eyes, the world reduced to the pulsing core of her body and Adam's overriding voice. When she reached his chair, she withdrew her hand, the slithery sound explicit in the stillness of the room, and submissively held out her fingers smeared with glossy liquor.

"You're soaked," he murmured, reaching an idle finger out to trail through the gleaming liquid. Looking up at her, he slowly surveyed her from her slender legs past her lush thighs and moist pubic hair to the curve of her hips and belly, her splendid breasts flushed pink in arousal. And when his gaze rested at last on her face, he coolly inquired with the faintest of smiles, "Did you come to my room to get fucked?"

The blunt word struck her senses like a hammer blow, the lascivious word so graphic, so exacting, so lush with promise she could feel a drenching balm flood her vagina.

"Answer," he gently prompted, although beneath the soft spoken word was an iron firmness.

"Yes . . . no . . . I mean . . ." Gripping the bunched folds of her skirt tightly at her waist, she stood before him like a nervous schoolgirl, her carnal passions so intense she was breathless, seething, heedless of all but her frantic need for release. And he was waiting for his answer, his dark brows drawn together in a frown. "Yes," she blurted out, avoiding his cool eyes, "yes, I came here . . . for that."

"You weren't thinking, though, were you? You could have met a man on your way down here," he chastised, a sudden chill in his tone, her sexuality so ostentatious she was temptation incarnate. "Anyone would have known you were naked under that blouse."

"I was careful not to meet anyone." She needed him so desperately, her voice had taken on a pronounced deference.

"What would you have done if you'd met a man? Fuck him first?" He was driven by his own unaccountable demons.

"No. I want only you."

"James saw you," he accused.

"Only for a minute," she hurriedly replied. "We parted at the stairs. I came down the servants' stairway."

"I don't like other men looking at you."

"Adam, please, I'm sorry." Her voice was only a whisper. "I should have worn something else. I should have worn a corset and a chemise and petticoats and a heavier blouse. But no one saw me."

"How fortunate," he sarcastically murmured, "because no man could resist you if he saw you like that." With her skirt bunched at her waist, her sex was lushly on display.

"Adam, please," she softly pleaded. "You're wrong."

"You didn't flirt with James? Look at me," he curtly ordered, impelled by a brutal covetousness. "You're sure you didn't have intercourse with anyone tonight? What about Ellis Green? Did you give him a taste of that?"

Adam brusquely queried, reaching out to run his finger roughly down her damp cleft, "before the Fisks' ball?"

Flora moaned, a spiking rapture stabbing through her senses. "I haven't had intercourse . . . with . . . anyone," she said a moment later, her voice trembling, ". . . since you left me."

His head came up suddenly from the tantalizing view, and his eyes held her in a steady gaze. "Say that again."

"I haven't . . . slept with anyone . . . since you."

Inhaling deeply, he took in her luscious form as he absorbed the extraordinary information. Why did it matter so? he wondered, awed by the possessive feelings Flora engendered. Why indeed, he more pragmatically considered as he slowly exhaled. What man wouldn't want all that succulent female passion for himself alone? Locked away for his own private use. It was a masculine emotion as old as time. "Look what that does to me," he quietly said, "knowing you've been without a man so long." His erection stretched the fine wool of his trousers.

"I'm dying to feel you, Adam," she whispered. "It's been thirty-three days. . . ."

His brows rose briefly at the exactitude of her memory. "And you're eager . . ."

"Very much," she softly replied, a drop of pearly fluid sliding down her thigh, her gaze on his enormous arousal.

"Then all you have to do, *bia*, is take off your skirt," he smoothly said, "and your celibacy will be over."

While Flora unhooked her skirt with shaking fingers, Adam slipped his white satin suspenders off his shoulders and opened the buttons on his trousers. Intent on the voluptuous sight of her bobbing breasts as she struggled with the small hooks at the back of her skirt, he watched her, absorbed by the lush wiggles and jogs. At last, when she managed to wrench the final hook loose, she still had to ease the skirt over her hips, the great globes of her breasts swinging out as she bent slightly forward to force the skirt downward. Once over the flare of her hips, the riding skirt slipped down her thighs with ease and fell to the floor in a muted rustle, leaving her standing before him stupefyingly ripe and waiting.

"Now come here, darling," Adam softly said. "And let's get reacquainted."

Still dressed, he lounged in the large chair, his embroidered silk waistcoat unbuttoned, his starched and pleated shirt crisply white in the golden lamplight, his tie loosened at the open collar of his shirt, his patent-leather dress shoes and tailored trousers the height of Parisian elegance. The only Absarokee touch in all the fashionable garb were the pink shell earrings occasionally visible beneath his long sleek hair.

She moved forward, barefoot, nude, like a novice courtesan in her trembling meekness, overwhelmed by her wanton need, beyond sophisticated repartee, entranced by the sexual heat enveloping her.

"Put your foot here," Adam ordered when she came to stand by his chair, and he pointed at the cushion beside his left leg. He helped her steady her right foot when she lifted it, waiting until she was balanced before leaning back in his chair again. His view was explicitly clear. He could see how plump and swollen she was, how wet, how vividly crimson the inside of her throbbing labia. Gazing up at her wide-open sex, he reached up to gently stretch her, and she moaned at the surging rush of pleasure. "You look . . . very eager," he murmured, sliding his fingers inside a small teasing distance, then out again.

"Lord, Adam," she whispered, quivering under his hands. "You're torturing me. . . ."

"Do you want something?" His voice was quiet, deliberate as he gazed at her, open and glistening between his splayed fingers.

"Let me feel you. . . ." She was submerged in a great intoxicating desire, gorged with sexuality.

"Do you want to sit on me? Do you think I'll fit in there? It looks very small."

"Please, Adam." She was trembling.

"You always were impatient," he murmured, removing

his fingers, placing her foot gently on the floor. "Here," he said, putting out his hand, "let me help you up."

He steadied her nude body as she climbed onto his lap, sliding his hands around her waist after she straddled his legs, lifting her, helping her guide the cresting head of his erection to her slick, heated entrance. As she settled down on him, he felt exquisite pressure, her passage too small despite her copious lubrication. "You're very tight," he murmured, adjusting his upward movement.

"It's been so long . . . ," she softly sighed, her hips gently rotating, drawing him in more deeply.

He eased upward slowly, careful not to hurt her.

"You're very large." A gasp of pleasure punctuated her declaration as Adam forced himself farther.

"We're happy to see you again," he said with a smile. "Careful now," he cautioned, holding her immobile for a moment, letting her catch her breath, caressing her hips in a soothing rhythm, as if calming her fevered body. "More?" he murmured some moments later when her trembling had quieted.

"Yes, please." She spoke on a small caught breath of anticipation, as though he were offering her another serving of dessert and she didn't dare appear gluttonous.

He invaded her another small distance.

"Again?" he quietly asked seconds later as her breath came in small panting exhalations. "Now?"

She nodded, and he pushed upward into her yielding flesh until she whimpered, her sounds of ecstasy unblushing ardor, a spangled flourish in the stillness. And when she could listen again, he quietly said, "Now you must do something for me. Hold your breasts up. I want to kiss them." He remembered how she liked to have them sucked, how he could make her climax just from his sucking.

She knew what he was thinking, what he was going to do, and her vagina throbbed in an answering rhythm. Some nights at his house he'd sucked on her until she'd climaxed so many times she was weak from pleasure, until she'd pleaded with him to stop.

When she cupped the great mounds of her breasts, her nipples had already swelled and lengthened, as if the message had been instantly delivered from her heated brain, their normal pinkness altered to a luscious bright red. Her hands looked small trying to support the opulent flesh, her breasts overflowing the capacity of each palm, their pale weight spilling over her fingers.

"Give me the right one first," Adam softly said, because she'd turned slightly to offer him her left breast—the one he knew was more sensitive, more erogenous. "I'll kiss that one next," he offered, touching the curved top lightly, "if you promise to be very quiet. You can't scream, because the neighbors will complain. And then the manager will come, and I'll have to leave you to make excuses. You wouldn't like that—if I had to leave you." He smiled into her heated eyes and whispered very low so she had to strain to hear his command. "The right one now."

She twisted her torso to accommodate him, her memory of the nights at his ranch piquant encouragement to obey.

"Lift it higher," he quietly ordered. "Use both hands."

She took the breast in both hands and raised it to where his mouth waited. And when his lips closed over the nipple, she felt the bewitching pressure in her toes and spine and wildly, deep inside where Adam's erection stretched her wide. And she suffocated the delirious scream that rose in her throat.

"Very good," Adam murmured, lifting his mouth from her nipple to praise her constraint. "You didn't wake the neighbors." He languidly licked the tip of her nipple before he drew it back into his mouth with a strong, hard pressure.

She could feel herself open as he sucked on her, the stirring quiver and quake of her breast as he nursed on her, palpable in her cupped hands; she could feel his arousal sink deeper as if he knew how to operate the code for the secret door.

A master at gauging minute degrees of arousal, Adam lifted his mouth at last when she was hovering on the brink of orgasm, almost beyond reason, and the cold air on her wet nipple brought her to a shuddering awareness.

"Now the other one," he said with that authority in his voice that intoxicated her libido, as if she had no control over her body, as if he possessed her, owned her, mind and soul. "You've been so quiet, you deserve a reward."

His words flared through her brain like a beacon flame in the dark of night. The reward unmistakable.

"Bring it closer." He rested his head against the back of the chair and waited for her to lean forward to offer him the breast that always brought her to climax. "I think they're bigger than they were . . . ," he murmured, sliding a fingertip over the thrusting nipple. "Are you sure no one's been sucking them?"

"No one. I'm sure." She squirmed on his erection.

"None of that now," he warned, holding her hips so she couldn't move. "Sit still. And if no one's been sucking on them, why are they so large? And this . . ." He ran a palm over the creamy mound she held out to him. "It's bigger too. Have you gained weight?"

"I don't think so." She spoke in the merest whisper, her body defenseless against his touch, nearly orgasmic, throbbing so fiercely all her senses were centered on her drenched and pulsing vagina.

"Are you ready to climax?" His breath was warm on her nipple.

She didn't answer, her mind so inflamed she had difficulty concentrating on his voice.

"I asked you a question." He ran his tongue over the turgid crest.

"Yes," she said, trembling at the enormous effort it took to gather her thoughts, her breast quivering in her hands.

"You mustn't scream," he cautioned, his voice inflexible, stern.

Subject to his tone, his whim, when he held her on the orgasmic brink, she quickly said, "I . . . won't." And pressed the large nipple against his lips.

He opened his mouth slowly so she could feel the slippery passage of her nipple over his lips. He paused then, licking the hard peak, nibbling on it, teasing it with his tongue. And when he closed his mouth and softly bit down, the first shuddering spasm coiled deep inside her.

He knew there was nothing she could do to stop the flow, and he drove deep inside her in a hard, steady rhythm, intent on meeting her climax, on joining her fevered journey to paradise. And seconds later, when he sucked hard and ravenously like a man starved for sustenance, her climax exploded, as he knew it would, and he released himself into her sweet welcoming body, filling her with great hot rivers of sperm, invading her so deeply she screamed at the reeling pleasure. Holding her hips between his large hands, he pressed down with such savage intensity she peaked for agonizing moments on the delirious, rapturous crest.

She clung to him as the convulsive violence surged through her body, her orgasm so riveting, so prolonged, so excruciatingly acute that shaken from surfeit, she collapsed insensible in his arms.

He held her sudden weight for a moment, then lifted her free and settled her in his lap, his own breathing still labored, his heart drumming at ramming speed, a faint, triumphant smile gracing his handsome face. Brushing a lock of hair from her forehead as she lay in his arms, he gazed at her fair beauty, at the sublime grace of her lavish form, at her ultimate yielding to him.

She was a woman of inestimable glory, dramatic, sumptuous, his own resplendent prize. His gaze came up and traced the gold-filigreed hands of the clock. For forty-six and a half hours more, he pleasantly mused. His smile reappeared as he glanced at the four deuces lying on the nearby table. He should have them framed.

Pulling his jacket across the table, he gently covered her nakedness, adjusted her head comfortably against his chest, and, lying back in the large chair, he shut his eyes.

Chapter Twelve

A delicious languor warmed her body; her skin was so keenly attuned to sensation, she could feel her pulse tremble on its surface. A blissful, luxurious contentment pervaded her senses as if she were lazily lying in a summer field under a hot sun. Her eyes opened slowly as she came up from the gossamer world of sweet clover and liquid sunshine, her heavy lashes lifting drowsily, her mind still quiescent and dreamy, and then a faint smile touched her mouth.

She saw him. And the bliss and contentment had a name.

His eyes came open as if he could feel her gaze on him, and he smiled down at her with a tenderness she hadn't seen before. "How do you feel?"

"Perfect."

"You look perfect," he softly said, tugging her a minute degree closer, bending his head to brush her forehead with a kiss.

"I've never felt like this . . . ," Flora whispered, the warmth and power of his body enveloping her. "Is this nirvana?"

"Very close, I think . . ." His smile touched her with warmth. "Or at least our own personal nirvana."

"Has this ever happened to you before?"

"No."

"Nor to me."

The cryptic words were sufficient to two people touched with sensations unique to them both. But Adam Serre preferred less volatile topics, considering the limited duration of their time together, and he said with a smile, "This is our first morning alone without children or fathers at the breakfast table. Could I interest you in a sunrise and then some breakfast?"

"I'd be delighted," Flora amiably replied, understanding his sudden change in subject matter. She leisurely stretched in his arms. "Does this sunrise come to us, or do we go to it?"

"Which would you prefer?" he inquired with a grin.

"Now, you're good Adam Serre, but you're not *that* good," she replied with an answering grin.

But in the end he did make some adjustments in the sunrise, or at least *their* sunrise, because he rearranged the furniture in the sitting room so the sofa faced the east windows. He found a robe for Flora and one for himself, and after he carried her in from the bedroom and placed her on the wine velvet couch, he handed her a menu and said, "You order while I get into something more comfortable than last night's clothes."

He undressed while she asked, "Do you want eggs? Bacon? Ham? Porridge? Toast?" and numerous other items on the menu, to which he invariably answered yes. Looking over the top of the menu at his hard, taut body currently sans shirt and about to be divested of trousers, she said, "How do you stay so lean when you eat so much?"

Seated at the end of the sofa, he glanced at her over his muscled shoulder and said with a wicked grin, "I burn it off."

She felt the color flood her cheeks.

"But why don't we eat first?" he went on in a silky murmur. "You need sustenance."

"I suppose as a practicing libertine," she retorted, "you understand the merits of good nutrition."

"I certainly do," he smoothly replied, sliding his trousers off. Tossing them aside, he turned to look at her. "But if that temper in your voice is directed at me, perhaps I could soothe your cranky mood *before* breakfast. . . ."

"Thank you, no," she retorted, resentful of his damnable assurance. "I don't want you to touch me."

"Darling, now, why would you say that when you know you like to be touched?" He settled back as if they were discussing the philosophical case for the decline of Rome.

"I don't *need* a reason," she said with a sulky pique as he lounged opposite her on the couch, his powerful, bronzed body glorious to the eye. "Lord, Adam, do you always have an erection?"

"With you I do."

"Should I be flattered?"

He shrugged. "Probably," he calmly said, "but why not be fucked instead? It's a little early anyway to wake up the kitchen staff."

"How can I turn down such a well-bred invitation?" she purred with dripping-sweet sarcasm and one arched eyebrow.

"Suit yourself." Crossing his arms behind his head, Adam shut his eyes. And waited.

He'd silently counted to twenty when he heard the first small rustle. She was untying her robe; he heard the swish of silk on silk as the knot slipped free. And then the couch cushion dipped under her weight as she moved from her side to his. He stopped counting when he felt her fingers close around his erection, and long, pleasurable moments later, as her warm mouth drew in the swollen crest of his penis, he slowly opened his eyes.

Her red curls lay in a tumble on his hard belly and thighs, the nape of her neck pale white in the dawn light. Tracing a fingertip down her graceful back, his hand ran over the curve of her bottom, under it, cupping her hot crotch. Slipping his fingers inside her, he held her securely, her body moving up and down on his invading digits as her mouth serviced him.

Could one die of too much sex? Flora wondered for the first time in her life, her orifices filled, the heat in her brain burning away all thought but an indescribable hunger for Adam Serre. How could she want him so intensely? She'd intended to ignore him lying there; she'd always prided herself on her self-control. He could wait, dammit. But he was the ultimate temptation, like original sin in Eden, the glorious pleasure he offered explicitly visible, hard, long, swollen so large, the sight of it sent a shiver down her spine.

And she couldn't wait. And he'd known it.

He lifted her off him after a time because he wanted to feel her under him in submission, because he wanted to ram himself so deep inside her, she'd feel him in her throat, because he felt an ungovernable need to endlessly possess her. He wanted to bury himself in her and ravage her ripeness; he wanted her to need him desperately, as he needed her.

And when she cried out and wept at the end when their climaxes shattered their nerves into fragments, a gratifying sense of victory assailed him.

This man who, until Flora Bonham, had only played the game.

They lay in each other's arms afterward while the pleasure settled from manic to a more manageable level of enchantment, kissing each other, basking in a lush surcease, watching the sunrise color the sky in magnificent flame and glowing apricot.

Exalting in their sweet harmony.

When a hard rap on the door ruptured their quiet repose. "Chambermaid with morning coffee, sir," a female voice called.

"It must be James's doing," Adam said, coming to his feet with a sigh. "His idea of humor," he added, reaching for the robe he'd dropped on the arm of the sofa. "Just a minute!" he shouted so the maid could hear. "Do you want to go into the bedroom?" he asked, gazing down at Flora.

She shook her head. "I don't know anyone at the hotel

except Papa, and it's obviously not him. How can it matter? Hand me that robe you gave me."

Adam tossed her the green silk jacquard garment, swept a glance around the room to find some suitable surface for a coffee tray, and, deciding on a small pier table near the door, said completely out of context of time, place, and circumstances, "I should take you to Paris sometime."

"Let me check my schedule." Flora understood his odd impulse. She felt the same comfortable contentment, as though they'd spent years in hotel rooms together, as though they'd wakened to morning coffee in strange cities for decades.

He tied her robe for her and rolled up the sleeves until her hands showed. "Your cheeks are rosy like a child's," he murmured, brushing his knuckles delicately over her flushed face.

"You do that to me," she whispered, wanting him with an insatiable longing as though her senses were attuned to his merest touch, as if the light brush of his fingers signaled her body to open for him and offer itself for his pleasure.

"I'll be right back," he softly said. He smiled down at her with a lover's warm smile.

Pushing herself into a sitting position when he walked away, Flora twisted around and, kneeling with her arms on the back of the couch, watched Adam move toward the door. He was broad-shouldered and lean beneath the burgundy silk of his robe, his bare feet graceful, quiet as a whisper on the carpet, the rhythm of his stride unvarnished beauty, perfection of fluid muscle and power.

As he turned the latch, the door swept inward with unexpected force, and a strangely dressed chambermaid with a pale-blue gown beneath her starched apron and a feathered hat in her gloved hands burst into the room.

"I hope you don't mind, Adam, but I had to see you and—" At the sight of Flora leaning over the couch, Henrietta Fisk's explanation came to an abrupt halt. Suddenly surveying the room, she took note of Adam's clothing lying on the carpet, at the rearranged furniture, at Flora's tousled hair and dishabille. And her anger ignited like a flare. "How *could* you!" she explosively cried, as if she had prior rights to Adam's time and person. "How *could* you when I want you and Auntie said *I* was going to have you!"

Adam was already easing her back through the threshold before she'd finished. "You shouldn't be here, Henrietta. Your aunt won't like it, your parents won't like it. And you're very wrong about me. I'm not involved in your life." His voice lowered then, and his remaining communication was hastily murmured into Henrietta's flushed, stormy face as he placed her outside the doorway with a gentle propulsion. "Now, go back home, *right now*," he quietly ordered. "*Hurry.*" He shut the door.

And locked it.

Leaning against the door, he ruefully said, "Is this where I'm supposed to say, 'You're compromised. You must marry me and save your reputation'?"

Flora softly laughed. "If you weren't already married, perhaps—"

Her facetious answer struck him oddly.

His words were to have been a wry jest, as was her answer.

But they both noticed how the earth seemed to stop for a moment.

How many times had she been proposed to? Flora reflected in the sudden suspended lull. And how many times had she politely refused?

"*Will* this compromise you, and if so, how much?" Adam asked when the brief moment passed, his sincerity plain, his voice touched with a nuance of regret.

"No, of course it won't," Flora replied. "There isn't a soul in Helena who has the ear of London society, and even if there were, my escapades have been the stuff of gossip for so long, another story from some far-flung frontier won't raise an eyebrow. Now, come here and entertain me. I need someone to erase the disconcerting image of Henrietta's red, blustery face."

"Someone?" he softly disputed, his jealousy of the men in her life an incredulous constant.

"Only you, darling," Flora whispered. "I want only you in all the world and star-filled heavens."

Walking over to the couch, he kneeled, took her face in his hands, brushed his lips lazily against hers, opened her mouth with a small pressure, and tasted her, his kiss slow, gentle. "You'd really enjoy Paris . . . ," he murmured against the softness of her lips.

"I would with you . . . ," she said, her voice hushed. Her arms rested on his broad shoulders, her fingers were caught in his sleek dark hair. "And you can't have her."

He leaned back a small extent so he could see her eyes, his expression questioning.

"Henrietta."

His brows came together in a frown. "Lord, I don't want her."

"She's too young for you."

"She's too stupid for me," he softly corrected.

"Just so long as we understand each other," Flora purred.

"Are you giving orders now?" he gently queried, smiling faintly.

"About that I am. I don't want any more interruptions."

"Is our schedule too full?" he murmured, slipping her robe off her shoulders.

"I certainly hope so," Flora whispered, leaning forward to kiss him. With her movement her breasts rested on the sofa back, pale mounds on the wine velvet, grandiloquently disposed, largess for his pleasure.

Kissing her lightly, he stroked the satiny mounds, his warm palms exerting a light pressure downward. "I think I'll keep you like this, without clothes . . . so you'll always be ready for me to touch. So you can service me anytime. . . ."

Flora's eyes had drifted shut, her body so receptive to Adam, his lightest touch triggered a flooding sensuality. And when his head lowered, when his hair drifted over her breasts, she moaned deep in her throat even before his mouth closed over her nipple. After the last hours her body was too primed, too heated, to sustain prolonged foreplay, and moments later she clutched great handfuls of his hair, pulled harshly to lift his head, and, looking directly into his genial, amused eyes, said, heated and low, "I don't want to wait another second, Adam Serre. Is that clear?"

His smile was dulcet understanding. "Would mademoiselle have a preference in—er—" His fine teeth flashed white in his bronzed face. "A particular position?"

"Why don't I leave that to your imagination?"

"Good choice," he teasingly said. "Now, don't move."

His vault over the sofa back was an effortless synthesis of muscle, power, and perfect balance, and it was perhaps four seconds before he was buried deep inside her, but Lady Flora seemed not to notice the discrepancy in timing, for her eyes were shut as she leaned forward over the couch back, her breathing already unquiet, agitated. Clasping her large breasts solidly in his hands, his muscled chest pressed hard against her back, Adam's lower body glided in and out with long, firm strokes, deliberate, measured, penetrating to the extreme limits of Flora's yielding flesh.

And in leisured due course, Lady Flora's third climax that morning was, in the words of their unorthodox chambermaid—*divine*.

A short time later as Flora and Adam were feeding each other tidbits of their breakfast between sweet smiles and teasing banter, Henrietta was feeding her anger in her aunt's bedroom. Molly Fisk, a middle-aged, slightly plump matron, who generally slept until noon to preserve what looks remained to her, was propped up on her pillows doing her best to absorb the suddenness of Henrietta's appearance.

"You should have seen her," Henrietta fumed, pacing the Aubusson carpet like an infantry soldier on the march. "All sleepy eyed and half-undressed. The slut."

"Henrietta, dear, please take care for my French carpet. You'll wear a path. And, darling, ladies never walk with that long a stride. It's not comme il faut. Now, come, sit by me," she went on, waving the hand peaking from beneath the lacy cuff of her nightgown at a small chair near her bed, "and we'll talk about this."

"I want to scratch her eyes out," Henrietta sullenly declared, approaching her aunt's large tester bed, hung with white satin looped in azure silk, in a slightly modified stride. "She's old," the young girl blurted out, plopping down onto the chair with such gawky solidness her aunt shuddered for fear her delicate Louis Quinze would crumble. "She has to be twenty-three if she's a day, and everyone knows when you're not married at twenty-three, you're nothing but an old maid. I don't know what he sees in her."

"Who exactly are you speaking of, dear?"

"Lady Flora!" Henrietta bemoaned. "She was in Adam's room this morning with no clothes on—well, almost no clothes on. And Adam had on only a silk robe. But he looked so-o-o gorgeous, Auntie," she added, adoration in her voice.

"Adam's room at the hotel?" her aunt repeated with suppressed horror.

"Of course his room at the hotel. Where else would he be?"

Molly Fisk could name a score of other places Adam could have been and had been in the past, from brothels to fine ladies' boudoirs, but such information wasn't allowed eighteen-year-old virgins. "Did anyone see you?" she inquired, sensible of her role as protector of Henrietta's reputation.

Henrietta looked at her blankly, and for a moment Molly Fisk's heart shuddered to a stop. The fool. "Recollect now," she earnestly prompted. "Did you meet anyone in the lobby who recognized you? On the stairs? In the hallways?"

"I don't think so. . . ."

Molly's mind was already racing with possible excuses.

It was Sunday, after all. She quickly glanced at her niece's ensemble. Henrietta at least had had the good sense to dress appropriately. Her blue morning gown and small hat would be suitable for church or Sunday school. She could have been on her way to teach Sunday school. Thank God, Molly silently reflected, she had enough influence in the community to make such an unlikely story pass inspection. "Well, I hope you're right," she briskly replied. "And anyone of consequence would naturally still be abed. Only the working class are up that early. As for Lady Flora being in Adam's room, she's a most unusual woman, and men find that sort of spirited female *interesting*," she finished with a thoughtful moue. She'd heard nothing but glowing praise for Flora from her own husband. "As for what Adam Serre sees in Lady Flora, it's quite plain. She's beautiful, wealthy, and unconventional. Clara tells me Lady Flora's refused most of the eligible bachelors in England as well as several on the Continent."

"How does she know?" Henrietta pettishly queried, displeased with evidence of Flora's allure. "I don't believe you." Her scowl did nothing to enhance her unprepossessing face.

"Clara Lockwood has a cousin married to a baronet from Surrey. Her cousin's husband is a distant connection of Lord Haldane. While Lady Flora may be a spinster at age twenty-six, not twenty-three, my dear, it's quite by choice. As is her strange interest in Indian life. But one never questions the eccentricities of wealthy aristocrats, darling, as you would be wise to understand. And those nobles of great wealth like the Earl of Haldane, Lady Flora, and your own fond interest, the Comte de Chastellux, must be considered very much above the rules governing lesser mortals, much as we may deplore their unorthodox ways. Do you understand me, Henrietta?"

"No! Papa makes ever so much money too, and so does Uncle Harold, and we aren't above the rules."

How exactly to explain that her father and uncle were in many ways a law unto themselves without revealing too much of the sordid world to an innocent girl? "Do you remember when your papa had the President to dinner?"

"Of course. Mama had the entire house redecorated."

"Well, you see, your papa is friends with the President because he's a very powerful and rich businessman. Now, you didn't see President Johnson having dinner with your milliner, did you?"

"Aunt Molly! Why ever would he want to?"

"Exactly. And in the same way, aristocrats are very special like the President, and like your father in the business world. But aristocrats are influential not only because of their wealth, but because of their bloodlines. You can't buy that, you see, and it sets them apart. Laws set them apart, as well, in their native countries. They do what they want to do, and if Adam Serre and Flora Bonham have a fancy to spend a month in his hotel room, I for one wish them well. And when they emerge from that hotel room, then we'll see what we can do to interest Adam in you."

A smile erased Henrietta's frown. "She won't be staying long, will she?"

"I understand Lady Flora leaves for the Yucatán at the end of the summer. And there are a great many terrible fevers and diseases in those tropical climates."

"She may die!" Henrietta exclaimed with elation.

"It's a possibility," her aunt agreed with a lesser degree of enthusiasm but an equal interest. Since Adam's wife had left with what appeared to be more finality than usual several months ago, Molly Fisk had viewed Adam Serre as the perfect candidate for her nephew-in-law. Unlike most of the younger sons of nobility sent out to the American West to rusticate until their scandals had abated in Europe, Adam Serre had enormous wealth. He wasn't just a younger son living on an allowance who could eventually look forward to a comfortable life on a modest country estate in England or France—he was a younger son of a very *rich* duke, or more accurately now, the younger *brother* of a very rich duke. "So, you see," Molly went on in her reasonable tone, "we need only wait until Flora

Bonham leaves. You're a lovely eighteen-year-old girl. What man wouldn't find you attractive?"

"How perfect! It's July already. In another month or so, I'll have Adam all to myself. Do you think he's angry with me for bursting in on him?" An unusual discretion entered her voice. As the spoiled daughter of doting parents, she rarely questioned her motive.

"Why don't I apologize for you? I'm sure Adam will understand your youthful enthusiasm."

"Would you, Auntie? That would be divine! Oh"— Henrietta clapped her hands together—"I can hardly wait for the summer to end!"

Molly Fisk wasn't a fool. She understood Adam Serre could have any woman he wanted here and abroad, but she also understood he'd chosen Montana for his home. Only a certain kind of woman would be willing to live her life on the frontier. Of those women, why not young Henrietta, with the advantage of her father's millions? Why not, indeed. Her matchmaking plans were back on track. "Now we won't say anything about this to your uncle, and should someone have seen you this morning, I want you to simply deny it. I will as well," she added, saving her Sunday-school story for reinforcement if necessary. But there was no point in confusing Henrietta with added options. She was a simple young girl. "You were here with me having an early breakfast in my room. I'll talk to the servants. There. How nice. Everything is settled."

Chapter Thirteen

With the extremely warm July weather, the windows in the suite were opened wide, the lace curtains stirring occasionally as a breeze flowed through them, the sounds from the street below also drifting through the gossamer fabric.

It was just before midnight Monday night, the sky vaporous gray through the veiled windows, the sounds of carousal lessened but never completely extinguished in the thoroughfare outside. The bed curtains hung limp in the sultry heat, the ticking of the clock the only sound in the shadowed bedroom. Adam sat with Flora on a chair he'd pulled close to the open windows, her nude body resting on his lap, her head on his chest, her breathing the regular cadence of peaceful slumber.

He found sleep elusive. It was the heat, he told himself, avoiding the more complex reasons having to do with his powerful response to Flora Bonham. Their time together was almost gone. Gazing down at her, he reflected how pleasant it would have been to have met her years ago, before Isolde and all the complications she had presented to his life.

But in the next pulse beat he cautioned himself to a more cool-headed reason. Persistent sex with Flora Bonham *could* have something to do with his warm feelings toward her, he reminded himself. The emotions assailing him were difficult to separate from the intensity of their carnal bond. If past experience was any indication, he'd find it difficult to remember her name by winter. But even as he rationally considered the possibility that this was another transient liaison, a niggling doubt questioned such cool logic.

Flora stirred in his arms, snuggling closer like a sleepy kitten, and a smile touched Adam's mouth. She made him happy; her simple presence could make him smile.

He was lowering his head to gently kiss her when a barrage of gunshots exploded outside. And a second later the cry followed, "Meagher's dead! Meagher's dead!" the clamorous yell louder as the messenger galloped down the street toward the Planters House. Another volley of gunfire punctuated the screams, calling the town to attention.

The second round of shots at close range woke Flora.

Lacing her arms around his neck, her eyes drowsy with sleep, she murmured, "Another gunfight?"

"A messenger with news of Meagher's death." Adam's deep voice was without inflection. But he gathered her firmly in his arms and suddenly rose from the chair. "I'm going downstairs for a minute," he softly said, carrying her over to the bed. "And find out the details."

"He won't be after your clan now. . . ." She wasn't fully awake yet, and her words were only a murmur of sound.

"I'll be back in a few minutes," Adam quietly said, placing Flora in the center of the bed, lingering a moment to kiss her.

She clung to him. "Ummm . . . don't go." Obsessed, greedy for the feel of him, she pulled his head back down. "Stay . . . ," she whispered against his mouth.

He relented temporarily, tasting her sweet mouth in a lingering kiss that elicited a delicious purring sound from the lady beneath him. "My unquenchable darling," he whispered with a smile, extricating himself from her clinging arms, "give me five minutes and I'll be back."

"You won't forget me, now," she said, her voice low-pitched and sultry, her lithe body stretching in an unforgettably sensual way.

"I'll definitely remember that," Adam murmured, grinning. "Don't go away."

He dressed with masculine swiftness and exited the bedroom with a wave and a blown kiss while Flora felt that first faint quiver of dread.

This was how she was going to feel when he was gone from her life in another few hours—empty, abandoned, bereft of his energy and spirit. She shivered in the sultry summer heat. Shaking away her melancholy, she resolutely took herself to task. She wouldn't dissolve away from the loss of one man, no matter how beautiful and accomplished he was. Her life was too full for her to wallow in self-pity and despair over the termination of a love affair.

Abruptly rising from the bed, she walked into the sitting room as if escaping the site of so much of their passion. She'd better control her sensibilities, she warned herself. But they'd made love everywhere in the sitting room, too, she realized as her gaze swept the room. Snatching up a shirt Adam had dropped onto a chair, she slipped it over her nakedness, feeling a sudden need to cover her body as though she could shield herself from passion with a linen shirt. She began pacing, agitated by her desolation, her emotions in turmoil. The men in her past had never affected her like this. Never. They were charming diversions to her life, but they didn't impinge on her emotions. Or they never had. Until now. Threading her way around the bulky furniture, she crossed and recrossed the room, restless under the charged tumult in her brain.

To her horror, when Adam walked back into the suite short minutes later, she stopped, looked at him, and burst into tears.

"I'm sorry . . ." She hiccuped, mortified, tears streaming down her cheeks.

"What happened?" Adam softly exclaimed, striding swiftly toward her.

"Nothing . . . I'm fine . . . ," she gasped, weeping in great gulping sobs, looking like a small child in his overlarge shirt, her legs bare, her toes curled into the flowered carpet.

Sweeping her into his arms when he reached her, he hugged her close. "I shouldn't have gone," he whispered in self-reproach. "Tell me what happened."

His compassion, the particular aptness of his words, only brought on fresh tears, and perplexed, he searched her face. But she only uttered a muffled, "Nothing happened," when clearly something had. Debating how to comfort her, he moved to the couch, sat down, and, holding her in his lap, sympathetically said, "Just tell me." He lifted her chin gently so their eyes met. "I can make it better."

"I'm . . . being . . . silly," she stammered, gulping hard to control her weeping. "I must be . . . tired."

"Did someone come in while I was gone?" He gently brushed the wetness from her cheeks.

She shook her head, forcing back the tears flooding her throat.

"You didn't hurt yourself?"

She waggled her head no again, her curls a wispy caress on his chin.

"Would you like to sleep? I should have let you sleep more."

"It's not your fault," she quietly said, her tears nearly stanched. "And I really don't want to sleep."

"What do you want to do?" he asked in an attempt to cheer her. "Tell me and we'll do it."

"Go to Paris," she replied, her teasing smile trembling for only a second.

"I'll pack," he softly replied, touching the susceptible corner of her mouth with a light brushing fingertip. "We'll have dinner with the emperor."

"And you'll take me to the races."

"I'll definitely take you to the races." His voice went very quiet. "Every man will envy me."

"I'll stay at your house."

"I won't let you out of my sight," he affirmed, holding her tight.

"We'll dance at the Tuileries."

"Or at St. Cloud."

"And every woman will envy *me*," she whispered.

"Our holiday will last forever."

"Forever," she said very, very softly. "Now kiss me before I cry again."

And he did with a special tenderness as though she were fragile. He kissed away the damp trails her tears had left on her rosy cheeks, he kissed her delicate earlobes and silky lashes, he kissed the sighing warmth of her mouth.

She found his kisses fortifying, her distress melting away in his arms. "You're an extraordinary man," she murmured, her fingers laced through his hair, her spirits recovered, her smile restored to its former glory. "Tell me how you do it."

"To begin with," he teasingly said, "I always have a good breakfast and see that I get plenty of sleep and—"

"You never sleep."

"Sometimes I do. This isn't one of those times, for obvious reasons."

"Because of our limited time."

He looked at her closely before he answered, gauging the stability of her mood. "Yes," he said. His sigh ruffled her hair. "With Meagher dead, I should ride north," he quietly added.

"How soon will you be leaving?" Pride kept her voice level.

"Right after you do. The camp probably has the news by now, but the militia will have to be monitored for a short time at least. And then if all goes well, if the volunteers disband soon, I'm hoping to take my horses to Saratoga for the August races."

"Lucie tells me she's going along this time," Flora said, politesse serving as barricade to her feelings.

"I'm hearing the same thing. She wants to see Magnus run."

"You should win with him." It was remarkable, she thought, how her smile could be detached from emotion.

"I'm planning on it."

"If you need to leave earlier for the camp—"

"No," he quickly interjected.

"You're sure? I don't want to feel guilty about a foolish wager."

"I'd like to stay longer if I could." His voice was soft as velvet.

Her smile held her old assurance. "We've another four hours, anyway."

"Four and a half," he said with a grin. "What kind of chocolate should I order this time? Chocolate with ambergris?"

"Are you trying to seduce me?" Her voice was fluty with heated allure.

"Of course not," he murmured with a faint smile. "Only comfort you." Brillat-Savarin referred to ambered chocolate as chocolate of the unhappy, for its pleasant capacity to allay suffering of any kind. "Or would you prefer Russian chocolate?"[10]

"I'll have both," she softly replied. "Will you feed it to me here or in bed?"

He gazed at her for a moment, his dark eyes heated, covetous, as though he'd not touched her before, as though he were a hot-blooded youth offered his first woman. "I'll see what you like best," he murmured, remembering where he'd indulged her in the days past. How he'd fed her chocolate mousse in the chair by the window one afternoon while she'd pleaded for his touch; how he'd offered the little meringue-and-almond chocolate drops to her as she lay on the sofa—in exchange for her kisses. And the Dobos torte, eaten in bed at first, had reminded them both of Budapest and later of a particularly memorable bath.

"You're too good to me," she whispered, a sweet, restless coquetry in her voice.

"Why shouldn't I be? You're peerless delight."

She smiled. "For four and a half hours more, at least."

"No," he quietly said, sensitive to the impression she'd made on his life. "For always in my heart. . . ."

But Flora eventually stayed an extra half day because she couldn't bring herself to leave, no more than Adam could let her. And when she finally forced herself to go, they both found their last good-bye difficult.

"I'm sorry," Adam quietly said, holding her lightly in his arms, leaning against the door so she couldn't walk away for a few moments more.

"It's too soon," she softly replied, understanding his cryptic words as if he'd gone on at length about the disarray of his marriage.

"After marriage to Isolde," he ruefully admitted, his voice very low, "it might always be too soon." In his darkest moods he wondered if the scars of his marriage might never be erased.

The reasons for it.

The day-to-day misery of it.

The combative residue of it.

He'd never be completely rid of Isolde.

"I understand," Flora said, sensible, pragmatic, a rational focus having long determined the direction of her life. "Thank you for everything," she said with a smile. Reaching behind her, she gently removed his hands from her waist and stepped back.

Adam sighed at the inevitable and then returned her smile. "You're entirely welcome," he softly said. "And thank you, too, for a rare pleasure. Lucie and I will miss you." He pushed away from the door and released the latch so it swung partly open.

Flora's smile was less easy suddenly, for she would truly miss them both. But her life had never revolved around any man; she had no intention of bartering her independence for that dependency, no matter how poignant her feelings of loss. "Good-bye, Adam," she whispered.

And picking up her valise, she walked out of the room.

Chapter Fourteen

With Meagher's death and the return of Governor Green Clay Smith, the Montana militia was reorganized. All commissions issued by the late acting governor Meagher were reduced to complementary ranks. And though Governor Smith issued a call at the end of July for volunteers for a new six-month enlistment, when General Terry, commander of the Department of Dakota, visited Helena and conferred with him, Terry suggested that nothing had occurred in Montana to justify the alarm over hostile Indians.

He expressed the opinion that the troops should be mustered out.

It had all begun with political ambitions as the major impetus, augmented by the greed of the volunteers. A small successful Indian war would have restored Meagher's reputation as a bold military leader and placed his name prominently in the eastern papers, while the possibility of bounty had driven the troops. But Meagher's enemies had begrudged him that celebrity and put an end to his ambitions when he ostensibly fell overboard into the Missouri River the night of July 1 and disappeared forever.[11]

By the last days of July it was clear the danger was over, and Adam's clan was safe once again from the unpredictable forays of the drunken volunteers. Immune to the political and financial machinations only beginning now that Governor Smith was back in the territory and Meagher's faction was in disrepute, Adam set his affairs in order with his clan and ranch crew and left for Saratoga. In their overland journey to the railhead at Cheyenne, his party avoided the hostile Lakota ranging the Powder River country, a full complement of scouts accompanying them as protection for Lucie should difficulties arise. From Cheyenne his horses traveled in Adam's specially appointed stable car, his own private quarters housed in a second railcar, with grooms and cooks and nursemaids for Lucie seeing to the ease of their journey.

They reached Saratoga the first week in August along with twenty thousand other summer visitors descending on the country village for the August season at the Spa. Every hotel was filled: the large Union Hotel, the equally gigantic Congress Hall, the exclusive Clarendon, where Adam settled his entire party, and all of the numerous other hotels down to the smallest boardinghouse far off the fashionable thoroughfares.

The leisurely pace of social activities never varied: breakfast between seven and nine; a stroll to any of the score of springs for a drink of the waters; a morning concert, then a light luncheon served in the larger hotels to a thousand guests by a staff of up to 250 waiters; another walk after the meal to settle one's food; some visiting on the lengthy piazzas lining the fashionable promenades; an afternoon concert with any number to choose from, since each hotel invested in its own musicians; and the de rigueur event of the day at four—the carriage procession to the nearby lakes. At night numerous balls, informally referred to as hops by the initiated, offered amusement while men with other interests could gamble their fortunes in the discreet private clubs where women were barred from the gaming rooms.

It was an unhurried schedule of eating, drinking, sleeping, talking, walking, reading, riding, dancing, nonstrenuous activities catering to pleasure and requiring at least five changes of costume during the day so the ladies could see and be seen in the full glory of their wardrobes and jewels.

Adam and Lucie spent their days at Horse Haven, the old course turned training track, overseeing their horses' practice runs for the August race season. Saratoga offered the best racing in the country, drawing from as far away as the West Coast visitors and horse owners anxious to see the prime thoroughbreds in America pitted against one another during the thirty-day season.

The first track, built in 1863, had been immediately superseded by a larger course and grandstand the following year to accommodate the intense interest of the Spa visitors. Ten thousand spectators attended the daily races, with betting beginning at nine each morning and the first race starting at eleven. The purses ran from $350 to $1,000, but the real money was in the stakes betting and the auction pools, where private bets ran up to $200,000 a day and the auction pools went up to astronomical heights. The millionaires who brought their stables to the small upstate village each August bet as heavily on their bloodstock as they did on their cards each night at the casinos. The demimondaines, beautifully dressed and carefully chaperoned—for Saratoga still espoused a strict tradition opposed to sin—were displayed like so many colorful flowers in their fine carriages. For where best to meet the wealthiest of men but at the track?

Unlike Newport, the other summer retreat for the wealthy that sheltered its inhabitants behind the exclusive barriers of multimillion-dollar villas, Saratoga offered entrée to anyone with the price of a hotel room. So a mélange of eastern financial titans, western bonanza kings, transportation tycoons, statesmen, society dilettantes, and sporting members of the turf aristocracy rubbed shoulders with Middle America on the verandas, at the springs, at meals in the enormous communal dining rooms, in the gambling emporiums, and on the shady walks. And the colorful array of humanity, symptomatic of America's melting-pot culture, where every man with drive and gumption had an equal opportunity to make his fortune, came together once a year at the Spa to offer a remarkable spectacle—the democratization of elegance.

However, there were those wealthy visitors who preferred their own residence, and to accommodate them, enormous mansions lined the tree-lined streets, elaborate concoctions and whimsies in the newest eclectic styles: French châteaus, Swiss chalets, Italian villas, Dutch Renaissance manors, Greek Revival temples in white clapboard, and Victorian Gothic concoctions ornamented with towers, turrets, nooks, crannies, and filigreed details like frosting on a cake. The sprawling mansions celebrated with a theatrical flair the obscene wealth of their owners.

In contrast to the new flamboyant "cottages" erected with the nouveau riche wealth accumulated by profiteers during the Civil War, more sedate homes of the old moneyed families, built in the Federal style of previous decades, sat with stately calm and uncluttered facades, pristine white and grand behind wrought-iron fences and flowering borders. In such a home Flora's Aunt Sarah had lived each August since Saratoga had been only a sleepy village known for its medicinal waters. And so she dwelt again the season of 1867, a widow for the past ten years, an avid horse breeder, and a remarkably youthful-looking woman at fifty.

Sarah Gibbon knew Adam Serre as a fellow turf aficionado, having met him in 1863 when the first races were run at Saratoga. They weren't close friends but social acquaintances, as were many of the wealthy horse breeders who congregated at Saratoga each summer.

The Comte de Chastellux had brought his daughter this season, Sarah noted with a mother's eye for children —the girl had his coloring and fabulous eyes. But he'd not brought his wife, she also noted. Rumor had it his marriage was more unorthodox than most.

In the height of the summer it was so hot on the plains, Four Chiefs's village had moved into the mountains to escape the sweltering temperatures. Other clans had also moved to the higher elevations, and much visiting occurred between the various camps. The men and women raced their horses, competed in games, gossiped, and gambled, and at night everyone danced under the starlit sky. It was a time of good cheer and familial contacts. And Flora and her father were kept busy recording the events of the summer camp, describing the various games and dances, observing the courtship rituals, deciphering the complicated substructure of the Absarokee family and clan relationships.

Flora submerged herself in her work again, but thoughts of Adam wouldn't be dislodged from her mind regardless of how much she devoted herself to her studies. She understood there were limits to love affairs, boundaries one didn't defy. Intellectually, she understood the parameters.

One simply said, "Thank you. It was nice," and stored away the memories like the remembrance of a perfect sunny day or a fine ride or the feeling when a marvelous new discovery was revealed in one's research.

But this time logic failed to withstand her longing.

And her father knew.

One afternoon, seated in the cool shade of a mountain pine, George Bonham and Flora watched the daily races taking place on a grassy flat below them.

"You could go to Saratoga too," the earl quietly said, his gaze on the galloping horses.

Flora's head abruptly turned from the race scene. "Is it so obvious?" she said, her eyes trained on her father.

"Only because I know you," he replied, turning to look at her. "And Henry said you fought back tears on the trip back to camp after leaving Helena."

"Thank you for having him wait for me. I didn't realize I was so transparent in my designs that night of the Fisks' party. And if Alan hadn't been with you, I would have told you the truth. But he's so pious, I was afraid he'd have an apoplexy if he heard my plans."

Her father smiled. "Alan looks at the world with too

much solemnity, but he's a superb artist, so he's allowed his puritan idiosyncracies." The earl, as a product of his class, and heir to one of the oldest, wealthiest families in Yorkshire, understood aristocratic privilege to an infinitesimal degree. "Even without hearing your conversation with Adam at the poker table, I could anticipate the outcome. Your sudden interest in traveling with James came as no surprise."

"I was planning on hiring guides to accompany me back to camp. And Adam had men he could call on to guide me."

"I preferred having you travel with someone I trusted."

"You're very dear, Papa," Flora softly said, and then she exhaled in a lingering sigh. "I'm feeling out of my depth for the first time in my life. It's a very strange sensation."

"Perhaps you're in love. It makes one less pragmatic."

She looked at him with a curious alarm. "Do you think so? Maybe it's simply ennui," she dissented, answering her own question. "I feel so rudderless, in limbo . . . utterly without direction. It's very odd. I find myself considering Adam Serre from every conceivable posture—as friend, mere acquaintance, lover—none of the classifications offering the slightest possibility of a workable future." She sighed again. "But going to Saratoga won't solve anything."

"You might discover love can't be dealt with in an empirical manner."

"Why not, Papa, when everything else responds to the methodology?"

George Bonham gazed at his daughter for a moment, wondering if their preponderantly scholarly existence had blinded her to the magical qualities of life. "I don't know," he quietly said. "I only know the experience is breathtaking, rare, and if possible—not to be missed."

"Adam may not agree." Tracing an idle finger through the fallen pine needles littering the grass, she added, "I think love is very low on his list of priorities."

"But you don't know for certain, and since Sarah has plenty of room at her summerhouse, why not find out?"

"Is love like the search for the source of the Nile, with the trip alone being worth the effort?"

"Or like Ludwig Ross's theory of an Aegean civilization that demanded years of exploration to substantiate. The answers aren't always readily evident."

"He may not want to see me." She was resisting, the thought of chasing after Adam Serre anathema to her liberated soul.

"Well, Sarah certainly will, and," her father went on with an indulgent smile, "I expect numerous men at Saratoga will find your presence gratifying."

"It's a very long way to travel for a man." Especially, she thought, for a man who was so in demand he needed a dance card to keep track of the females in his life.

"But not so far to go for love."

"Papa, you're a romantic," she exclaimed with a modicum of surprise.

"I knew love once with your mother, and if you could be as fortunate, I'd wish you that same happiness. You've been miserable since Helena. Admit it."

"But, Papa, how demeaning to chase a man halfway across the country. He's much too arrogant already. I couldn't."

"Have you ever considered he may feel flattered?"

"Have you ever considered he may have a dozen women with him? You know how the men arrive at Saratoga and rent the private cottages at the hotels for their fictitious nieces or cousins or secretaries."[12]

"Such possibilities didn't stop your mother. She arrived at my hotel room in Boston on the second day after we met, with her maid in tow and a packed valise, drove away from my suite the woman I was entertaining, and informed me she was going to marry me."

Flora smiled at the image of her petite mother raising havoc with her father's hotel guest. "And you agreed?" She'd never heard the details of their elopement.

"I had to. She wouldn't leave my room. She threatened to have her father and brothers sent for. And I was mad for her even though I had a fiancée in England. So you see," he added with a smile, "how indiscreet your heritage."

"What ever did you tell your fiancée?"

"I sent word of my marriage and told her I'd honor the financial agreements of our marriage settlement, which tempered her anger considerably. She found herself another husband very soon."

"And you and Mama sailed off around the world."

"Within the week. Her family was amenable to my title; I didn't have need of her fortune—a positive in her Yankee family's view of me, and I loved her. Everyone came to a happy understanding."

"So you think I might have some success barging into Adam's hotel room and repeating Mama's drama," Flora said with a grin.

"You're considerably more reserved than your mama; I don't expect you'll precisely follow her scenario. But at least go to Saratoga and resolve your emotional tumult."

"I've never considered myself reserved." She had in fact viewed herself as wholly unconventional. "I wish I'd known Mama better," she softly said, her memories of her mother the nebulous images of a six-year-old.

"Your mama was very young, very beautiful, very spoiled, and the love of my life. You remind me of her every minute of every day, although you're not in the least spoiled." He spoke with the unconditional love of a father who wished his daughter every happiness life could offer, and if Adam Serre was the means to that happiness, he would see that she had him. "Now consider, darling," he went on, "we can have you in Cheyenne in five days."

"Why don't you come with me?" Flora said, not realizing she'd made up her mind.

"I have to keep Douglas and Alan busy here," her father replied. "But we'll meet you again at the end of August. I'll send Henry with you."

"I don't know . . . ," Flora murmured, her gaze unfocused on the races below, her brows drawn together in a faint frown as she debated the possibilities.

"Of course you do," her father insisted, already composing his letter to Sarah in his mind. Sarah had married off two daughters; she'd know precisely how to deal with Flora's predicament. Not that he was thinking of marriage so much as having Flora happy again. And Adam Serre seemed to hold the key to that emotion. "Think of the shock on Adam's face when he sees you," he teased.

Flora grinned. "That *would* be worth eight days' travel. Do you think he'll remember me?"

The earl laughed. "Darling, I expect you're very hard to forget."

Chapter Fifteen

❧

Flora arrived on her aunt's doorstep in high season with the full influx of summer visitors in place, slightly apprehensive of her motives for coming, tired after eight days of travel, and grateful for her father's insistence on sending his valet along.

Henry, a diminutive Cornishman with a flare for languages and an indefatigable energy, had escorted her across America with ease and astonishing organizational skills. Her luggage had actually arrived before them as had her father's second and third telegram, so Sarah was waiting with open arms and a welcoming smile.

"Darling, how wonderful you've come," her aunt cried, hugging Flora. "It's been ages since I've seen you. Come right in and tell me everything," she cheerfully added, taking Flora by the hand and leading her into the cool interior of the shaded house on Franklin Square. "You must be hungry."

"Henry saw that I was never hungry," Flora said with a smile. "As he saw to everything else."

"Which is why your papa pays him so well. He's a jewel. Even your mama liked him, and she begrudged sharing your papa with anyone. Let's sit out in the garden where it's cool," she went on, pulling Flora through the

small formal drawing room toward French doors opening
onto a green, flowering bower.

When they were seated and the servant had left after
bringing tea, Sarah said, "Your papa sent a telegram, but
you know how cryptic those messages. What brings you
to Saratoga on such brief notice?" She was being diplomatic, for George Bonham's three telegrams from Cheyenne had been lengthy, although for the sake of
discretion, proper names had been omitted.

"Papa talked me into coming," Flora said on a small
sigh. "And I've had eight days to have myriad misgivings
about this trip. He seems to think Adam Serre can offer
me some measure of solace."

"Are you in need of solace?" Sarah Gibbon spoke with
a discretionary calm, for Adam Serre seemed the least
likely man to bring solace to a woman.

"I'm not exactly sure what I want, and had you asked
me that same question a few months ago, a man wouldn't
have been the answer to my unsettled feelings. My work
has always come first; it's been my greatest pleasure."

"And now Adam Serre's brand of pleasure has infringed
on that private reserve."

Flora shrugged her shoulders and reached for a small
cake. "Do you eat when you're frustrated?" she queried,
taking a bite of the pastel-frosted confection. "Thank
God Henry was along to see that I had sweets to sustain
me." Her smile was self-indulgently cheerful.

"I do find a bonbon or two helps my disposition at
times," her aunt agreed. "But what do you *think* you want
to do now that you're here?" Sarah persisted, wanting her
niece's interpretation of the events detailed in her
brother-in-law's telegrams.

"Make Adam Serre pay for my damned discomfort,"
Flora said with a grin, "and for the extra pounds I probably put on thanks to my utter frustration."

"You look splendid, darling. No need to make him pay
for that, but then it never hurts to gain some revenge for
that male nonchalance they're trained to cultivate from

the cradle," she sweetly added, her smile accompanied by a wicked tilt of one brow.

"I'm afraid my plans have rather been in that direction," Flora amiably declared, "despite occasional manifestations of conscience cautioning me to more proper recourse. After eight days of deductive logic, vigilant reason, and the full array of philosophical scruple, I'm fairly convinced I'm here to disrupt his life and seduce him."

"Surely not a difficult task with Adam Serre. Seduction is his forte."

"Actually it may be a very *difficult* mission. He said only, 'I'm sorry,' when last we parted."

"A familiar posture for him, no doubt. And for you as well," Sarah reminded her niece. "As I recall, you've disposed of a great number of lovesick swains in a similar fashion."

"And now I'm paying penance for my misdeeds," Flora replied with a small smile. "I find myself besotted as never before, and I'm here to discover whether I miss him so intensely only because he's suddenly gone, or in truth."

"And when you find out, then what?" her aunt softly inquired.

"I'm at an impasse then," Flora plainly said, a permanent relationship beyond the current framework of her life—that possibility having always been relegated to some nameless future with some nameless man for reasons that would be clear to her at the time. "My immediate pleasure is simply in saying hello to him and watching his reaction. A small test of my seductive powers. Do I sound totally malicious and without scruple?"

"Darling, every young woman here is out to seduce. Some for love, some for profit, others for pleasure alone. You're not in exclusive ranks, believe me. And frankly, my dear, Adam Serre is long overdue for amorous reprisal. He's walked away from more than his share of romantic entanglements. Do *I* sound unscrupulous?"

Flora laughed. "We must have conscience enough that we're questioning our ethics."

"How reassuring," Sarah said with a smile, "for this is a

town of illicit love and sanctimonious poseurs. We must keep up appearances at least. Now, enough about needless piety," she declared, a practical woman at heart, which accounted for the success of her shipping firm, her dead husband's shipping firm, and her well-run stock portfolio. "What we need first is a wardrobe for this seduction. You must come with me to the Bellington ball tonight."

"Adam's not likely to be at a ball. I'd be more apt to find him at the racetrack or the gaming rooms."

"I have it on good authority that Caldwell King is bringing his party to the Bellingtons tonight, and Adam gambles with Caldwell every night. Have you brought anything suitably dazzling with you? We'll have the dressmaker over directly tomorrow morning, but in the meantime we must make do tonight with what we have."

"I have a beaded chiffon over silk that Worth spend a month completing."

"What color?"

"Parma violet."

"Perfect," Sarah declared in a breathy whisper. "With diamonds of course," she added in a husky contralto.

"Of course," Flora replied with a delicious wink.

After a profitable day at the races and an early supper with Lucie, Adam was in his dressing room changing into evening attire of white tie and tails. Lucie was in attendance, seated on a chair beside the cheval glass, swinging her buttoned green leather shoes, keeping up a running inquisition.

"Where are you going first?"

"To Morrissey's Club on Matilda Street."

"The little redbrick house?"

"That's the one."

"Are you going to lose money?"

"I hope not."

"Can you take me there someday?"

"Only to the dining parlor, darling. There are rules against ladies inside the card rooms."

"That's stupid."

"You're right." He smiled down at his daughter, still dressed in green-trimmed muslin to match his racing colors.

"What's the difference if I see the cards? I see your cards all the time when you play poker with me."

"Exactly, it's very odd, I agree."

"If there are no ladies there, why are you dressing up?" He shrugged. "More rules."

"I hate rules."

Adam grinned into the mirror as he adjusted his white tie, his daughter's perceptions of constraint much like his. "There are entirely too many," he said. "It's better back home on the Musselshell."

"But our horses are running really good, aren't they, Papa? So the long trip was worth it. And Magnus has won every race he's run."

"Every one. I can't get profitable odds anymore," he added with a grin. "But he's a joy to watch," he went on, reaching for his coat. "Next season we'll run him in the Grand Prix."

"And I'm going with you this time."

"Absolutely." He settled the finely tailored garment onto his broad shoulders.

"I'm old enough not to need Cloudy all the time now."

"You certainly are, sweetheart," he said, brushing her dark curls, her presence in his life like breath to him. "You'll like Paris."

"Will Maman be there?"

"I'm not certain, darling. She doesn't like racing as much as you and I," he blandly replied, avoiding the more pertinent reasons they weren't likely to see her.

"Are you going to see Uncle Caldy tonight?"

"He's coming to fetch me."

"Can I stay up until he comes? He always brings me candy and he laughs really loud. It makes me giggle."

"He makes everyone laugh, and yes, you may stay up."

"You're so easy, Papa."

He looked down at her from under his dark lashes, his faint smile genial. "Am I really?"

"You always let me have my way."

He grinned. "Should I say no more often?"

She looked up at him with identical dark eyes, her gaze open and artless. "I *like* having my own way."

"That's what I thought," Adam gently said. "Give me a kiss now, because Caldwell will be here soon, and I won't see you again until morning."

Kneeling beside her chair, he hugged her, and she gave him a wet kiss and a glowing smile.

"Are you going to kiss any ladies tonight?" she asked as he stood upright again.

He hesitated for a moment. "I don't think so."

"Rosie says you kiss *lots* of ladies, and Flossie says she wishes you'd kiss *her.*"

His eyes widened briefly, and he carefully said, "You probably misunderstood."

"Uh-uh. They say it ever so much. They talk about you all the time and sigh and giggle. I think they like you, Papa."

"Why don't we go downstairs and wait for Uncle Caldy in the lobby," he abruptly declared, taking a parent's conventional escape route of distraction. "You can slide down the banister."

"Yippee," Lucie cried, jumping from the chair with her usual boundless energy. "You're the bestest papa in the whole word," she exclaimed, already halfway across the room.

Perhaps he'd better send Rosie and Flossie back home to Montana, he reflected. The last thing he needed, he thought, lacing the gold chain of his watch through his waistcoat buttonhole, was problems with Lucie's young nursemaids.

Chapter Sixteen

The old colonel's ball at the Union Hotel was a crush. The sweltering August weather wilted fashionably frizzed hair and starched white collars, producing an unladylike sheen of sweat on many a petticoated, crinolined, and corseted female. The terrace doors were thrown open in hopes of catching any slight coolness or breeze, and the run on iced champagne gave rise to a bright and lively gaiety.

Sarah and Flora came late, avoiding the worst of the evening's heat, interested less in the dancing than in the Caldwell King party, which wouldn't arrive until after some play at the casinos.

Sarah introduced her niece to their host and hostess, the colonel and his niece, Mrs. Morton. Mr. Bellington's wife was on prolonged holiday in Europe—a pattern with many of the wealthy wives whose husband's interest had waned. One of America's richest men, Colonel Bellington had an eye for beautiful women, and he immediately turned his attention on Flora. It was several dances and champagnes later before she could politely extricate herself from his lecherous grasp.

"He's almost completely without manners," Flora breathlessly remarked to her aunt, leaning against the brick of the Union Hotel's piazza wall. "I thought I might have to literally pry his hands from around my waist."

"He's from a rough background," Sarah noted. "And he's very aware of what his wealth commands."

"Not my body, however," Flora heatedly retorted. "Has anyone ever publicly brought him to his knees? I was sorely tempted."

"Not to my knowledge, although many a young beauty has made a profitable sum from his heated interest."

"Thank God I've no need of his money. He hasn't a modicum of finesse. I'm going to sit here in the garden and cool off, although you needn't entertain me." Sarah had a bevy of friends at the party. They'd met a dozen of them in the ladies' powder room—all women who'd been coming to Saratoga for as long as Sarah, and who knew every family and visitor of note. "I'll come back in later."

"You're sure, now?"

"I'm positive. It's peaceful here and a few degrees cooler. Now, go and find out what gossip Elizabeth Stanton is dying to tell you. She was practically bursting at the seams."

"She couldn't tell me in front of Charlotte Brewster."

"I gathered as much," Flora said with a smile. "It must be succulent. I'll hear the details tonight."

Strolling down the veranda lit at intervals with ornate gaslight fixtures, Flora found a wrought-iron bench in a secluded corner and sat down. The music from the ballroom was muted by the great length of the portico, the night shadows seemed to separate her from the noise and bustle of the crowd, even the couples strolling in the garden were far enough away to offer her solitude.

It was all very well in principle to take her father's advice and come east to see Adam, she reflected; Sarah, too, supported her. But now that she was here, now that she was actually a part of this frenzied mass of humanity tonight, she didn't have the remotest interest in intruding on Adam's life. Maybe she was tired; maybe it was too hot. Perhaps she didn't feel seductive in such a sweaty throng.

Or possibly the old colonel's unwelcome designs had put everything in perspective.

She didn't pursue men. At least not purposefully. She'd never felt the need.

Relaxing against the cool metal of the garden bench, she exhaled a small sigh, relieved to have reconciled her motivations. How pleasant to be comfortable again with her emotions. Life was a positive journey, not a negative manipulation of people and events. She'd visit with her aunt for a few days, take in some of the races, and then return to Montana. The lure of the cool mountains was definitely an attractive incentive to leave this sultry heat.

Her eight days' travel took their toll as she lounged in the shadows of the wisteria vines, or perhaps the several glasses of champagne made her drowsy, and, lulled by the distant music, she dozed off.

A short time later when Sarah saw Caldwell at the buffet table, she approached him. As longtime friends, they cheerfully greeted each other.

"I thought I'd find you here," she teased. Caldwell always gravitated toward food, his appetite for everything in life gargantuan, like his size.

"Couldn't miss the colonel's spread, Sarah," he boomed. "Your diamonds outshine mine, tonight, darlin'. You look right purty." Caldwell was known as White-Hat Caldwell for the large white Stetson he wore, and his diamond rings, tie pin, and studs dazzled the eye.

"I'm in a festive mood tonight. Two of my horses took first today."

"Don't I know it, darlin', with mine relegated to second and third. I'm going to have to buy that dark roan beauty you have and bring him to my stud."

"It's too hot for him in Texas, Caldwell. You need more barb blood down there."

"Damned if I don't, but bejesus, that roan's a real goer." After introductions were exchanged with those of Caldwell's party she didn't know, the conversation was predictably of horses, with much time spent discussing the day's race card.

When Caldwell excused himself briefly to sample a morsel of lobster a few feet down the sumptuously arranged table, Sarah casually turned to Adam and said, "Have you met my niece, Flora Bonham? She's here from Montana, although I'm not altogether sure in that large a territory whether you would have had the opportunity to know each other."

Adam's heart seemed to stop for a second, and his shock must have been obvious, for she looked at him curiously. "Is our terrible heat bothering you?" she pleasantly inquired.

He assured her it wasn't, and when Caldwell reentered the conversation a second later, Adam found himself unable to concentrate on their continuing dissection of that day's race schedule. It suddenly didn't matter which horse had won or what the winning times were or whether Leonard Jerome or Travers was entering his three-year-old the following day.

Flora was *here*?

Not just in Saratoga, but at this ball?

"Where is she?" he heard himself say, his voice too curt for politesse, his voice sounding as though it were echoing in his ears from a great distance.

"Pardon me?" Sarah Gibbon said with infinite calm, an important question suddenly answered to her satisfaction.

"Your niece. Where is she?"

"Do you know the little filly?" Caldwell queried, his Texas drawl as florid as his diamond rings and enormous girth.

"We've met," Adam said.

"She never mentioned it," Sarah cordially said, "but, then, I expect Flora met a great number of people in Montana. Do you know an Ellis Green?" she adroitly added.

"Yes," Adam replied, his voice suddenly cool. "Is he in Saratoga too?"

"I haven't the faintest idea," Sarah tranquilly declared,

"with a crowd of this magnitude. It's almost unmanageable, don't you think?"

"Do you know where she is?" Adam enunciated each word with a distinct clarity.

"I saw her last on the piazza . . . that way, I think, or was it that way?" Sarah airily motioned. "Oh, dear, my sense of direction is so . . ." Her words trailed off as Adam briefly bowed and left. She smiled up at Caldwell. "My, what a precipitous young man," she sweetly declared.

"I'd say he's off to woo that niece of yours, Sarah," Caldwell jovially said. "I reckon she's in for a surprise."

"She certainly will be," Sarah Gibbon said with the gloating smile of a matchmaker. "He's remarkably hot-blooded."

In swift, stalking scrutiny Adam searched the entire length of the quarter-mile piazza, not certain whether he'd find Flora with Ellis, not certain what he'd do if he found them together. But when he finally discovered her behind a half screen of wisteria vines, he simply stood arrested for a moment, her beauty more breathtaking than he'd remembered.

Her skin was pale against the violet of her gown, her hair piled high in studied disarray with wispy tendrils framing her face. She half reclined on the filigreed settee with one leg on the seat, the other fallen over the edge of the garden bench. Her head lay against an ornate scalloped shell design, her hands were lightly clasped in her lap, the beaded bodice of her gown sparkled in the subdued light as her breasts softly rose and fell with each breath. The diaphanous chiffon of her gown lent an illusion of nudity in the shadowed light, as if her flesh were only lightly veiled by glimmering jewels. And the diamonds at her throat and ears shimmered icy cool against her skin.

He shouldn't have come looking for her. He'd tried not to for that small amount of time it took to listen to Sarah Gibbon's explanation of Flora's presence in Saratoga. And now that he'd found her, he wasn't sure what to do—what was possible or impossible with her slumbering form so available, her thighs lushly open beneath the filmy chiffon and silk. His fingers flexed, an unconscious gesture of repressed action, and he drew in a deep breath of restraint. He pulled up a chair and sat down, a compromise measure to less prudent impulses pressing the boundaries of good taste. He didn't suppose her aunt would benignly overlook public lovemaking or an abduction.

As he gazed at Flora—rocked by indecision . . . one second thanking the spirits for bringing her to him . . . the next, half rising to leave—he remembered other times when he'd watched her sleep, when she'd not been dressed so elegantly—when she'd not been dressed at all.

He sat back down again, his fingers clamped hard on the chair arms.

"Don't you dare, Bertie, what will people say if they see, Bertie, no!" And a high squeal of delight pierced the quiet corner of the veranda. "Bertie, no, no, no . . ." But the voice was playful, teasing, drifting away now toward the opposite side of the garden.

Flora wakened with a start at the feminine cry, and it took her a moment to remember where she was, for Adam Serre was seated very close, his dark eyes trained on her.

"You're here," she whispered, still half-asleep, her words a tentative measure of reality.

"I came looking for you."

His voice was deep and low as she remembered, and the vague possibility she was dreaming vanished at the familiar tone. She still wasn't fully awake, or she would have responded to the intensity in his voice. "Have you been here long?"

He shook his head. "A few minutes. I saw your aunt inside, and she mentioned you were here."

"Sarah seems acquainted with everyone at Saratoga."

"She and Caldwell are friends. I was with his party."

"I know that."

His brows rose.

"Sarah knew it too. I came here to find you."

"As I did just now. Although," he said with a small, bitter sigh, "I don't have a damned thing to offer you."

"That's all right," Flora replied. "I don't want anything."

"And yet there's much I want," he softly said. "You look very beautiful tonight," he murmured. "All glittering undress."

"My seduction dress. I came here to seduce you, but . . ."

"But?" No more than a husky intonation, subdued like the light in their cloistered corner.

"I decided against it. I found myself unnerved by the artifice and the unwonted intrusion in your life. It's enough to be friends."

"I don't know if it is for me." His head moved in a minute gesture of negation, exposing a glimmer of pink shell earring.

"I won't be staying long," Flora said, realizing suddenly how difficult it might be to resist. "Just a few days; surely we can act like adults," she added in bolstering defense.

He smiled. "Tell my libido that."

"I know about your libido," she said with a tentative smile. "But there are masses of women here. And you're not the celibate type."

"Nor you, which is a real problem for me." His voice took on an edge. "Is Ellis here?"

"I don't think so, but I just arrived this afternoon." Her lacy brows came together in a small frown. "And I'd never sleep with Ellis. He likes docile women."

Adam grinned. "Surely not your style."

She smiled back. "Not in memory. Friends now? Come, Adam, say yes. I'd adore seeing Lucie while I'm here."

He inhaled deeply, his expression shuttered, and then, slowly exhaling, said, "I'll try." He smiled. "And Lucie will be ecstatic. You've become the bellwether for pleasure in our family."

The word "family" hurt for a moment, the sweet intimacy at Adam's ranch her own gold standard for idyllic happiness, but she managed a courteous smile, as was expected of well-bred ladies. "Have your horses been winning?" she asked on a less personal note.

He nodded. "Magnus is taking every race he enters. Come see him run tomorrow. Lucie would love it." He paused. "And I would too."

"I'd enjoy that." Flora spoke in her modulated social voice, the one without undue feeling. It was a test of her nerves.

"I'll have a carriage come for you at half-past ten tomorrow morning." He stood abruptly. "I think I'll go back to the casino now. If I stay here much longer, looking at you in that seduction gown"—his smile was tight— "I might have to put it to the test."

And if he'd stayed, she thought, watching him walk away, broad-shouldered, powerful, his stride all fluid grace, his dark beauty as extravagant as his passion, she would have allowed him anything.

She shivered in the humid heat.

It was much easier in the bright light of day to repress her most ardent longing, particularly with Lucie in tow, and their day at the races was pure delight—the very best of harmonious friendship. Conversation centered on horses, speed, jockeys, stables. Lunch with Caldwell and his friends was raucous, the discussion amusing, energetic, hysterical at times, and Flora laughed more than she had in ages, her enjoyment giving Adam enormous pleasure.

Adam's thoroughbreds won all their races, so both Flora and Adam made a tidy sum on the betting.

"I'm going to have to buy some bauble with my winnings," Flora gaily declared. "Something completely useless."

"I'll take you to Tiffany's tomorrow," Adam said.

"When?" Her face was wreathed in smiles.

"Whenever you like. They'll open the store anytime."

"Tomorrow morning is fine."

"At nine, then, before the races."

"Perfect."

How easy it is to love him, she thought.

How easy it is to make her happy, Adam cheerfully reflected.

The day sped by, the mood serious at times when Adam's horses were running. He watched every move of horse and jockey with a stopwatch in hand, taking note of the minutest details. At other times Lucie kept them busy with her questions and comments, her Baby DeeDee a participant in the conversations as well. And after the races that afternoon, when they brought Flora back to Sarah's, at Lucie's insistence Adam agreed to come in for tea.

"You don't have to go gambling until nine o'clock, Papa, so we have plenty of time for cakes and tea," Lucie had cheerfully maintained when Adam had hesitated at Flora's invitation.

How could he refuse such logic?

They were seated in the garden under the shade of the elms with a silver tea service gleaming on a table set near a bed of pansies, their white wicker chairs arranged in a half circle around it.

"Don't you just love frosting?" Lucie declared, licking her fingers with relish.

"It's my favorite," Sarah agreed, "which is why I always have Cook make these cakes for tea. Flora was just telling me yesterday how much she liked them."

"I like any sweets," Flora said with a smile.

"But chocolate best," Adam said.

And the look passing between her two adult guests caused even a worldly woman like Sarah to take pause. "You're not drinking your tea, Mr. Serre," she said in the sudden hush, feeling decidedly de trop. "Would you care for something stronger?"

It took Adam a moment to respond, and when he turned to his hostess, he said almost abstractedly, "Brandy would be fine."

"Papa doesn't usually drink tea, although Maman would always complain and say he was—what was that long word, Papa? It started with 'un.'"

"Uncivilized," he said.

"It's just a matter of taste, darling," Sarah quickly interjected into the abrupt silence. "Many men find tea much too weak. My dear husband always preferred a cup of rum. It came from his days at sea when he was running the China clippers. Rum was his favorite—hot, cold, with sugar and lemon, with eggnog, well . . . just about any form of rum . . . pleased him." Realizing she was nervously running on, Sarah came to an abrupt conclusion. "Let me call the maid to bring you some brandy," she quickly added, ringing the small bell on the table with obvious agitation.

Adam debated saying he didn't really need brandy but realized that would only further fluster her.

Flora wondered how a few words could bring back a flood of memories with such clarity. Adam had often fed her the rich chocolate desserts she'd ordered at the Planters House. She recalled the tempting variety of ways.

"What's a clipper?" Lucie's chirpy question punctuated the humid quiet like a drumroll.

"Let me show you some paintings of clippers," Sarah immediately replied, not sure whether she wasn't making a cowardly retreat or kindly leaving the two lovers alone. "They're big sailing ships, darling, and I've several paintings of my husband's favorite ones in the library."

"I've never seen a big sailing ship. Only the steamships on the Missouri. My nanny Cloudy came up the river on a steamship," she added in clarification of her knowledge. "I'll just take one of these cakes with me in case they're all gone when I come back." And with the spirit of an adventurer, she followed her hostess without a backward glance.

"She certainly isn't timid," Flora said with a smile, watching Lucie skipping alongside Sarah.

"*I'm* sitting here at the tea table," Adam said with a grin.

"When you don't drink tea."

"And making your aunt very jumpy in the process."

"You shouldn't have looked at me like that."

"I'm sorry. Actually, I'm not sorry about that," he candidly admitted, "but about a dozen other things in my life that are keeping me from touching you."

"Which subject makes *me* very uncomfortable because my notions of restraint are much like Lucie's." She smiled. "Almost nonexistent. And I'm trying to be mature about this."

"It's an edifying experience, at least—this notion of honorable intentions. I'll be taking cold baths with great regularity."

"How sweet."

He looked at her from under his dark brows and muttered, "Don't press me."

"Would I be sorry?" She felt safe in teasing him because he was so noticeably under control.

He grinned. "I don't think so."

"Immodest man." Her voice was ingenue flirtatious.

"Damn you, you just feel secure because we're in your aunt's garden."

"And Lucie's here."

He laughed; then his eyes took on a speculative look. "But she goes to sleep quite early," he said. "Which room is yours?" His gaze swept the garden side of the two-story mansion.

"Good Lord, Adam! You can't come to my room. The servants would talk. I'm not even sure Sarah would approve, tolerant as she is. This town lives on gossip, and I wouldn't want to implicate her in any of my—"

"Indiscretions?" he mildly interjected.

"You're definitely an indiscretion, darling. Henry tells me Morrissey's taking bets on whether your nursemaids stay or go."

"This *is* a damned small town," Adam noted with astonishment. "Lucie just told me last night."

"Losing your vigilant perception, monsieur?"

"Apparently," he murmured. "And for your information, they're on their way home."

"Did I ask about your entanglements?" she said with feigned artlessness.

"They're not my entanglements," he muttered. "Dammit, how the hell did Morrissey know?"

"So soon, you mean. Sarah tells me he has most of the servants in town on his payroll. So kindly stay away from my bedroom, or they'll be betting on how long you stayed."

"I'll be careful no one sees me."

"That's not the right answer."

"I'll be *very* careful."

"Adam!"

"Look, this is all very new to me, this carnal restraint. I hope cold baths work." His smile was boyish, sweet, and impossible to resist. "If they don't, I'll kill any servant I meet in your hallway to suppress gossip."

"I can see who will have to be firm about this denial."

"Right," he dryly said. "The lady who offered me twenty-four hours of sex as a side bet."

"That was different."

"How?"

"I hadn't . . . well, completely resolved the issues in my mind."

"And now you have."

"More or less."

His brows rose. "That seems unusually firm."

"Well, it is." Her voice sounded childish even to her ears.

"Good," he smoothly declared, his eyes half-lidded. "I'm glad one of us can handle this competently. Because I'm not real sure about myself."

"Maybe we shouldn't see each other." A tentative avowal.

"No," he emphatically said. He had no intention of giving her up, even if her company was constrained by prohibitions.

She smiled from her wicker chair under the cool shade of the elm trees. "I was hoping you'd say that."

"You're very confusing." His voice was clipped, restrained.

"I like being with you under any conditions."

"Yes, I know the feeling, and on that disturbing note, I need a brandy—a bottle, I think. Where the hell is that maid?"

The maid appeared shortly with the brandy, having been sent out by Sarah, and Adam commenced to enjoy tea with a new appreciation, although the degree of innuendo in his conversation increased in direct ratio to the decreasing amount of brandy in the bottle. By the time Sarah and Lucie returned after a lengthy interval in the library admiring clipper ships, Flora found herself blushing on occasion at the softly put double entendre. And after Adam and his daughter took their leave, half a bottle of brandy later, Sarah said to her niece with breathless awe, "If you manage to keep Adam Serre at bay, my dear, it will be not only a miracle of vast proportions, but a testament to your self-denial. He's unutterably tempting. And impatient."

"Also the object of every female's lust from nursemaid to lady. He's had enormous practice."

"But Lucie said her nursemaids were sent back home. Cook is helping until they can find someone suitable. Surely it's a gesture of some kind."

"You needn't defend him, Auntie. He already told me very plainly, he can offer me nothing."

"Surely not a surprise to you. Did you expect more?"

"No." Flora traced with a fingertip the embroidery on the napkin lying on her lap. "But I find I want more."

"You're serious about him," her aunt murmured, her expression sympathetic.

"A very ridiculous posture with Adam Serre, wouldn't you agree?" Abruptly crushing the linen napkin, Flora tossed it onto the table.

"I don't know him well enough," her aunt carefully said, although she had her own perceptions of Adam Serre's regard for Flora. A man of casual conquests in the past, he seemed curiously possessive of her niece's time. He'd asked what entertainment they'd be attending that evening and promised to come. Adam Serre at Charlotte

Brewster's party for her granddaughter, Sarah reflected, would be a startling sight.

"And I know him *too* well," Flora retorted with a grimace. "He's simply intent on overcoming my resistance. It's part game, part true interest, but predominantly motivated by carnal impulses."

"Unlike other men, you're saying?" her aunt archly queried. "Most of the men wooing women here are consumed with the same fundamental desires, my dear. Don't be too hard on the boy. He seems devoted to your entertainment. And his darling child adores you."

"And I her. Isn't Lucie the most wonderful child? She's charmingly inquisitive, never difficult, and so precocious, I forget she's only four."

"Adam clearly worships her. Not the pose of an unfeeling man."

"I'm not taking issue with his capacity for tenderness or emotion, simply with the duration of his interest."

"Are you actually contemplating settling down in one place on the globe"—Sarah tipped her head slightly and cast a speculative eye on her niece—"after all these years of wandering?"

"It's quite mad, I know. And it's only the most fitful consideration, along with more powerful self-chastising impulses for even thinking of Adam Serre with permanence. At base I'm furious with myself for falling in love with a flagrant libertine, and a married one at that."

"His marriage surely is in name only," Sarah reminded her.

"Nevertheless . . ." Flora sighed. "I have my romantic notions too, Auntie. When I think of how many marriage proposals I've turned down, it's ironic. Every one of those men pledged their hearts and souls to me—like modern troubadours."

"Apparently you weren't in the market for a troubadour," her aunt dryly remarked.

"Nor do I find a profligate rogue a sensible candidate for—what? I can't even say 'husband'; he's already someone's husband," she fretfully noted.

"I've always rather thought the word 'sensible' out of place when it comes to love," Sarah declared. "Ask your father, if you doubt it."

"I know," Flora quietly replied. "He told me about Mama insisting on marrying him, about how much they were in love. Papa sent me east because of his romantic notions." She sighed again. "Unfortunately, Adam Serre doesn't have a nodding acquaintance with romance."

"Perhaps he can learn," Sarah very softly said. She had an idea or two that might foster an appreciation of the finer points of romance in Adam Serre. And she intended to set her campaign in motion tonight. "Why don't you take a short rest now, darling," she suggested, "so you'll be refreshed for the evening? We don't want any dark circles under your eyes."

"Please, Auntie, I'm not a prize heifer being readied for market," Flora protested. "I don't have to be toddled off for a rest so I'll be in prime form for the buyers."

"Forgive me, dear," Sarah apologized with a cheerful smile. "Force of habit, after all these years. Both Bella and Becky were prone to show their fatigue under their eyes. You look magnificent. Perhaps you'd like to read instead until we have to dress for dinner. But if you'll excuse me, I've some letters that need a reply." She grimaced. "It's an unending duty, but if I want to receive mail, I must answer mine," she went on with a benign smile. "We're promised to Charlotte's for dinner at eight. A simple gown will do, for it's essentially a family party."

"I'm not sure I want to go," Flora caviled. "The idea of being pleasant all evening seems a drudgery, and Adam probably won't arrive until very late. He doesn't even leave for the casinos until nine."

"Humor me, darling," her aunt cajoled. "You're not planning on staying in Saratoga long, and I want to show you off to all your mama's old friends. Your mama was the one, you know, who designed your strange education. The night she lay dying on that wretched ship in the Strait of Malacca she insisted I write down her wishes, and she wouldn't shut her eyes until each item of study was documented. Your papa and I both signed the note; she wanted our word, you see, and then, when she was content we understood her proposals, she had you brought in. Reaching for your small hand, she whispered she loved you, and only then did she close her eyes. She fell into a coma within minutes—only sheer force of will had kept her conscious until then. But Susannah was the most determined woman I ever knew, and she'd be pleased you turned out so much like her."

"I remember thinking she was only sleeping," Flora softly said. "She looked so peaceful with her eyes shut and her hair brushed out on the pillow."

"Your papa had just bathed her and washed her hair and put her locket with your and your papa's picture around her neck. She wanted to look her best, she'd teased, even on her deathbed. Susannah was very beautiful—like you," Sarah softly added. "It broke your papa's heart to lose her. She would have followed him to the ends of the earth."

"Papa didn't tell me she was dead . . . for several days. I thought she was too sick to see me."

"Your father couldn't accept her death himself. She'd been such a vibrant woman. Even at the very last Susannah insisted on ordering the world to her wishes as if she could hold back the specter of death until her plans were complete."

"She probably wouldn't approve of my sighing regrets."

"*She* always said she didn't have time for regrets."

"And I'm childishly feeling sorry for myself when I'm so fortunate in countless ways. Forgive me, Sarah, for my deplorable complaining. I shall be pleased to go to dinner at Charlotte's. I'll be ready at eight."

"Capital, my dear," her aunt said, gratified her plans were *entrain*. "Everyone will be pleased to visit with you. Now I'm off to my miserable letter writing."

"You'll appreciate this, Susannah," Sarah Gibbon murmured, smiling heavenward as she sat at her desk a short time later, penning Charlotte Brewster a note. "Didn't

you always say faint hearts never win anything? Help me
with the wording, now," she said half-aloud, prone to ask
her sister for advice in times of need.

She mentioned first in her hasty missive to her friend
Charlotte that Adam Serre would be joining the party at
her invitation, sometime during the evening. She wasn't
sure he'd come for dinner. Then she proceeded to request
a certain seating arrangement at the dinner table, specifically for her niece and young Lord Randall, who was at
Saratoga visiting his aunt Charlotte. The consensus was
that he was vastly handsome, charming as his rakehell father had been in his youth, and in the market for a rich
wife. Seeing Flora at the dinner table with Charlotte's
handsome nephew should force Adam Serre's hand, at
least marginally, she smugly thought, sealing her missive
with a dab of wax.

Minutes later one of her footmen was speeding toward
Charlotte's house, a short block away. And now, Sarah
reflected, what gown would be suitable for her niece tonight? She wanted to present a certain image, and Flora
had explained to her last night on the way home that a
dressmaker wouldn't be required since she'd decided
against her plan of seduction and would be returning to
Montana in a few days. Yes, she was very sure, Flora had
declared when her aunt had mildly questioned her motives.

How sweetly naive, Sarah had thought at the time: to
give up one's love for principle.

Since Adam Serre probably wasn't so high-minded, she
reflected with the cynicism of experience, she wished to
add a certain fillip to Flora's allure tonight. A simple purity would be effective, lending an unapproachable quality
to her beauty. Perhaps a gown of white linen or a summer
gown of pale muslin. No diamonds. She wanted to avoid
any appearance of sophistication. Pearls would be perfect,
especially in this heat. With some pastel ribbons in Flora's
hair. Sarah smiled as she sat at her boudoir window overlooking the elm-lined street. She hadn't had so much fun

since she'd married off her two daughters to the most eligible bachelors on the East Coast.

If she went to help Flora dress at six-thirty, she mused, that should be time enough to implement the perfect image. Now, if the darling girl would only cooperate. She had her mother's strong will, but she also had her flirtatious bent. The question was, How much of the truth would bear revelation?

As it turned out, Flora was receptive to a simple gown with no more explanation required other than the stifling heat. "Of course, Auntie," she agreed. "White linen would be perfect. And only one petticoat, if you don't think me too daring. I refuse to sweat beneath an armor of irrelevant froth. It's much too hot to be concerned with useless propriety."

"What a sensible girl," her aunt exclaimed, signaling the maid to take away the white linen for a final pressing. "And just small pearl earrings, don't you think?"

"Or no earrings. I'd like to dispense with silk stockings too in this heat, but I suppose it would be considered too shocking," Flora lamented.

"No earrings. How clever. You'll look ever so much cooler," Sarah appreciatively noted. "And I'd like to say yes to bare legs too, dear, but it would be altogether too risqué. How silly all the rules of etiquette when the temperature is ninety, but unfortunately there are minimum standards." She had other reasons beyond those of etiquette, however, that discouraged the notion of stockingless legs. Her plan was to tantalize Adam until he clearly understood the extent of his affection for Flora. A temptation, as it were—just out of reach.

But she rather thought Flora's nude legs might be *too* much of a temptation. Lust had a tendency to overrun an analytical approach to desire. And she definitely wanted Adam only to *think* about his need for Flora the next few days.

Chapter Seventeen

That evening at Morrissey's Adam seemed distracted, enough so that two of his companions at the card table asked him if he was sober.

"Unfortunately, yes," he said, his tone so clipped no one mentioned his inattention again.

But when he glanced at his watch shortly after ten, tossed his hand onto the table, and said, "I'm out," in the middle of a heavy round of betting that he'd initiated, everyone registered their surprise in vocal accents of astonishment.

"I'll be back later," he simply said, pushing his chair back and rising.

"When later?" Caldwell drawled in his normal tone, which was just below a bellow. "Should we save your chair?"

Adam hesitated minutely. "No, I'll find a spot when I come back." And on that nonexplanation he strode from the private room on the second floor of Morrissey's club.

"It's that redhead from Montana," Caldwell grunted, turning over Adam's cards and spreading them out so the straight flush was revealed in undisguised splendor. "She must be damned hot, to walk away from this hand."

"She's from London," someone said.

"Yorkshire," another man corrected, "via several jaunts

around the world. Her father is that earl who dug up a collection of ancient bronzes during one of those uprisings in China. It made the *London Times*'s front page. Donated the passel to the British Museum."

"She there too?" Caldwell asked with some curiosity.

"That's what the paper said. Shot a couple of the bandits herself."

"Damn! I hope she don't blow a hole in Adam's head. He didn't seem in a mood tonight to take no for an answer," Caldwell said in so quiet a voice, heads swiveled to observe the phenomenon of Caldwell King muted.

His card-playing compatriots would have been even more surprised had they viewed Adam in the environment of a family party for a very young lady he didn't in the least know. Dinner was almost over when he arrived, but he was seated for dessert, where he proceeded to ignore the lady on his right, to whom etiquette required he speak. Except for making the most bland replies to her conversational forays, he focused his heated attention instead on Flora Bonham and her dinner companion, Lord Robert Randall.

The Comte de Chastellux was noticeably restless when the covers were removed, the ladies left, and the port began its passage around the table. He conversed pleasantly enough with the men, taking compliments on his horses and their winning style, but he drank considerably more than his share, a fact noted by his host, who had orders from his wife to see that the men appeared in the drawing room in no more than an hour—specifically the Comte de Chastellux, and still walking under his own power, Mr. Brewster understood. He didn't know Charlotte's plans or care to know them. She'd simply made it clear he must not dally over the port and cigars if he wished his household to be run with his comfort in mind.

Such stern warning kept Ezekiel Brewster's eye sharply on the clock and on the count's liquor consumption, for he'd suffered his wife's wrath only once before and learned from the experience.

At ten minutes short of the hour, the men returned to the drawing room.

"How opportune," Charlotte exclaimed with a beaming smile as the men entered the beautiful Adams drawing room that had survived unscathed the ruinous redecorating blighting so many Federal homes. "You're just in time for charades."

Adam inwardly groaned. This evening was going to test the limits of his good manners. It wasn't even possible to get near Flora, for she was hemmed in by females—one on either side of her on the sofa, others in nearby chairs.

He took a seat near the door and endured a round of inept pantomime along with a cup of very weak tea. After the second charade had stumblingly continued through numerous clues for almost twenty minutes, he brusquely said, "Hold, or cut bow strings, *A Midsummer Night's Dream*, act one," simply to end his misery.

His tone of voice must have signaled his hostess, for Charlotte suggested a change of pace—a short recital of her granddaughter's piano repertoire. As the guests moved to the embrasure holding the piano, Adam maneuvered through the throng, forcibly took Flora by the arm, and propelled her to a distant corner of the drawing room, where he said a shade bluntly, "Please sit."

Dropping down beside her on the settee, he murmured, "This is torture."

"Too much excitement?" Flora sweetly queried.

He grimaced. "I have future recitals to look forward to, no doubt, once Lucie becomes more proficient on the piano."

"Perhaps you could help select the music. And Lucie's performance will be more animated than Charlotte's granddaughter, I suspect. Isn't the young girl bland?"

"Which one is she?"

"The one at the piano, darling. Pay attention."

"I'm still numb from forty minutes of appalling charades. And," he added with a grin, "I prefer watching you. You look very cool tonight—without your petticoats."

"Leave it to you to notice."

"Every man here tonight noticed, *bia.*" He slipped into a more comfortable sprawl and crossed his legs at the ankle. "Particularly when you left the dining room. Your new beau, Lord Randall, couldn't take his eyes from you." Adam was relaxed and smiling again now that he had Flora to himself. "Will I have to call him out?"

"And disgrace me?" she replied, flirtatious, smiling. "You're a married man."

"I'm also a jealous man." His glance strayed to the lord in question and narrowed slightly. "He needs to be warned off," he grumbled.

"I hope you're not serious, but if you are, Adam, no. I'll be leaving in a few days, anyway," she added.

"Rumor has it he's looking for a rich wife since his father gambled away the family resources."

"Now, if only I was in the market for a simple nobleman with nothing to recommend him but his looks and smile," Flora sardonically replied. "I'm afraid I'd grow bored in short order, though. He spoke of himself almost exclusively. I know his tailor and his clubs, his prowess at the hunt and at cricket, and had I not stopped him, I would have had a recital of the aristocratic ladies he's bedded."

Adam grinned. "You're not enamored, then, with his golden good looks. I'm relieved."

"I find myself enamored instead with a half-blood married to another woman," she quietly said.

His smile disappeared, and she thought for a moment she'd lost him with her candor.

He glanced around the room as if finding himself in an alien sphere and then, turning back to her, murmured, "I find myself wondering how much you mean to me that I'm at a stranger's house in hopes only of speaking with you." His eyes were grave, his voice low, constrained. "I don't know what to do."

"Nor I," Flora whispered.

"I can't even ask you to leave here without scandal."

"Nor could I if you did. These are my mother and aunt's friends."

He smiled faintly, as if he found some humor in his suffering. "I've had tea twice in two days. A record in my reprobate life. Is this love?"

"It is for me."

His eyes seemed suddenly to impale her with their sharp gaze. "When did you know?" His voice was hushed.

"Yesterday, today . . . I'm not sure, Adam . . . maybe only this instant. I don't want this any more than you do," she fervently murmured. "I'm trying to deny it. Really I am."

"Why?" The softest of sounds.

"Why? Good God, Adam," she whispered. "For all the obvious reasons. Because you're married already. Because I'm selfish. Because I won't share you. Because you don't know what love is," she finished almost in a fury.

The other guests were beginning to cast surreptitious glances their way, the intensity of Flora's vehement response vibrating across the room—in resonance if not clarity.

Adam outstared the curious gazes until each flustered guest succumbed to his icy regard and reluctantly returned their attention to the pianist.

"Maybe I do know what love is," he quietly said, turning back to her, his eyes restive and moody. "Maybe it's sacrificing a straight flush to arrive here before dinner's over," he slowly said. "Maybe it's thinking you look like an angel tonight in that plain gown with ribbons in your hair," he added, sudden tenderness in his voice. "Or maybe it's telling myself I can't touch you when that's all I want to do every minute of the day," he tensely added. "Maybe it's an unwelcome celibacy and cold baths that don't do a *damned* bit of good. Maybe it's not *fucking* you," he heatedly finished.

Tears came to her eyes for his struggles and his indomitable strength, for his ardent desire and terse resentment. For his appearance here tonight.

"Lord, Flora, don't cry," he pleaded, sitting up, instantly contrite. He quickly searched for some means of escape for them, but the only exit was past the entire roomful of guests. "Tell me what you want me to do," he murmured, taking her hands in his, "and I'll do it."

"I don't know," she whispered, happy, sad, skittish with indecision.

"I'll come to see you in the morning," he abruptly declared. "We'll go somewhere and talk. There are too many people here, the music is incredibly bad, and I'm ready to put my fist through the wall."

Her smile reassured him. He was uncomfortable with tears. "And you have to spend your winnings at Tiffany's," he added, comfortable, at least, with pleasing women. "I'll feed you breakfast at Crum's first. He'll open early for me. His trout and fried potatoes are the best in the world."

Flora's smile widened. "Is the serious discussion over?"

He grimaced. "I sure as hell hope so. I don't like to see you cry. Am I excused now?" he asked like a young boy chafing to play outdoors.

"If you can make your way out," Flora answered, glancing dubiously at the audience around the piano. "The gauntlet looks daunting."

Adam grinned. "Watch me. I'm very good at this." Releasing her hands, he patted them lightly. "Now, go to sleep early, *bia*, and I'll pick you up at eight." Rising, he winked at her and strolled away. Stopping at his hostess's chair, he leaned over and spoke quietly to Charlotte. She instantly smiled, nodded, smiled once more, and when Adam bowed over her hand and kissed her fingertips in farewell, she was visibly beaming.

All eyes avidly followed the Comte de Chastellux as he exited the room. And as soon as he was gone from sight, a buzz of conversation rose in competition with the faltering rendition of a Bach étude. Glances were cast in Flora's direction, some curious, some envious, others of a minute scrutiny as if to say, "Tell me all the details. . . ."

She blushed under the contemplation, or was it only the rosy glow of happiness? Adam hadn't said he loved her, but he clearly wished to please her. "Celibate" . . . he'd said the word in moody, sulky ill humor, but he'd said it.

The sound strummed through her mind. He was celibate for her. It was an Adam Serre declaration of love.

Sarah quizzed her niece on the short walk home that evening, but Flora only said she was pleased Adam had come.

"It looked as though you had some angry words," Sarah persisted.

"Not exactly," Flora ambivalently replied, too much in tumult to disclose her feelings, or the possibility of truly loving Adam. "He said I looked like an angel in this dress."

Sarah's smile was hidden by the shadowed night. A victorious first skirmish in her campaign, she complacently thought. "What did you think of Bobby Randall?" she asked to gauge the efficacy of her plan. "He seems a handsome, charming blade."

"He's the most dreadful bore. Adam's taking me for breakfast in the morning."

"How nice," her aunt replied as if the two sentences were a single happy thought. "The mornings are so wonderfully cool for an outing." Definitely an evening of successes on several fronts, she cheerfully reflected. "How fortunate, then, that we're getting home early so you can get your beauty sleep," she tranquilly added.

Adam, on the other hand, was missing his sleep, having returned to Morrissey's to sit in on the poker game again. He was in an expansive mood regardless of the monumental problems in his personal life. Flora had said she loved him. It was enough; it was everything. He played more recklessly than usual and still won.

"Damn you, Adam, how the hell can you keep getting those hands? It's been a dozen in a row now," Caldwell grumbled. "No wonder you're smiling, although you were in a helluva good mood when you came back in here too. Was the lady friendly?"

"Friendly enough," Adam cheerfully said. "We talked."

"Right, and I'm a Sunday-school teacher."

"Don't you ever just talk to ladies, Caldy?" Adam

blandly retorted, gazing at his friend from under his dark lashes.

"Not unless they're damned plain, Serre, and to my recollection that flame-haired beauty you've been wooing so assiduously ain't within shouting distance of plain."

"We listened to a piano recital," Adam related with a faint smile.

The declaration gained everyone's attention.

"You serious?" one of his friends said, his eyebrows rising to his hairline.

"You'd all do well to cultivate a little culture," Adam cheerfully remarked, the cigar smoke thick enough to cut, the table littered with liquor glasses. "You needn't spend all your time at Morrissey's."

"Don't," one player laconically noted. "There's the track too."

"Suppose you're going to be winnin' there, too, Serre," Caldwell muttered, tossing his chips onto the large pile in the center of the table. "I'll raise."

"My horses are resting tomorrow," Adam pleasantly said. "And so am I." He met the bet and raised it another five hundred.

And so the play continued as it did every night in the private room on the second floor while the liquor bottles emptied and stakes rose. Until shortly after one, when the door abruptly burst open, and a disheveled, very drunken gentleman swayed on the threshold. Bracing his hands on the doorjambs to steady himself, he cast an unfocused gaze on the men at the poker table. "Where's . . . that bastard redskin?" he demanded, lurching forward a step as he lost his balance.

"Any *particular* bastard redskin?" Adam politely inquired, his eyes on Ned Storham's young brother.

"Aha!" the inebriated man exclaimed like an actor in a bad melodrama, his fingers clenched white against the door frame to hold himself upright. "I foun' you."

"Unfortunately," Adam calmly said. "You should go and sleep it off, Frank."

"Don' wanna sleep. Wanna kill you."

Adam sighed, glanced at his cards, and shoved some markers into the pile. "Maybe some other time, Frank. I'm in the middle of a game."

"Gonna shoot you," the drunken man emphatically declared, fumbling with his coat pocket.

Calmly setting his cards down, Adam rose to his feet.

"Want my derringer?" Caldwell quietly inquired, his gaze on the intruder in the doorway.

Adam took the gun, pushed his chair back, and, walking around the table, strolled toward the teetering man still attempting to extract something from his pocket.

"This isn't wise, Frank. You're too drunk," Adam said as he soundlessly moved across the plush carpet.

"Wise my ass," Frank muttered, a smile appearing on his face as his fingers finally closed on the revolver in his pocket. "Damned if you're gonna take our grazing land." Pulling the weapon free with a convulsive jerk, he pointed it directly at Adam.

"Your brother is going to be really angry if you get yourself killed, Frank," Adam murmured, his gaze shifting between the wavering gun barrel and his assailant's resentful face. "Let's put the gun away. Someone might get hurt."

Frank laughed. "Hurt? You're gonna get *killed*, Injun. Start singin' your death song."

As Frank took a tottering step forward, Adam's hand closed with blurring speed on the shaking gun barrel and wrenched it from the drunken man's grasp in a smooth twist of his wrist. He tossed it to Caldwell, then took the befuddled man by the shoulders and turned him around. "Now, why don't you go back to your hotel room, Frank?" Adam gently said. "Your head's going to hurt like hell tomorrow." Shoving him out into the hall, Adam called for one of Morrissey's men.

A burly ex-fighter came on the run.

"He's had too much to drink, Finn. Will you see that he reaches his hotel?" Adam handed five gold pieces to the bouncer.

"Yes, sir, Mr. Serre. Right away."

The disruption put a mild pall on Adam's good mood. Frank Storham in Saratoga was a loose cannon he'd rather not deal with. Frank drank too much and, unlike his older brother, who had made his fortune in the cattle business because he worked hard, didn't mind taking what wasn't his and paying for hired guns to fight his battles. Frank had inherited the Storham temper and none of the brains.

"You all right, Adam?" Caldwell inquired when Adam returned. "I had him covered in case the fool could function well enough to pull the trigger."

"Thanks. I'm fine," Adam replied, sitting down and picking up his cards.

"One of your enemies from Montana?" one of the players asked.

"His brother has his eye on my land."

"Got enough men to defend it?" Caldwell inquired, familiar with range wars in his native Texas.

"So far. Lord, I'm getting tired. This is my last hand."

"Good. Then the rest of us will get a chance to win," Caldwell said with a broad smile.

But Adam didn't go back to his hotel room when he left Morrissey's. He found himself walking toward Franklin Square, and a few minutes later he was standing before the neoclassic facade of Sarah Gibbon's house, his gaze on the lighted second-floor window.

Chapter Eighteen

❧

The knock on her bedroom door was a firm double rap, and Flora's hand froze in arrested motion over her head, the hairbrush in her hand suspended in space, her face in the gilt-framed mirror before her registering shock.

He wouldn't dare, she incredulously thought, even as the solid reality of the sound echoed in her mind, the knock so like him—not diffident, but strong, sure. Glancing at the small jeweled clock on the dressing table in front of her, she checked the time. One-thirty. Could she have been imagining noises in the night? she nervously equivocated. Perhaps a servant had been checking the gaslights in the hall and accidentally banged against the door.

But even as she attempted to discount the truth, she watched the door behind her open in mirror image and saw a tall familiar figure in evening dress enter her bedroom. Shutting the door in a whisper of sound, Adam smiled at her.

The hairbrush fell from her hand and she froze where she sat, every sound in the large house magnified a thousand times in her ears. Sarah would hear. The servants would know. Everyone was listening to Adam's footfall crossing her floor.

Coming up behind her, he touched her hair first, sliding his hand down its shimmering red-gold length as if marking her as his possession, vetting her and branding her in one simple gesture. Then his fingers slipped forward, glided up her throat, gently gripped her chin, and lifting her face slightly upward and toward him, he bent his dark head low.

"I couldn't wait," he murmured against her soft mouth. "I don't know how to be friends. . . ."

"You're drunk." Her voice was hushed, the taste of brandy fragrant on her lips.

"I don't think so," he whispered, slipping his hands under her arms and raising her from the small satin-covered bench. "I wish I were," he murmured, turning her, pulling her hard against his body, his hands on her lower back warm through the cotton eyelet of her nightgown.

"So you'd have some excuse for coming here." Her palms lay on his satin lapels, the familiar feel of him initiating a rush of pleasure, her senses immune to the danger of his presence.

"Yes."

"But you don't."

"I haven't thought of one."

She could feel the strong beat of his heart under her hand. "Perhaps you love me."

He grimaced and the silence was profound.

She smiled at his resistance in the context of such obvious necessity. "We *could* just be friends."

His brows drew together in a scowl.

"But you came here for something else, didn't you?"

Another silence while she surveyed the dark beauty of his face as if searching for her answer in the subtle play of light and shadow.

"I came here because I can't live without you," he said at last.

"I know," Flora softly replied, her fingers stroking the fine silk of his lapels, the feel of him beneath, hard, strong. "I've missed you."

Adam glanced at the clock on the dressing table.

Like a drenching in ice water Flora was reminded of the style of his liaisons. Short, sweet, numerous. "Do you have another engagement?" Resentful, instantly jealous, she tried to pull away.

"You haven't lost your hot-blooded temper," he teased, his arms unyielding.

"Don't patronize me," she snapped, locked hard in his embrace despite her resistance, hotspur anger in her eyes. "Am I keeping you from something, dammit?"

"I have to be back when Lucie wakes up."

"Oh, Lord," she whispered, a mortified, flaming blush coloring her cheeks. "How humiliating."

"No more than my coming here," he quietly said. "When I shouldn't."

Unguarded desire trembled through her senses, the heat of his body burned into her palms. "How long can you stay?" she murmured, beyond shame, helpless against her need.

"Three hours, probably four. It's up to you"—he smiled—"and the servants' attuned hearing."

"I should send you away," she whispered.

"But you won't."

"No," she softly said.

"Good," he murmured, his gaze bare of well-mannered civility, flame hot. "Because I wouldn't go."

Reaching for the blue ribbon threaded through the scooped neckline of her summer nightgown, he gently pulled on the bow.

She didn't move in the quiet of the bedroom, aware of the tremulous beating of her heart, aware of the delicate touch of his fingers as he untied the silk ribbon and then loosened the gathered fabric. He slowly slid the fine eyelet over her shoulders, the brushing warmth of his hands flaring through her body, the intoxicating pleasure feverish, familiar, and she thought: How long has it been?

Weeks.

Hours were too long to deny such soul-stirring rapture, and it had been weeks since he'd touched her.

Now that he was standing before her, tall, powerful, aroused, she wondered how she'd ever been able to rationalize away her longing.

His palms glided over the verge of her shoulders, shoving the light material aside, slipped down her arms, midway to her elbows. And the pale gown slithered to the floor.

He looked at her without speaking, his hands drifting lower until his fingers touched hers and delicately slid through them. Lifting her hands to his lips, he gently kissed her knuckles.

"You're trembling," he murmured, his gaze intent beneath the shield of his lashes.

"It must be the cold," Flora whispered, her smile discounting her words and the sultry summer heat.

"Do you need someone to warm you?"

"I thought that's why you came."

It stopped him for a moment, the candid truth beneath the casualness of her reply, the utter lack of coyness.

"I saw your light," he said.

"From Morrissey's?"

He grinned. "Is this a quiz?"

"No," she said, glancing at the bed before her gaze returned to his. "Why don't you latch the door?"

How did she always manage to disconcert and arouse in equal measure? he thought as he moved away. And when he turned back from locking the door and saw her waiting for him, lounging against the lacy pillows like a practiced courtesan, he questioned his sophistication. A grudging displeasure pervaded his mind.

Dropping into a chair near the bed instead of joining her, he restlessly slid into a sprawl, not certain why he was there, suddenly not certain what he was going to do. She looked very beautiful, playful and inviting, like a Boucher nymph—all pink, blooming flesh. But less cherubic, he noted, more voluptuous and womanly.

"I came to Saratoga to seduce you," Flora gently said, surveying Adam's moody sprawl. "Will I have to, after all?" she softly inquired.

"No."

"You have that sullen look of a man doing something against his will."

"And you know all about men."

"Are you jealous? Tell me, because I am."

His gaze went oblique for a moment before it met hers again. "Yes," he said. "And I can't escape it if I ride ten thousand days and nights. I want you in my hands. I want you to be kissed only by me. I'm haunted by the pleasure I take in possessing you."

"The pleasure isn't exclusively yours," Flora gently reminded him, "nor the inescapable need to possess. And don't look at me like that. I don't say this to other men."

"I'm sorry," he gruffly muttered. "The violence of my feelings threaten any sense of detachment."

"Your customary sense of detachment, you mean."

His gaze came up, volatile, fitful, and he looked at her from under lashes longer than anyone's. "I see you everywhere—in my dreams, in shop windows, in the mirror in place of my own image. I'm not sure—"

"You want to be in love?"

"I'm not sure I want the calamitous changes in my life."

He looked spectacularly beautiful, all dark eyes and hair and sullen restiveness, his powerful body elegant in black tails, diamond studs twinkling down his starched shirt front, his hard, flat belly sleek beneath a white satin waistcoat, a large sapphire ring on his right hand catching the light.

"I don't have your misgivings," Flora said, sliding her legs over the side of the bed, pushing herself upright. "Love doesn't frighten me."

A swift surprise showed in his eyes, and he watched her with a guarded wariness as her feet touched the floor and she moved the small distance from the bed to his chair.

"The fetters alarm you, don't they?" she murmured, gracefully kneeling at his feet. "You don't want to be undone by love."

"I don't know what I want," he quietly said, aware the rhythm of his breathing had changed when she knelt before him.

Placing her hands on his knees, she parted his legs so she could move between them. "There's always one certainty, at least," she softly said, feeling the warmth of his thighs on the underside of her arms, knowing he could have stopped her at any time. "In this friendship of ours." Her fingers slid under the placket on his perfectly fitted trousers, closing on the top button. "We agree on that, I think," she whispered, her eyes on his as she slipped the first button free.

She undid his trousers with the compliant deference of a well-trained houri while Adam gripped the chair arms to restrain his violent impulses.

Her hair smelled of perfume, the scent sweet and heavy, the pale satin of her shoulders and the mounded fullness of her breasts only inches away, tempting, tantalizing as Persian love poems, his for the taking.

Was he willing to contemplate the enigma of love? He thought for the first time in his life. And if he did, what was the price of his freedom?

But tumultuous feeling overwhelmed any further insightful musing, for Flora's hands glided over his arousal as she tugged his shirt up, and he suddenly lost interest in speculative theory. Her small hands were warm on his stomach, brushing his clothing aside, languidly spreading the fine wool of his trousers over his hips to expose his erection.

A small cry escaped her, a swallowed, abrupt sound, the shape under her hand recognizable. "You're carrying a gun," she softly challenged.

Adam drew the weapon from his pocket. "For the servants," he pleasantly said, placing it under the chair.

"The truth," she firmly demanded.

"Caldwell gave me his derringer at Morrissey's," he replied, his voice devoid of inflection.

"Why would he do that?" Her hands rested on his thighs, her gaze held a critical scrutiny.

He shrugged. "He's the cautious type."

"Why?"

"No reason, darling." He smiled, brushing a light fingertip over her quirked brows. "You look delectable in your pearl earrings," he said, flicking the pendant pearl dangling from her earlobe. "And nothing else," he added in a hushed murmur. Shifting on his spine, he leaned foward, and taking her face between his hands, he kissed her, a long, slow, delicious kiss that made her forget the violence that was so much a part of Adam Serre's life. And when he released her mouth and lounged back again, he'd forgotten Frank Storham's disruptive presence.

He waited then as she knelt between his legs, familiar with that look in a woman's eyes—her gaze heavy with passion. And when her head lowered over him, he shut his eyes.

Her mouth was warm, soft, engulfing, her hands on his erection skilled. The scent of rose and jasmine drifted into his nostrils, Saratoga vanished, the bedroom disappeared, his world narrowed to a gliding mouth and exquisite, intense sensation.

His size intoxicated her, his readiness tantalized, like a personal invitation to sensual delight. She felt the heat between her legs, whetted desire restless in her blood. And a sense of power touched her too, offered its own degree of pleasure. She could hear his harsh breathing and the catch in the rhythm when she held him deep against the back of her throat. She could feel him lift his hips when she paused a lengthy moment at the apex of her ascent, and his deep groan of satisfaction as her mouth descended again evoked a small internal smile.

His hands slipped through her hair, cradling her head, grasping incredible pleasure in his hands. And she held him in thrall.

Until suddenly he lifted her head.

"I'm not finished," she murmured, looking up at him through tousled curls.

"You're finished," he gently said, rising in a flawless fusion of muscle, sinew, and bone, pulling her upright, no longer uncertain about motive or purpose, sure of what he wanted.

Carrying her to the bed, he settled her down and, swiftly moving over her, lowered himself between her legs. He entered her with dizzying speed, driving in with exactitude and force, pressing to the depth of her womb so she moaned in ecstasy, overpowering rapture so acute she held her breath to sustain the trembling splendor.

Then Adam Serre proceeded to do what he did so well, clothed or unclothed, disquieted or resolved, regardless of setting or circumstance. Like an acquired skill with a lariat or the consummate artistry of a well-trained pianist, he knew how to make love. He knew how to move: how fast; how deep; how slow; how hard. He knew how to kiss a woman's mouth and the tender warmth behind her ear; how to suckle her nipples and draw his tongue lightly over the curve of her breast or the pouty fullness of her lips. He knew when to lift her hips to meet his plunging invasion, when to be gentle and when not to be. He understood the delicate balance between violence and pleasure, between harshness and tenderness. He was accomplished at bringing a woman to climax simply by caressing her or talking to her. He was very good.

But he did it a lot, Flora thought, as peaking ecstasy climbed through her body.

It was one of his professions. And if she hadn't been quivering just short of release with her own selfish pleasure, she might have resented his proficiency.

Their climax when it came was like running downhill, breathless, bursting, wild. But immediately afterward, as if cooled by a sudden cloudburst of remembrance, Adam rolled away. Lying on his back, eyes closed, he struggled with his compelling need for Flora, with the obstacles and consequences.

Sparks were still detonating in small flashes along Flora's nerve endings, the heat of her body diminishing slowly from blue flame to red to flickering gold. And she didn't recognize germane elements of reality, only her own pulsing enchantment.

When she finally turned to look at Adam, he was sprawled beside her, his arms thrown over his head, his breathing still fast and hard. Undressed like a man in a brothel, she thought, with only the minimum clothing undone.

"Do you want to leave?" she asked, sensitive to the cool silence of his pose.

He didn't answer, and she wondered if she really wanted to know. Rolling on her side, she noticed how close his eyelashes were, black silk, long like a baby's but thicker. What would he do if she touched them? she incongruously mused, when she should have been considering his deadly preoccupation.

Then his eyes opened, the pupils large in the semidarkness, shadowed by his heavy brows, and his smile appeared, sudden and warm. "Maybe I'll leave in a thousand years," he said.

"In that case," Flora murmured, cognizant of the difficulties in his life, her own smile ripe with delicate accord, "you're overdressed."

She divested him of his clothing while he obligingly helped, kicking off his shoes, raising his hips to slide his trousers off, shrugging out of his coat while she tugged at the sleeves. But when she straddled his hips to unbutton his waistcoat, his concentration suddenly lapsed, her hot bottom instant enticement.

"I'm glad you decided to walk to Franklin Square tonight," she fondly said, slipping a fabric-covered button through a buttonhole.

"I didn't have a choice, *bia,*" he murmured with a lazily quirked brow.

"Because this brought you here." She touched his arousal, sliding her finger up the swollen shaft, circling the ridged pulsing crest.

He smiled. "It's stubbornly enamored."

"Of me?" She pulled his shirt loose from the diamond studs in a sweeping tug of her wrist.

His grin offered instant delight. "As you see." He lay beneath her, half-undressed, his shirt and waistcoat open, the white fabrics stark contrast to his bronzed skin, to the muscled power of his tall frame. "Are you ready?" His voice was a low whisper, the question rhetorical; she was soaking wet between her legs, her own honeyed fluids mingling with his ejaculation. And when he touched her breasts, she pushed herself against his hands and breathed deeply, her eyes closed, her face lifted upward with a groan.

He fondled the ripeness of her breasts, cupped them, softly massaged the nipples. Gently swaying as he caressed her, she glided back and forth over his erection in languid incitement, the rush of her breathing the only sound in the silent room.

"Lift up," he murmured, sliding his hands over to her upper arms and raising her. "Would you like me to come in you again?" he whispered, his fingers stroking her swollen labia. "Would you like that?"

"Yes," Flora sighed, luxurious feeling ravishing her senses, an insatiable hunger for him transcending all else. "Fill me to overflowing. . . ."

"I'll see what I can do," he lazily murmured, adjusting her on his hips, guiding himself into place, slowly penetrating her throbbing tissue, encouraging her hips with his hands once he was inside her, easing himself in by slow degrees until she'd absorbed him completely.

Then, bracing his feet, he pushed deeper, surging upward so forcefully, she screamed, the sound ringing through the silent house—hot, insatiable, unmistakable.

She instantly tensed under his hands, even while the savage heat of passion bombarded her mind, clashed with any faint-hearted apprehension, outstripped caution.

Swiftly cupping her head, Adam pulled her facedown and kissed her. "No one heard," he murmured against her mouth, covering her ears with his hands. "No one." He had no intention of stopping or relinquishing this night of carnal passion—not, at least, this side of death. He softly kissed her, soothing, pacifying kisses, his hands lightly covering her ears, blocking out the world, the rhythm of his lower body persistent, bewitching, unsated.

He didn't care if the door came crashing down. He didn't care if all of Franklin Square poured into the room. He was on fire, Flora was shaking, flowing with desire, both their bodies slick with perspiration, gratification shudderingly close.

Surging upward again, he felt flame scorching his brain.

She could feel her womb opening up, wanting him to come in and fill her, fulfill her, replenish, ravish her. She clung to him, felt him swelling, swelling inside her.

The frantic rush of their breathing accelerated, flooding the shadowed room with the audible cadence of lust, and then their two fused bodies stopped.

A second hung suspended in the filmy heat.

Until their orgasms exploded, unspeakable pleasure melted through their senses, hot, rippling, fierce. With a small, inarticulate cry, Flora slumped across Adam's shoulder, her hair streaming over his face, filling his nose, his mouth, covering his eyes.

He smiled with her hair in his mouth.

It tasted faintly of rose, like her.

After they'd rested, after they'd kissed like adolescents, closemouthed, tenderly; after they'd murmured giddy love words to each other that made them giggle. After they'd smiled into each other's eyes with the innocence of new-found happiness, they made love in the simplest of ways. With his body balanced between her parted thighs, he joined in her silky wet heat, moving in harmony, his palms warm on her smooth shoulders, her hands pressed lightly at the base of his spine.

They explored and discovered, swimming and sliding, their kisses soft, warm, his sex harder and harder, plunging, withdrawing, thrusting, and rising until she couldn't wait anymore, and sensing it, he moved in so deeply, rivulets of ecstasy seared her brain, dissolved into his as he followed her in orgasmic release.

Enfolded in the tremulous overflow of rapture, Flora reached up and touched Adam's cheek afterward, wordless, her eyes still filled with wonder. He was perfection. Dangerous as an addiction, an undiluted drug of pleasure, framed above her by a lemon-colored light that limned his wide shoulders and sleek head. As she basked in the exaltation of his allure and the charitable afterglow of lovemaking, his shadowed form suddenly slipped away, moving off the bed with a supple agility.

"Where are you going?" Her voice sounded distant to her ears, a three-o'clock-in-the-morning voice, someone else's voice.

"Not *too* far without any clothes," he said over his shoulder, the smile in his voice caressing her across the room. Moving with a horseman's loose gait, he walked to her dressing table and, bending over, picked up the hairbrush she'd dropped on the floor. Returning to the bed, he kissed her gently, climbed back in, and lifted her docile body—the lethargy of climax still blanketing her senses—arranging her in a seated position between his legs. Kissing the curve of her shoulder, he murmured Absarokee love words into the soft curls behind her ears, his voice deep, hushed. And began brushing her hair.

Aware of the momentous implications, Flora was enchanted by his devoted gallantry. But she found herself wondering with a modicum of skepticism, as he smoothly wielded the brush with a flowing deftness, whether he'd often indulged in such love play. Although a heartbeat later she debated whether she really wanted to know.

Her natural curiosity overcame more sensible caution, however, or perhaps she was feeling immeasurably secure, with his prevailing spirit tonight so charmingly affectionate. "Have you ever done this before?" She'd half twisted around so she could see his face when he answered. "You don't have to answer." But then her voice changed midsentence to a more impassioned tone. "I want to know."

He smiled at the discernible change. "How serious I am? How enamored?"

"You could say 'love,'" she gently chided with a delicate, tantalizing smile. "I was just wondering if I should die of love right here, right now, or scratch your eyes out instead for your facile charm."

"Don't die of love, darling. I want you too badly."

"Are we betrothed, then?" she playfully teased. "Should I select a wedding gown tomorrow?"

"I've never done this before," he said instead, a lifetime of evasion difficult to disregard.

"Never?"

He shook his head.

"Not with all the scores of women?"

Hundreds, he thought, and smiled no with a small shake of his head. But he gave no further explanation because he had none, no words to explain, no prearranged reason in his brain. He'd acted on impulse, but amazingly he didn't feel dread at the consequences. It surprised him He'd been waiting for the overwhelming terror to strike. A man attuned to the mystical rhythms of his world, he particularly took note of that lapse.

But he only kissed her then, as she lay against his shoulder, and showed her in ways other than words how much he cared. And much later, when he finally had to leave or risk being seen, fully dressed again, Adam turned back to the bed where Flora lay in languid repose and, gazing down at her, said with a small sigh, "We have to talk . . . about . . . this . . . us. I don't want to rely solely on chance meetings and lust."

"You needn't be chivalrous, Adam," Flora murmured, smiling up at him. She was beyond recriminations and demands, her body sated, her senses replete, enchantment pungent, like the scent of roses crushed in one's hand. She knew he cared; she was content. "Come to me when you can."

"I don't like the casual sound of that." His voice was minutely curt.

"I'm sorry, darling. Don't misunderstand. I just mean I'm willing to meet you anywhere, anytime—your rules."

After their long weeks of separation, after their recent incredible hours together, he found he couldn't risk having her sail away for Tikal or Timbuktu or even somewhere innocuous like the Midlands for the upcoming hunt season. More pertinent to a man who'd never viewed a woman with any degree of permanence, he couldn't bear the thought of another man touching her. He softly exhaled, a decision reached sometime in the heated hours of their passion. "I don't want that," he firmly said. "I want more." Then, smiling at his own seriousness, he murmured, "I'm beginning to think this insanity is love, *bia*." Leaning over, he kissed her soft cheek and whispered, "I'll see you at eight."

It was five-thirty when Adam reached his hotel room; enough time to bathe, dress, and visit with Lucie for a short time before he left to take Flora for breakfast.

"Are we going to the track, Papa?" Lucie exclaimed when she came bounding into his bedroom shortly before six and climbed up onto his unused bed. "Should I have Cook find my clothes?"

"We'll go later today, darling. I've a breakfast appointment first." Almost finished dressing after his bath, he slipped some bills into his trouser pocket.

"Don't forget you promised Flora a ride to Tiffany's at nine. And if you go without me, bring me back something," she added with the eternal request of children to their parents.

"What do you want?" He picked up his watch from the bureau top and slipped it into his waistcoat pocket.

"A toy." Her answer never changed.

"Is Cook keeping you entertained?" Loop the chain, snap it shut. He looked at himself in the bureau mirror; sleep might be useful one of these nights, he thought. His eyes were more heavy-lidded than usual.

"She knows hundreds of stories about wild animals 'cuz she was raised in a cabin with her papa who trapped and she didn't have a mommy very often like me, so that's why she knows all the stories. Her papa told them to her."

Lucie's knowledge of the staff's personal lives never ceased to amaze him. He thought Cook had come from St. Paul with Mrs. O'Brien; they seemed of the same age, they both had grandchildren. "You'll have to tell me some of the stories. I like animal stories," he said with a smile, sliding a small gold signet ring his father had given him on the fourth finger of his right hand.

"She had her own pet owl too. Can I have a pet owl? I'll take really good care of it and it can sleep in my room."

"We'll have to think about that, dear. I'm not certain an owl would *like* to sleep in your room."

"Could I have a squirrel for a pet, then? Cook had two squirrels for pets and a baby wolf and a chickadee who sang for its supper every night at the same exact time. Isn't that the most amazing thing you ever heard?" Her voice trilled with excitement.

"We'll definitely have to get a pet when we return to Montana. Maybe Cook can help you train it." He ran his fingers through his damp hair, shoved it behind his ears, and turned to his daughter. "Would you read me a story before I have to leave? I haven't had you read to me in two days. And we'll go on a picnic with Flora later, so you and Cook tell the hotel restaurant what you want in the picnic basket and we'll be back at noon."

"I know noon on the clock, Papa. That's easy. I'll read you the story about the little girl who travels with her baby doll to Paris. I like the pictures." She spoke with the same energy that fueled her mind and spirit and small body.

She sat on his lap in a chair by the window, and he helped turn the pages. She brought a peace to his life, a grounding, a joy. She knew the words practically by heart; he did too after rereading the book so many times. And when Cook came in later to check on Lucie's wishes for breakfast, the plans for the day were arranged.

"We may go back to Montana early," Adam told Cook, who stood politely in the doorway, her starched white apron so crisp it crackled when she walked. "It depends on a number of things. So if you don't mind looking out for Lucie for a few days, I think we'll forgo hiring new nursemaids here."

"Lucie's not a speck of trouble, Mr. Serre. She likes my stories about Pa and the animals, but if you decide to return to Montana early, I can't say I'd be disappointed. I miss my Ben."

"That's her husband, Papa," Lucie said, interpreting her father's blank look.

"Forgive me, Mrs. Richards," Adam apologized. "I haven't slept much. The name didn't register immediately."

"Never mind, Mr. Serre. I reckon you got lots more on your mind than remembering everyone's names. Now, you should be dressed too, Miss Lucie," she added. "Maybe we could take a walk to that toy store down the block after breakfast, if it's all right with your father."

"Yowiee!" Lucie gleefully cried, jumping from her father's lap. "Let's see if they have any fuzzy animal toys. Say yes, Papa," she added, figeting in her excitement, "and don't forget to bring me something back."

"Yes to both," Adam said with a smile. "And thank you, Mrs. Richards."

As Adam waited for his carriage to be brought up to the entrance of the Clarendon, he debated the next step in his relationship with Flora.

His marriage, of course, was a dominant roadblock to any permanence. He could arrange a divorce in Montana, but Isolde would ignore it. The Catholic church didn't recognize divorce, nor did the laws of France.[13] And knowing Isolde, she would continue to consider herself his wife.

He needed an annulment.

Almost reflexively, he drew in a deep breath at the finality of the word. At the commitment it implied in terms of his attachment to Flora. Despite his wretched marriage, he'd always avoided the ultimate dissolution. Out of inertia, perhaps, or a sense of family duty. Or maybe for selfish reasons—since he and Isolde had lived separate lives, he'd been spared any restrictions on his activities, and his status as a married man had protected him from demanding lovers.

Was he truly ready for such a serious measure?

Did he really want to be free of his marriage?

Would he regret the loss of his liberty—for Flora expected faithfulness. Was he capable of such devotion?

Smiling at his driver as his carriage rolled up to the hotel, he stepped into the open carriage and said, "Good morning, Monty. At least one of us is fresh and alert, I see."

"Some of us use a bed for sleepin', boss," the wiry ranch hand said, echoes of the Georgia hill country still in his voice after years in the West.

"The thought's beginning to take on a definite appeal, Monty," Adam replied as he sank into the soft leather upholstery. "Ten Franklin Square this morning."

But a block down Broadway, Adam suddenly said, "Stop."

"Forget somethin'?" Monty asked, easing the horses over to the side of the street.

"I just need a minute to think," Adam murmured.

Should he wire James to begin the annulment proceedings? Adam mused, indecision rife in his mind, his gaze unfocused on Monty's straight back. If he intended to go through with an annulment, James should start the legalities; any negotiations with the Vatican were sure to be protracted. Isolde would be obstructive. A certainty there. As was her mercenary family's greed; they'd sent a phalanx of lawyers to deal with the marriage settlement.

On the other hand, *if* the proceedings were to take years, a few days one way or the other scarcely mattered. He needn't make so momentous a decision this morning.

Perhaps the afterglow of last night with Flora would fade.

Perhaps she would annoy him this morning.

Her untrammeled independence didn't bode well for obedience in a wife.

If indeed he wanted that submission.

If he wanted another wife at *all*. He sighed; he squinted into the sun; he decided to decide later. "Go on, Monty—Franklin Square," Adam asserted, visions of his discordant marriage instinctively cooling his ardor. Sliding into a lounging sprawl, he gazed up at the canopy of green leaves and sparkling sunshine overhead, unanswerable questions assailing his mind. Should he or shouldn't he? Did he wish to lose Flora or keep her? *Would* he lose her if he did nothing? Swearing under his breath, he longed for a very large cognac.

They were turning onto the approach street to Franklin Square when Adam suddenly shifted upward on the seat and abruptly said, as if he might change his mind were he to be less impetuous, "Go to the telegraph office first."

Bringing the horses to a halt, Monty shifted around, not sure he'd heard correctly, so softly had Adam spoken.

Adam smiled. "Yes, I'm sober, although I'm not certain I might want an excuse later for doing this. The telegraph office, Monty, *before* Franklin Square, and you can congratulate me. I'm getting married."

"That a fact." Monty Blair was too polite to mention Adam's current wife, although no one at the ranch expected her back. And if he was talking marriage, it had to be the redhead from England. After her stay at the ranch, bets were taken by the staff on how soon she'd return.

"An *eventual* fact," Adam replied with a grin. "If Lady Flora will have me. I have to let James know."

"Don't expect he'll be surprised." Monty had been driving for Adam for a decade; he'd watched the young count forced into his marriage; he'd seen Isolde's reaction to Aspen Valley and her husband. And he was aware of all the concessions and adjustments Adam had made for his wife over the years. "Reckon things will be different with Lady Flora," he laconically said. "Congratulations, boss."

"Thanks, Monty," Adam replied. "I'm in a damned good mood." His smile shone white in his bronzed face, and then his dark brows rose and fell in swift merriment. "I think. . . ."

Flora was sitting on the front steps of Sarah's house when Adam's carriage drove up, and by the time his driver had stopped in front, she was standing at the curb looking fresh-faced and girlish in a primrose, sprigged muslin gown, her straw bonnet hanging from her wrist by its grosgrain ribbons.

Jumping down from the gleaming black victoria, Adam helped Flora in and then settled on the padded seat opposite her.

"I didn't want to wake Sarah," Flora explained as the carriage began moving. "She generally sleeps late in the morning, so—"

"—you were sitting on the steps like an urchin," Adam finished with a smile. "A very beautiful urchin, by the way. Could I interest you in a home," he teased, "to get you off the streets?"

"I could possibly be tempted," Flora coquettishly replied, fluttering her eyelashes in mock flattery. "Would the work be hard?"

"Sometimes," he said. "It depends . . ."

"On?" A flirtatious lift of one brow.

"On my mood," he softly said.

"I'd have to cater to your moods? Ummm . . . perhaps I should think about it."

"You're not allowed to think about it," Adam brusquely retorted, and without regard for gossip or scandal, he reached over, lifted Flora into his arms, and pulled her onto his lap. "You're only allowed to say yes," he whispered, holding her tight.

"Are you abducting me against my will, Mr. Serre?" Flora murmured, the froth of her primrose skirts surrounding her in heaps and piles so she seemed fragile, vulnerable.

"It's a thought," he said with a degree of sincerity, not inclined to let her leave him again. "Kiss me."

"They'll run us out of town, darling," she warned, quickly glancing around to see if they were observed.

"You're too shy," he murmured, kissing her instead, a light, delicate, restrained kiss. If he'd allowed himself to really kiss her, there'd be scandal indeed. "And I won't be here much longer should they wish to run me out. I'm going back with you."

"When?" Heaven within reach.

"In a day or two. I have to see my horses readied for travel."

"Utter bliss," she murmured.

"It gets better," he said. "Wait until you taste George's fried trout."

George Crum[14] had first learned to cook as a guide in the Adirondacks, having been taught the finer aspects of cooking by a Frenchman who employed him. He'd worked at Moon's Lake House with his sister-in law, and after gaining fame for his culinary expertise, he opened a restaurant of his own on a low hill at the south end of Lake Saratoga. A mixed-blood of mulatto and Stockbridge Indian heritage, he kept his expenses down by having his five Indian wives serve as his waitresses. They were all devoted to him, as were his customers. His tables were so crowded he had no need for reservations, and tycoons, socialites, and celebrities waited their turn with ordinary guests. And despite the rustic quality of his restaurant, no objections were made to his prices, which were as high as New York's fashionable dining salons. His gifted skills as chef were worth the cost.

Flora and Adam were greeted on the front porch by George and his wives.

"I promised Flora your trout," Adam said as they climbed the few stairs to greet their host. "And thank you for opening early. It's hard to find privacy in Saratoga."

"How much privacy you needin'?" George replied, his bony face creased in a smile. His long, straight black hair attested to his Indian blood. "This your second wife now?"

"That's what we're here to discuss, so give us your table out on the porch by the lake and bring us something sweet right away, because I think she's going to hit me."

"Want some tips on managing your wives?"

"One is all I can handle at a time, George," Adam said with a smile, taking Flora's hand. "I'm not diplomatic like you. And bring champagne too. We're celebrating."

They sat at a small table overlooking the lake, holding

hands across the white linen, smiling at each other as if they alone knew the secrets of the universe, the magical beauty of love.

"Forgive George," Adam said into the peaceful summer air. "We've been friends too long."

"Everyone's forgiven today. I feel unbelievably happy."

"I already wired James to begin annulment proceedings. I'll talk to your father in person when we return to Montana. I need you with me."

He spoke quietly, with very little inflection, his fingers tightly clasping hers, and she felt that small restraint in tone, in the fierce pressure of his hands.

"Do you love me?" she asked.

"I must," he carefully said. "I do," he corrected himself and then with a faint sigh added, "I'm not sure about love; I've never been in love before, but I desperately miss you when you're gone, and I want you to be my wife so you'll never go away again. And to that purpose I'm willing to try to buy off the Vatican, Isolde, and her family. If not for that daunting prospect, and the vicious scars of my marriage, I'd be more certain. I wonder too at times what you're doing with me."

"I don't have the vaguest idea," Flora cheerfully said.

He grimaced. "Perhaps we have a problem here."

She shook her head so her curls swung back and forth on the delicate lace of her collar, her smile carefree, her joy a kind of radiant abandonment, boundless and prodigal. "I may not know precisely and absolutely why I love you, darling, but I know what love is now. It's everything," she said, her tone both tender and blissfully happy. Her brows arched in teasing query. "Do I need particular reasons?"

"No, so long as you're with me." His life had been more restricted than Flora's by family and duty; Isolde too had tempered his belief in happiness. And his clan's struggle to survive against the enroachments of settlement had made him aware of the stark reality of greed. It had nurtured a possessiveness in him. "I'm impossibly jealous," he quietly said.

"As I am," Flora replied with equal gravity. "I've never met Isolde, and yet I despise her for the time she's spent with you. And all the other women too."

"You needn't be jealous of Isolde. I never touched her after . . ." He paused, debating how much to say. "After our marriage," he neutrally finished. "As for the other women . . . that's over, and it's long past time to end the sham of my marriage."

"If you can."

"Generally large sums of money expedite annulments, but Isolde's family is influential too." He sighed. "There's no certainty."

"You needn't marry me," Flora gently said, understanding the complications. "I'm content simply to be with you . . . content like this, holding your hands, knowing you're near."

"But I want to marry you." He'd never said that before, never thought he'd understand with such clarity what marriage could offer. "I'd like to have more children, too." He smiled. "If you don't mind."

Flora's halcyon glimpse into paradise faded away. In all her jubilation she'd forgotten. "Maybe you won't want to marry me, after all," she softly murmured, pulling her hands away and clasping them in her lap.

"Why wouldn't I?" His voice was circumspectly calm, but he was watching her intently.

"Because I can't have children," Flora whispered, forcing down the lump forming in her throat.

Only the slightest flicker in his eyes denoted his fleeting shock. "It doesn't matter," Adam softly replied, leaving his chair to move around the table. Slipping his hands under her arms, he lifted Flora to her feet and, taking her chair, pulled her down onto his lap. "It doesn't matter," he whispered, his arms enfolding her. "Truly."

"I wish I could give you children." A tear slid down her cheek.

"Hush, don't say that. I don't care." He wiped away the wetness with his thumb. "I just want you."

She told him then in a rush of tears and broken phrases

about her illness in Egypt, how she rarely had menses after that, how the doctors—so many doctors—had told her the high fever and infection had destroyed her capacity to have children. "None of it mattered to me . . . until now," she ended on a gulping sob.

"Please, *bia*, don't cry." He gently rocked her in his arms as if she were a distraught child. "I love you," he whispered. "I'll always love you. I've loved you from that first night at Judge Parkman's." It was the only time he'd ever told a woman he loved her; it was the first time he realized how powerfully Flora had affected him all those months ago in Virginia City. And for a man who had studiously avoided the declaration in all his amorous play, he found the sentiment pleasing on his tongue, satisfying.

"Maybe you'll change your mind later," Flora despondently said. "When you miss having more children."

"We have Lucie," Adam gently said. "She's more than enough to keep us both on our toes, believe me."

"She *does* like me," Flora murmured into his shirt front, a small ray of hope entering her gloom.

"Lucie adores you; I adore you. Come, now, darling, dry your tears. This is a day of celebration, and I've a wager for you. Tell me what you think my annulment will cost, and closest estimate to the actual figure wins—what —ten thousand?"

Flora half raised her tear-streaked face. "You're just trying to coax me out of my doldrums, but it won't work; I'm feeling very sad." Her bottom lip was pouty like a child's.

"I'll say twenty thousand for the prelates," he thoughtfully murmured, ignoring her reproach because he was intent on distracting her. "Twenty thousand for Isolde, and another twenty thousand for her family's honor."

Flora's head lifted completely from his chest. "Are you talking about the real world?" she incredulously inquired. "Twenty thousand won't even get a monsignor to read your application. As for Isolde, while I don't know her, I gather she moves in very expensive circles. Twenty thousand buys five or six dresses at Worth. You've been in Montana too long."

"Really," Adam calmly said. "What sort of numbers are you betting, then?"

"Damn you." She'd fallen for his bait.

"You're intrigued," he said with a smile. "Admit it. Humor me, darling, tell me what this is going to cost me."

Since Flora had overseen the expenses of all their expeditions, she had a precise knowledge of prices throughout the world. "I dislike being manipulated," she remarked, her tone still mildly resentful.

"Don't answer, then." He'd dealt with a pouty Lucie many times.

"You think you're clever, don't you?" But the sadness was gone from her eyes.

"Fine, don't give me a figure," he blandly replied. "We don't have to wager."

"I don't need your money."

"Nor I yours. It's just for fun."

"Maybe we should wager something else," she tentatively suggested, a gambler at heart.

"What do you have in mind?" His smile had taken on a roguish cast.

"Not that, you libertine. Let's say, breakfast in bed for a month."

"You can't cook."

"I could carry it up."

"I don't want breakfast in bed. Everything spills."

"My, we're fussy. You think of something."

"Can I be salacious?"

"No."

"We're not even married yet, and you're becoming virtuous. Maybe we should rethink this proposal of marriage," he quipped. "At least with Isolde I was free to indulge my libido with other women."

"That's not allowed in *my* contract." Flora's eyes had taken on a deadly glare.

"Do you think you could stop me, little one?" Adam teased.

"A bullet between the eyes would be effective."

His eyes widened in mock alarm. "Am I supposed to be faithful, then."

"Absolutely."

"And you must as well," he quietly said, the humor gone from his voice.

"My pleasure, Monsieur le Comte. Are we done now with our ultimatums and demands, because I dearly love you above all things. And you select the wager." She grinned, carefree once more. "I just want a chance at the amounts, because I know I'll win."

"We both won already," Adam softly said, warmed by the joy in her eyes, his own heart filled with love.

"I knew that before you did. I knew that when—"

"—when we first talked of Siberia. I wasn't going to touch a woman that night. Not after my recent nasty wrangling with Isolde."

"But I changed your mind."

"Without a doubt, *bia*." He smiled. "I've often thought of buying that landau from the judge and enshrining it."

"It does have fond memories," she noted with a lingering smile.

"Are we agreed, then, my sweet seductress?" Adam murmured, holding her close. "Marriage as soon as my annulment is obtained. The absolute moment we receive word. I'll have a preacher or parson or shaman standing by."

"Agreed," Flora cheerfully replied. "Papa will be ecstatic too. He practically pushed me on the train. In the meantime, apropos our nameless wager, because you know how I love to win, I say fifty thousand for the Vatican, no less than two hundred thousand for Isolde, and another hundred thousand for her ducal family. I'm within pennies on this, darling, you don't stand a chance."

"James is very tightfisted. I think you're high. I'll go ten thousand less for the Vatican, half your estimate for Isolde —he hates her thoroughly—and nothing for her family. Isolde's father ordered James to take his coat once, mistaking him for a servant. That impertinence will cost him dearly."

"But, then, they know you're in a hurry. Which will adjust the price accordingly."

"I don't care what it costs. I only care about you," he said, taking simple pleasure in the words. "Isolde is gone, and I mean to see she's permanently out of my life. Whatever the price."

"I'm so happy I found you that night at Judge Parkman's," Flora merrily declared.

"And I mean to *keep* you happy," Adam murmured, nibbling on her earlobe.

"You can eat that later, Adam," George Crum called out, leading a procession of his wives down the length of the porch, all bearing trays of food. "Give this a try first."

Adam invited their hosts to join them, and after pulling over another table, they all enjoyed breakfast alfresco, overlooking the peaceful shores of Lake Saratoga. Fresh trout, fried to crisp perfection, bass boiled with wine and herbs, woodcock, snipe, quail in subtle, pale sauces were arranged on white china platters. George's signature Saratoga chips, potatoes sliced paper thin, fried and salted, piled high in a large glass bowl, disappeared with predictable speed. His delectable invention was already on menus around the world. A luscious variety of fruits completed the meal: pineapples, tamarinds, pomegranates, peaches, apricots, and grapes. The whole washed down with sparkling champagne.

It was a perfect morning in a perfect world. Good food, pleasant company, Flora and Adam's future sweetly assured.

As figurative frosting on the cake of their happiness, they stopped at Tiffany's when they returned to Saratoga. Flora bought herself a small brooch of pearls and emeralds, a reproduction of a Renaissance piece depicted in one of Raphael's portraits. And Adam insisted on buying her a ring. "An engagement ring," he whispered.

She shook her head and nervously glanced at the clerk, who might have heard. "Hush. What will Sarah say if we're in the *Herald*'s gossip columns tomorrow?" James Gordon Bennett, who owned the *New York Herald*, took special interest in reporting the indiscretions of the wealthy at Saratoga. Every day brought new scandal in the morning paper.

"A friendship ring, then, a pearl or an emerald to match your pin," he murmured, and before she could respond, Adam said to the clerk in a normal tone of voice, "Show us your emerald rings."

Ignoring her quiet protests, Adam selected a large oval emerald surrounded by diamonds, slipped it on the fourth finger of her left hand, kissed her in front of the prudently expressionless clerk, and said, "I'll take it."

All the employees at Tiffany's understood that the wealthy lived by different standards from the normal populace, and if the Comte de Chastellux, whose horses outran the best in the country, and who also happened to be married, chose to engage himself to a beautiful young woman with a ring priced at thirty thousand dollars, it wasn't a lowly clerk's place to take public notice of a nobleman's eccentric whims.

The clerk did, however, offer the tidbit of information to the *Herald* reporter who regularly paid him for his insight into the lives of the rich and famous, and the young Tiffany employee added twenty dollars to his income that day.

Lucie and Cook thought the new brooch and ring beautiful, although Lucie preferred her gold mechanical parrot bank with diamond eyes that flapped its wings and opened its beak for the coins. After their picnic that afternoon, when Flora returned home, Sarah admired the new jewelry with a more personal interest in its significance.

"Adam calls it an engagement ring," Flora said, smiling. "A quaint term under the circumstances."

"But very lovely. How long do you plan on being engaged?" Sarah placidly asked.

"Until his annulment is secured."

"That can be a lengthy process."

"In the meantime we're going back to Montana."

"Are you happy?" It was a rhetorical question, for Flora was so obviously in love, her eyes shone with joy.

"Extremely." Flora spread her arms wide and smiled. "Immeasurably."

Her aunt beamed, pleased with her part in the match-making. "All my best wishes, darling. Your papa will be pleased, and now that all is reconciled, I don't imagine you'll need me to entertain you this evening."

"We're going to dinner and then a play."

"An improvement over the piano pieces last night," Sarah said with a smile.

Chapter Nineteen

Edwin Booth was performing a scene from *Hamlet* first, followed by lighter fare: a comedy of manners lately imported from London. The theater, although of a lesser size, had the same magnificence as Europe's finest: red velvet seats; muraled ceiling; magnificent crystal chandeliers; gilt and ormolu-trimmed boxes; an audience elegantly dressed and ablaze with jewels.

Edwin Booth, returned to the stage after a year's retirement following his brother's assassination of President Lincoln, was in top form. The slight, dark-haired actor gave a stirring rendition of Hamlet's most famous soliloquy.

Flora and Adam viewed the performance from a well-placed box, enjoying their first night out. They drew the eye, but, then, the Comte de Chastellux always did, and the beautiful lady on his arm tonight, rumor had it, might be replacing his wife. Although the *Herald*'s gossip column, being printed even as Mr. Booth emoted, wouldn't appear until morning, the few short blocks of fashionable Broadway had been abuzz with the tantalizing news since afternoon.

The *Herald* reporter had mentioned the Tiffany's anecdote only discreetly to a few friends, who of course mentioned it discreetly to a few more, and so it went. . . .

During the short break between performances, the houselights came on, and several members of the audience trained their opera glasses on Flora and Adam and openly gawked. Familiar with being stared at, Flora decided American audiences were simply more overt in their curiosity; Adam had long ago learned to ignore the interest his looks and profligacy inspired. But when several members of the audience actually pointed and then whispered to their companions, Flora leaned over and murmured, "It can't be my jewels; there are dozens with more diamonds on, including several men. Why the acute fascination?"

"You're dazzling, dear, or maybe Hamlet bored them," Adam casually said, surveying the audience, his gaze sweeping the floor, the box seats. "I'm looking forward to the next"—his pause was infinitesimal—"performance," he finished. But his glance returned to the boxes stage right, where his brain had registered an ominous image. Blond hair, a familiar crescent hairpiece of large diamonds —a woman leaning flirtatiously over the shoulder of the man in front of her.

She was laughing now, her head thrown back, the expensive diadem purchased with his money catching the light from the chandeliers in sparkling brilliance.

His wife.

Adam's stomach tightened. She had that effect on him, like an evil demon reentering his life.

She had to have seen them, with so many glasses trained on them. When had she arrived in Saratoga? Why had she come? Were there no country-house parties of interest this year; had Cowes lost its appeal? *Why* was she back?

He made excuses during intermission, not wishing to join the crowd in the lobby in the event Isolde was there. Knowing Isolde's malignant tongue, he didn't want to risk his wife meeting Flora. "Why don't I go out and bring us back a champagne?" he suggested. "It's such a milling mob out there, you're bound to be crushed."

And it was. Pushing and weaving his way to the bar set

up under two enormous potted palms in the lobby, he asked for a bottle of champagne and two glasses.

There was no question who the woman was when she entered the box. Winterhalter's portrait had done her justice, Flora thought. She was the graceful ideal of his stylistic female image: delicate; fair-skinned; a heart-shaped face with large doe eyes; and a dainty nymphet body perfect for the frothy, full-skirted styles of the Second Empire. But he'd painted out the malice in her eyes.

"I hear rumor my husband has promised to marry you," the Comtesse de Chastellux coolly said, moving down the carpeted stairs. "I thought I'd come over to disabuse you of that notion." She sat down in full view of everyone and smiled at Flora as though she'd not brutally demolished her future.

Isolde's sudden appearance, when she was supposed to be in Europe, had a disconcerting effect, but long familiar with aristocratic cattiness, Flora replied with a studied calm, "I suppose I can't exactly say it's none of your affair, but in truth, I think you're years too late to influence Adam's plans."

"My, how cool a tart you are," Isolde murmured, her smile a shade tighter. "I hear you're quite an attraction in Mayfair; Adam always did have an eye for experienced women."

"You speak from personal knowledge, no doubt. Is the baron here with you?"

Isolde's porcelain complexion took on faint color, and when she replied, the coolness had disappeared from her voice. "Adam won't be able to marry you because he's married to me and France doesn't allow divorce. I just thought I'd make that plain."

Although Flora knew Isolde had no intention of cooperating with Adam, the blunt denial dispelled any illusions. "Apparently you couldn't bring the baron up to the mark," Flora said, a fine insolence in her voice. "Adam will be disappointed to hear the news."

"What a little bitch." Isolde's pale-blue eyes took on a

haughty air. "For your information, my life is no concern of yours."

"Nor is mine remotely within your sphere of influence. I suggest you attempt to bully those more easily intimidated," Flora answered, familiar with arrogance. "I've held off bedouin tribesmen and Chinese bandits armed with more than your vicious intent. You've picked the wrong person to terrorize."

"I can make your life hell." Isolde sat very straight, her voice no more than a whisper.

You already have, Flora thought. "You can't anymore," she said instead. "You arrived too late."

"Actually, I rather think it's too late for you." Isolde's smile reappeared. "Why don't I let Adam explain everything to you tomorrow?"

It was a lengthy interval before Adam worked his way back through the crowd and up the stairs to the second floor.

Striding down the corridor fronting the boxes, he heard Isolde's voice before he saw her, and in that split second he debated a score of options, none ethical or legal. He wasn't smiling when he lifted the velvet curtain at the back of their box. He was grim-faced as a hanging judge.

Both women turned at his entrance, Flora's expression relieved, Isolde's veiled wickedness as he remembered.

"Good evening, darling," his wife cooed. "I came to see the engagement ring you bought for this sweet woman. It's the latest gossip in town. Didn't you know?" she innocently inquired as his brows drew together in a fierce scowl. "He's such a generous man," she added, turning to Flora with a mocking smile.

"What are you doing here?" Adam harshly said, standing dark and forbidding at the back of the box.

"I'm just being sociable. I've heard so much about your newest paramour, I simply wanted to meet the darling girl."

"You don't know how to be sociable, Isolde. Kindly leave."

"Not even a welcome-home kiss, darling? I'm so looking forward to the healthy air of Montana."

"We changed the locks the last time you left, Isolde. Save the train fare."

"And I suppose you're planning for this woman to become your new chatelaine?"

"My plans are none of your concern."

Her brows rose. "My, my—I think she said the same thing."

"Twice warned, then, Isolde. If you don't want to leave, we will. I have no interest in talking to you."

"What of our daughter?"

"What of her?" But his voice held a new caution.

"I came back to spend some time with dear Lucie."

"What the hell are you conniving?" Adam growled. "You haven't spent five minutes alone with her since she was born."

"I find I miss her dreadfully."

"If the baron didn't contribute enough to your bank account, Isolde, I'd be happy to help you out. But leave Lucie out of your plans. I don't want her life disrupted any more than it already has been."

"What of my mother love, my need to nurture my daughter?" Isolde gazed at Adam with soulful eyes. "You can't deny me that."

"You should consider the stage as a new avocation," Adam sarcastically drawled. "Since I'm not as good an actor," he went on in a level, carefully modulated voice, "I'll state my position simply. Stay away from Lucie. I don't want her hurt again."

"Apparently you're not in a reasonable frame of mind," Isolde pleasantly declared, rising from her chair in a shimmer of diamonds.

"If being reasonable means giving you what you want," Adam quietly said, motionless, watchful, "no, I'm not. Not ever again."

"I wouldn't recommend buying your trousseau," Isolde tranquilly said to Flora as she turned to ascend the shallow bank of stairs. "You certainly found big tits this time, darling," she mockingly said, advancing up the stairs toward Adam.

"Jesus, Isolde. What the hell's wrong with you?" he growled.

"She's going to be a cow when she gets pregnant," his wife gibed as she swept by him in a cloud of perfume and a rustle of peach-colored tulle, her smile cold as ice.

"I'm sorry," Adam said with a sigh as he came down to join Flora, setting the bottle and glasses on a chair. "I wish I could have spared you her crudeness and malice."

"I've met other *fine* ladies like her," Flora sardonically replied, her sympathy for Adam more marked since meeting Isolde in person. She was more vicious than she'd expected. "Don't worry, darling, I'm relatively unscathed. But what of Lucie?" she gently asked. "How dangerous will Isolde be to Lucie's peace?"

Sitting down beside her, Adam sprawled low in the chair, stretched his legs out, leaned his head against the padded back, and briefly shut his eyes. "Her talk of mothering Lucie sets off alarm signals," he murmured. "She might as well have said she planned on becoming a nun." Turning his head, he gazed at Flora. "I think we should leave tomorrow. Whatever Isolde wants can be negotiated with Lucie out of range. Isolde in a nurturing pose makes me want to check my ammunition."

"Montana sounds like paradise after my few short days back in fashionable society." And after five minutes with Isolde, she thought. "I can be packed in fifteen minutes. " Flora smiled. "Since I only came here to find you, and now I have, my mission is complete."

Adam grinned. "A plainspoken woman."

"Subterfuge isn't my forte."

"A decided blessing after Isolde. Do you want some champagne?"

Flora shook her head. "You'd better check on Lucie."

"My thought too. I'll see you home and come for you in the morning. I'd like to leave early."

.   .   .

After saying good night to Flora, Adam returned to the Clarendon and found Lucie peacefully sleeping. He explained to Cook that they'd be departing earlier than anticipated and under no circumstances was she to allow Isolde into the suite. Next he had his driver take him out to the track to make arrangements with his grooms for the transportation of the horses. If it was too difficult to prepare everything by morning, Adam told them, they could follow later.

Joseph convinced him the horses could be ready by dawn, so Adam made arrangements next at the station to have the stable car brought up with his traveling car. Both would be waiting on a spur rail, he was assured, by five-thirty, ready to be hooked up to the train scheduled to depart at eight o' clock for Chicago.

Adam stopped at Morrissey's last to say farewell to his friends. They'd been expecting him later that night for a few hands of poker and, having also heard the Tiffany's anecdote, greeted him with ribald congratulations on his marriage plans. After cheerfully accepting the crude teasing over a last drink, Adam described the incident with Isolde at the theater and advised them of his abrupt departure.

"Sensible thing to do," Caldwell remarked, taking a cigar from the humidor on the table. "Gonna cost you a pretty penny to buy her off, ain't it?"

"Worth every cent, believe me," Adam said.

"Should have done it before," a banker from Atlanta asserted. "Now that you've found someone else, she's going to ream you."

"Talking from experience, Grant," a millionaire iron-rail manufacturer facetiously remarked. Everyone knew how much Grant Putnam's new young wife had cost him.

"I don't mind a million or so one way or another, but Winnie was damned greedy, I'd say, for a lady from the Natchez Trace country. I'm supporting everyone of her deadbeat relatives in high style."

"But, then, you've got some fine consolation at home,"

Caldwell declared. "Can't say which of my four wives consoled me best."

"Now, boys, just want to remind you that there are some of us who still love the wife we married the first time," a wealthy congressman from New York cheerfully said.

"Ain't knockin' first wives, Taylor. Just saying it's damned hard to find that perfect one," Caldwell said with an expansive smile. "Not that I'm not doin' my share of tryin'."

"Since my father selected my first wife," Adam interposed, "this time *will* be my last."

"Sounds like a man in love to me," Caldwell boomed. "Send us a wedding invitation once you've got the Vatican paid off."

"I know a lawyer in Washington who could help you," the congressman said. "Name of Tom Barton. Smoothed the way for an annulment of a twelve-year marriage with six children. Said it went like silk on silk soon as an agreeable price was reached."

"I'll have James contact him, although attorneys in Paris are also essential," Adam said. "But thanks, I'm interested in speed."

"Got the little lady in the family way already?" Caldwell inquired with a grin. "Have to turn up the legal wheels full speed if'n you do."

"No," Adam quietly replied. "I just want my life back."

"She's a beauty. We wish you luck and happiness," the congressman said. "But with your luck, hell, you don't need any from us."

"Appreciate it, just the same," Adam replied. "And we'll send out invitations, so plan on a trip west sometime this year."

"Think we can get through the Powder River country? Hear Red Cloud's kicking up trouble on the Bozeman Trail."

"We'll bring down an escort if needed," Adam said. "The Lakota are traditional enemies of ours." He didn't mention they'd come with gifts last year, looking for allies. None of these men would understand.

"Always forget you live with—"

"—the Absarokee," Adam kindly interjected to help out Grant Putnum, who wasn't sure how to refer politely to his heritage. To most easterners, Indians were either noble savages or dangerous savages without discrimination for tribe or individual.

"Hell, my grandma was a Comanche, Grant," Caldwell pointed out. "If'n your family settled out west early enough, that's how the family tree looks, or else there wouldn't be no family tree. Don't have to go tippy-toeing around being polite just 'cuz Adam here has a shade darker skin and that long hair and those damned earrings like some Gypsy. He's just a man same as us, even if he is too damned good a poker player for my bank account. Don't mind saying, Adam, my games are going to be a tad more profitable once you get on that train for Montana."

"And I'll be considerably more comfortable once I've put some distance between myself and Isolde," Adam said, rising from his chair. "Good night, gentlemen." He smiled. "We'll see you next at my wedding."

Walking out onto Matilda Street, Adam turned in the direction of the Clarendon, quickly estimating the time remaining to see to the packing. He'd left instructions with Mrs. Richards to assemble some minimum clothing and supplies for Lucie and herself. He'd see to his own things. His railway car was well stocked, and what they left behind could be packed by the hotel and shipped later.

His most pressing obligation now was seeing that Lucie was safely away from Isolde. Knowing Isolde's utter selfishness, whatever her plans for Lucie, they wouldn't be advantageous to a child.

Preoccupied with his plans for departure, Adam didn't notice the man farther back in the crowd keeping pace with him. There were a good number of strollers enjoying the summer night despite the late hour; all the hotel dances were still in full swing. Music drifted on the summer air, the sounds of laughter and conversation eddied around him as he wove through the crowd on Broadway, his swift stride moving him past those enjoying a more leisurely pace.

After passing the Grand Hotel, the crowds thinned, only the small Clarendon remained on this section of Broadway. Adam occasionally glimpsed stars now between the branches of the elms overhead, the scent of flowers from the hotel gardens sweet on the air, the summer evening idyllic. The portico lights of the Clarendon gleamed in the distance. Only a few minutes more . . .

A gunshot exploded, shattering the tranquillity.

Adam dived for the ground and rolled, his survival skills honed to a fine edge by raiding and war parties. Even as he plunged for cover, he was returning the fire, the revolver he'd carried in a shoulder holster since seeing Frank Storham last night blazing into the darkness. He assumed his assailant was Frank, although the dark figure that had slipped around the large elm tree was momentarily concealed from view.

The initial screams from pedestrians at the sound of shots lapsed, and Broadway was suddenly empty, the crowds vanished in a stream of fear. The doorman was gone from the Clarendon entrance, the night utterly still, the distant gaslights from the hotel porch the only illumination under the shadowed elms.

"Almost gotcha, Injun!" A voice of elation. Frank's voice. "Gonna kill you when you least expect it, damned if I ain't!"

The constable in Saratoga wasn't going to be much help, Adam understood, nor was Frank likely to come out and face him now that he realized his target wasn't unarmed. If he wished, he could wait for Frank to slip away, but that would leave a dangerous man free to ambush them later—perhaps on their way to the station, or on the trip home.

Or he could go and get Frank Storham.

Not a difficult choice.

As he reloaded his revolver, Adam gauged the distance

between himself and the tree across the street—roughly thirty yards of wide-open space, of moonlight . . . and shadow. The shadows would help, and he didn't expect Frank was sober. Two advantages in his sprint across no-man's-land.

Snapping the loaded cylinder back into place, he checked the street one last time. Untenanted silence. Pushing himself upright, he leaped in a bound the low hedge that had served as cover, hunched low, zigzagging with agility and speed, twisting to one side and then the other to avoid the hail of gunfire aimed at him, diving across the last few yards into the protection of some shrubbery, pumping out two rounds as he finally caught sight of Frank's form.

At Frank's piercing scream Adam was already rolling to the right; he rose to his knees and fired again, dropped, rolled, stood upright, and fired three swift rounds into a target that was fully visible now.

And he watched the dark figure of Frank Storham crumple to the ground in a grotesque, doomed languor, falling to his knees first, his arms slack at his sides and then slowly toppling over.

He shouldn't have felt the eerie chill; he'd seen men die many times before. The Absarokee were assailed by enemies, surrounded by tribes wanting their lands; warfare was a way of life.

But Ned Storham had purchased a small army to protect his grazing lands and allow him to expand beyond its perimeters. When he learned how Frank had died, Adam expected he'd need an army of his own to guard his valley. Not an unexpected eventuality even without Frank's death, but a more imminent one now.

Stupid, drunken fool, he scathingly thought, gazing at the widening pool of blood spreading under Frank's body. He didn't have his brother to back him here, and he wasn't fast enough to survive on his own. But even in death he was still a damnable menace.

Sliding his Colt into the holster under his arm, he

slipped into the shadows and walked away from the Clarendon. He didn't have time to stay in Saratoga for a formal investigation into Frank's death, not with Isolde breathing down his neck. He'd approach the hotel from the north and enter by the rear door.

Chapter Twenty

～⚬～

The scent of camellia warned him, but seconds too late.
He was already inside his suite. Or more pertinently,
Isolde was already inside.

And warned or not, he couldn't retreat with Lucie
asleep in her room.

He stood with his hand still on the door latch, his back
against the closed door, exhausted, impatient, painfully
aware Isolde was going to exact a high price for her presence.

"How did you get in?" he softly said.

Seated on the sofa, she faced him across the lamplit
room. "The night clerk was so very accommodating when
I told him I was your wife." She was ablaze with diamonds, the richness of her toilette reminding him dis-
agreeably of their wedding, when the papers had reported
on the noteworthy value of her jewelry along with all the
other details of the aristocratic nuptials.

"Where's Mrs. Richards?" He spoke very quietly, his
hands at his sides as though ready for a gunfight.

"With our darling daughter, of course. You needn't
glare like that, they're both quite safe."

The word "safe" brought with it apprehension. "Who
else is here?" he asked.

"Just my driver and maid, darling."

"Where?" His gaze swept the room.

"Why, protecting Lucie and Mrs. Richards." Her reply held menace.

"You obviously want something, Isolde," he carefully said, prepared to negotiate. "Why don't we come to some agreement and you can be on your way?" He wanted her out of the suite and away from Lucie as soon as possible. He'd pay any price to protect his daughter. "You must want money. You never wanted anything else from me. Tell me how much."

"What a cynic you've become, sweetheart. Your new little whore must be having a bad influence on you."

"Look, Isolde," he murmured, controlling his urge to strangle her and be done with it. "We can trade insults all night, but I'm in a damnable hurry, so if you'll speak plainly, I'd appreciate it. I'm leaving for Montana on the eight o'clock train."

"How convenient. We'll go with you."

"No." Blunt as a hammer blow.

"Darling," Isolde gently reproached, "how terribly rude. Do you mean to tell me I can't come to Montana with you?"

"That's exactly what I mean." He would manage to keep Lucie safe without the ultimate price of Isolde back in their life.

"I'm afraid, then, I'm going to have to disagree," she calmly said, drawing a derringer from beneath the frothy folds of her skirt.

For a stark moment he couldn't believe it. Twice in less than an hour, he thought. The dark spirits were looking for his blood tonight. He inhaled, slowly let his breath out, and quietly said, "What the hell is this all about, Isolde? You know killing me won't make you any richer. You're clearly left out of my will with the exception of the more-than-generous sum we agreed on for living expenses."

"I'm interested in having sex with you tonight." She could have been saying "Pass the salt," so expressionless was her tone.

"Have you lost your mind?" For a man who prided himself on sangfroid, his astonishment showed.

"Really, dear," she mildly observed. "You've always entertained a great number of ladies. It won't take long."

"I'll pass." With the same firm conviction he would reject the guillotine.

"I don't recall asking for your approval."

"Is this a command performance?"

"Merely a necessity."

"I won't under any circumstances. Shoot me," he blandly said, the range on her derringer not sufficient to do more than wound him; his revolver, on the other hand, could kill her nicely.

"Why don't I have my servants shoot Mrs. Richards instead?" Isolde said as if she were selecting a new hat from a number of choices. "She's so much more expendable."

She might. With Isolde he couldn't be certain. He'd seen her beat a servant with a riding crop once, and if he'd not come in on the scene and stopped her, the girl would have been severely hurt. "Do you want to be fucked there on the sofa?" Adam coolly replied. "Or somewhere else?"

"The sofa will be fine. Let me call my two witnesses."

And then he understood. Two witnesses were required to corroborate conjugal relations. Could she have anticipated his desire for an annulment after meeting Flora? But even children didn't matter in an annulment, and certainly not conjugal relations. The second possibility was that she was pregnant and in the market for a legal father. The baron must have shirked his duty. His vote was for possibility number two.

How ironic. The woman he loved couldn't have children, and the wife he despised wished him to be the father of her child.

Again.

When Isolde's servants came into the sitting room from Lucie's bedroom, Isolde's handsome young driver gave Adam pause, and he considered perhaps he was standing in as father for a servant's child. Isolde's maid was a bold piece who cast a slow, appreciative glance his way and licked her lips as though she were anticipating the coming occasion with personal pleasure.

Adam calmly watched without expression when Isolde had her maid lock the door to Lucie's room as a precaution against Mrs. Richards's escaping. He took note of the time with a swift glance at the mantel clock, for he intended to be on the train when it left—with Lucie and Mrs. Richards safe and *without* the added baggage of his wife and her entourage. It wasn't a matter of negotiating anymore; it was a question of survival.

"Is all in readiness?" Adam sardonically inquired as Isolde handed her derringer to her maid and the young manservant took a revolver from his coat pocket. "I can't remember when I last performed for an audience. It was in my adolescence, I think, when debauch was a delight in itself."

The manservant gazed at Isolde with a transient lasciviousness as Adam spoke, and Adam decided the paternity of Isolde's child was definitely at issue.

"Kindly do what you do so well, Adam," Isolde coolly said, kicking off her silk slippers and lying back on the sofa, "and we can all be on our way to Montana."

"I'd forgotten how romantic your sensibilities are," Adam murmured, moving toward her. "It certainly puts me in an amorous mood."

"As I recall, mood has nothing to do with your amorous propensities. All you need is an available woman."

"Well, we'll certainly put rumor to the test now, won't we, darling? I pray I don't disappoint you. Do you still squeal when you climax?" he inquired, watching the young driver with an oblique look.

Apparently she does, he thought with amusement; the man's face had flushed a rosy hue.

Sitting on the couch at Isolde's feet, he slipped his shoes off, smiled at the witnesses, and sardonically said, "Pay attention, now, I don't care to repeat this." Then, turning to the woman who had made his life hell on numerous occasions the last five years, he added, "Shut your eyes and think of money."

Leaning forward, he pushed her skirt up with both hands and, taking her by the shoulders, moved as if to adjust her beneath him. But his left hand flashed downward, slid under his trouser cuff, closed on the bone handle of his knife, and wrenched it from its scabbard. Jerking Isolde upright, he swung her around so she faced their audience and pressed the razor-sharp blade against her throat. Two drops of blood trickled down her pale neck.

"Now, then," Adam serenely said, "let's discuss this situation. Not you, Isolde, you could bleed to death if you so much as move. I can't guarantee my temper at the moment." And he took vengeful delight in her wide-eyed fear. In all the years of their marriage he'd never raised his hand to her, but she'd finally demanded too much. "Hand me both those guns first," he ordered the servants, sliding his revolver from his holster and aiming it at the driver. "Don't dally. I'd really like to kill my wife. I may anyway," he thoughtfully added, "but if you cooperate," he went on with a tight smile, "at least I won't kill you." He had no intention of firing his weapon unless absolutely necessary. With the limited time before train departure, he couldn't afford the imbroglio sure to follow a discharge of firearms inside the Clarendon.

The guns were immediately turned over because neither servant cared to die for Isolde. She didn't inspire loyalty. After disarming them Adam directed the maid and driver to the bureau drawer that held his latest poker winnings. "You may divide it between you," he said, "and then kindly leave Saratoga. There should be enough money to satisfy you both."

It took some time for the servants to count the money, but when the last bill had been tallied in a perfect division of spoils, they cheerfully left.

"You should pay your help better, Isolde," Adam suggested as the door clicked shut behind them, "and they might be willing to put up a slight struggle for you." Releasing her, he pushed her away, tired of her machinations, genuinely fatigued, pressed by time to arrange his departure. "If you need money," he said, leaning back against the sofa, the weariness in his voice profound, "tell me and I'll write you a draft. But I don't want to see you again."

"You can't get rid of me that easily, Adam," Isolde replied with a loathsome smile. "We're married and we'll stay married, despite what you wish." She held the final card, the unbeatable one, with divorce illegal in France. "Your engagement to that Englishwoman will have to be eternal." She reclined against the sofa arm in a casual languor as if they were enjoying a late night tête-à-tête.

"Maybe I should just kill you now," Adam said with disgust, sick to death of her viciousness, of her venal self-interest. "I could strangle you, pack your body in a trunk, and toss you off the train our first night out. *Don't* press your luck. Now, if you want money, tell me. I won't offer again."

His voice held a morbid finality Isolde hadn't heard before. An astute observer of the male sex and a business-woman at heart, she sensibly said, "Fifty thousand."

"Go to Morrissey's in the morning and they'll give you the money." His voice was no more than a murmur, his eyes half-shut.

Reaching down for her silk slippers, Isolde slid them on and, rising, straightened her skirt as if they'd just shared no more than a cozy chat. "You know a divorce isn't possible," she coolly said, "even if I was obliging enough to give you one. And you know how your brothers feel."

"I don't care how they feel. If I did, I'd be a martinet like them with my major interest court politics and the price of the emperor's favor."

"Napoleon's made them extremely wealthy."

"Our father *left* us wealthy. Napoleon's friendship just helped. Maybe you chose the wrong brother to ensnare."

"I don't like court."

"Reason enough, I suppose," he sarcastically drawled. Looking up at her, he wondered what made her so malevolent. Although, knowing her family, he thought, it was understandable. "I don't care to discuss any of this with you," he deliberately said, and rising from the sofa, he moved away. The camellia scent surrounding her almost made him nauseated. "Just go."

"I didn't think I'd ever see you in love, Adam," she said, intent on a last uncharitable comment before she left. "It's quite unmistakable. Like a sad young boy," she chided. "But, then, I shouldn't complain," she went on with a flaunting smile. "It's made you more generous than usual."

He turned away from her because he didn't trust his temper, concentrating on the garden scene outside the window. And when he heard the door click shut, he exhaled like a man reprieved from a death sentence.

He didn't unlock Lucie's bedroom door until he'd secured the suite door behind his wife. As if her spirit might still return to harm his daughter.

Adam found Mrs. Richards seated beside Lucie's bed, his daughter blessedly asleep. "They're gone," he quietly said. "Did Lucie know—"

"The darling slept through everything," Cook quickly interjected. "Thank the Lord. I just knew you'd send them on their way once you came back, Mr. Serre, but I don't mind saying, those two servants made me a mite nervous. They'd steal the gold from a dead man's teeth."

"I appreciate your taking such good care of Lucie. I'm deeply in your debt."

"Is *she* coming to Montana?" Mrs. Richards inquired, her tone contemptuous.

"No," Adam firmly declared.

"Good!" Cook declared, rising from her chair. "I'll finish packing, then. I was almost done when *she* came in," Mrs. Richards darkly noted.

"Just take what we can carry ourselves. The rest can be sent later. I don't want our departure to cause attention."

"Yes, sir. I understand, sir."

Chapter Twenty-one

⊰⊱

When the train pulled out of the station at eight, Adam allowed himself a small sigh of relief. Henry had reported that he'd seen no sign of Isolde and privately told Adam he'd detected no coffin being loaded onto the baggage cars—both remote possibilities, but not to be disregarded. The morning was sunny and still slightly cool, the horses and their grooms were settled in the stable car, Lucie and Flora were playing cards, Mrs. Richards was arranging supplies in the small kitchen. There was a very good possibility they could travel west without incident. A gratifying prospect at such short notice. He was in extreme good humor.

Once they arrived at the railhead, complications might ensue; Ned Storham could be waiting. He would be apprised of his brother's death by then, but Adam had already notified James and expected an escort to see them home.

Four days on the train, another four on the trail, he thought, the rhythm of the wheels pulsing under his booted feet as he stood on the small open platform between his traveling coach and stable car. Once they reached his ranch, they were safe. He could protect his valley from attack.

"Papa, come play with us," Lucie shouted through the open door. "Flora is showing me a new game."

"In a minute," Adam replied, taking one last look at the countryside passing by. Peaceful, bucolic—a pleasant change from his night past. He allowed his fatigue to seep into his consciousness. Lord, he was tired. He'd hardly slept in days.

"Lucie has your talent for cards," Flora said, smiling up at him as he walked in to join them. "She already knows all the rules, and we've been playing for only ten minutes."

"She has a good teacher," Adam said, dropping into a chair beside Flora, his gaze affectionate. "Deal me in, and I'll see if I can make it a little harder for you two to win."

They played for another half hour while the smells of breakfast cooking wafted in from the kitchen, both adults taking pleasure in Lucie's obvious delight, both acutely aware, as well, of each other.

Their eyes met over their cards and they'd smile, a private, lazy smile. And when they spoke, their voices seemed hushed in a sweet intimacy. Adam's railcar offered shelter from the world, protection from the public, from the too recent showy glitter of the beau monde. They were isolated, a small family again, Lucie's busy chatter a familiar, pleasing melody.

"I'll be glad to get back to the ranch," Adam said as Lucie explained her cards to Baby DeeDee, his voice conveying infinitely more meaning than the simple words.

"It was nice, wasn't it?" Flora replied, understanding.

"I've never really had a family of my own." His eyes held a sweet tenderness.

"I've never had a family," Flora murmured.

His smile offered cloudless pleasure. "You have one now."

That night after Lucie had been tucked in, when Mrs. Richards and Henry had retired, when the only sound in the plush sitting room was the perpetual cadence of the wheels on the rails, Adam gazed at Flora seated across from him and softly said, "I've been watching the clock since dinner. Do you know how long it's been since I've slept with you?"

Flora nodded, suddenly unable to speak, acutely sensitive of his nearness, disquieted by her own intense need. They were alone but not alone, and he was tantalizing. Adam was barefoot in the summer heat, dressed casually in beige linen trousers and a white shirt, his hair tied back, his lounging pose etched on her mind as if longing were caustic.

"Are you bothered by the"—his head tipped toward the closed bedroom doors—"close quarters?"

She shook her head no and murmured, "A little," her agitation apparent.

"No one will . . . interfere," he quietly said.

"On orders?" She blushed at the thought of having their lovemaking discussed.

"No." He didn't elaborate, he only added, "I haven't seen you in that shade of blue before. Your gown's lovely."

"Sarah bought it for me. She said men like blue." Her cheeks flushed a deeper rose hue. "I didn't wear it tonight because of . . . that. . . . I mean . . . I wasn't—" She nervously stopped, her gaze dropping before Adam's mild scrutiny.

"Does it seem different now?" he softly queried.

She nodded before she looked up, and when she spoke, her voice held a tremulous quality. "It's not playing anymore, is it? Or teasing flirtation, or a summer liaison that ends when autumn comes. I'm not sure suddenly about . . ."

"A lifetime commitment?" His voice was carefully modulated.

"I've traveled as long as I can remember, Adam," she said in a very small voice. "I've never stayed in one place for any length of time." Her fingers unconsciously pleated the soft lawn of her skirt as she spoke. "What if I miss my research, the new cultures, my traveling?"

"Why don't we travel together?" He spoke casually,

but his gaze was watchful; he already had a wife who preferred traveling alone.

Flora's restless fingers stilled. "You wouldn't mind?"

He smiled. "I'd love to go. Maybe not right away," he added, "because Ned Storham is going to be one helluva problem for a while, but in a few months, six months, no more than a year, either he wins or I do, and then you can take me anywhere you want."

"I love you so much. . . ." Her eyes filled with tears. "I thought you'd want me to—"

"—give up everything?" He slowly shook his head. "Why would I want you to change when I fell in love with a strong, wild, talented woman who's spent a good part of her life trying to understand mankind's common bonds? Don't change. Just let me share your adventures."

Jumping up, Flora threw herself into his lap, flung her arms around his neck, and hugged him fiercely. Covering his face with kisses, she laughed and cried and told him how much she loved him in the Absarokee words she'd learned from the women in Four Chiefs's camp.

Adam held her close, his eyes wet with emotion, some of the soft words achingly familiar, bringing back long-ago memories of childhood and mother love, other phrases more specifically those of a woman to her lover, blissful, joyous sounds, teasing, coaxing—but all of them words of his people through timeless ages. And for the first time he fully understood the profundity of love, its depth and breadth and fullness, as if a lifelong quest were over.

The world was new for them that night. Love was new. Their bodies and souls untouched by the past, the sensation of bliss so intense, so graphic, Adam wrote the word on the steamy compartment window late that night and, lying on his back with his arms flung over his head, trying to catch his breath, he murmured, "Consider that written in diamonds. . . ."

Flora playfully licked her finger and swiftly wrote the word on his chest while he smiled at her.

"You're branded mine . . . ," she breathlessly said,

falling on top of him and kissing his fine, straight nose. "I hope you're available for the next millennium."

"For you I am."

"Just for me?" A female possessive demand, an absolutely new sensation for Flora Bonham.

"Only for you. . . ." He grinned. "Although I may suffocate soon from the heat. Let me open the window."

"They'll hear," she whispered as if the other occupants of the car were listening.

"Everyone's sleeping. The train wheels are so noisy, a gunshot would go unnoticed. You're supposed to be grown-up and sophisticated." His grin widened as he looked up into her indecisive face. "But if you don't want to, I'll gladly melt away for love."

"The wheels *are* rather loud."

"I'll just raise the window partway."

"How far?"

"Only enough for your newfound modesty."

"The other bedrooms are so close."

He grinned. "I won't let you scream."

She punched him.

He tweaked her curls.

And the lighthearted melee began. In the rolling tussle Adam shoved the window wide-open, then stopped Flora's protest with a heated kiss, and before very long thoughts of propriety had vanished from her mind.

The night air swept into the small bedroom, washing over the rumpled bed and sweat-sheened occupants, bringing in the sweet smell of new-cut hay and clover, the rush of coolness mingling with the racing heat of their passion.

The first night together after their long separation was the stuff of dreams, sumptuous and balmy and tender.

It was also feverish tumult and heat.

It was perfect love.

Adam fell into an exhausted sleep toward morning, his lapse into slumber occurring with split-second suddenness. One minute he was talking to Flora, and when she turned back from picking up a pillow that had fallen to the floor, he was asleep.

He lay facedown on the bed without a pillow or covers, his arms gracefully framing his head, his stark profile vivid on white linen, his muscled back awesome in its fluid power, his long athletic legs sprawled wide, his feet dangling over the end of the bed.

"You're mine," Flora whispered, an inescapable sense of possession overwhelming her. And leaning over, she gently kissed his cheek.

He stirred in his sleep and his hand reached out for her.

Twining her fingers through his, she murmured, "I'm here."

A faint smile appeared on his beautiful mouth, and he gently squeezed her fingers.

It seemed as if they inhabited their own private world as the train raced west, the following two days ones of peace and rest and contentment. They didn't exit the coach at any of the train's scheduled stops, for Adam was concerned with leaving a trail. He wasn't sure if Frank had come to Saratoga alone or with cohorts, but if they were being followed, he wanted as little evidence as possible of their route. But in Chicago's bustling station, as they were waiting to depart, Lucie spied a vendor with pink lemonade hawking her wares.

"I want pink lemonade, Papa!" she cried. "Hurry, hurry, she's walking away!"

They were all seated in the small parlor section with the windows opened wide to mitigate the sultry August heat, watching the mass of humanity streaming by on the concourse.

Responding to his daughter's urgency, Adam went to the window and called the vendor over.

"I want a big drink, Papa. I love pink lemonade," Lucie urged.

Adam smiled, purchased a large cup of lemonade, and handed it to her.

"Look! There's ice too. This is the bestest." And she

drank a big swallow. After several more laudatory comments and some coaxing, Adam obligingly drank some of the lemonade too. Flora declined the invitation to taste it, pointing to her glass of iced tea Mrs. Richards had just brought in.

By sunset they'd cleared the station, the city, and its straggling outskirts and were well out in the country again, where they enjoyed the passing scenery over dinner.

Shortly after their meal Lucie vomited. Adam was instantly alarmed, although he cautioned himself to a more cool-headed reaction; she'd probably just eaten something that hadn't agreed with her. But summer fevers were dangerous, he knew, and particularly lethal to young and old. Carrying Lucie to her bedroom, he helped put her to bed and then sat with her, holding her hand, wishing they were closer to home, where the air was clean and fresh, knowing they had six more days of travel to reach their valley.

Flora read to Lucie when she asked for a story, her little-girl voice a startling wisp of sound, drastically altered from her normal spirited tone. She lay very still and pale on her bed, her dark eyes listless, her small hand limp in her father's grasp.

"I'm so thirsty, Papa," she whispered, but when she was given water, it didn't stay down, and by evening, after retching several more times, she was so weak she couldn't raise her head. Her pulse had weakened, the surface of her body had become cold, intense cramps were affecting her legs and arms. She barely opened her eyes now, and her skin was dry, indication of the intense draining away of body fluids.

Adam sat beside the bed, terrified by Lucie's rapid deterioration, by her stillness. "This train has to be stopped," he said, his voice absolute, fear coiled tight in his stomach. "We need a doctor."

"I'll have Henry tell the engineer we need a doctor in the nearest town," Flora said, rising from her seat at the foot of the bed. Exiting the room at a half run, she moved through the parlor in search of Henry. Fearful of Lucie's symptoms, she hadn't dared voice her suspicions. She didn't have the expertise to diagnose or treat cholera, and Adam was already wild with worry.

"We'll find a doctor soon," Adam whispered to Lucie, gently stroking her forehead, her cool skin frightening to the touch. "Papa's here, I'm right here, the doctor will know what to do, we're almost there . . ." His voice dropped to a whisper. "And then we're going home. . . ."

When Henry appeared in the doorway a few minutes later, Adam looked up and asked, "How long?" his voice taut with alarm.

"Forty miles. The engineer will telegraph ahead to have the doctor at the station. Another half hour," Henry sympathetically said. He recognized cholera too; he'd seen it often in their travels.

Adam nodded, his attention immediately returned to his daughter, oblivious to everything but the fearful threat to her life. The drastic change in her condition in so short a time terrified him, and head bowed, he silently prayed to The One Who Made All Things, asking his spirits to hear him even in a strange, faraway land. "I need your help, Ah-badt-dadt-deah, and your strength to save my only child. She's my sunshine and happiness, the sweet promise of my life. Please hear me tonight, send me your help. She's so young," he whispered.

He could still remember the incredible joy he'd felt when he'd first held his daughter in his arms. Cloudy had brought her in to him minutes after her birth and had said, "She's yours now, Monsieur le Comte. We'll see that she's happy, won't we?" Lucie's eyes had been wide-open, and she'd gazed up at him from a cocoon of soft white blankets with such a pensive earnestness, he thought she must have understood Cloudy's words. And he'd whispered to the pink-cheeked baby, "Welcome to Aspen Valley, Lucie Serre. And Cloudy's wrong. *You're* going to make *us* happy."

She'd instantly become the center of his life, and he'd

learned under Cloudy's strict tutelage how to bathe her and feed her and change her nappies. He sang his own songs to her when he rocked her to sleep—Absarokee lullabies his mother had sung to him.

He'd listened to her first word—"horse"; he'd been there to catch her after her shaky first step. And he'd helped teach her to ride her first pony when she was two. She always woke him up in the morning, kept him company at meals, recited her lessons to him. And made him smile.

He couldn't lose her.

His world would fall into darkness.

Unclasping his earrings, he slid them from his ears and carefully placed them beside her pillow. "Save her, Ahbadt-dadt-deah," he murmured. "She's my life."

Flora fought back tears at the sight of her betrothed relinquishing, to save his daughter, the talisman that protected his life. His anguish tore at her heart, and she longed to hold him in her arms. But she stood quietly in the doorway, not wishing to interfere, knowing he was in his own world with Lucie.

"Breathe, darling," Adam whispered, bent low over her still form. "Keep breathing . . . that's a good girl." He watched intently for her breath, holding his own as he scrutinized her tiny chest. And then an almost infinitesimal movement lifted the blanket. "That's Papa's girl," he murmured, his relief trembling in his deep voice. "Breathe again, there, that's right . . . now again . . ." as if he could will the air into her lungs.

The doctor was waiting when their railcars were detached onto a siding at Walker. She was a tall, strong, forthright woman who took one look at Lucie's blue coloring and dry skin and pronounced the dread word "cholera" without evasion. "It's prevalent this time of year," she said with matter-of-fact clarity. "August and September are our worst months, but if we keep everything absolutely sanitary, make sure the water is boiled, and see that this little girl keeps down some liquids," she went on, the certainty in her tone bringing immediate comfort to everyone, "we'll manage to have you on your way in a week."

The doctor was rummaging through her bag as she spoke, searching for some aromatic powder of chalk. "Knew I had some," she exclaimed, pulling out a glass bottle. "Just a touch of opium in the chalk will allay the pain and help the medicine to stay in her stomach," she declared. "How are you feeling, Mr. Serre?" she inquired, her voice casual but her gaze clinically acute.

"I'm fine," Adam said. "Particularly now," he added, his heartened spirits obvious. "Now, are you certain the medicine will—"

"She's a sturdy young child, Mr. Serre," the gray-haired doctor interrupted. "Helps a lot when they're not frail. She'll be better in a few days. Looks like you need some rest too."

"Lucie's my only child."

It was an answer the doctor understood. "Once she's kept some water down, you might want to think about some sleep," she suggested. "The next few days will be tiring."

"Could you stay here until Lucie is well?" Adam asked.

He didn't say "Name your price," because he was too courteous, but plainly that's what he meant, Dorothea Potts reflected, and one glance around the elegantly appointed railcar gave graphic indication of his wealth. Not to mention his stable car alongside on the siding. Or the beautiful English lady who had been introduced without explanation simply as Lady Flora Bonham. Decidedly these were people of means.

"I can stay as long as other patients don't need me, but I do keep office hours, Mr. Serre. This community depends on me."

"Of course, I understand," he politely said. "Whatever you can arrange will be appreciated."

A short time later, after Lucie had taken her medicine, kept it down, and fallen back to sleep, they were seated in the small parlor going over the general progress of the disease.

"Her normal color will start coming back first," Dr. Potts said. "We should notice that by tomorrow. Another day or so and she'll feel like some food again. Something simple and plain. And I don't want to be alarmist, Mr. Serre," the doctor went on, "but you're going to be mighty sick too from the looks of it. Feeling nauseated, I'd bet," she added, gazing at him with a practiced eye.

"I don't think so."

"Can't fight it off that easily, Mr. Serre. Here, let me take your pulse." And after monitoring it for an interval, she said, "Why don't I have some nursing help sent out here? You're going to be down in bed by nightfall. We don't quarantine anymore, but it's hard work keeping everything clean."

"I have to take care of Lucie," Adam replied, his voice carefully modulated. "I can't afford to be sick."

The doctor smiled. "Whatever you say, Mr. Serre, but your daughter will most likely be sleeping peacefully through the night now. How are *you* holding up, Lady Flora?" Dr. Potts asked.

"I still feel well. I think it's possible pink lemonade may have been the culprit. Adam and Lucie drank some from a vendor at the station in Chicago," Flora explained.

"You might be lucky enough to avoid it, then," the doctor declared, "but sanitation is absolutely essential. Carbolic acid, lots of soap and water, boiled water for everything."

"I'll be scrupulously careful," Flora promised, already aware of the merits of sanitation with cholera. She and her father had stayed with one of three Russian regiments bivouacked near Samarkand in the summer of sixty-five, when cholera was rampant and killing so many. But the officer in charge of the regiment hosting them had sentries guarding the stream running through camp, allowing no one near the water; all water for washing and drinking had to be boiled first by the cooks. Not one member of his regiment contracted cholera, while half the men in the other two regiments camped in the same vicinity died.[15]

The doctor stayed with them until Henry appeared with two nurses he'd been sent to fetch—two hearty farm girls who looked so capable, Flora's fears were instantly allayed.

Adam had insisted on sitting with Lucy until her breathing stabilized, although he looked increasingly afflicted. At midnight he'd collapsed precisely as the doctor had predicted.

The course of his illness was as swift as it had been with Lucie, and by midmorning Adam was reduced to a state of prostration. He called for Lucie in his opium dreams, his anxiety poignant, and when Flora took his hand and spoke to him, he opened his eyes and whispered in a thready rasp, "Lucie has to get home."

"In a few days we'll all be home," Flora reassured him. "Lucie's much better." She hadn't vomited since morning, and her skin was less blue.

"Have to get there before Ned," he muttered.

"Ned Storham?"

"Have to get there before Ned." He seemed not to have heard her. His gaze turned suddenly lucid. "How's Lucie? Is the doctor here?"

"Lucie's improved," Flora gently said, having repeated her message numerous times already. "The doctor's sitting with her."

"Good." Grimacing as cramps attacked his arms and legs, Adam groaned deep in his throat, a tormented sound, and then his eyes fell shut again, overcome by the opium in his bloodstream.

The next three days were a regimen of medicines and forcing liquids as the effects of the disease ran its course, of snatched sleep and vigilance to see that neither patient relapsed—a possibility, Dr. Potts warned. Without proper convalescence patients could relapse up to three weeks after an apparent cure. The doctor stayed as often as she could, and the local ladies saw that food was prepared, linens were clean, the patients bathed. Flora first knew with certainty Adam was on the mend when he opened his eyes the morning of their fourth day in Walker, looked up at the strange woman bathing him, and shouted, "Flora!" in a powerful voice that had none of the husky whisper synonymous with cholera.

When Flora appeared at a run, he politely said to the stranger, "Excuse us for a moment," and when the lady left the bedroom, he relaxed his grip on the sheet pulled up to his neck and murmured, "Who the hell was that?"

"A nurse. You're feeling better," Flora replied with a smile.

"Not quite well enough for that kind of shock," he grumbled. "I'll bathe myself from now on. Where are we? Is Lucie all right?" He tried to sit up as he suddenly remembered his daughter's illness, but weakened by the disease, he fell back in a sprawl. "Is she alive?" he whispered, the strain of any sudden moves more than his ravaged body could sustain. "Tell me."

"She's very much alive, darling, and feeling very well. We've had to try to keep her out of your room since yesterday, when she decided she'd been in bed long enough."

"I want to see her." An intense longing resonated in his voice.

When Lucie came running into his bedroom a few moments later, he smiled and opened his arms. Lucie had the rosy glow of health again, and with a cheerful smile and her black curls bouncing, she threw herself into his arms.

"It was so-o-o scary, Papa, when you were sick," she lamented, hugging him tight.

"I know," Adam murmured, holding her small body close. "You were sick first, and I was scared too."

Flora swallowed a lump in her throat, the two dark heads pressed together, the small arms wrapped tight around Adam's neck a poignant sight. Aware of her own special bond with her father, she understood how Lucie depended on Adam's love.

"Flora took care of us, Cook said," Lucie proclaimed, turning around to beam at Flora, her exclamatory delivery restored with her health. Bouncing into a comfortable position beside her father, she said, bright-eyed and cheerful, "You should marry her, Papa, and then we can always be together. Wouldn't that be perfect?"

Adam's smile touched Flora, its message private, bewitching. "That *would* be perfect," he softly said.

"You can get 'vorced," Lucie proposed, dangling her legs over the side of the bed and swinging them beneath the ruffle of her nightgown. "Montoya's 'vorced and so is Ben or he was. He's not 'vorced now," she emphasized in case her father wasn't following her explanation. "He's married to Cook. So why *don't* you, Papa?" she casually said, having found what she considered a perfectly workable solution.

"It's a good idea, darling. We'll have to think about it."

"I'm hungry," Lucie proclaimed, jumping from the bed, divorce abandoned to more important considerations. She stopped as if remembering her manners. "Would you like something to eat, Papa? Cook has chocolate cake, and the doctor said I can have one teeny piece if I eat all my broth."

Chocolate cake was beyond his palate at the moment; Adam was thinking more along the lines of a glass of water. "Maybe later," he answered, smiling at the familiar image of his daughter bouncing from foot to foot. "Enjoy your treat."

"You definitely look on the mend," Flora said when Lucie had gone. "How do you feel?"

"*Almost* good enough for chocolate cake," he said lightly, and then he added in a more grave tone, "I can't thank you enough for all your help. You've had an ordeal."

"The nurses did most of the work."

"So modest," he said with a smile. "When did you sleep last?"

She shrugged. "I slept."

"I'm not used to this, you know. You're spoiling us."

Leaning against the doorjamb, one of Mrs. Richards's

aprons over her couturier gown, Flora said with a faint smile, "Anyone would do the same."

No, he thought, Isolde would have jumped ship at the first sign of illness. She'd never sat with Lucie even when Lucie was healthy. Children annoyed her. "No, they wouldn't," he quietly said. "I'm very grateful and I'm very lucky to have found you," he softly added.

"We found each other," Flora replied, smiling. "With a little help from Papa and Aunt Sarah."

"An energetic family," Adam teased.

"We believe in results," Flora said with a grin.

"Then I'd better get well," Adam lazily drawled.

By the next day Adam's recuperation had progressed so well, he was taking issue with the convalescent diet of light soups, milk, and farina. "I think Dr. Potts has been an angel of mercy, but she probably has other patients who need her more," he pointedly remarked, gazing at his bowl of cooked farina with a critical eye. "I'll thank her when she returns from her office hours today. Why doesn't Henry go into town and get a bank draft to cover her charges?" He pushed the bowl away. "You have to be sick to eat this. I don't suppose there are buffalo ribs in town," he said.

On Adam's orders Henry made arrangements at the station that afternoon for their railcars to be attached to the morning train. Luckily the doctor pronounced them healthy enough for travel, for Flora had the distinct impression they would be leaving regardless of her opinion. Shortly after five the following day, just as the sun lightened the sky, they resumed their journey home.

That put them two days behind Isolde, who was also traveling west on the Union Pacific. The Comtesse de Chastellux had a variety of reasons for returning to Montana, and none of them included divorce.

A coffin containing Frank Storham's body was transported in the baggage car of the same train Isolde occupied, while his brother Ned was riding south to the railhead to pick up Frank's remains.

James and the Earl of Haldane had arrived in Cheyenne

only to find a second telegram waiting at the Forsyth Hotel with news of the delay due to illness. The postponement increased the chances that Ned Storham might arrive at the railhead before Adam.

James was hoping to avoid that volatile confrontation.

Chapter Twenty-two

❧

The risk became serious when Ned rode into Cheyenne two days later escorted by his hired guns. Over breakfast the next morning James and the earl considered their options.

"This isn't the place for a battle," James said. "We have to see that Lucie and Flora are out of danger. Once they're secure, we can deal with Ned Storham and his men. We should have killed them all last spring," he softly murmured, adding another spoonful of sugar to his coffee. "But"—he sighed—"Adam held a more benevolent view."

"And we have no idea when Adam and Flora are arriving," George Bonham thoughtfully remarked. "Only that they're delayed."

"A damnable tightrope."

"So we just wait?" The earl abruptly rose from the table and walked to the window overlooking the street. Gazing down on the busy thoroughfare fronting Cheyenne's best hotel, he softly queried, "What of the local sheriff?"

"He won't do anything."

George Bonham turned back at James's blunt answer. "You're certain?"

"To take on Ned's bunch is virtual suicide, and he

knows it. The courts might convict one or two of his killers, but that wouldn't help him once he's dead. And the courts out here are fairly . . . shall we say, *flexible* in their verdicts. Hell, we don't even need courts to convict and hang in these territories. The Vigilantes hung thirty-two men a few years ago in Virginia City.[16] No one stopped them; no one even mentioned bringing them to justice."

"How many men do we have in town?" Their main force of Absarokee was camped well off the trail in the hills north of town. Those who'd accompanied them into Cheyenne were ranch hands who wouldn't cause as much notice.

"Eight. It should be enough, provided we have an idea of Adam and Flora's arrival time. I'd rather not meet every train *en force* and in the process alert Ned to the fact Adam hasn't reached Cheyenne yet. I'm hoping he's assumed Adam preceded Frank's body home."

"You have Curly watching the station?"

James nodded. "Let's hope he can give us sufficient warning."

Instead a brief telegram arrived at the hotel on Saturday: "30 LL 8." It was signed "CiCi."

"Adam's not coming into Cheyenne," James said, smiling as he handed the telegram to the earl. "We're meeting him at eight, the morning of the thirtieth at Lucas Landing, the last stop east of town."

"You're sure it's from Adam?" The cryptic message had an ominous tone.

"CiCi is a name only I'd recognize. He's being cautious . . . thank God . . . seeing how Ned Storham's paid guns are keeping the station under tight surveillance." James didn't mention that the nickname was a phonetic allusion to the initials of Adam's title, Comte de Chastellux—a playful one having to do with a beautiful lady's licentious coaxing "*ci-ci*" (here, here) to attract Adam's attention at a Parisian revel one night. She was successful, of course, at catching his notice, and the sportive name took hold.

"Will it be possible to leave undetected?" Although James and the earl had kept to their rooms, their presence in town might have been known to Ned.

"Our men can ride out of town singly over the course of the next twenty-four hours. I'll have Joseph give them the message when he comes up later today. You and I will leave late this evening, and we'll all meet at Lucas Landing tomorrow night."

But when Joseph came up to James's suite, he had news of his own. The train had just deposited a stylish lady on the platform, Curly had reported. The Comtesse de Chastellux had disembarked into the August dust and heat, modish and grand with her silk parasol shading her from the hot sun, and before she'd walked more than a few yards toward the station, a familiar figure had intercepted her path. The two seemed to find much to talk about, Curly had said. And then Ned Storham and Isolde had departed in the same carriage. They were at the Palace Hotel now.

James swore.

"She wasn't expected?" the earl inquired. In his experience women like Isolde never relinquished money and title without a protracted struggle.

"Adam wired that he'd paid her to leave—permanently. Apparently she arrived in Saratoga; I don't know the details."

"That should have been interesting for Flora," her father said with a smile.

James groaned. "More than interesting, if I know Isolde."

"Her presence doesn't change our immediate plans, does it?"

"No, but there's always hell to pay when Isolde's in the vicinity. I hope Adam has some idea how to deal with her, because my impulses tend toward the draconian."

•　　•　　•

The morning of the thirtieth was bright with sunshine and shimmering heat already at eight in the morning when James, the earl, and a small escort watched from a distant ridge as Adam's two carriages were unhooked onto a siding. Nothing moved in the two railcars until the train disappeared from sight, and then the doors to the stable car slid open, the ramps were set into place, and the horses led out.

James watched Adam carry Lucie down, while Henry helped Flora onto the ground. Mrs. Richards was the last to leave the coach. Adam looked directly up at James and smiled into the telescope lens. Then after everyone was mounted, with Lucie in Adam's arms, the small party made for the ridge where James and the earl waited.

James had remained out of sight so the train crew wouldn't report that Adam had been met by an armed escort. Every advantage mattered in their journey north; they were only three hours ahead of Ned Storham. Traveling as they were with women and a child, those few hours would be critical against a pursuing party that could ride faster.

But Isolde was a wild card in the equation.

Her presence might change everyone's plans.

Adam greeted James with a smile, said, "Good morning, sir," to Flora's father, and thanked everyone for riding south to see them home. Flora added her thanks, kissed her father hello, murmured, "Saratoga was smashing," and grinned when Lucie said, "Georgie, we're going to get 'vorced and then marry Flora."

At his daughter's premature announcement, Adam abruptly interrupted his conversation with James and, turning to the earl, said, "I'm sorry, sir, I'd planned on asking you with more formality . . . once the situation is . . . well—"

"No need, my boy," the earl interposed. "I'm an accomplice too, like Lucie, for I was the one who sent Flora east. I hope everything is eventually reconciled." He didn't mention Isolde, nor did James until they were well on their way and James found the opportunity to speak to Adam without Flora hearing.

"Isolde arrived in Cheyenne on Saturday," he quietly said, his gaze monitoring Lucie as she conversed with the earl riding on Adam's opposite side.

Adam's eyes grew hot with temper. "You're sure."

"Curly saw her."

"I don't know why I'm surprised," Adam said, low and clipped. "She's pregnant and looking for a father for her child."

"You again."

"I thought I'd dissuaded her, but more fool me. Damn bitch. Once is enough and I told her that."

"She left the station with Ned Storham."

"That might slow him down," Adam said with the faintest of smiles. "She travels with a dozen trunks."

"Does he need her?"

Adam shrugged minutely. "I wouldn't want to second-guess Ned's intelligence. In the past he's relied on murder more than cleverness, but those two together could be a disconcerting combination. It depends what Isolde offers him or pretends to offer him."

James slowly shook his head. "I don't think he's likely to bite at her bait, whatever it is. Ned's style is generally straightforward ambush."

"Maybe Isolde will change his mind."

That was exactly what Isolde had been trying to do since Saturday, but Ned Storham didn't trust women. Not that he was necessarily prescient in terms of Isolde's honesty; his resistance had more to do with a deep-seated suspicion toward the opposite sex.

And her proposal was mighty strange, even for the raw, untamed frontier.

"I ain't never bin interested in marriage, Countess," he reiterated, maintaining his resistance as their conversation went over familiar ground. "Don't want to be leg-shack-led."

"It's only a formality, Ned. How many times do I have

to tell you?" Isolde asserted, her exasperation forcibly concealed. The man's intelligence was as stolid as his compact, sturdy body. Neither seemed easily moved. "If Adam dies, my daughter inherits Adam's estate," she explained again, sitting ramrod straight, her be-ringed fingers grasping her parasol handle so she wouldn't slap his ruddy face in her impatience. How many times had she gone over this with him? "Naturally, any court would consider me her proper guardian. I'm her mother, after all. Despite what arrangements Adam's made for a trustee, I'm sure a judge in Montana would be prompted to concur with my guardianship. And a suitably large bribe would no doubt assure that judgment. I don't want Adam's land. But you do. I *do* want his money, however. So if we were to marry after Adam meets with an accident of some kind and dies, no one would take issue if I, as your wife, were to cede you the land. With the court's blessing I can manage my minor child's fortune, and we'll both be happy. After a decent interval we could be divorced; Montana's divorce laws are so lenient. Now, consider, Ned, isn't that easier than attacking Adam and his tribesmen in an encounter where you might run the risk of being injured or killed? He murdered your brother, you can be sure, even if proof is lacking. You could be next."

"Frank was stupid."

Although she agreed, surely this wasn't the time to voice such an opinion. Any lone man who attempted to kill Adam was going to die. "Perhaps he misjudged his opponent," she politely said.

"Damn right. He was stupid. Drank too much, too."

This was the closest she'd ever come to gaining Adam's fortune for her own, and she intended to take full advantage of the bizarre set of circumstances that had placed Ned Storham in a position to listen to her. How could she have known Adam would kill Frank? How could she have arrived so opportunely in Cheyenne? How could she have possibly arranged for the man who coveted Adam's valley to be so terribly naive about women? Surely she was blessed that stupidity ran undiluted in the Storham blood.

Now, Ned may have been naive about aristocratic women who wore diamonds, but he was skilled at taking what he wanted. And one of the reasons he was willing to listen to the countess was that she was offering a bold way of acquiring Aspen Valley. He wasn't quite sure it would work; he wasn't sure at all she wouldn't outmaneuver him in the end. Man or woman, he knew shifty eyes when he saw them. The countess never looked at you directly. He noticed that first off.

But, then, he had a rogue posse at his command, and if her proposal didn't work, he could always shoot his way in, the way he'd planned in the first place. There might be a blowup when the count was killed, but no one wanted the Indians to have that country anyway. Everyone in the territory coveted that splendid grazing land. The government had tried to treat for all the country north of the Yellowstone last year, but the negotiations broke down. It was just a matter of time before whites owned that Indian country.

That would most likely make an inquiry into the count's death little more than a formality. He was part Indian, after all.

"Tell you what," Ned said, trying to smile but not quite managing a sincere performance. "Why don't you ride north with us, and we'll figger this out on the way?"

"Why, thank you, Mr. Storham. I'd be delighted." It was a strain for her to smile too, but Isolde was more artful after years of practice. "I look forward to our little . . . discussions."

Murder was on both their minds, their primary target identical, but as with all scoundrels, their secondary targets were more equivocal.

With a cold-blooded pragmatism, they viewed each other as only temporary allies.

Isolde's new alliance with Ned Storham assured a peaceful ride north for Adam, Flora, and their sizable party, once they reached the Absarokee camp in the hills. With twenty warriors added to their ranks, they passed unmolested through the troubled Powder River country and reached Four Chiefs's village on the evening of the fourth day.

Many of the clans had gathered together for the last summer visiting before the cool weather set in and the buffalo hunts began. The camp was large, spreading east and west along the wooded banks of the river, smoke from cooking fires rising from hundreds of lodges into the purple sky of twilight.

James and Adam, together with Flora and her father, had agreed the large camp offered not only temporary protection from Ned Storham's designs, but a refuge for Lucie to recoup from her illness. Although over the worst of the disease, she still tired easily and hadn't yet completely regained her appetite. A week or so in the fresh air and sunshine would be beneficial.

An advantage not to be discounted for Adam, as well. Although no one dared suggest he needed the rest, his weight loss was still evident. And with Ned Storham and Isolde as possible partners in crime, everyone would require full stamina.

As they rode into camp, they were greeted from all sides with cries of welcome, the mood festive in the gathering of the clans, everyone in good spirits during the fellowship of the summer visits. Alan and Douglas were standing before the earl's lodge, smiling, pleased to see them safely returned.

Their Absarokee escort had ridden off to their own families, but Adam and James dismounted with the earl and Flora, while Lucie ran off to see Alan's drawings.

A slight awkwardness ensued when Henry began unstrapping the saddlebags from Flora's mount and then hesitated, not knowing where she would be staying.

"Why don't we all meet for dinner?" Flora suggested. "In the meantime, I'm going to spend some time with Papa and see what's transpired since I was gone. We'll bring Lucie with us when we come."

No one disagreed with her diplomatic solution. Henry

carried in the Bonhams' luggage, and Adam and James took their leave.

"So tell me, now," George Bonham said, taking Flora by the hand and leading her to a comfortable spot near a chokecherry bush, "are you pleased you traveled to Saratoga?"

"You're ever so smart, Papa," she said, dropping onto the cool grass. "I couldn't be happier."

"And you don't mind that I interfered? I worried the whole time that I'd bludgeoned you into something you detested."

"Next to Sarah, you're a rank amateur when it comes to pressure. She was absolutely determined to see Adam in my net."

"She succeeded, apparently."

"Oh, yes. I think she quite enjoyed herself."

"I thought she might." His concern showed then behind his pleasant smile; his eyes were suddenly solemn. "How will you manage Adam's wife? I hesitate to ask, but she exists."

"James is arranging an annulment."

His grave look disappeared. "Really. In that case your future isn't so ambiguous." Long-term love matches outside of marriage were common enough where divorce was still rare, but if Flora wasn't obliged to exist in that amorphous social half world, he would be better pleased.

"We're planning on marrying as soon as the annulment is granted."

"I'll see that Prendergast is put on the case too. He has enormous influence at every level of the Vatican. So all is well," he said with obvious satisfaction. Flora's happiness was of first importance to him.

"All is extremely well, Papa. We'll be going back to the ranch after a short stay here."

"Tikal is postponed?"

"Temporarily."

"Do you mind?"

"It's not permanent, and Adam has promised to travel with me on occasion. I'm content."

"Lucie likes you. An important consideration."

"And you," Flora said. "So you'll have a grandchild after all, Papa," she softly added.

"That never bothered me, darling. It was more than enough to have you."

"Will you stay with us in Montana for a time?"

He smiled. "I can be persuaded very easily. Four Chiefs has opened up a vast new culture for research. So I've two reasons for staying."

"How perfect. Then we'll all live together in sweet felicity at Aspen Valley," Flora said, "like the agreeable endings in one of Mrs. Burnett's romances."

Apparently Adam hadn't mentioned the death of Frank Storham and the expected repercussions, the earl thought. Or Isolde's presence in the territory. Time enough, though, to face those stark realities. Their journey back had been eventful enough. "I'm looking forward to it," he said with a smile.

James and Adam had been arranging strategy against Ned Storham while Flora and her father were reviewing the past few weeks. Both men agreed that Lucie and Flora would be more secure in camp than at the ranch until the conflict was resolved.

They also agreed they'd have to go out and find Ned before he could amass too large an assault force.

"He's in Virginia City or Helena looking for men," Adam noted. "After the breakup of Meagher's militia—" He shrugged.

"—there's a good supply of underemployed Indian fighters," James sarcastically finished.

"We'll leave in three days," Adam declared. "I want to see that Lucie's definitely on the mend before I go. Dr. Potts kept warning us of relapse. And," he added, "it will probably take that long to convince Flora to stay behind."

At the same time Adam and James were selecting their departure date, Isolde was on the trail to Helena, the heat like a blast furnace for the third consecutive day. Although they stopped often to rest their mounts, the ride was taking its toll on Isolde's delicate constitution. She rode sidesaddle, as was expected of a lady, her serge riding habits a solid barrier against any breeze, the adverse conditions debilitating to a countess who had always considered physical activity an obligation of the laboring class.

Her cramps began that night, and the following morning she noticed spotting when she changed her underclothes. Even Ned Storham hadn't withstood her demands to bring along one small portmanteau, and she changed daily. The remainder of her trunks were being freighted up at a more leisurely pace.

Those first small signs of blood weren't a displeasing observation. They were, in fact, an enormously convenient relief. If she could rid herself of her driver's child, it would save her the hideous bother of being pregnant for seven more months and further save her the nuisance of having to farm out the brat to some wet nurse. She had no intention of raising a servant's by-blow.

Isolde allowed herself a smile of satisfaction in the shade of the alder bushes where she was dressing that morning. It looked as though her affairs were falling nicely into place. Her young manservant had begun putting on airs when she'd taken him into her bed, and she would have had to buy him off very soon anyway. How convenient that Adam had saved her the expense.

Now, if this miscarriage would proceed to its inevitable conclusion, by the time she reached Helena, she would be in an excellent position to reclaim her place at Adam's side.

Temporarily, of course.

And then, after a conveniently arranged "accident" to her husband, she would be busy spending his fortune in Europe. Lucie could be sent off to a boarding school somewhere. England, perhaps. That would be suitably distant.

Dinner in Adam's lodge that night was festive, the food prepared by several of his numerous relatives. Talk was predominantly of the coming buffalo hunts, and Flora managed to understand most of the conversation, with Adam interpreting on occasion when a new phrase escaped her. Her father had become quite fluent over the summer, as had Alan and Douglas, so she had a full complement of helpers when she struggled for an appropriate word.

Several women were included in the party—cousins, aunts, wives of the male guests, and with the covetous eye of a woman in love, Flora noticed a glance or smile pass between Adam and a beautiful young woman on more than one occasion. They seemed to share a past, a casual intimacy; they referred to a common adolescence in anecdotes and joking repartee.

Her name was Spring Lily. She was currently unmarried, and her children seemed of special importance to Adam.

With determined restraint Flora concealed her jealousy during the long evening. Larger issues than petty jealousy faced Adam. She needn't add to his difficulties by acting like a petulant child. Ned Storham was an imminent problem, and finding his way clear of Isolde would test Adam's patience and fortune. She should maturely deal with her jealousy. Adam loved her. How could it matter that Spring Lily seemed to know Adam so well? He was allowed a past. There. A reasonable approach. An adult fairness. Evenhanded. Nonjudgmental.

But Flora's smile occasionally took on a marginal tightness in the course of the evening. Despite her attempt at an impartial self-control, her resentment would flare when Spring Lily leaned too close or smiled too intimately or shared a fond reminiscence. Then Adam gave Spring Lily a brushing kiss on the cheek when she left, and the smile directed back at him was noticeably alluring.

And she was the last to leave, of course; she probably would have preferred staying with Adam, Flora heatedly thought. Which was what Flora said a shade explosively the minute Spring Lily exited.

Glancing quickly at Lucie asleep on fur robes in a corner of the lodge, Adam took Flora's hand in a firm grasp and pulled her outside. Since the door flap was open against the summer heat and the lodge skins raised to allow the cool night air in, he began moving away from the encampment toward the river, preferring not to entertain the neighbors with their argument.

"Spring Lily's in love with you, isn't she?" Flora hissed, trying to wrench her hand free, her braced weight solidly resistant to the pressure of Adam's hand, mature logic in full retreat.

"We're friends," he said, his voice a low rumble, his gaze sweeping the surrounding lodges. It was still early; no one was sleeping yet except the children.

She noticed he didn't need clarification in terms of the woman, damn him. He knew exactly who she meant. "I imagine you have lots of friends here," she heatedly said. "And all of them were just waiting for you to come to the summer camp so they could seduce you. Is Spring Lily a special favorite of yours?"

"She is," he said, giving up on winning the tug of war with Flora, sweeping her into his arms instead. "Because she was my brother's wife," he added, striding away into the darkness, his hold on Flora's struggling form visetight.

"She'd like to be a lot more than that, believe me," Flora hotly remonstrated, trying to wriggle free. "I saw that enticing smile when she left."

"I'm capable of saying no." They were beyond the last lodges now, and Adam spoke in a normal tone of voice.

"So she asked you!" Flora exclaimed. "Put me down, dammit, put me down this instant."

"Sorry." His voice was somewhere between a growl and a grumble as he purposefully moved down the path to the river. "We're going to clear up a few misunderstandings right now," he emphatically declared. "Beginning with your needless jealousy. I haven't looked at another woman since I met you."

"Like hell. What do you call that kiss when Spring Lily left?"

"A courtesy."

"I'm sure she appreciated your politeness," Flora snidely said. "How polite are you going to be to all the other women vying for your favors? You can take me to the ranch tomorrow. At least there I don't have to see the longing in their eyes."

The river gleamed in the moonlight as they approached, the cottonwoods lining the shore whispered in the night breeze, and without answering, Adam walked to a small rise on the bank and stood for a moment gazing down the ribbon of sparkling current flowing away to the west. "We shouldn't fight about this," he softly said. "Look, the moon's covered with a haze. A storm's coming." And then, lowering himself to the ground, Flora's weight in his arms seemingly incidental, he settled onto the sweet-smelling grass. "I love you," he quietly said, not relinquishing his firm hold on her, his eyes shadowed in the moonlight. "I've never loved anyone else, except Lucie. I've told everyone in camp I'm marrying you, and if women look, I can't help it, but I'm not looking back—not that way." His voice turned to a whisper. "I don't know how to say it any plainer."

How simple he made it all sound, how uncomplicated by the tumult of emotions jostling in her mind. "I'm not used to this, Adam," Flora murmured, her hostility muted by his sincerity, her resentment draining away. "I'm not familiar with loving someone, with this insane jealousy." She sighed. "I hate myself for acting like one of the spoiled ladies I always found so childish. I apologize." Her smile gleamed in the moonlight. "At least I didn't make a scene during dinner."

"I appreciate your restraint. You saved me from relentless teasing. A man is supposed to be able to control his woman."

"Heaven forbid I should embarrass you." A small snap had reentered her voice.

"Truce, darling," Adam quickly replied. "That's just a male viewpoint. The women have their own perspective.

Although we both know who's in charge," he softly went on, "don't we?"

"I think so," Flora sweetly replied.

"The strongest one," Adam whispered, swiftly rolling over and pinning her body to the ground.

"The smartest one," Flora breathed, reaching up to brush his mouth with her lips.

"The strongest *and* smartest," Adam murmured, shifting so his weight rested on his elbow, lifting her skirt slowly so the cool night air bathed her legs. "Ummm, you feel luscious. . . ." His hand drifted higher, sliding between her legs, his fingertips touching her pouty softness.

She raised her hips the slightest small distance, so his fingertip slid in a fractional degree, so he felt her damp heat, her readiness. "I was wondering," she breathed, her voice a sultry contralto, "if I worded this properly, if I appealed to your masculine strength with just the right degree of deference, whether you might . . . make love to me." Caressing the long, hard length of his arousal, her fingers slid over the sleek leather of his leggings until she reached the distended crest of his erection and she squeezed.

His groan trembled deep in his throat, and she watched his eyes drift shut. "It's just a thought," she murmured, maintaining the pressure of her fingers. After a very long interval, while he shuddered under her hand, he reached down to release her hold, his eyes slowly opened, and, gazing down at her with a tilted smile, he murmured, "I'm convinced."

"You see." Her smile was demure, like an innocent young maid.

He laughed. "Your point, darling," he graciously said, "but I have a feeling the tables may be reversed later"— his amused glance deliberately surveyed her—"when you're, shall we say, intensely *interested* in . . . orgasm."

"You're ungallant."

"But currently available."

"I don't need you."

"Why don't we see . . ." He slid his fingers deep inside her and gently stroked, her response instant, as he knew it would be.

"Ummm . . ." Her breathing had altered. "Maybe we . . . could reach some . . . agreement."

"I'm listening." It was a delicious game under a moonlit summer sky. "What are you willing to give up?"

Everything, she thought, to feel you inside me. "I'll think of something tomorrow," she evasively said instead. "Take these off." And she began tugging at the tie to his leggings.

Withdrawing his fingers, he covered her hand with his, staying her effort. "I don't think so," he gently said. "You're not cooperating."

A small silence ensued, and then she said so softly he barely heard her, "I won't be difficult about Spring Lily."

He smiled. It was an enormous concession. "And I'll let you give orders," he said with a reciprocatory charm.

"How nice."

"Exactly."

"Are we going to move on to other things now?"

"I was thinking we would."

"What if people see us?" The grassy knoll overlooking the river was exposed if anyone were to stroll down the bank.

"Would you rather not?" He already knew the answer.

"You're too damned casual."

He'd had much practice, he thought, but in lieu of that controversial note, he said instead, "I'll cover you."

"I'd like that," she whispered, wanting to feel him over her and on her and inside her, wanting to be over-whelmed, wanting to feel his strong back under her hands, wanting the power of his violent, unrestrained desire to make her weak with longing.

"Hurry," she said.

"We've all night. I don't have to hurry."

"You do for me." A small heated tempest underscored her words.

"Ummm . . . ," he murmured with a smile. "This

sounds familiar. Are you going to be sexually demanding?"

"Always."

His lashes drifted down so his eyes were narrowed shadows. "I like the sound of that."

"I thought you might."

"That must be why I love you." And then his expression changed, the moonlight exposing a gentle tenderness. "For that and for a thousand other reasons too," he said in a velvety whisper.

"Or ten thousand," Flora softly murmured. "I'm defenseless," she breathed as his lips brushed hers. "Helpless in love."

"And I'm here to help you," he whispered, his voice husky, seductive. Reaching for the tie on his leggings, he pulled the leather knot open.

Impatient, driven by strange impulses coursing through her blood, Flora stripped her skirt off in economical, swift gestures, slipped her blouse and chemise over her head in one frantic tug that ripped the delicate dimity undergarment.

"Is this a race?" Adam teased, taking the torn chemise and blouse from her hand, dropping them onto the grass.

She took a deep breath to steady the reckless heat flooding her body. "I think it might be," she said, her voice softly tremulous. "Do you mind?"

He smiled. "Darling, it's every man's dream."

"Well, then," she said with the barest touch of impertinence.

He laughed. "Apparently the lady isn't interested in foreplay."

"Adam—!" The sound was somewhere between an order and a wail.

She was orgasmic the moment Adam entered her.

The absolute frantic first second.

As though her senses were aflame, as if love overwhelmed all rational thought, as if the trigger to orgasmic delight that moonlit night was Adam's simple presence. Briefly shaken by her instant, staggering climax, she won-

dered how defenseless she'd become because of love. But
Adam was still hard inside her, filling her, stretching her,
and within seconds—cerebral debate was obscured by
more intense, immediate pleasure.

She minutely shifted her hips, absorbed the un-
abashedly luxurious tremor, and then languidly stirred
again, searching for reaffirmation of the delirious sensation.

Accomplished at recognizing female appeal no matter
how voiceless, Adam deftly responded, moving gently inside her, exploring the silken perimeters of her heated
interior, carefully at first in deference to her recent orgasm, and then less gently.

She came again, almost at once, and he took note after
her third swift climax how impetuous her response, how
fevered. And gallantly, he brought her to orgasm twice
more before he sought his own release. Rendered almost
insensible by the explosive assault on her senses, by the
agonizing pleasure, Flora lay adrift from the reality of the
summer night, transported to a delectable, sensual world,
her mind absorbed by the pulsing rapture strumming
through her body. When she finally opened her eyes,
blinking against the brilliant moonlight, she gazed at
Adam lying beside her and whispered, "I love you too
much. I'm dizzy with longing. I crave your touch, your
kisses, your sex." Her dark eyes looked up at him with
awestruck trepidation, as aware as he of her frenzied response. "It's terrifying."

"It's love, darling," Adam softly said, as if she'd wakened frightened from a dream, touching her cheek with a
gentle brushing finger, understanding the frantic need,
the ungovernable feelings, the intoxication that made one
forget even the deep-seated fear of marriage.

"Tell me you'll always love me." She'd never felt such
disquietude; she'd never felt as though she were complete
only in his arms. "I must be tired," she uneasily added,
wanting an intelligible reason for her vulnerability.

"I'll always love you," he simply said, sympathetic
to her emotional struggle; he'd engaged in a similar one

in Saratoga. "I'll love you beyond the slippery log," he softly added, his voice hushed like the summer night. "Beyond the mountaintops . . . now, this minute—tomorrow . . . and through eternity."

"Good," she said with a small sigh. "Are you sure? Oh, Lord," she restlessly murmured, "I feel so strange. . . ."

"Love is like a living force," Adam softly said. "It stimulates and agitates, it colors every aspect of the world. It makes the flowers sweeter, the sky bluer, alters the meaning of happiness—"

"—precipitously ends a life of restless journeying," Flora quietly interjected.

"Or gives immeasurable joy to a life," Adam said. "We've found each other; we'll share a future together. It needn't be terrifying." He added with a smile, "I'm looking forward to your taste in furniture."

"Anything that folds, can be packed, or Henry can buy in transit." Her mouth pursed slightly. "Which means some adjustments are in order if I'm experiencing this radical compulsion to put down roots."

"Anyone who can shoot their way through Chinese bandits will manage competently, I'm sure," Adam assured her.

"This bewilderment is temporary, then."

"You're probably still fatigued from our long journey west," he politely said, respectful of her uncertainties. "Would you like to sleep? Here or in the lodge?"

"Actually, no." Her voice was touched with a familiar heated allure, one undeniable certainty pulsing through her blood.

"Really . . . ," he playfully drawled.

"Are *you* tired?" Reaching over, she ran her palm over his broad shoulder, down his muscled torso, his ribs marginally evident since his illness. "Would you mind, then . . . I mean—if you're really not too tired . . . although I realize maybe it's too soon—"

"Look," he said, interrupting her tactful rush of words, glancing downward.

"Oh—" A small sound of astonishment.

"Anytime, darling."

She smiled in the moonlight, an innocent smile of artless joy. "Thank you," she whispered.

Toward morning, after a night of memorable sensation,
Adam rolled over on the crushed grass, rummaged
through his clothing, and handed Flora a small beaded
pouch. "I meant to give you this after our guests left."

"But I interrupted your plans."

He grinned. "No complaints, *bia*."

When she pulled the drawstring top open and tipped
the leather bag upside down, a sparkling brooch fell into
her hand.

Bliss was written in diamonds on her palm. A delicate,
simple design executed in very large gems. "It's beautiful," she whispered, remembering the sweetness of their
first night on the train.

"You're *my* bliss," Adam quietly said. "I wanted you to
know that."

"I'm going to cry," Flora breathed, swallowing the rising lump in her throat. "I never cry."

"I don't mind if you cry." It always astonished him—
the extent of her self-denial and strength. Sitting up and
taking her in his arms, he cradled her the way he did
Lucie when she was sad.

"My emotions are in shambles," she apologized, hic-
cuping against his chest, tears streaming down her face. "I
don't know why I'm crying." She rubbed the tears from
her cheeks. "I just love you so much."

"We're even, then. Because I love you with the same
ungovernable feeling. Tell me, do you like it?" He
touched the twinkling diamonds lying in her hand, wanting to distract her from her sadness.

"I adore it," she murmured, licking away a tear that had
funneled into the corner of her mouth. "I adore you
madly for your sweetness, but how in the world . . . how
did you—"

"James did," he interposed, wiping her cheeks with the
back of his hand, kissing her gently on the forehead. "He

had the pin made in Cheyenne while he was waiting for us. I telegraphed him instructions."

"Do you think we're too lucky?" she asked, her voice shaky, oversensitive to every nuance of emotion, giddy with love, plagued by uncommon dread. Wondering in her strange new susceptibility if life was too perfect and recompense would be demanded.

"No, we're just *truly* lucky. Period," Adam firmly said, his arms tightening around her. And he had every intention of seeing that their luck continued.

Chapter Twenty-three

❧⟡❧

When Flora woke in the morning, she felt queasy, as if she'd eaten something that didn't agree with her. But she resisted her mild nausea during breakfast, concentrating instead on Lucie's questions, not wishing to alarm Adam. He'd immediately think cholera, and she was certain her unsettled stomach was less severe than the symptoms she'd seen on the train.

When Adam left after breakfast to survey the horses they'd be racing later in the day, she and Lucie stayed in the coolness of the shaded lodge and practiced some of the new Absarokee phrases; the earl had taken notes on the previous night.

A short time later their lessons were interrupted by Spring Lily and her children. "They couldn't wait to play with Lucie," Spring Lily explained, standing in the doorway. "Would you mind if we came in?"

"Please do," Flora politely said, her jealous fears put to rest last night. And she'd promised to be pleasant to her.

When the children immediately ran off, Spring Lily entered the lodge, handing Flora a small willow bowl of sweetmeats made from berries, nuts, and syrup. "A peace offering," she said with a smile.

"Was I that obvious?" Flora replied with a slight blush, taking the bowl. "Forgive me. Adam told me how much you and your family mean to him." Picking out a sweet, she put it in her mouth.

"He has love only for you," the slender, dark-haired woman said. "Everyone can see that. I'm pleased he's found someone to make him happy. His wife ruined his life for too long, and now that she's back, who knows what trouble she's planning for him?"

Flora choked on the sweet, shocked by the sudden disclosure. *Isolde in Montana?* Anarchy convulsed her brain. Her stomach seemed to lurch in reaction, and suddenly she felt her breakfast coming up. Clamping her hand over her mouth, she mumbled, "Excuse me," and bolted from the lodge.

Spring Lily found her a few moments later kneeling under a plum bush, her skin pale, a fine sweat on her face, her breakfast emptied on the ground.

Handing Flora a wet cloth, Spring Lily helped her up and guided her back to the lodge. There, over only minor protest, she insisted Flora lie down.

"I'm fine now," Flora weakly said, resting on a bed of buffalo robes. Or as fine as she could be considering that trouble in the form of Adam's wife was back in Montana. "Hearing of Isolde's return was a—" She swallowed hard to repress the bile rising in her throat. "It was a surprise," she whispered, nausea threatening to overtake her again.

"Was your stomach unsettled this morning?" Spring Lily asked, ignoring her comment on Isolde, having long ago dismissed Adam's wife as useless. She was more interested in the state of Flora's health.

"Just a little."

"Have you been sleeping more? Feeling tired?"

"I *have* been tired, but our trip from Saratoga was draining, with both Lucie and Adam ill." Flora took a tentative inhalation of fresh air. "As soon as we all have a few days of rest, I'm sure I'll be less fatigued."

"Are your breasts tender?"

The conversation had suddenly altered, Spring Lily's last question decidedly personal. Or at least her stomach took it personally. When she'd repressed the sudden lurching amazement, she carefully said, "What are you asking?"

"Forgive me if I'm interfering," Spring Lily courteously replied, "but you have that pale-greenish look of baby sickness, and I was curious. Adam would be pleased, I know. He adores children."

"It's impossible." But even as Flora said the word, another wave of nausea overwhelmed her, and she struggled up on her elbow, trying to tamp the sensation.

"Let me make you a cup of tea. It helps."

"I'm afraid you're wrong," Flora whispered, trying to breathe slowly, as if the measured rhythm would mitigate the waves sloshing around in her stomach.

"Just try some. With all my pregnancies I could never hold down anything in the morning the first three months unless I drank a cup of tea first."

"I mean you're wrong about my being pregnant," Flora murmured, leaning back on her elbows and shutting her eyes. "I hope I'm not getting cholera." She felt miserable.

"I haven't seen cholera," Spring Lily noted, "but I *have* seen your ailment. And if you're worried about Isolde, Adam will see that she leaves. I heard him tell James he'd have her out of the territory within the month."

The name Isolde jolted her stomach again, and Flora stifled a moan.

"Don't move," Spring Lily quickly said. "I won't say another word until I've made the tea, and then you'll see how much better you feel." She understood how hearing about Adam's wife could be traumatic.

So while Flora lay utterly still, trying to repress her nausea, Spring Lily quickly went to fetch a small pouch of herbs from her lodge. When she returned, she heated some water and made them both a cup of tea, comfortably familiar with everything in Adam's lodge.

"I like a weak brew and plenty of sugar," she said, scooping in two large measures of sweetening. "Here, see what you think," she went on, helping Flora into a seated position and holding the cup to her mouth.

It was a miraculous transformation. Within minutes

Flora felt restored, the waves had ceased to toss, she could think about something other than vomiting, and she took note of the children again playing tag in a small grassy meadow between the lodge and the river.

"There, now, isn't that better?" Spring Lily's smile was warm in the perfect oval of her face.

"Immensely," Flora said with a grateful sigh. "Thank you very much."

"You have to tell Adam. He'll be ecstatic."

"I'm afraid you're misinterpreting," Flora gently said. "I can't *have* children, you see, because of an illness I had years ago. Several doctors have agreed on the diagnosis."

"I'd say they're wrong."

Her words held such certainty, Flora considered the possibility for the first time in her life. A transient flitting thought, immediately discarded. A dozen doctors couldn't be wrong, despite Spring Lily's conclusion. "I wish you were right, but—" Flora slowly shook her head.

"Well, at least the tea cured your stomach," Spring Lily politely replied. Adam's woman would know soon enough when her belly began growing large with the child, she thought. There was no need to convince her today. "When you're feeling better, let me introduce you to some more of Adam's relatives. Everyone is anxious to meet you. He's happy again, and all his family is pleased he found you."

Or, maybe, found *us*, Flora giddily thought with a small rush of secret longing.

But she didn't mention her upset stomach to Adam, for she knew he'd worry, and she rationally dismissed the improbable dream from her mind as well. She told Adam only of Spring Lily's visit when he returned. And asked him about Isolde.

"You needn't protect me from unpleasant subjects," she said, gazing at him sprawled against his willow backrest. "I'd rather know."

"There was no point in spoiling our holiday here. James just told me recently, and there's nothing we can do at the moment." He touched his earring, an unconscious gesture to ward off evil.

"You're going to need more than your medicine to see her out of your life," Flora said, her smile benevolent, charmed by his intrinsic spirituality. His earrings were restored now that Lucie was well, and he had the look of an Absarokee warrior in elkskin leggings and moccasins, his torso bare in the summer heat.

"We'll worry about her later," he casually replied. "At the moment I'm more interested in swimming. The water looks damned inviting in this heat. Let's take Lucie."

They spent a lazy day *en famille*, swimming in the river, lying in the sun, riding up into the hills late in the afternoon when the heat of the day had dissipated. And that night after Lucie fell asleep, they sat under the stars, listening to the drums accompanying the dancers, the rhythm pulsing through the darkness to their secluded hermitage on the riverbank.

They made love with lingering slowness, both touched by a special enchantment, the majesty of the vast night sky a dazzling canopy above them. Bliss was written in the stars that night in the summer of their love. And they lay in each other's arms till the moon sank toward the amber streak of dawn.

Very early the next morning, it was Adam who held her head when Flora vomited, wiped her face when she was through, and carried her back to the lodge.

"I was afraid of this," he said, tucking her back into bed. "It was just a matter of time until you succumbed to cholera too. Luckily we still have Dr. Potts's medicine, and I'll take care of you until you're feeling better." Ned Storham would have to wait, he thought, rearranging his schedule. They'd have to put added scouts out to detect Ned's forces should they approach the Musselshell.

"It's not cholera," Flora faintly said, her stomach still indisposed and shaky. "I threw up yesterday morning too, but Spring Lily made me tea and it helped. I didn't feel sick again the rest of the day. If it was cholera, darling," she noted, "I would have been continually sick. Would you mind making me some weak tea?"

When he brought her the steaming cup a short time later, he sat silently as she propped herself on one elbow and drank it, his gaze contemplative, his training as a scout evident in his utter stillness, his concentrated observation.

"It's very effective," Flora gratefully murmured, setting the cup down, tentatively moving into a seated position. "Spring Lily says the two large spoonfuls of sugar are key. I'm an absolute believer after two successive mornings of nausea."

"What do you think it is?" he softly asked. Adam glanced at Lucie peacefully sleeping on her soft bed and remembered Isolde's bouts of morning sickness.

Flora shrugged. "I don't know, but I do know it's not cholera. Look, my skin is pink; it's not dry, my voice is perfectly fine, and I throw up only in the morning. When Spring Lily jumped to conclusions, I had to disagree."

"What conclusions?" His eyes held a quiet intensity.

"The usual ones, apparently, with this kind of nausea. She wasn't aware of my circumstances. Once I told her, she understood."

"That you can't have children, you mean." His voice was low-pitched, subdued.

"Yes. Do you mind that I told her? I somehow feel as if I'm betraying you by not being able to bear your children. Maybe I shouldn't have mentioned it to her."

He shook his head. "That's fine. There's no need for secrecy. Did she agree with you?"

"At first she didn't, but I think it was clear once I explained."

"You look better now," he gently said. "You're not so white. How do you feel?"

"Very well. You make a wonderful nurse. I think I'll keep you."

"You couldn't get rid of me if you tried, *bia*," he said with a warm smile. "I'm here to stay."

•   •   •

Later that day when Flora lay down to keep Lucie company during her nap and promptly fell asleep, Adam went in search of Spring Lily.

He found her with a group of mothers overseeing their young children at play, and when he asked to talk to her, her companions all giggled and tittered, the whispered word *"ba-baru-sabish,"* meaning "super" passing between them, their gazes openly admiring.

"They thought you'd be back in circulation again, when your wife left. They're hoping you still might be," Spring Lily said with a teasing smile as they moved away from the female gathering. "I haven't mentioned that your wife's back again."

"Not for long," Adam brusquely replied. "Although we may not be able to arrange her departure as soon as I expected. Flora seems to be sick."

"She threw up again this morning." It was a statement, not a question. "Do you want to walk or come to my lodge?"

"I'd rather not walk."

He wouldn't have come looking for her unless he had a serious purpose; they would have more privacy in her lodge.

"Is Flora feeling better now?" Spring Lily skirted a group of children playing hoop.

Adam nodded. "I made her tea to your formula. Flora tells me you had some idea what might be causing her indisposition."

"She didn't believe me." Arriving at the entrance to her lodge, Spring Lily gestured him in.

It was cool inside, the site shaded by a large cottonwood. Settling into a comfortable position against an ornate backrest, Adam carefully said, "Tell me what you think."

"Your woman is pregnant."

"How can you be so sure? Flora tells me some past illness precludes such a possibility."

"The doctors, you mean, who told her so. Do you trust doctors?"

He lay perfectly still, digesting the startling possibility. "Some are better than others," he said at last. "The woman doctor who treated us for cholera was capable."

"The doctors haven't seen Flora, though, have they? It's simple enough to see the signs. Are her breasts tender, slightly larger? Is she tired all the time? Is she sick every morning?" She smiled knowingly. "Is she amorous?"

His eyes flared wide for a moment at the last question. "Flora wouldn't appreciate my telling you," he quietly replied. But she *was* noticeably more ardent; a condition he would have considered impossible had he not so recently experienced it.

"You don't have to take my word for it, Tsé-ditsirá-tsi. Wait a few weeks and you'll see for yourself."

"I hope you're right," he said very, very softly, his hushed words vanishing into the cool, dappled light.

"You should have had more children before," Spring Lily said. "But your new woman is healthy and young; she'll give you many babies."

A smile transformed the harsh planes of Adam's face. "I don't know if I actually believe it," he slowly murmured, as if he were trying to come to terms with the momentous idea. "It's very soon—a little more than three weeks."

"The baby is strong inside her; it wants you to know."

"She takes no precautions against pregnancy," he quietly noted. "But she said she's never had to. Couldn't it be cholera instead, or some other illness?" His practical nature required more substantive answers.

"She's nauseous only in the morning," Spring Lily reminded him.

"Hmmmm . . ." Indecision vibrated in his murmured response. "She's had lovers before . . . and never been pregnant." He shook his head. "If she was capable of having a child, why wouldn't this have happened before? She's twenty-six."

Spring Lily shrugged—a small, dismissive movement. But her smile held a gentle consideration for his naïveté. "You're a tyro in these matters, Tsé-ditsirá-tsi. Do you remember White Elk's wife? How she was barren the first three years of their marriage? And when they adopted his brother's son, she became pregnant. Or Pretty Woman, who shed countless tears over her lack of children, and in the summer of victory over the Lakota at Bear Mountain, she found herself with child. I know a score of other women too who have borne babies after years of childless marriages. Should I go on?"

He gazed at her, a half smile on his lips. "Do I detect a certain smug certainty?" he pleasantly inquired.

"I recognize that peaked hue on Flora's face," Spring Lily said. "It's an unmistakable green."

"Say it's true—"

The silent rebuke in her raised brows stopped him.

"The thought pleases me," he corrected himself, the sheer wonder of it reflected in his eyes. Hope shone plainly. He sighed then because he dared not indulge in such cloudless dreams with Ned Storham threatening his very existence. Time enough for blissful fantasies if Ned was defeated. "I'm going to have to leave very soon," Adam said with a sigh of regret, harsh reality intruding. "Ned Storham and Isolde have combined forces, it seems. Will you see to Flora's comfort while I'm gone and help care for Lucie when Flora's not feeling well? I know I can ask this of you."

"I promise, Tsé-ditsirá-tsi. Your family will be safe in my care. But will she let you go?"

It was a volatile subject when it came up a week later.

Adam had postponed his departure as long as possible, but he had to leave without fail by morning. Word had reached him that Ned Storham was scouring the country far afield, looking for men ready to risk their lives for gold. They were assembling in Helena by the middle of the month.

Seven more mornings of sickness had convinced Flora of the blissful fact she was indeed pregnant, and though she didn't understand the nuances of how or why, she was already fiercely protective of the small life inside her. She strongly objected to Adam's risking his life.

"I'd like this child to have a father when it's born," she vehemently said, the small evening fire in the center of the lodge illuminating her moody resentment. "Send the others out."

"I can't ask my friends to fight for me." He kept his voice neutral; he didn't want to leave in anger. "A man has to have the courage to defend his country and family."

"Hire gunmen, as Storham does. Let them fight your battles." Her eyes were dark, stormy.

"They're undependable." He'd been trained as a warrior; she didn't realize what that entailed.

"What about the law? Certainly they won't allow your land to be taken from you illegally."

Land was taken away every day by those with better weapons or influence or both. "The judicial system won't keep Ned Storham off my land," he quietly said.

"You can't go! Do you think I want to lose you now!" she cried. "Don't you care about this child? Don't you care about me? I should have *known*," she heatedly added, "when you had Spring Lily take Lucie tonight. You *knew* you were leaving."

"There isn't anyone else to fight my battles," he softly said. "No court to slap Ned Storham's hands and make him go home, no aristocratic privilege to protect me— only myself. I won't take any chances, I promise."

"That doesn't mean anything, dammit," she hotly retorted, "when you're riding out to face an army of hired thugs led by a man who kills anyone in his way. Why did you have to shoot his brother?"

How did she know, he wondered, when he hadn't told her! And his surprise must have shown because she fretfully said, "Papa mentioned it by mistake. He can't keep track of what you withhold from my innocent ears. Dammit, you shouldn't have killed Frank Storham."

"I tried not to the first time, but if I hadn't killed him, none of us would have ever been safe."

"So you just shot him?" She wasn't being reasonable, only thin-skinned and maternal.

"You don't understand," he said, the rising anger in his

voice tightly restrained. "This isn't Mayfair or Pall Mall," he said, "but a territory where you survive as long as you can defend yourself. There's no one but myself to protect my land. Out here people take things from you if you're weaker. Do you know how many men I've seen shot down or hanged in cold blood?

"This isn't civilization with civilized rules or expensive lawyers to fight your battles in court where no one gets bloody. They want to kill me, do you understand?" he softly said. "And unless I kill them first, they will. I'm sorry you're upset. I wish I could comfort you. I wish I didn't have to constantly fight off encroachments on my land. I'd like to die of old age in my bed with you beside me. But to be able to do that," he slowly enunciated, "I have to kill Ned Storham and probably someone else next year or next month or tomorrow. I have valuable land— some of the best range land in the territory. And I'm keeping it."

"I hate when you talk like that, I hate your warrior code!" Flora exclaimed, agitation trembling in her voice. "I don't want you to die!"

"I'm not going to," Adam firmly said. "I'm coming back to you and Lucie and"—he smiled—"our child."

"Promise?" A small, fearful whisper. Defeated by her own sense of logic, justice, and reason, she resigned herself to the inevitable. Ned Storham wasn't going to disappear without violence.

"Promise," he softly said, reaching across the buffalo robe to draw her into his arms.

"When?" With her cheek pressed against his shoulder, the sound was muffled and low.

"I don't know." When Ned Storham is on his way to hell, he thought, and Isolde traveling back to Europe. "Very soon, I hope. Kiss me now and tell me about the baby. I want to talk of more pleasant things. Are you wishing for a boy or a girl?" he softly queried, holding her gently. "Do you think Cloudy will ever let us hold it—or will Lucie? Are you as happy as I am that we're having a baby?" He gently stroked her hair.

"I'm so happy, there's no measurement, no words. And if you weren't leaving me . . ."

"Not for long," he whispered.

"Truly?" She felt like a small child in her fear, a strange sensation after a lifetime of successfully facing challenges.

"Word of honor."

But Adam had been gone only half a day when Flora found herself debating a variety of ways she might be of help to him. She understood why he had to face Ned Storham and that her presence would add risk to his undertaking. But why couldn't she offer aid in some adjunct role? She wasn't a novice with a weapon.

Wasn't she obliged to support him for the sake of their child, and for Lucie? she reflected. Shouldn't she help diminish the odds against the man she loved? Why shouldn't she assist in protecting their future too?

Walking over to her father's lodge, where the men were packing an assortment of Absarokee clothing to send back to the museum in Göttingen, she casually declared, "I've been thinking of following Adam and James. Would you be willing to come along?"

The earl looked up, saw her face, and set the basket in his hands aside. "I know how you feel, but Adam wouldn't approve," he said. "He's concerned for your safety."

"Are my concerns for his safety inconsequential?" Her voice held a restless edge.

"I'm not arguing the point, darling," her father soothingly replied. "I'm only suggesting Adam would rather you stay in camp."

"Well, I'm not staying. Are you willing to come with me?"

Henry stopped folding a beaded shirt and looked at the earl. Alan and Douglas, too, watched their employer.

"Of course you know I will." If the earl had been averse to danger and adventure, he'd be living in Yorkshire. He'd found it as difficult as Flora to stay behind. "But what of Lucie?" he queried. "Will she be alarmed if we leave?"

"Why don't I ask her?" Flora promptly said, feeling in control of her life again.

Dressed like the other children in camp, Lucie was indistinguishable from her friends and cousins, and in the way of children having fun, she had to be cajoled away from her play for a moment of conversation.

Kneeling before her, Flora said, "Would you mind if I followed your father and James on their war party?"

Lucie's gaze returned to Flora from a quick perusal of the running game in progress. "Are you going alone?" the young child asked, familiar with war parties. "Papa never goes alone."

"No, Georgie, Alan, Douglas, and Henry would all come along too. I wouldn't be alone, and Spring Lily will take care of you until we return."

"I'll be right back!" she shouted to her friends before returning her attention to Flora. "May I go back and play now?" she politely inquired. "We're playing horse race and I'm winning."

Trauma was averted.

Lucie had been raised in the midst of a large, extended Absarokee family; she was assured of her father's love; her nanny would defend her against demons from the depths of the stygian gloom. And successfully, Flora reflected with a smile.

She was a child secure in her varied worlds.

Chapter Twenty-four

❧❧

Adam and James entered Helena alone, intent on the simple mission of persuading Isolde to leave. She was staying with Harold and Molly Fisk, Adam discovered after they'd arrived. A sensible precaution, he thought. But, then, she always knew how to protect her interests.

That meant he'd have to deal with Isolde in a more civilized manner than he wished. His first impulse had been to tie her up, toss her into the stage for Salt Lake City, and have the driver see that she transferred at that point for the East. Knowing Isolde's resilience, she'd no doubt be back on the return run, he ruefully acknowledged, so he'd have to make his position *extremely* clear this time.

Deathly clear.

After he and James settled in at the Planters House, they bathed and dressed. While Adam called on his wife at the Fisk mansion, James had his own agenda—gathering information on Ned Storham's current whereabouts.

Both men wore their guns.

It was late morning and very warm, even up on the hill where the wealthy had built their homes. Adam's face was grim as he walked up the brickwork path to the front door; the task of running Isolde out of the territory would have been more easily done in a private setting.

That was precisely why she was ensconced at the Fisks.

Molly came forward in a welcoming flurry of navy silk and rustling petticoats when Adam was announced, crossing the formidable space of the drawing room in a breathless rush.

"How absolutely wonderful to see you again. Wasn't I just saying yesterday how splendid it would be if Adam were to come into town?" she exclaimed, turning to the other two occupants of the room for confirmation.

Henrietta flushed in her excitement and stammered an inaudible greeting.

Isolde calmly said, "How nice to see you again, Adam."

"Come in, come in, dear boy," Molly asserted, guiding Adam with a hand on his arm. "Can I get you tea?" One look at Adam's expression, and she said, "Perhaps a bourbon and branch water? Is it too early?"

"A double, please."

"Ice would be nice today, wouldn't it?" she added, responding to his abrupt reply. "Sit down and I'll have one for you in a jiffy."

And after a fussing interval with a maidservant, she turned back to them all with a smile. "You must tell us about Saratoga," she said as the maid handed Adam his bourbon. "I hear your racers won some very good money." What she really meant was "Tell us about Lady Flora." Isolde had already been quite explicit. But, of course, there were always two points of view.

"We went out to test Magnus and some of our other young ones, and they performed well," Adam replied, wondering how long he could manage to be polite. Or if he even cared to.

"Harold says we'll definitely go for the season next year. Henrietta's dear papa always goes to the Spa; he says it's a marvelous place to do business. And wasn't it a shame about poor Frank Storham? They just buried him yesterday. Not that I had any fondness for the man," she hastened on, "for he always drank more than was quite acceptable. But, well . . . he's dead," she maladroitly noted. "It does make one consider the frailty of life."

"James mentioned his death to me," Adam said. "The Storhams seem to put themselves in dangerous positions. And, then, Frank did always have an unsteady gun hand." He spoke without inflection, his face a mask.

"Ned's saying you killed him," Isolde casually said, smiling at Adam over the rim of her teacup.

"Ned can say anything he pleases," Adam replied, "but since he wasn't in Saratoga, it would be difficult to take his accusation seriously."

Now that he'd found love, he wondered how he could have suffered Isolde's bland malice for so long. She was completely without compassion or feeling. He had no illusions about her friendship with Ned Storham. She and Ned in combination couldn't be improved on for cold-blooded greed.

"Who would possibly believe Ned Storham anyway?" Henrietta hotly interjected. "He's an uncouth bully. Auntie won't have him in the house," she declared.

"How sweet," Isolde cooed. "The darling girl is defending you, Adam. Another conquest?" she queried, her voice fragrant with spite.

"I'm afraid Henrietta's right," Molly affirmed, stepping in to mitigate Isolde's contentious venom. "I've told Harold he can't invite the man to the house, regardless that Ned Storham has large deposits in Harold's bank. He's much too vulgar."

Henrietta smiled at Isolde with a stabbing triumph.

"He must be a very tedious man," Isolde coolly said, "but, then, so many are rough-and-tumble out here. Will dear Henrietta be coming out at court anywhere?" she deftly went on, plunging her retaliating stiletto with precision. "I know how difficult it can sometimes be to find a sponsor." What was left unsaid was the contrast between the parvenu nature of Henrietta's American fortune and Isolde's ancient ducal lineage.

"I'll be coming out in London," Henrietta proudly retorted, the subtlety of Isolde's thrust lost upon her. She was proud of her father's money, and it wasn't new to *her*, for he'd had it as long as she could remember. "I'm just eighteen."

Adam smiled faintly. Henrietta's riposte was masterful. He supposed Isolde, at twenty-seven, did seem aged from her vantage point, he thought, recalling Henrietta's flirtatious comments on the attraction of "older" men.

"How bright the world looks at eighteen," Molly tactfully declared, mildly unnerved by the hostility in the air. She'd forgotten how antipathetic the Serres' marriage was. "I imagine we all remember those blissful days."

"I hadn't met you yet," Isolde said to Adam, her gaze icy.

Deciding not to respond in kind, Adam neutrally said, "I don't think I even saw France for most of my eighteenth year."

"Which accounts for your interesting barbarism." Isolde's voice was sugar sweet.

"What part of it do you find interesting, madame?" Adam coolly inquired, the sudden snapping of his temper almost audible in his chill rebuke. Draining his bourbon, he set his glass down, stood abruptly, and turning to his hostess, said in a voice so cold, "Would you please excuse my wife and me? We have business to discuss, and my time is limited."

Molly stood as if propelled from her chair, glanced at her niece, who understood that tone of voice too and was already rising, and stammered, "Of course . . . I understand. . . . Henrietta, come."

In seconds Adam was alone with his wife for the second time in a month.

His anger showed. In his clenched fists, in the heated depths of his eyes, in the rigidity of his spine as he stood limned by the pale light of the lace-curtained window behind him.

"Will you shoot me with that gun?" Isolde coldly asked, all pretense of civility gone, the hatred in her eyes flagrant.

"It's a thought," he bluntly said. "Several of my friends have persistently encouraged me."

"James, I suppose, the hateful man. You won't, of course. You're too ethical."

"At least one of us is."

"Ethics are for bourgeoisie."

"The Serres outrank your family, Isolde, and they're aware of the term. But I didn't come here to argue philosophy with you. I'm here to tell you to leave Montana and don't come back."

"I still have rights as your wife, Adam. It's not going to be that easy. And I didn't journey through this dusty, hot, miserable country to abruptly leave again. By the way, I took some of my things from the ranch last week. Apparently you haven't been there for some time. Mrs. McLeod was difficult, as usual."

"Cloudy misunderstands your charitable nature," he sarcastically drawled. "I'm surprised she let you in the door."

"I explained I wouldn't be staying at the ranch."

"Incentive, then, for her tolerance. But you won't be staying in Helena either. I want you to return to Europe."

"How authoritarian you've become. I'm afraid I can't accommodate you. I have other plans."

"Ned Storham can't help you."

"Perhaps I disagree."

"He'll be dead in a few days."

"Or you will."

"Don't count on it."

"But I am."

He sighed, relaxing marginally, all this very old battle ground, none of it useful to the purpose of his visit. "Suit yourself," he said. "I'm not here to negotiate or argue." He paused for a moment, wanting to be certain she was listening, so there wouldn't be any mistaking his message, and then, moving closer, he quietly said, "Either be on the stage for Salt Lake City tomorrow morning, or I'll see that you are."

She looked up at him with bland eyes. "You don't frighten me."

"That's because I've always been too pleasant. I'm very serious now. Don't discount my sense of purpose."

"You're not even going to offer me more money to leave you in peace with your new paramour?"

"No." He was done buying, paying, cajoling, looking the other way, ignoring the fact that his life was passing by while other people were enjoying happiness. By the merest stroke of fate, because of a duty visit to Judge Parkman's one night, he now had an opportunity to possess what other people possessed: a family, love, peace and contentment, happiness, perhaps more children if the spirits were kind. "No," he firmly repeated, his hand unconsciously moving to his Colt. "Not a penny more."

"You sound very dramatic." Her ladylike pose hadn't altered, her hands lightly clasped in her lap, her perfectly coiffed head tipped slightly to one side as though she were listening intently, the tips of her perfectly aligned shoes peeking out from beneath her rose-colored tea gown.

"If you're not on the stage tomorrow, you'll be the recipient of some real drama, Isolde. Be warned."

"Such brute purpose, darling. Should I quiver in fear?"

His teeth shone briefly white in a grim smile. "Fine. Pleasant journey, Isolde." And he walked from the room.

"We'll see whose journey is more pleasant," she softly said as the door closed behind him, and leaning over, she picked up her teacup with a satisfied smile.

When Adam exited the room, he found Molly waiting in the foyer, nervously wringing her hands. Her sigh of relief brought a genuine smile to Adam's face.

"I wouldn't do the deed here, Molly," he pleasantly said. "Rest easy, although it's damned tempting right now, considering she just told me she expects me dead in a few days."

"Ned Storham's deal with your wife," Molly unreservedly declared. "I didn't want to take her in, Adam. I hope you know that. But she's your wife. I couldn't say no."

"I understand all the myriad ramifications, Molly. No need to apologize. I was wondering, though," he went on, smiling down at her, "what your plans were for the evening."

"What would you like my plans to be?" she asked with a smile of her own. She'd always had a soft spot in her heart for the rakish Comte de Chastellux, and if she'd been twenty years younger, she would have been tempted to forget her marriage vows for a night or two with the charming rogue.

"If you were to take a ride out to the hills west of town to view the sunset this evening before dinner, I feel sure Isolde would prefer staying home. Take Henrietta too."

"How long should we be gone?"

"An hour should be enough."

"I hear you've fallen in love at last," she gently said.

"For once the gossip is right," Adam admitted with a faint smile. "So I'm trying to set my life in order. I paid Isolde in Saratoga to leave the country. I was surprised to hear she'd come to Montana."

"I imagine her pregnancy motivated her journey," Molly matter of factly asserted.

"Is she telling everyone it's mine? It's not, of course. Should I place a disclaimer in the local paper?" he sarcastically murmured.

"No need, my boy," Molly soothed. "She had a miscarriage."

Ever suspicious of Isolde's machinations, he asked, "Did she tell you that?"

"We're not on such intimate terms, darling, but unlike your wife, who thinks servants are subhuman, my maids talk to me. I know everything that goes on in my household. Isolde was bleeding heavily when she arrived several days ago. But I'm informed now the countess's health is fully restored."

"It couldn't be something else . . . I mean . . . how—"

"No," Molly interjected, curtailing Adam's embarrassed query. "I'm absolutely sure." She smiled. "Would you like the details?"

"No," he quickly replied, breaking into a beaming

smile. "Jesus, Molly, do you know what you've just given me?"

"Freedom?" she archly said, her eyes amused. "A new—" her sentence ended in a startled gasp as Adam pulled her into his arms and kissed her soundly.

"Thank you, Mrs. Fisk," he said with a wide grin as he steadied his hostess on her trembling legs. "I shall be eternally grateful," he solemnly pronounced, the gravity of his declaration mitigated at the last by a throaty chuckle.

"Thought you should know," Molly cheerfully noted. "Knew you'd be pleased. The countess has a real art of irritating."

"I've noticed that," Adam said, his grin irrepressible. "Why don't I have you to lunch this afternoon to celebrate Isolde's imminent departure? Say the Planters House at two?"

"I suppose this means I have to change my plans for Henrietta," Molly teased.

"You're welcome to bring her along."

"Such pretense, Adam, from a man of your intelligence."

"You didn't really think you had a chance of implementing those plans, now, did you?" he softly queried.

Molly shrugged. "Harold told me I was crazy."

Adam smiled. "He was right, darling. What about Ellis Green?" he playfully suggested. "He has plenty of money for Henrietta's papa."

"Maybe I should invite him to dinner." Her statement was simultaneously thoughtful and teasing.

"But not tonight."

"No. We'll dine alone tonight. Harold prefers a quiet dinner."

"That would work extremely well for me," Adam murmured with a faint smile. "At two, then?" And bowing over her hand, he took his leave.

Before Harold Fisk went home from the bank that day for his midday meal, he tracked Adam down. When he'd run into James earlier that morning, he'd learned Adam was in town. He found James and Adam inspecting the condition of a stout carriage at the livery stable.

"Needing a stagecoach?" Harold queried, walking into the stall where the coach was parked.

"I hope so," Adam said with a brief smile. "I saw Molly this morning."

"And our houseguest, I'll warrant." Harold's mouth was a straight, grim line.

"My condolences on having to put up with her."

"Can't say she's very pleasant, but, then, she never was."

"Isolde may be curtailing her visit," James said.

"None of my business, I'm sure," Harold quickly replied, then, swiftly glancing around as if spies were on his trail, he added, "Actually, she's partly the reason I came looking for you. Just found out word of Ned Storham's travel plans. Seems the two of them came up from Cheyenne together. Not a pretty picture," he declared, wiping his forehead with his handkerchief. His face was visibly flushed even in the cool, shaded stable interior. "You know everyone fights his own battles out here," he prudently noted, "but I thought you'd like to know Ned's on his way to the Musselshell." He took another quick look around before he murmured, "No one will interfere and no one will miss him."

"I appreciate the information, Harold," Adam said, although he'd already received news of Ned's direction from his men in Virginia City. But the offer of carte blanche was reassuring. Not that he couldn't adequately defend his position, but it never hurt to have other influential men on your side.

"Seems to me your land claim is as legal as they get," Harold emphatically stated. "Our damned governor couldn't even get a private act of Congress passed."

"My father had personal friends in Washington," Adam noted. "He wanted my mother happy and her clan protected."

"Well, just wanted to say good luck. The men with Ned are mostly scoundrels. They'll run."

"That's what I was thinking," Adam said.

"And our weapon arsenal is first-rate," James added.

"Good . . . good . . . glad to hear it." Banker Fisk was noticeably agitated. Ned Storham had a great deal of money in his bank too, and it wouldn't look right—his choosing sides. There were those who privately looked askance at Adam's half-blood heritage, although none of them would openly acknowledge their feelings. The Comte de Chastellux was too powerful. "You know Judge Parkman will cover you if any Storham heirs make trouble."

Adam smiled. "So he said. I received a message at the hotel. Thank you, Harold." He put out his hand, genuinely appreciative of Harold's efforts when he had many other wealthy depositors to appease.

"I'll be saying good-bye, then. Bring Lady Flora to dinner—later." He nervously smiled.

"Our pleasure," Adam replied. "Maybe Flora can win some more of our money."

"Only yours, Adam," the banker said with a chuckle. "She plays too rich for my blood."

Flora and her father rode into Helena at midafternoon. They'd kept a steady pace from the camp on the Yellowstone, stopping to sleep for only a few hours the previous night. Henry, Alan, and Douglas followed, the entire party dust-covered and warm—the fall day cloudless and bright with sunshine.

Flora drew eyes as she passed down the street, dressed as she was in trousers and a tailored shirt. Women rarely rode astride; female legs were generally concealed beneath voluminous skirts, and an armed woman was unusual enough to elicit stares. The fact that the leather of Flora's rifle and pistol holsters had a well-worn sheen only added fascination.

The wide brim of her flat-crowned western hat shaded her face, but her beauty was unmistakable, as was her luxurious auburn hair tied with a narrow black ribbon at the nape of her neck. Even had she not been dressed and armed like a man, her splendid looks would have drawn attention.

Some townspeople recognized her from her previous visit. Helena society was small. Others who stopped to gaze at her from the sidewalks bordering the main street wondered who she was. Her name passed from those who knew to those who didn't, the flurry of question and answer, tittle and tattle, following in her wake as the party from the Yellowstone rode down the sloping street to the livery stable.

"That's Lady Flora . . . her father's riding beside her . . . an earl from England . . . they travel all over the world."

"Ellis Green was sweet on her."

"She took the count from Aspen Valley for two hundred thousand at Harold Fisk's one night . . . five-card draw . . . plays poker like a man."

"Don't look like a man."

"Count didn't think so either, rumor has it."

Tucked between the Miners' Bank and the new law offices of Cordell Harper, Letitia Granville's millinery shop had a bow window with a clear view of the street. And since Cordell's voice carried through the open doorway as he stood outside his office with his law clerk, Letitia and her two customers took note of the horsemen riding by.

"Damn, she's a beauty. She could have any man in the territory, even if she weren't titled and rich as Croesus." Coming from Cordell Harper, who had the most avaricious mind in town, the compliment suggested the infinite measure of Flora's beauty. "Howdy, Lady Flora!" he shouted. "Hey, over here! How-de-do!"

When Flora turned with a smile, Letitia's customer seated at the small mirrored table momentarily stiffened, and her pale-blue eyes narrowed into grim slits. A second later the Comtesse de Chastellux untied the pink silk bow of the bonnet she'd been trying on, lifted it from her blond curls, and, handing it to the plump proprietor hovering over her, coolly said, "Charge it to my husband and send it to the Fisks." Putting her mauve velvet toque back on, she swiftly adjusted the languid fall of feathers, cast a practiced glance into the mirror to see that the tilt of the bonnet was properly perched over the curls on her forehead, and rising, walked from the shop without a word.

"Did you see that?" Letitia whispered to the principal's wife, keeping one eye on Isolde's departing form. "Her husband's lover . . ." The milliner's rotund form quivered with excitement.

"*I* saw the count and Lady Flora dancing together the night they met at Judge Parkman's in Virginia City," Effie Humphries fervently declared, "and I swear, Letitia dear, those two raised the temperature in the room a good thirty degrees. Every lady there had to dab the sweat from her upper lip when they walked outside."

"I heard the stories of what happened *then*!" Mrs. Granville's voice was breathy with scandal. "Where do you think the countess is going?"

"If we're careful to stay out of sight," the principal's wife whispered, putting her finger to her mouth in warning and indicating the doorway with a nod of her head, "we can watch."

Isolde paused on the sidewalk for the brief time necessary to survey the street in the direction Flora had ridden, her nostrils flaring at the sight of the riders dismounting at the livery stable. As if scenting her prey, she drew in a breath, smiled, and moved determinedly in their direction.

"Why don't you go ahead to the Planters House?" the earl said to Flora as he began unbuckling his saddlebags. "We'll be along shortly."

"I won't even politely demur," Flora replied with a faint smile. "A soft bed sounds heavenly after a day in the saddle."

"Maybe you could order some lunch for us," her father suggested, lifting his saddlebag free. "And something cool and wet," he added with a grin.

"Done," Flora responded with a nod. "Do you think

Adam's still here?" she asked. Although his trail led them to Helena, once in town, it was impossible to follow.

"I'll find out," her father assured her. "Go, now. It's been a long ride."

She had the loose-gaited stride of a horseman, Isolde disdainfully noted, taking in Flora's long-legged tread as she moved up the gentle rise toward the Planters House. Although with her mannish attire, it shouldn't be surprising. Adam had been out in the wilderness too long, his wife spitefully thought, her stylish high heels delicately clicking down the wooden sidewalk. He'd lost his taste for femininity.

Or perhaps the earl's daughter had found a new way to amuse him. Could it be Adam had tired of conventional females? Regardless of the reasons, Isolde tartly thought, she wanted the hussy—whatever her appeal—to understand that Isolde de Plesy de Chastellux would *remain* the Comtesse de Chastellux. Adam's title was hers by marriage, and she wasn't about to relinguish it simply because he'd taken a fancy to his newest bed warmer.

Isolde's pale curls caught the sunlight, so Flora noticed her when she was still some distance away.

"Damnation!" Flora swore. Even though she knew Isolde was in the territory, what the hell were the odds she'd walk into her at *this* precise moment, on *this* afternoon in Helena? Damn! What bloody bad luck!

Just walk by, she cautioned herself. Ignore the countess. A modest number of pedestrians populated the immediate vicinity. Surely, under the circumstances, Isolde wouldn't make a scene.

But she steeled herself.

Seconds later Isolde stood blocking her way, the width of her crinolined skirt a bar to Flora's passage, her posture aggressive, her chill gaze taking in Flora's unusual clothing. "Does he like you dressed like that?" the Comtesse de Chastellux scornfully inquired, insult in every syllable.

"Better than he likes you in any attire," Flora calmly replied, although she experienced a sudden longing for her riding quirt to mitigate Isolde's derisive sneer. "Now, why not stand aside?" she went on in a carefully neutral tone. "There's no point in conversing. We've no grounds for agreement on anything."

"We're sharing the same man," Isolde murmured with malicious sweetness, leaning slightly forward so her elegant skirt swayed like a silken pendulum. "Surely that's common ground enough."

"We're not sharing anything except the air in Helena. You don't have him to share."

"A court might disagree."

"But a court can't give him back to you. Why not let him go?" Flora quietly suggested. "You don't love him."

"An inconsequential emotion," Isolde replied with a contemptuous snap. "We're *irrevocably* married." And she noted with gratification the sudden flaring pain in Flora's eyes.

"All good wishes, then, for a prosperous future," Flora softly murmured, sensible of the futility of their conversation, beginning to move around Isolde's spreading skirts.

Lifting her furled parasol, Isolde stopped her.

"You'll never keep him," the countess coldly said, holding the flat of the parasol against Flora's waist. "Even if he survives Ned's plans for revenge, he'll tire of you, as he has all the others. Females have always kept him company —in great numbers. But, then, you knew that, didn't you?" She smiled faintly at the distress she was causing. Flora had gone quite pale.

"We're having a child," Flora said into the small silence, wanting the cold, brutal woman to know, defending herself against Isolde's cruelty with a brutality of her own.

"Really." Not a flicker of emotion registered on the mannequinlike face. "It's not a very original ploy."

"It's not a ploy at all, but a great miracle. I don't expect you to understand." And taking the wrapped silk of the parasol in a hard grip, Flora wrenched the ebony handle from Isolde's gloved fingers.

A flinching shock suddenly displaced the countess's haughty disdain. "Look," Flora said with a small sigh of restraint. "Why not find someone else to harass? I don't want Adam's title. Mine is quite sufficient. You can remain the Comtesse de Chastellux with my blessing." She placed the parasol against the brick wall of Sherman's Emporium.

"While you publicly usurp my position, you impertinent jade!" Isolde spat. Finding herself braver as she snatched up her parasol, she heatedly added, "I'll see that you rue the day you crossed my path. I'll see that you're cut from society."

"Society rarely interests me," Flora replied. "But when it does, rest assured, my fortune allows me continuing entrée. You certainly know that incontrovertible fact, Isolde. Money opens all doors. Oh, by the way," Flora said with a grin as she began walking past Isolde, "my tits are getting bigger already."

She shouldn't have said it, she thought. She'd suppressed the flip remark several times in the last few seconds. It was unladylike, perhaps unkind, certainly too irreverent for such a seriously daunting occasion.

But then she saw Isolde's expression alter to a vivid, lethal intensity, and she didn't mind anymore that she'd been uncharitable.

"I should have had you killed in Saratoga," Isolde said so softly, it sent a small chill down Flora's spine.

Half turning back to the lady who was dressed for the Parisian drawing rooms and boulevards, Flora said, "Go home, Isolde. Go away." Her voice dropped to a murmur. "I won't let you win. And I can kill you myself if I wish."

There was a distinct sputtering sound behind her as she resumed her journey to the Planters House. A minor victory of sorts, Flora thought with a smile. How often, she wondered, had Isolde been left speechless?

Chapter Twenty-five

When Adam, Molly, and Henrietta walked out of the dining room of the Planters House, Flora and Lord Haldane were in the lobby. The earl, having arrived shortly after Flora, was at the front desk arranging for a room, while Flora waited for him in a comfortable chair. Lounging with her head against the padded back, she first caught a glimpse of Adam from under the veil of her lashes.

Her eyes snapped open, her mouth curved into a smile, and she was rising from her chair when she saw him turn to his right and put his arm around Molly Fisk, who came into view from behind a fluted pillar. As they moved down the passageway leading from the restaurant, Henrietta appeared on Adam's left, and Flora's smile abruptly vanished.

Gazing at the friendly scene, she cautioned herself to restraint—no doubt some reasonable explanation existed.

Adam immediately saw Flora as she emerged from behind one of the numerous potted palms decorating the lobby, and, considering her unexpected appearance, she gave him high points for poise. "You're a long way from camp," he calmly said, dropping his arm from Molly's shoulder, taking in her dusty trail clothes with a swift glance. "I thought you were staying on the Yellowstone." The faintest rebuke lingered in his tone.

"Obviously," Flora retorted. "Am I interrupting anything?"

"Adam was kind enough to take us to lunch," Molly interceded. "We're celebrating the imminent departure of my houseguest, the Comtesse de Chastellux."

"Celebrating?"

"Isolde's leaving for Europe tonight," Adam said.

"Are you sure?" Skepticism arched Flora's brows. "I just saw her on the street, and she seemed intent on maintaining her position here."

"Accept my apologies . . . then . . . for Isolde." His last, he hoped. "She's always difficult."

"More than difficult, I'd say. I wouldn't count on her leaving."

"Perhaps she simply wanted the last word," Adam suggested, taking Flora's hand in his, not wishing to dwell on Isolde's presence in Montana. Flora didn't seem unduly upset by her encounter, and by nightfall his wife would be gone. "She won't want to be here once the weather turns cold," he said, explaining Isolde's departure plans in a highly edited recital, "and an early snow could close some of the travel routes. She'd never take the chance of missing the Parisian season. So I think she's actually going this time," he declared. "Thanks in large part to Molly's assistance in arranging for Isolde's trunks and luggage. This lunch is small payment for her aid," he said with a smile.

"How very strange this must seem to you," Flora said to Molly, understanding the reason for Adam's cheer. "But thank you very much."

"We've our share of strange stories out here on the frontier, Lady Flora," Molly replied. "Some of them pretty violent, and the countess never did take to the country. She always complained about the dust," Molly added with a smile, surveying Flora's utilitarian clothing coated with trail dirt.

"I'm afraid she wouldn't approve, then," Flora noted, glancing down at her coated boots and trousers. "But I only just arrived and haven't had time to change yet."

Adam quickly surveyed the lobby. "You didn't come alone, did you?"

"Of course not," she calmly replied. "Papa's arranging a room, and Alan, Douglas, and Henry are still at the livery stable."

"You shouldn't have ridden that far. Are you tired? You must be, and hungry too, I suppose," he said with a grin, her appetite prodigious since her pregnancy.

He suddenly seemed unaware of the others, his concern obvious, the affection in his voice low, intimate, causing any third party to feel de trop. "I think we'll be on our way now," Molly obligingly said. "Thank you for the lunch, Adam, and our best wishes and congratulations to you both."

"Adam told you about the baby!" Flora exclaimed. "We're ecstatic, aren't we darling?" she jubilantly said, gazing up at Adam.

Choking, Adam disguised his shock with a small cough. "Absolutely thrilled," he manfully agreed.

"We're expecting in the spring," Flora explained, obviously elated. "Or at least that's what Spring Lily tells me. I'm a total novice. Adam had to convince me finally that it's true."

Molly would have liked to have witnessed that exchange, entertained by the notion that the man who'd been caution itself when it came to his choice of amorous partners—always preferring women enlightened about birth control—had to explain impending motherhood to his naive lover. "How opportune the timing," Molly graciously declared. "Spring is a perfect time to have a baby."

"Anytime would be a perfect time," Adam said, pulling Flora into his arms in full sight of everyone in the crowded lobby.

"You're making a scene," Flora murmured, gazing up at him with a languorous smile.

"*Now* I'm making a scene," he corrected, lifting her into his arms, smearing his black frock coat and embroidered vest with the fine gray dust from her clothes. "Good afternoon, Molly, Henrietta," he said with a dismissive nod and a lighthearted smile. "We have a few things to discuss." And strolling away toward the stairs, he kissed her as an audible gasp from onlookers momentarily silenced the buzz of conversation in the luxurious lobby.

"He's really, truly in love with her, Auntie," Henrietta mournfully declared, watching Adam carry Flora up the flight of red-carpeted stairs in great, long strides. "Did you see how he looked at her? How he smiled at her when she said they're having a baby? I'll never have him now," she lamented.

"I'm afraid you're right, darling," Molly commiserated, patting her niece's gloved hand. "It's a shock to me as well. I never thought I'd see the day when Adam Serre fell in love. Although I'm pleased for him. He's had his share of misery the last few years. If the countess was going to stay much longer," Molly averred, "I'd kill her myself. You needn't worry, though, darling," she soothed. "You're young, pretty, and very rich. You won't lack suitors."

"But none as wickedly handsome as Adam," Henrietta fretfully replied.

"Let's think about this on our way home," Molly suggested, taking her niece's hand and moving toward the street entrance. "What do you say to having Ellis Green over for dinner tomorrow? He's certainly an attractive man. I know it's short notice, but your uncle will ask him for us. Now, who else could we invite? Do you think Maud Henley would like to come with her new husband? Or perhaps that nice Mr. Belton."

"Oh, Auntie," Henrietta sighed, marginally restored from her doldrums. "Do you think Ellis Green would ever notice little old me? He's so handsome."

"I've a feeling he'll not only notice you but like you immensely," Molly assured her. Henrietta's millionaire father would be of distinct interest to Ellis, she knew, for Ellis had political ambitions, like all his family. He'd understand with that male practicality that made politics the art of compromise how useful it would be to align himself with a family as influential as Henrietta's. She'd have Harold mention to Ellis when he invited him that Henrietta's very generous marriage portion also included a stately home in Washington.

"He's ever so tall," Henrietta cooed, "and his manners are divine." A smile lifted the curve of her large mouth. "What should I wear, Auntie?"

Apparently her heart wasn't permanently damaged by Adam's loss, Molly dryly noted. But at eighteen, whose was?

"You shouldn't have come," Adam said, kicking the door of his hotel room shut, "but now that you're here, I can't think of anyone else I'd rather spend the afternoon with." His smile was very close.

"Doing what?" Flora playfully murmured. "Although I warn you, after seeing Henrietta lusting after you, I'm in a decidedly possessive mood."

Leaning against the door, Adam gazed down at her with amusement. "We probably don't want to be disturbed, then. Should you tell your father where you are?"

"Oh, Lord!" Flora ruefully exclaimed. "I forgot! Put me down. Where's the bell for the maid? Adam! Put me down."

"Relax, darling," Adam said with a grin. "He saw us."

"Are you sure?"

"He waved and smiled, so I'm *pretty* sure," Adam teasingly replied.

"You're supposed to be nice to the mother of your child," Flora said, pouting with a decidedly seductive allure.

"I intend to be in just a minute," he murmured, the heat in his gaze tantalizing. "And indulgent and pampering and *very* gratifying."

"In that case," she whispered, sorcery in her voice and violet eyes, "you're forgiven."

They spent a heated, sensual afternoon in bed while James entertained Lord Haldane.

"I don't know if I can convince Flora to stay behind," the earl replied to James's concern, their conversation

over drinks focused on the campaign against Ned
Storham. "Actually, I doubt I can."

"Adam won't allow it at a certain point. I know him."

The earl smiled. "We'll have to see what happens, then,
for Flora is extremely stubborn once she's made up her
mind. I gave up directing her life long ago. And I confess
to a certain ambivalence. She's a very capable shot to have
on your side."

While James understood that the Absarokee culture allowed female participation in warfare under certain circumstances, he felt Adam would personally forbid Flora to
accompany them on such a dangerous mission. Wishing
to exact revenge for his brother, Ned Storham was intent
on Adam's death—with the possession of Adam's land
enormous added incentive.

"What weapons did you bring along?" James asked, debating whether any might be of use to them.

"We've new Winchester rifles and Colt revolvers, also
several of my custom hunting rifles. They're sharp-
shooter's rifles with a distance of fifteen hundred yards. I
thought they might be of use on this expedition." He
knew that because of the Absarokee's modest force of warriors, they fought a guerrilla-style warfare, rarely utilizing
frontal attack in battle. They couldn't afford the high ca-
sualties.

"How proficient are Alan and Douglas with weapons?"
A strategist, James always considered all options.

"Both are excellent shots. Alan prides himself on not
unduly marring the coat of an animal specimen. He likes
to use a small bore rifle with a twenty-two round that kills
with a minimum of damage. Douglas is equally good.
Henry learned about firearms as a boy fighting off the
customs men in his native Cornwall. He never wastes a
shot. But Flora's most skilled. I think Adam's already seen
her shoot."

James had too, that day at the ranch. Her marksman-
ship was impressive. She sighted-in swiftly, handled the
pump action on her weapon with fluid skill, and fired a
startling number of rounds in a few seconds. "She's going

to be a soul mate to Adam, no doubt," James remarked. "But surely she has to consider her pregnancy."

"I tried to caution her; I'm sure Adam did too, but I'm afraid she disagrees. She wants to help protect Adam so their child and Lucie won't be deprived of a father." The earl shrugged, a negligent dismissal of James's growing scowl. "I'm here to support her in whatever decision she makes." He smiled at his dinner partner. "It's been my role for a very long time."

At that moment Adam was lounging on the bed, gazing at Flora, who lay beside him, her face marred by a frown. "Darling, you know how much I love you," he gently said, "but you really can't come along. This isn't a gentlemanly game of war with rules and etiquette and prisoner exchange for ransom. This isn't a lady's game, and don't scowl at me like that. I realize you can do most anything I can do. I know you can shoot as well as any man, probably better than most, but if I take you with me, I'll be spending all my time worrying about you and the baby. I can't afford the distraction, darling. You'll be in the goddamned way."

"You think you're right, don't you?" she grudgingly said.

He exhaled in frustration because they'd been arguing for some time. "I know I'm right," he firmly declared. "I've been going on war parties since I was fifteen, and part of the reason for the success of my medicine, or whatever you want to call that special spirit that carries one to victory, is the fact that I'm totally focused, with *no* distractions. Lucie understands; maybe it requires a simple faith like hers. She realizes I'll always come back to her. But I need to know that whatever decision I make in battle won't be compromised by doubt or apprehension or caution. In combat you're operating on pure energy, which vitalizes your mind and your limbs and the source of your strength. Let me go and take care of Ned Storham without having to wonder if one of his hired thugs is going to put a bullet through your beautiful head. Please, darling," he softly whispered.

"I don't want to say yes," Flora reluctantly acknowledged. "But if I do," she went on, understanding her presence could be an actual danger to him, "what will you do for me?"

"I'll be back very soon," he promised, relieved she'd finally relented. "Wait for me here, if you wish. It's closer to Virginia City."

"Is Ned in Virginia City?"

"Last we heard," he evasively said. "We were going to leave this afternoon, but since you arrived, it won't hurt to postpone our departure until morning." They'd be cutting the time close, but it wasn't an impossible ride. "Let's go downstairs for dinner tonight," he coaxed, gently brushing the curve of her bottom lip. "Do you know we've never eaten dinner in the dining room? Let me show you off. Did you bring a gown"—he smiled—"or will we have to brush off your trousers?"

"Now am I supposed to be gracious and appeased?" she murmured.

"I'd really appreciate your cooperation, *bia*." His grin reminded her of the boy beneath the man. "Am I being suitably humble?"

"I have a gown," she said in succinct answer. "Will I be rewarded for this benevolent understanding?"

"Perhaps something from Tiffany's."

"I'm not Isolde."

"Something more personal, then." His smile held seductive promise.

"How clever of you."

"A kiss?" he playfully suggested.

"It's a start," Flora murmured, reaching over to slip her fingers through the heavy silk of his hair and tugging his head close.

A heated interval later Flora said, "That's the third occasion you've checked the time. Am I keeping you from a pressing engagement?"

Six-thirty, Adam noted, before turning his full attention on Flora. Leaning over, he kissed her rosy cheek. "I was planning on meeting James to look at a thoroughbred Daniel McGillvray has for sale," he lied. "But James can go alone." It didn't look as though he could comfortably leave to check on Isolde's departure. But his men and James could manage without him.

"Why don't you go? I have to wash my hair if we're dressing for dinner. It'll take some time to dry. Is McGill-vray's far?"

"No, just up the hill." A small wave of relief washed over him. He preferred seeing for himself that Isolde left. "I'll be back in half an hour," he said. "You're sure you don't mind?"

Flora smiled up at him. "I'm sure." She indolently stretched, then glanced at the clock. "I probably won't even have my bathwater by the time you're back."

So that evening while the Fisks were viewing the setting sun from a vantage point on the hills west of town, and the servants were enjoying their leisure after having been given the night off, two men entered the Fisk mansion and surprised the Comtesse de Chastellux as she was writing a note in the library. Quickly gagging her and binding her hands and feet, they carried her out of the silent house and carefully placed her in the coach parked outside the kitchen door.

"You're dressed for travel, I see," Adam said, appearing at the open door of the carriage with Isolde's note in his hand. Gazing in on his trussed wife attired in a riding habit, he said, "How convenient that you were on your way out. However, I'll tell Ned when I see him that you changed your mind about marrying him. A shame, because I'm sure you would have killed him in a much more brutal way than I could contemplate." Shrugging, he pocketed her note. "Unfortunately, I can't wait to find out. I'm pressed for time. Good-bye, Isolde, it's been a hellish five years." Closing the coach door on the hatred in her eyes, he locked it and handed the key to one of his men, who would accompany the driver to the railhead.

"Will she stay away?" James quietly inquired as they watched the carriage roll down the hill.

"Probably not," Adam bluntly said, "but once the annulment is finalized, I don't care."

"Are we ready for Ned Storham now? Stopping him should be slightly more bloody than the disposal of Isolde."

"That depends on how much loyalty his money will buy. My guess is, not an enormous amount. But we'll find out very soon."

As it turned out, Adam and Flora went downstairs very late, because Adam returned in time to join Flora in her bath and then, dressing for dinner, took another amorous interval; so before they stepped from their room, it was almost ten o'clock.

James and the earl joined them from the bar where they'd retired after their dinner, and the foursome spent an agreeable evening together. No one brought up the controversial subject of Flora's participation; conversation was devoted to less contentious topics.

And much later that night, as they lay in each other's arms, Adam murmured, "I didn't know you could love so totally. I love you in bed like this with your body close to mine or at dinner in public among crowds and throngs like tonight—all with the same deep passion."

"We're very lucky," Flora softly said. "I didn't even believe in love—passion perhaps, but not love. Do you know how close I came to avoiding the party at Judge Parkman's?"

Adam smiled. "I knew I was obliged to make an appearance, but my intention was to offer my congratulations and leave as soon as possible."

Flora grinned. "And then I seduced you."

"I'll be forever grateful, *bia*," he gently said. "You've given me my life back."

.   .   .

Adam slipped away that night after Flora fell asleep, wanting to avoid any added arguments in the morning, wanting to find Ned Storham and crush him. He'd never felt such ruthless intent even after years of warfare and raiding, his urge to destroy the man who threatened his newfound life a pitiless resolve, an all-devouring quest.

"Let's get this over with," he curtly said to James as they met that morning, as if Ned Storham's head were the bloody price for peace.

They rode south through the gray shadows of predawn, forty of them mounted on their war ponies like lethal weapons of destruction, honed by years of training, urged on by the need to protect their country, their families, their future.

When Flora woke at first light, she dressed quickly in riding clothes and went to wake her father. He was seated at a table set for breakfast in his room, booted and spurred, reading the paper.

"I've been expecting you," he said with a smile. "There's weak tea here for you and some dry toast. You overslept."

"Adam's unbelievably stealthy. I wouldn't want him to be out to murder me in the night. And the baby makes me sleep more." She smiled as she sat down opposite him and reached for the teapot. "You look as though you're ready to go somewhere."

"Just waiting for you to make your appearance. I assumed you were planning on a ride south when you didn't mention the pursuit of Ned Storham last night at dinner. Didn't want to openly lie to Adam, did you?" he added with a grin, and folding the paper away, he lifted a silver cover from a plate of ham.

"So perceptive, Papa," Flora replied, her smile half-hidden behind the rim of her cup.

"How many years have I been watching you get your way, darling?" he inquired, placing a slice of ham on his plate. "And I must admit—from a safe distance of course, for you do have a baby to consider now—it would be interesting to avail ourselves of a bit of target practice on those hired gunmen. I don't suppose you want any of this," he added, placing the cover back on the serving platter.

"Not unless you relish my throwing up ham. I'll take some along for lunch, though. By that time I'll be ready to eat anything and everything."

"I had the hotel pack us some food," her father casually said, spooning some scrambled eggs onto his plate. "Are you going to be all right?" he sympathetically queried, looking at her pained expression.

"Put the cover back on those eggs if you don't mind, Papa. There. I'm fine now. The smell . . . it's too early." Settling back in her chair, she sipped on her heavily sweetened tea.

"They left at four," her father declared, cutting his ham.

"A little over an hour ago," Flora noted, glancing at the clock. "Are the others ready?"

Her father nodded as he chewed on his food.

"So I'm the only one holding up our departure."

Swallowing, the earl said, "They're not that far ahead, and the Absarokee take care not to tire their mounts when they anticipate a long ride.[17] Take your time with your tea."

Alan, Douglas, and Henry were waiting at the livery stable with the horses saddled, the packs in place, the weapons all in prime condition. They'd protected Lady Flora in scores of remote corners of the world, and by contrast, Montana Territory was considerably less dangerous.

Additionally, each man was an adventurer at heart, or he would have spent his life in more conventional pursuits and locales. In truth, a certain joie de vivre was in evidence that morning.

"If you need your jacket, I tied it behind your saddle," Henry said, helping Flora mount. "Your Tanser rifle is in your front gun case, the Winchester's in back, the Colt is slipped smooth as silk into this holster," he went on, indicating the tooled leather sheath to the right of her pommel. "There's a canteen of water right here," he added, patting an engraved steel flask. He sounded like a nanny taking care of his child, although the directions were for more lethal concerns. But he'd attended to Flora's well-being for so many years, neither saw anything strange in the instructions.

Flora smiled her thanks and proceeded to check all her weapons for ammunition, a rote procedure she'd learned very young.

"Do we know what this Storham fellow looks like?" Alan quietly asked, his tall, lanky form casually disposed in his saddle, his carrot-orange hair framing an elongated face with dark, intense eyes like a militant saint.

"Short, stocky, ruddy complexion, sandy hair, Mexican silver on his tack, and traveling with a renegade bunch," Douglas succinctly enumerated. A methodical personality, he was always prepared with background information. "He's not a particularly fast draw, I hear. He relies on his hired guns and ambush."

"We don't want to get close enough to see his ruddy complexion," the earl significantly noted. "We're along only to help, not contribute to the assault force."

"We're along to see that my child and Lucie have a father," Flora softly declared. "And we'll do whatever we have to do to assure that end."

The men exchanged swift glances.

The earl had been quite clear in his directives last night: Adam Serre was to survive this campaign. Not, however, at the risk of his daughter's life.

Flora's fearless courage seemed in sharp contrast to her demure appearance that morning. In a tucked white linen blouse and black riding pants with her hair pulled back in a thick braid and small pearl earrings dangling from her ears, she had the look of a modest young lady.

"Don't worry, Lady Flora," Henry replied. "The count won't be needing much help with those warriors riding at his side, but we're more than ready to lend our assistance."

Chapter Twenty-six

❧

They picked up Adam's trail southeast of town, fresh signs indicating a large party riding fast.

"They must have word of Ned Storham's whereabouts," the earl said as he remounted his horse. "The war party's traveling out in the open in daylight, not concerned with concealing their route. If Ned was close, they wouldn't be exposing themselves."

"Will we overtake them?" Flora asked, her concern obvious.

"They're moving at a swifter pace than I thought, but we won't be far behind."

The telegram Adam had received in Helena from his men who were following Ned Storham had not only noted his direction but the strength of his party.

Fifty men hired to hunt down Indians would be a mixed lot, Adam knew. Their expertise with weapons, their courage, their motivation beyond money, would all be at issue when an actual engagement occurred.

Whereas his men, trained to a warrior's life, were determined to protect their country. Additionally, they were well armed, in contrast to the common Indian dilemma of inadequate weapons and ammunition. Everyone carried a large supply of cartridges.

The odds were slightly more even this time.

They were riding for the bluffs east of the big bend of the Elk River, where they'd wait for Ned Storham's troop in a strong defensive position.

The morning was fine, warm and sunny with no hint of autumn in the air. Summer was lingering on the best hunting ranges on the northern plains, on the land his people had fought to defend against strong enemies since dim memory, Adam thought, gazing over the lush prairie rolling away to the south, the hazy blue of distant mountains rimming the horizon on either side. Ned Storham had no claim on this beautiful country, no right to invade it. Today they would take their stand against him and with Ah-badt-dadt-deah's help, they would strike him down.

That night their scouts came in with reports that Ned had reached Fort Ellis late in the afternoon with his troop of fifty, and two wagons carrying supplies. The men were camped within the walls of the fort.

New scouts were sent out to observe the progress of the advance the following day. The troop should be approaching their position by early afternoon. In council that night Adam and his men went over the details of their battle plan, assigning positions to their defenses, discussing alternative options should Ned's attack begin to outflank them, trying to anticipate any contingency in the coming assault. And after considerable discussion, satisfied they'd considered all possibilities, they all wrapped themselves in their robes and slept. Tomorrow would be a violent day of reckoning, a bloody day to count coup.[18]

An order from Governor Smith only recently arrived at Fort Ellis turned out to be of great service to Ned Storham's mission. Since regular army troops were finally being sent into the territory, the governor had ordered his militiamen to muster out. In the official order the governor sent the volunteers the "heartfelt thanks and gratitude of the people of Montana."

When the order was read, the disgruntled troops felt

that something more tangible than "heartfelt thanks" was
due them. They'd been promised Indian booty, and during the summer campaign no profitable plunder had ever
materialized. During the course of the evening, over several five-gallon kegs of whiskey, Ned was able to capitalize
on their displeasure. He offered the men who'd just lost
their new six-month contracts an opportunity for better
wages than the territorial government allowed, as well as
the lucrative prospect of real Indian plunder. The Absarokee bands in Aspen Valley were prosperous, with large
herds of horses, and Ned Storham promised the militiamen all the loot they could find.

At midmorning Adam's scouts galloped into camp, their
horses lathered, their news alarming. Ned Storham had
crossed Willow Creek with two hundred armed men.

Everyone worked furiously, throwing up stronger defenses, adding height to their breastworks, digging in,
moving some of the horses back into a small canyon for
protection. There was no point in falling back to a better
position, for no other defensive point existed between the
bluffs and Aspen Valley. And there wasn't enough time to
send for help.

Additional scouts were sent out to gather information
on the movements of Ned's troop. And then they readied
themselves for battle, stripping down to moccasins and
leggings, painting themselves for war, calling on their
medicine and spirits to aid them against their enemies.
Weapons were loaded, cartridge belts strapped on, sheath
knives adjusted, ponies accoutred with battle tack—rifle
scabbards, pistol mounts. And then they waited.

The small army came into view over a distant rise early
in the afternoon, riding in two columns, the sun glinting
off their weapons, the sound of men's voices distinct in
the open country. As they came closer, Adam's men
sighted-in their rifles, fingers ready on the trigger, calmly
holding their fire until the front ranks had passed and the
middle of the first column was within range. Ned didn't
ride as a leader would at the front of his men; he was well

protected at the rear. But they couldn't wait until the entire column had passed, and at Adam's command forty
rifles exploded in a deadly volley, white, acrid smoke and
flame bursting from the breastworks, the Winchester
lever-action five-shot pouring a withering fire into the
columns. Men toppled from their saddles, horse after
horse went down, and the column disintegrated in a con-
fused melee as the troops bolted for cover, falling back to
the protection of the two wagons that had stopped halfway down the slope.

At the pandemonium and turmoil the Absarokee warriors sprang onto their war ponies and took the offensive,
charging down the bluff, their war cry screaming into the
blue sky, their rifles cracking. With Adam in the lead, they
rode through the troopers and plunging horses, shooting,
striking the enemy down with their war clubs, slaughter-
ing dozens more as they ripped through the scattered
withdrawal. Then, wheeling and lashing their ponies, they
turned and swept back over the battleground to pick up
their wounded.

Dust from the horses' hooves and gunpowder swirled in
clouds, bullets cut the air, struck the ground, glanced off
to whine away as the warriors galloped back to pull their
injured up behind them. Dead, dying, wounded troopers
lay on the ground, slain and injured horses littered the
grassy plain, the squeals of the animals, the cries and
moans of the men rising through the dust into the sun-
filled sky.

The first assault was over.

After saving their wounded the Absarokee dashed back
to their defenses on the bluff to assess the damage, the
strength remaining to their enemy, to themselves. Only
four of their warriors had been wounded, none seriously
—a favorable portent to men whose medicine was their
very life. And settling in behind their breastworks, they
directed an unwavering rifle fire at the troopers barricaded behind the wagons.

No one had recognized Ned in the tumult. Was he still
alive? Had he fled? Who was directing the defense? But

when a fresh assault surged from behind the wagons and raced over the bloody field to press forward up the bluff, it was clear he was still in charge. No one with any experience in battle would have attacked the well-fortified position without superior inducement.

Deadly fire rained down on the luckless force, and more dead and mortally wounded sprawled at the base of the grassy bluff as the assault floundered and then collapsed.

As the afternoon wore on, with the Absarokee sharpshooters picking off any man who occasionally raised his head, concern rose that Ned might have sent back to Fort Ellis for reinforcements. Everything seemed too quiet, unearthly and hushed under the warm sun.

"I say they're waiting for reinforcements," Adam said, lightly stroking the knife handle at his waist.

"Or for dark, so they can retreat," James commented.

"Only to come back some other way, some other time," Adam said with disgust, gazing over their breastworks at the battlefield below.

"But if Storham didn't send for reinforcements," James added, "we *could* circle around them in the dark and finish them off."

"We can't wait that long. By that time they could have emptied out Fort Ellis and be here with another army." Restless against the inactivity, wanting to accelerate the conflict and put a final end to Ned Storham's intrusion into his life, Adam said, "I'm riding down to draw them out."

Although an act of extraordinary daring and bravery, such exploits weren't uncommon among the tribes of the northern plains, where individual courage and counting coup were the path to a chieftain's position. Adam had been a chief at twenty, and from his youth his medicine had been strong. Nothing could harm him.

For war parties warriors donned only light shirts and leggings, with all bright colors hidden away. But they carried dress clothing in parfleche boxes for their victorious return into their village. Taking his brightly ornamented clothing from his rawhide box, Adam adorned himself in full regalia: fringed and beaded shirt ornamented with ermine tails and scalp hair; beaded leggings with wolf tails at his heels; a bear-claw necklace; two eagle feathers tied in his hair, although had he been vain, he could have worn one for each of his many coups.[19]

Taking out his beaded mirror case, he added some ocher paint to his face, checked to see that his medicine bundle was tightly tied to a small lock of hair braided behind his left ear, and after talking quietly to his war pony, who would be carrying him past his enemies, he mounted. Sliding his Winchester out of its scabbard, he rode out from behind the breastworks and cantered down to the open plain below, riding straight at the barricaded wagons until he was within easy rifle range.

Then he turned his horse, raised his rifle high as if defying his enemies to harm him, and rode past their defenses through a rain of bullets, his beautiful beaded clothing sparkling in the sun, the eagle feathers streaming out behind him, his pony light-footed and swift over the grassy plain—untouched, protected by his medicine.

He heard Ned's screaming orders for his men to fire, he heard the rifle reports and whine of bullets around him, the cries of Ned's men who'd made themselves targets for the Absarokee, rising in anguish above the chaotic uproar. Then shots rang out from the bluffs behind the troopers, a frenzied round of firing, rapid-fire repeaters, and his mind distinguished the new, distinct sound amid the din of rifle fire.

Wheeling his mount, he galloped past the wagons again, his dark hair flowing in the wind, the leather fringe and ermine tails on his sleeves swinging, the blue figure on his shield mocking target to his enemies. As if he were a ghostly specter, no bullet touched him, and racing back up the hill, his war pony soared over the breastworks, coming to a plunging stop with faultless precision.

Springing from his pony, Adam dropped down between Standing Lance and James and, gazing at the bluffs behind the wagons, said, "Where are those repeaters?"

James pointed to the rise south of Ned's defenses where a steady firing was demolishing the troopers' exposed flank. "To the left . . . halfway up that bluff. They're picking off the troopers like flies."

"Damn her," Adam said, squinting into the sun. "She came." But he was smiling.

"I'd say Flora brought along a little help, too, from the sounds of those rifles. Look at what's left of Ned's hired guns. They're in a panic."

The shots were brutally on target, Ned's men completely unprotected from the south. As the deadly fire poured down, Adam unconsciously counted the rounds, the trenchant whine of bullets reechoing through the valley. At fifty he stripped off his beaded shirt and said with a faint smile, "Are we ready to mount up and finish this off?"

By the time the Absarokee came pouring down the hill short moments later, the troopers were in full retreat, fleeing from the lethal fire, streaming east toward the safety of Fort Ellis. Leading his men in pursuit, Adam paused a second at the wagons to survey the carnage, looking for Ned Storham. A quick glance at the dead and dying sufficed for him to realize his enemy still survived, and, quirting his pony into a gallop, Adam rode after the man whose rapacious greed had precipitated all the bloodshed.

He had forty miles before Fort Ellis to overtake Ned and kill him. Automatically glancing up at the sun, he gauged the time. Four more hours until dark. Raising his arm in salute to Flora, he pounded east.

Flora watched from the heights as the Absarokee scattered across the plains in full pursuit and Adam, galloping west, whipped his pony to more speed.

The late-afternoon sun bathed the plains in a golden glow, an idyllic, gilded landscape—radiant, lovely, deceptive tinsel over a bloody battlefield.

Then her hand went to her mouth in terror as she saw the head and shoulders of a man slowly rise from a coulee ahead of Adam, his rifle barrel sighting-in on his target. "Adam!" she screamed in warning. "Adam!"

Adam didn't hear her distant cry, but he caught the glint of the rifle barrel from the corner of his eye a fraction of a second before the weapon fired. Pressing his pony sharply left in an attempt to avoid the shot, Adam felt his horse stagger, slide, then fall as the bullet struck its chest. He hit the ground hard and rolled, bullets kicking up dirt around him. Diving for cover behind his dead pony, he flattened himself into the ground and reached for his Navy Colt. When he'd hit the ground, he'd lost his rifle, so whoever was shooting at him would have to come closer—within handgun range.

He lay perfectly still, waiting.

Flora was in the saddle a flashing moment after she saw Adam go down; the reins to her father's horse slipped through her fingers a second later, and before any of her party could stop her, she was spurring her mount down toward the valley below.

Swearing, the earl scrambled to follow his foolhardy daughter, vaulting onto the nearest mount. Henry's bay curvetted at the sudden strange weight on its back, and George Bonham swore again as he struggled to bring the animal under control. Precious seconds were lost before he followed Flora down the steep slope, Alan and Douglas close behind him.

Adam saw her coming, a small, boyish figure in trousers, her dark copper hair gleaming in the afternoon sun, wind-tossed with her braid coming loose, her long tresses whipping behind her as she rode full out down the hill, brave as any warrior. He smiled at her fearless courage, offered a swift prayer to his spirits to protect her, and then leaped up to draw the fire of his assailant before Flora came into range of the rifle leveled at him.

"No-o-o-o!" she screamed, the terror-stricken sound reaching him as he raced toward the coulee, his knife in one hand, his Colt revolver in the other.

Ned rose out of the coulee, his bulk outlined against the

blue sky, his sights aimed at Adam, his smile wicked with triumph as he pulled the trigger.

Adam stumbled as a .44 round tore into his shoulder, half fell to his knees as his brain absorbed the shocking impact of the corrosive pain. Catching himself with his knife hand before he dropped fully to the ground, he forced himself upright again, enduring the staggering agony with clenched teeth, commanding his legs to move by sheer force of will. Another few yards and he'd have Ned within pistol range. Under optimum conditions, even from this distance, standing utterly still with his hand steadied, he could pick his entry point, but since that option wasn't available, he needed to advance another dozen yards before he could fire. "I am an Absarokee," he silently murmured. "I have the heart of a grizzly. I am an Absarokee." The litany of his adolescence resonated through his brain, clearing his mind, calming him as his moccasined feet flew over the ground. He could see Ned's cruel smile now. Ten more yards. Eight.

And then the second bullet hit him.

He couldn't see out of his left eye when he aimed his Colt, blood suddenly obscuring his vision, so he swiftly adjusted for the discrepancy, aiming slightly more to the left, and emptied his pistol into Ned Storham's smiling face.

Sinking to his knees in languid slow motion, he waited for Ned to drop.

He did, falling out of sight into the coulee.

Flora reached Adam's side moments after he crumpled to the ground, and barely conscious, he warned her, "Go . . . Ned . . . you have to get . . . away." His voice trailed off, no more than a wisp of sound on the vast, open prairie. His eyelids drifted downward and he sank into darkness.

Flora had no thought for danger or Ned Storham as she knelt over Adam's body; she was only thankful Adam still lived. With a discerning gaze she scanned his bloodstained form. How dangerous were his wounds, how deep or le-

thal? Had any arteries been severed? His shoulder looked
as though an animal had torn it with its teeth, the flesh
mangled and ripped, blood covering his torso, his leggings
discolored where the red liquid seeped under his waistband. His head wound looked worse; the entire left side of
his head and face were smeared with rivers of crimson, his
hair soaked from the seepage.

Bending over, she placed her ear on his chest and,
breath held, waited to hear a heartbeat. A terror-stricken
moment passed before the faint sound reached her ear,
and despite his imperiled position from the devastating
wounds, she smiled.

His heartbeat was steady.

Nothing else mattered.

At her father's arrival minutes later, she looked up.
"Adam's alive. Find Ned Storham," she quickly said.
"He's wounded or dead." Clear-headed, succinct, concerned with protecting Adam from further harm, she
pointed to the coulee. "Over there."

Leaping from the saddle, her father ran toward the rim
of the coulee, with Alan and Douglas in his wake. Ripping
through Henry's saddlebags, Flora found the basic first-
aid kit Henry always carried, and taking some bandages
out, she tried to stanch the flow of blood from Adam's
wounds.

She would be scrupulous in the care of his wounds so
they didn't become infected, she promised in silent en-
treaty, as if some spirit might gauge her vigilance before
determining Adam's future. She'd see that he ate and slept
and did nothing strenuous, she pledged. She'd try to be
more humble and go to church, she added for the Chris-
tian gods, who rewarded humbleness and church attendance. She promised offerings to the spirits to propitiate
the Absarokee gods. And she'd take care not to overstep
any mystical boundaries, she compliantly affirmed, recalling the story of a Lakota chief who'd died in battle because he'd accepted food from an iron object and angered
his spirits.

Just let him live, she silently pleaded. His stillness was

frightening, the awesome power of his body suspended, as if his life lay in the balance. "I'll do anything," she whispered as she knelt over his inert form, the blood seeping through the bandage pressed to his shoulder wound, ominous in its unceasing flow.

She wanted to hold back the fluid draining his life away, she wanted to restore the mangled flesh and have him whole again. She wanted Ned Storham to pay for his unholy greed, her hatred so powerful in her grief that even if he was already dead, she wanted to kill him again.

It would always be like this, she unhappily thought as she knelt beside the man she loved, their forms minuscule on the rolling expanse of prairie. In a state where newspaper headlines screamed *Wipe Out the Indians*, Adam would continually be defending his land and his people. And she'd always be wondering if the next bullet was going to take him from her.

But please, God, not this time, she prayed, her tears falling onto the widening stain of blood on the cloth under her hand.

"Cryin' a whole damned river ain't gonna help him."

She knew who it was from the sneer in his voice, and leaping up, she lunged for the pistol in her saddle holster.

"Gonna get yerself killed," Ned said, cocking the hammer on his pistol, his hand steady as he leveled at her. "Now, just step away from that dead Injun real slow and move over here."

Sensible of the threat to Adam, she obeyed his raspy command, moving several feet away from Adam's sprawled body. Standing where he was, Ned was too distant to see Adam's faint breathing, Flora gratefully reflected, but she'd prefer he not come closer. "You're being tracked," she said, hoping to pressure him into leaving. "Three men are on your trail."

"Nice try," he said, his smile grotesque in his bloody face. "But they're way down the coulee followin' Bud Holt." He waved his revolver. "Move over here now."

She debated, trying to distract him with conversation until her father returned. He was wounded too, although she couldn't gauge the extent of his injuries. But since she had no way of knowing when her father would reappear, she couldn't take the chance Adam would move or make some sound, so she complied.

"Now we're gonna walk over to those two horses there," he carefully said as she approached, "and take us a little ride. Reckon I might need myself a hostage to get me back to Fort Ellis in one piece."

Three fingers of his left hand had been shot off, she noticed as she drew near, and she decided she'd try to ride on his off side if possible. The small .22 single-shot derringer in her trouser pocket could kill him at close range. She found herself remarkably calm, her mind busy with logistics, obsessed with getting Ned Storham away from Adam.

The man was wounded; she had a weapon.

It was forty miles to Fort Ellis, and he needed her.

Adam grew aware of the shining white light first; then he heard the voices. The light held a welcoming warmth, the distant voices triggered essential memory, and his mind struggled to connect the image and sounds. Incapable yet of sustaining thought, his brain synapses shut down, and he drifted back into the comforting oblivion of darkness.

Until two words registered on the membrane of his collective memory and dragged him back into the light.

Aspen Valley.

With Ned Storham's voice pronouncing the words.

As if an enfilade of doors opened in his brain, he suddenly knew where he was, what had happened. That his enemy still lived.

When the familiar sound of Flora's voice echoed in his ears, all his faculties came to attention, blind necessity pressing every sluggish nerve and afflicted sinew into readiness. Mentally he checked his capacity for movement as he lay on the ground, and, barring excruciating pain at the slightest pressure, his limbs seemed willing. Next he estimated their positions from their voices: south and slightly west, with Flora closer. How far? It took effort to refine and clarify detail, and he found his mind wanting to slip away. Regrouping his consciousness, he began again. How far, dammit? And miraculously the answer fell into place. Two horse lengths. He almost smiled.

"Mount up now, and slowly," Ned ordered. He'd removed the weapons from Flora's horse, and with his revolver trained on her, he held the reins of her bay with the remaining fingers of his injured hand as she slipped her foot into the stirrup.

At that point she could have swung up, whipped the horse, and probably escaped, and if Adam's life weren't at stake, she would have taken the risk. As it was, she carefully slid onto the saddle and calmly waited as Ned Storham heaved his bulk onto the horse. Not daring to glance at Adam for fear she'd draw attention to him, she tensely waited, every second seeming to stretch endlessly.

She was advantageously positioned on Ned's off side, her father was sure to follow her, she had her derringer, and Adam would be safe.

Or at least he would be the minute they rode away.

Surveying the scene from under his lashes, the sight in his left eye blurred, Adam saw that Ned would pass within a few yards of him. A distinct danger if he chose to finalize his kill with a few more shots into the corpse—a common enough practice after a battle, when the victors often walked the field murdering the wounded where they lay. He had to be ready to move at precisely the right time.

Not too early so Ned had a clear shot, but not too late either, or he'd be unable to save Flora. With his strength so badly diminished, he'd have only one chance to take Ned Storham down.

Riding beside Ned, her reins tied to his saddle pommel, Flora couldn't see where Adam lay, but as they approached the area, she deliberately said, "You don't look as if you're going to make the long ride to Fort Ellis."

Turning his head toward her and away from Adam's position, Ned growled, "You might be the one who don't make it unless you close yer trap."

Another few feet, Adam thought, estimating the pace of the horses and the distance.

"We'll see," Flora coolly replied. "You're bleeding pretty badly." He couldn't shoot her yet, she knew. Not until he'd eluded the Absarokee.

Now. Calling on his last reserves of strength, Adam lunged to his feet. Ned's horse broke stride at Adam's sudden movement, and half turning, Ned caught his first glimpse of danger.

Compelling his body to move, his teeth clenched against the agonizing torment, Adam closed the distance in two great strides. Jerking his bowie knife from its sheath with his good right hand, he reached up and plunged it into Ned Storham's body.

Ned held on for a moment as if he were nailed to the saddle, and then Flora struck his damaged left hand with all her strength, and, shrieking in agony, he tumbled from his horse.

His weight struck Adam's ravaged left shoulder as he fell, and Adam lurched, then rolled away in reflex action, the intensity of the pain incredible. He clung to consciousness with sheer determination, panting like a wounded animal, his ears ringing, white light flashing before his eyes.

Reaching for her reins and those of Ned's horse, Flora turned the mounts, and then, jumping down from her saddle, she lashed them off so she'd have a clear field of fire. Spinning back, she slid her hand into her trouser pocket to extract her small derringer.

She had one shot.

One chance to kill Ned Storham.

Ned was up on his knees, his left arm limp at his side, the revolver in his right hand unsteady but shifting toward Adam, where he lay sprawled on the prairie sod, the left side of his face smeared red from his wound, his painted torso streaked with blood, the bullet hole in his shoulder pouring scarlet rivulets onto the grass.

Flora raised the small handgun, stabilized her wrist on her left hand, and sighted-in on Ned's head.

"You're dead now, Serre . . . ," Ned panted, steadying his gun on his target.

"Say . . . hello to . . . Frank," Adam gasped, pushing himself into a seated position with his knife hand, sweat beading his forehead as waves of pain washed over him.

"You'll see him before I will, Injun." Ned's finger tightened on the trigger.

With his last ounce of strength Adam swung his right arm over his head and whipped his knife through the air.

The bowie knife had a ten-inch blade, so it had to be thrown with delicate precision in order to slide sideways between the second and third ribs directly into the heart.

Ned Storham died instantly.

Chapter Twenty-seven

Adam regained consciousness that night on the high banks above the Elk River as the travois he was lying on passed under the shadow of Sentinel Rock. The moon was hidden for a time behind the soaring sandstone peak, but the stars were brilliant in the sky, like perfect diamonds, and when he turned his head to gaze at the moon as it reappeared from behind the craggy outline of the landmark pinnacle, he saw Flora walking beside his litter.

He smiled. "I could smell your perfume, and I knew I was alive."

"Just barely, thanks to your damned notions of chivalry." She knew why he'd charged Ned Storham without a rifle, and her mood had fluctuated wildly between anger and relief in the hours since Ned's death.

"I heal fast."

"So you've been stupid before," she grumbled.

"I recall one night in particular," he said with a grin, "when I took a lady into Judge Parkman's carriage house."

"At least you weren't going to get shot," she muttered.

"I wasn't absolutely sure."

She smiled. "You're incorrigible."

"And damned lucky to have you for backup." He put out his hand. "Touch me so I know this is real. That you're really here. The sky's so beautiful it could be a dream."

Her small hand slipped inside his, and they felt the same mystical connection that had first joined them long months ago in Virginia City.

"I shouldn't have ridden into Storham's rifle range," Flora softly said. "You can say I told you so." He'd warned her about the danger of her presence.

"It was very brave of you to come to my aid, *bia*. You were a warrior. And one never knows in battle precisely how to react. I still don't."

"You have to show me."

"Maybe we'll have some peace now instead," he diplomatically replied. "I prefer raising horses."

"I can help you there."

"And I can help you interpret our Absarokee culture for your museums in Europe. Partners?"

"I'd like that," she murmured.

A sense of well-being enveloped them, as if they could accomplish anything together, as if they could see beyond the vision of ordinary men, as if the moon were shining for them alone tonight.

"You shouldn't be walking," Adam said. "Let me have someone get a horse for you."

"We're moving so slowly, I feel fine. And I throw up only in the morning. Besides, Spring Lily said exercise is good for the baby."

"She probably didn't have in mind the strenuous kind you just experienced," he dryly said. "If she's going to be your authority, I'm going to have to talk to her."

"She won't listen to you. Men don't know anything about babies, she says."

"This one's definitely going to learn," Adam said, gently squeezing her fingers. "I don't want to be left out—"

"—this time?"

"If you don't mind," he gently said. "The thought of you having my baby . . ." He paused to steady his voice, his ravaged body, his senses, suddenly overwrought—the image of Ned Storham within seconds of taking his life vivid in his mind, the bitter memories of Isolde's pregnancy painfully recalled. "I'm overwhelmed," he whispered. "And very happy."

"I know," Flora gently replied, her own happiness of equal measure. "This is the baby I was told I couldn't have."

"Ah-badt-dadt-deah gave it to us."

"You gave it to me," she whispered. There wasn't a minute of the day she didn't joyously think of the baby growing inside her. "A brother or sister for Lucie."

"Can I tell her?" His eyes sparkled in the moonlight like an excited boy.

"Knowing Lucie, she's probably already overheard a dozen conversations on the subject, but yes, do tell her. Tell everyone, tell the world."

"Is Lady Flora mildly excited?" he teased.

"It's a miracle, darling, or at least according to the learned physicians of the world it is, so not only am I duly impressed with your virility, I'm ecstatic."

"As soon as I can move without crying, I'll see what I can do about adding to your definition of ecstasy," he said.

"Don't you even dare think of moving for weeks. Do you know how close you came to bleeding to death? And if Henry hadn't dug that bullet out of your shoulder, you would have eventually died of infection. You are absolutely not to move for a very long time."

"Yes, dear." He had no intention of waiting for weeks. But his smile was accommodating, and when he said, "Whatever you say," she should have been warned at such contrition from Adam Serre.

They stayed at Four Chiefs's camp while Adam's wounds healed. Since Absarokee culture allowed a warrior more than one wife, shortly after their arrival Adam and Flora married, the simple ceremony witnessed by the entire village and celebrated with two days of feasting and dancing. On their honeymoon night Flora had first resisted when

Adam insisted on performing his conjugal duties. But he was very persuasive, and before long he overcame her demur and his pain in a sweet oblivion of mutual delight.

At the end of two weeks Adam became increasingly restless as a patient, his tolerance and meekness of limited duration. One morning at the end of September, after he'd brooded over breakfast, after Lucie had run off to play with her friends, he stiffly rose from his seat near the fire where he'd been moodily watching the flames and said, "We're going back to Aspen Valley today."

"You shouldn't ride yet," Flora protested. "It's too long a trip." She turned back to him from her task of arranging the bed. "You're still having headaches. You can hardly move without pain in your shoulder. No, I won't go."

"You're going." He was glaring at her.

"I don't take orders," she tartly said.

"Fine. Lucie and I will go. Come later. Oh, hell," he said with a deep sigh. "I'm sorry, but I can't sit still another day. I've done everything expected of me—eaten nourishing food, taken my medicine, rested until I'm soft as a woman. But I'm going crazy. I haven't seen my horses for weeks, or the ranch. Please come. We can travel in short stages if you like. I just want to go home."

He said the last word with such longing, Flora understood how obliging he'd been, how eager he was to see his valley again. "If you promise to go slowly."

He smiled, lighthearted, consoled. "Anything you want."

"I want to grow old with you, not see you succumb to your wounds."

"We'll take a week. Is that slow enough?" He'd not negotiated over personal issues since his father had died, his authority over his life supreme. That he deferred indicated the great magnitude of his love.

They compromised on five days, their journey a leisurely progress through an autumn landscape of great beauty. The cottonwoods and aspen had turned to shimmering gold, the kinnikinnick was blaze-red, and the air was so crisp and clear they could see for miles. Since the earl and his party had stayed in camp to continue their work, it was the first time they'd been completely alone, just their small family. When they rode through the mountain pass that opened into Aspen Valley and stopped their horses at the crest of the ascent to gaze down at the lush valley, Adam reached over to take Flora's hand in his. "Welcome home, Mrs. Serre," he softly said.

"Thank you, Mr. Serre." An overwhelming sense of possession, and a sweet sense of belonging, inundated her soul when she pronounced his name.

"How come you have drips in your eyes?" Lucie inquired with charming bluntness, leaning over to gaze at Flora from her pony on the opposite side of Adam's mount.

"Because I'm happy," Flora quietly said.

"Spring Lily said you might be crying a whole lot more now that you're going to have a baby. Is it because you're happy about the baby? I want a boy, you know, because he won't want to play with Baby DeeDee. Baby DeeDee wants a boy too." She spoke with the utter candor of very young children, certain her wishes were of utmost importance in the world.

"We can't be certain the baby will be a boy. Ah-badt-dadt-deah will decide," Adam said.

"I hope he decides on a boy," Lucie emphatically declared, adjusting DeeDee in her arms. "Don't you wish he will too, DeeDee?" she asked, listened a moment, and then said, "She's going to pray to Ah-badt-dadt-deah."

"Do you feel the pressure?" Adam murmured as Flora tried to keep from smiling at Lucie's candid preference.

"If it's a girl, we could name her Archibald."

"I'm not certain that will be satisfactory to Baby DeeDee. Maybe you should think of only masculine pursuits the next few months in an effort to make this work out properly."

"We could always have a boy next time."

His brows rose. "That's an idea."

"I thought you might approve."

" 'Approve' isn't exactly the word that comes to mind at the moment," he roguishly said.

"Something more seductive?"

"Definitely."

"Why don't I meet you in your bedroom in an hour or so?"

"*Our* bedroom," he corrected, "and why so long?"

"Because your staff will want to welcome you home, and Lucie will need your attention."

"Greeting the staff isn't that lengthy a procedure, darling," he replied, "and once Lucie sees Cloudy, we'll be of minor importance. Let's say our bedroom in twenty minutes."

"Two hundred dollars says an hour."

"You're on, you sweet, naive thing. Watch and learn." And nudging his sleek bay, he led the way down the trail.

Chapter Twenty-eight

❧❦❧

The staff was lined up on the drive when they reached the front door, and after Lucie jumped from her pony, ran to greet Cloudy with a big hug, and immediately disappeared with her into the house, Adam whispered, "You're about to lose two hundred dollars." As he lifted Flora from the saddle, Mrs. O'Brien immediately launched into a highly charged recital of Isolde's visit to the ranch.

Adam politely stopped her after several moments when she paused to take a breath by asking, "How many wagons did Isolde take when she left?"

"Ten, sir. We couldn't stop her. Well, short of shooting her, which Montoya said wouldn't please you, but I wasn't so sure—sorry, sir, but you know how she is . . . screaming at everyone and as rude as a mule skinner with a half-dozen bottles of whiskey in him, and, well, come in and see for yourself, sir. There's nothing left."

A short time later when Mrs. O'Brien had been soothed and the staff dismissed with thanks and appreciation for taking care of the ranch in his absence, Adam and Flora stood hand in hand on the threshold of his looted home. Surveying the large, empty foyer, the sitting room and reception room, to the left and right of the entrance hall, similarly devoid of furniture, Adam softly whistled in astonishment. "She even took the drapes. I thought Isolde hated them," he murmured, then added, "Maybe she didn't want you to have them."

"Drapes?" Flora said with a casual disregard, noticing the bare windows for the first time.

"You mean we're not going to have a decorator out here before you can draw an easy breath? And the shape of the bathtub won't cause you any sleepless nights?"

Flora smiled up at him. "Well, it might if I'm lucky."

Adam laughed and drew her close, so their bodies touched and she could smell the sweet sage from the prairie in his hair. "Perhaps we should take a look at it now." His dark eyes promised her pleasure.

"What a perfect host."

"Western hospitality," he murmured.

"I've heard of that. How long do you think this hospitality might last?"

His grin was pure seduction. "As long as you want. . . ."

Epilogue

~≈≋≋≈~

Much to Baby DeeDee's delight, a son was born to Adam and Flora in May, an event of great and momentous joy. And two years later another baby boy joined the family. By the time their daughter entered the world, Lucie was eight years old and past the self-interest of her four-year-old world. She'd been longing for a sister.

The Comte de Chastellux took his growing family on numerous travels over the years to please his wife's interest in anthropology, and in so doing, please himself.

James became Uncle James when he fell in love with Spring Lily and gave up the array of beautiful women who had serially infatuated him. It was a surprise to all when their simple friendship suddenly changed.

And the young children of the two men who had always been the best of friends grew up together in Aspen Valley, a large and raucous crew of mixed-blood children, bright, beautiful, wild, and unconditionally loved by their parents.

That wild spirit was nurtured by their families, tempered by the responsibilities of their lives, briefly constrained by the curriculum of eastern colleges, and eventually channeled into challenging careers in the new state growing up around them.

There were nine of them, four Serres and five Du Gards.

They called themselves Ravens-Who-Touch-The-Sky.

More conventional souls, resistant to the charm of their brash assurance or hostile to their wealth and power, called them less poetic names.

Notes

1. The word "Absarokee" is spelled a variety of ways in historical and contemporary sources. Robert Lowie (1905), Frank Linderman (1930), Glendolin Wagner and William Allen (1933), and Joseph Medicine Crow (1992) use the spelling "Absarokee." Since Lowie was the most thorough in his research and compiled extensive word lists in addition to his anthropological work, I adopted his spelling.

Variations found in other sources:

Rudolph Kurz (1851): Absaroka
Edwin Thompson Denig (1856): Ap sar roo kai
Edward Curtis (1909): Absaroke
William Wildschut and John Ewers (1918): Apsaruke
Rodney Frey (1950): Apsaalooke

2. In 1833–34, Alexander Philipp Maximilian, Prince of Wied-Neuwied, traveled from St. Louis up the Missouri River as far as Fort McKenzie (near present-day Great Falls, Montana).

As a student of Professor Johann Friedreich Blumenbach at Göttingen, Maximilian learned that rationalistic empiricism was the philosophical foundation for natural history and the study of man. Maximilian was especially interested in American Indians because his mentor, a leading Enlightenment theorist on the development of the human races, believed in the biological equality of all people. Blumenbach taught his students that climate, habitat, diet, and the means of human subsistence within a locale affect the development of races and cultures. In concentrating on the relationship between humans and nature, Blumenbach demanded close observation and the collection of plant and animal specimens and cultural artifacts.

Also essential to the anthropology of Blumenbach and Maximilian was visual documentation of peoples and their natural habitat, and it was in this context that Swiss artist Karl Bodmer contributed so much to Maximilian's expedition. The fervent belief of Blumenbach and his contemporaries in painstaking empiricism demanded that field-workers and collectors have great skill in observation and description.

For Blumenbach and the Göttingen "school" of explorers, discrete fact was the bedrock of science. In his work Maximilian came to see, to learn, and to record, and he labored to preserve as much as possible of the time and place in his journals.

Maximilian's manuscript journels, *Travels in the Interior of North America*, are in the collection of the Joslyn Art Museum in Omaha, Nebraska, and first editions of his work were published in German, French, and English between 1839 and 1843.

3. Edwin Thompson Denig, a fur trader at Fort Union for twenty-three years, left an account of the five Indian tribes of the upper Missouri. His broad experience among the Indians and his objective point of view enabled him to write about their cultures with concern and respect. In his work he estimates the Absarokee population in 1833 as 6,400. Smallpox devastated many of the Indian tribes in 1837, so only 360 Absarokee lodges were left after the illness, or approximately 2,480 people. By 1856 the population, according to his estimates, had reached 460 lodges or 3,680 people.

Indian agent Vaughan's estimate of population in 1856 is 450 lodges (3,600)—very close to Denig's total. In 1871 when the Absarokee were on the reservation for part of the year, Agent F. D. Pease's report listed 2,700 Mountain Crow and 1,400 River Crow. ("Crow" was the designation given to the Absarokee by the outside world.)

In relation to the large Lakota, Blackfoot, and Cheyenne tribes that surrounded their territory, the Absarokee were very small in numbers.

4. In July 1866 the Northwest Peace Commission met both the Mountain and River Absarokee on a steamer at Fort Union. The commission sought rights of passage to the Montana and Idaho mines, and establishment of posts by the army within the Indians' territory as bases of operations against the hostiles.

The treaty granted rights to roads, highways, and telegraph lines up the valley of the Yellowstone River to Virginia City and Helena, as well as the privilege of establishing depots and military and stage stations at suitable points of ten square miles each along the roads. The government agreed to expend for the Absarokee Nation the sum of twenty-five thousand dollars annually for twenty years, with two hundred dollars annually to each head chief.

Granting right of way for roads was a means of solidifying relations with Washington at a time when the Lakota were pressing hard on the eastern boundaries of Absarokee territory.

The treaty was never ratified—not an unusual circumstance once treaties reached Washington.

5. Like members of every society, the Absarokee had their own system of terms to denote kinship, and the importance of clan affiliations accounts for the extended range of close familial names.

Since clan membership was matrilineal, Adam would refer to a male cousin on his mother's side by the same term he used for a brother. The term would also be used in speaking to any of his mother's brothers. In the case of James Du Gard, referred to as "brother" when he was in fact a cousin, that term denoted a male cousin of maternal lineage. A male cousin on the paternal side would be referred to as "father."

6. In the myths, folktales, and religion of the Absarokee the Little People are supernatural dwarfs generally of a benevolent nature. They may bestow favors on mortals they pity, confer bounties in their own right, grant extraordinary powers, or opportunely rescue those in distress. They're sometimes called Little Helpers, and the nooks of the universe harbor these kindly beings.

7. In this instance it was perfectly acceptable for Adam to marry his sister-in-law, Spring Lily. In fact, if a brother (the clan designation for a true brother or a male maternal cousin or uncle) was killed, the widow often married her brother-in-law. It was necessary that the family be protected and supported. Adam politely chooses not to marry Spring Lily, but not because of cultural taboos. And as Spring Lily mentions, he's already taken on the responsibility of caring for her family.

8. As a young man, Thomas Meagher was active in the Irish political movements working toward separation from England. With the revolutions of 1848 sweeping Europe, England became increasingly concerned with the Irish factions advocating independence. In July 1848 Parliament passed the Suspension of the Habeas Corpus Act, which gave broad powers to the lord lieutenant of Ireland to apprehend and detain anyone he suspected of conspiring against queen and government.

On July 28, 1848, Meagher, along with several other men, was arrested.

Packing the jury was a common practice at the time, and when Meagher came to trial, he pleaded not guilty and then noted that in a Catholic county of a Catholic country, it was curious that only eighteen Catholics had been selected on a panel of three hundred jurors.

He was found guilty and on October 23, 1848, was sentenced to be hanged, beheaded, drawn, and quartered. As the son of a wealthy Irish merchant, Meagher's plight was immediately appealed. Two appeals were denied, but the death sentence was commuted to banishment for life to Van Dieman's land (Tasmania).

Three years later, after arranging an escape for six hundred pounds (about three thousand dollars), a considerable sum in 1852, Meagher arrived in New York and was welcomed as a hero by the large, active Irish-American organizations.

9. Having been informed that General Sherman was sending twenty-five hundred guns up the Missouri River from St. Louis, General Thomas Meagher gathered up a half dozen of his officers and made the long, hot trip from Virginia City to Fort Benton. His party arrived in Fort Benton on July 1.

It had been an unpleasant trip from Virginia City. For the previous six days the excessive heat had made traveling hard, and before the group had reached its destination, Meagher was ill. As he rode, tired and weak, down the main street along the riverbank, he overheard one of the bystanders say, "There he goes."

Ordinarily this apparently harmless remark would have gone unnoticed, but the rigors of the past few days had made Meagher worn and nervous. Since he had a number of sworn enemies in the territory, he interpreted the words as a threat.

The horsemen pulled up before Baker's store and dismounted. General Meagher retired to the back room, where the sympathetic storekeeper offered him the only therapeutic aid at hand—blackberry wine.

Johnny Doran, the pilot of the steamer *G. A. Thompson*, a fellow countryman from Ireland, invited Meagher to spend the night in one of the steamer's state rooms. That evening Meagher told his host that his life was threatened in town and asked for a gun. Nervous, Meagher asked Doran to stay with him, but Doran insisted there was no cause for worry.

Later that night a sentry pacing the deck of the *Thompson* heard a noise at the vessel's stern. Glancing in that direction, he saw a white figure moving about. He dismissed the matter, thinking it was one of the ship's officers preparing to retire. But as he wheeled about to resume his guard duty, a loud splash indicated a man overboard.

The night was black, and that time of year the Missouri was brim-full and swift. Meagher's body was never found.

10. The authority on chocolate seems to be Brillat-Savarin. His *The Physiology of Taste*, a wonderful kind of memoir/treatise comprising thirty years of research, wisdom, and good taste, and self-published shortly before his death in 1826, is the gastronomic classic against which all subsequent works are measured.

In reference to ambered chocolate he says: "If a man has drunk a little too deeply from the cup of physical pleasure; if he has spent too much time at his desk that should have been spent asleep; if his fine spirits have temporarily become dulled; if he finds the air too damp, the minutes too slow and the atmosphere too heavy to withstand; if he is obsessed by a fixed idea which bars him from any freedom of thought; if he is any of these poor creatures, we say, let him be given a good pint of amber-flavored chocolate, in the proportions of 60–72 grains of amber to a pound, and marvels will be performed." A modern translator of Brillat-Savarin points out to those unfamiliar with the additive, the amber should be ambergris from the sperm whale, not yellow amber. And an apothecaries' grain weight is 0.002083 ounce, or 0.0648 gram.

Apropos Russian chocolate: make a heavy syrup of bitter chocolate, sugar, and vanilla, cool it, and then blend it with its weight in rich whipped cream. Gobbets of this dark, thick sauce are then put in heated cups and hot milk poured over it from a silver pot.

11. The cost of the five-month campaign, in which the number of militiamen ranged from 80 to 250 for most of those months, totaled 1.1 million dollars. When the bill was sent to Congress, it was so excessive, no appropriation was approved. Protests from Montana flooded Washington, and finally, in 1870, Inspector General James A. Hardie was sent to Montana to determine the manner in which the money had been spent and to adjust the claims.

The inspector general discovered that claims from $200 to $220 had been put in for horses, many of which were unbroken Indian ponies. He allowed $80 per head on the 848 horses the militia had purchased. Wood had been purchased for $16 to $20 a cord when it was available for $6.25 to $7.50; $45 to $65 per ton had been paid for hay, which normally sold for $30 to $35 per ton. In one instance he discovered that Colonel James Fiske of the Volunteers had asked a livery stable keeper in Helena for some vouchers, which were signed, but on which no amount had been specified. He explained that these were to reimburse him for some money he had expended personally. Fiske then filled in the vouchers for a sum of $25,000 and sold them around Helena.

Supplies of all conceivable types were purchased. These included four dozen bunches of red tape at $1.50 per dozen, as well as alcohol and bourbon whiskey at $10 a gallon.

By May 1872 Hardie reported that $513,000 would extinguish all just claims. So an Indian war that never materialized, despite the efforts of the troops to produce it, cost the federal government a half million dollars.

12. In deference to the rich, who often brought their families and servants to the Spa for the entire summer, hotels as early as the 1820's allotted some of their space to cottage suites or actual cottages. Over the years their seclusion had made them so popular, the large hotels

eventually offered what they called apartment suites, which offered cottage privacy with the solicitude and service of an elegant hotel.

Each elaborate suite contained a large parlor, one to seven bedrooms, and a private bath. Visitors were announced by card, carriages were brought directly to the door, and if desired, breakfast, lunch, or dinner was delivered to the occupants in their suite or on the apartment's porch.

Each summer brought to Saratoga wealthy bachelors, and family men whose wives and children were vacationing in Europe, who wished female company after a day at the races or gaming at the club. Prior to the existence of the cottage suites, a difficult dilemma had existed, for the rich sporting bloods disdained the local brothels, and the village fathers resisted attempts to introduce the luxurious bordellos the wealthy men preferred.

Concern that these affluent men might abandon the Spa and transfer their free spending to a more hospitable resort required a discreet relaxing of the rules of propriety. Although the hotels kept their lobbies clear of light-skirt ladies on the prowl and refused to register guests who gave the barest hint of not being wed, if a guest was rich enough, such rules were overlooked.

On one occasion a wealthy Texan who had accumulated several million dollars and was known to spend it freely, followed the famous dandy Berry Wall and his manservant to the front-desk register of one of the prominent hotels. He studied the entry that preceded his—"Wall and valet" —looked at the pretty bit of baggage he'd brought with him, and wrote "McCarty and valise." Both he and his companion were admitted.

By tacit agreement the cottages were free of restrictions and surveillance by the hotel detectives, who guarded the entrance and piazzas against ladies of easy virtue plying their trade. The cottages were off by themselves, and the price of a cottage suite (as much as $125 a day) gave assurances that the guests who rented them were important enough not to antagonize.

Some rich indoor sportsmen found the arrangment so much to their liking that they stocked the larger suites with a variety of young and beautiful nieces, while younger bloods turned up with a bevy of stunning cousins. An oil millionaire was so swamped in business deals that he installed five pretty secretaries in his cottage apartment to help him handle all his work.

No one was fooled by these fictions, but the money spent by these wealthy men was too attractive to turn away.

13. After the revolution in France, in 1792 the legislative assembly laid down rules for marriage as a purely civil contract. Divorce was admitted to a practically unlimited extent; it was possible not only for causes determined by law and by mutual consent, but also for incompatibility of temper and character proved, by either husband or wife, to be of persistent nature.

The Code Napoleon of 1804 maintained the revolutionary principles pertaining to divorce.

In 1816, after the restoration of the monarchy, a new law abolished divorce, making marriage indissoluble, as it had been prior to the revolution.

On July 27, 1884, divorce was reestablished by law but permitted only for certain definite causes. On April 20, 1886, the law was simplified, although divorce by consent was still not permitted.

14. When George Crum shared culinary duties with his sister-in-law Catherine Weeks (Aunt Kate) at Cary Moon's Lake House, it was said he could take any edible and transform it into a dish fit for a king. And the eager customers who responded to the call for supper, which Aunt Kate blew on a fish horn, rarely disputed it.

The few who did complain and returned their orders to the kitchen were rewarded with the most indigestible substitute George could contrive. He enjoyed watching their reaction.

In 1853, the first season the Lake House was open, a

dissatisfied diner was the impetus for its temperamental chef to create unwittingly a delicacy of enduring flavor and international fame.

Dissatisfied with his french-fried potatoes, the guest sent them back to Crum with instructions to fry them longer and slice them thinner. Crum received the request with typical hostility. He sliced some potatoes into paper-thin shavings, bundled them in a napkin, and dropped them into a tub of ice water. Half an hour later he dumped the chilled slices into a kettle of boiling grease. When they were fried to curly crisps, he took them out, salted them, and sent them to the complainer's table, then peered into the dining room to watch the effect.

To his astonishment, the diner was delighted and asked for more. Other customers ordered the crisp potato wafers and found them just as tasty.

The next day Crum's potato chips, called Saratoga Chips by the Lake House's tourist-conscious proprietor, were on every table in the restaurant. A few years later they were listed on menus throughout the country.

15. The incident with the regiment at Samarkand is true, but I have taken literary license with the date. The actual event happened in the cholera epidemic of 1892–93, although there were also worldwide epidemics of cholera in 1848–49, 1853–54, and 1865–66.

At the same time the disease was striking the Russian army at Samarkand, a devastating outbreak occurred at Askabad. The cholera had almost disappeared in the area when a banquet was given by the governor in honor of the czar's name day. Of the guests one-half died within twenty-four hours; a military band, which was present, lost forty men out of fifty; and one regiment lost half its men and nine officers. Within forty-eight hours thirteen hundred persons died out of a total population of about thirteen thousand.

The water supply came from a small stream, and just before the banquet a heavy rainstorm had occurred, which swept into the stream all surface refuse from an infected village higher up and some distance from the banks.

16. With the discovery of gold, great wealth in negotiable material attracted many unsavory characters to Montana, and robbery and murder were prevalent.

The Vigilantes organized on December 23, 1863, to put an end to these outlaw elements. There was an executive committee consisting of Paris Pfouts, James Williams, and Wilbur F. Sanders. The remainder of the forty-five men who signed the original Vigilante Oath were organized into teams, each headed by a captain. During the winter of 1863, these groups ranged the mountain country from Virginia City to Fort Owen searching out the road agents. One of the early captives had confessed and given the names of his gang members.

By the spring of 1864, thirty-two men had been hanged. Many of the Vigilantes went on to become leaders in territorial and state affairs, and hanging as a means of swift vengeance (not necessarily justice, in many cases) continued through the nineteenth century.

17. Plenty-Coups relates a story to Frank Linderman about a pursuit of stolen horses. Blackfeet had stolen some Absarokee horses in the days after the tribes were on the reservation.

Where Park City now stands, we came to a few houses, and the white men who lived in them told us the Pecunies, or somebody, had taken most of their horses too. We talked to them as best we could with signs and a little English, and at last four white men who had lost good horses wanted to go along with us to get their stolen property. I believed them able to take care of themselves and agreed, which was one of the most foolish things I ever did.

They began to show me this soon after we started. Their horses had been eating hay and oats in a house, while ours had been pawing snow for grass in the windy hills. Naturally their horses could travel faster than ours, but because the trail was likely to be a long one, I tried to hold the white men back, telling them to save their animals for the trouble ahead. They would not listen but rode on, while we walked, until their animals grew tired. Then the white men camped. When I passed them by their fire, they wished me to stay with them, but I told them the Pecunies would not camp and that if we expected to catch them, we must keep going. I explained to them, as best I could, that the thieves were driving nearly one hundred horses and would be unable to go so far in a day as we could, if we kept at it. This did no good. They said their horses were tired out, and of course they were, having been ridden all day in the deep snow. So I left them, wishing with all my heart that I had not sent four of my men back to the Crow village when these white men joined me to go after the Pecunies.

They caught up with us late the next afternoon and at once began to talk about camping and eating, but this time I pretended not to hear them at all. I kept pushing on with my three men.

Then he goes on to relate how in the middle of the night he came upon the Pecunies and hurried back to tell the white men to stay where they were. He would try to steal the Pecunies' guns before they attacked them.

But I could not hold my white friends. They were unmanageable, and got on their horses to charge the camp in that dim light.

I ran ahead, waving them back, but they followed on horseback and began to yell. Yes, I am telling you the truth; they began to yell, and I dodged behind a boulder, leaving them out there sitting on their horses and yelping like coyotes.

They did not shout long. The Pecunies were not fools. I soon saw rifles poking over the rim rock. Down went a white man with a bullet over his eyes.

"Go back!" I called, making the sign. But my words did no good. There they sat on their horses, wearing too many clothes and looking foolish, until another tumbled off his horse with a ball in his forehead. This time the two others moved a little.

Eventually Plenty-Coups and his men killed two of the Pecunies, and the others withdrew, leaving the stolen horses.

18. Two Leggings's memoirs list the four important coups in this order: "Most praiseworthy was the striking of an enemy with a gun, bow, or riding quirt; then came the cutting of an enemy's horse from a tipi door; next the recovery of an enemy's weapon in battle; and finally the riding down of an enemy."

According to Lowie's interviews there were four types of deeds that were generally recognized as meritorious and counted for the title of chief: "the carrying of the pipe," that is, the leadership of a successful war party; the striking of coup (riding up to an enemy and striking him); the taking of an enemy's gun or bow; and the cutting of a horse picketed in the enemy's camp. The order is slightly different from Two Leggings's.

A chief was a man who had at least one deed of each type to his credit.

19. In Lowie's interview Yellow-Brow describes the way clothing could depict various types of coup.

The taking of guns from an enemy was symbolized by wearing a shirt decorated with ermine skins. Leggings fringed with such skins or with scalps denoted that the wearer had led an expedition that returned with booty. The striking of coups was indicated by wolf tails at the heels of moccasins.

Two Leggings's description of specific insignia denoting coups honors further adds to the explanation.

The winner of all four types of coup could decorate his deerskin war shirt with four beaded or porcupine-quill strips, one running from shoulder to wrist on each sleeve and one over each shoulder from front to back. Merely earning the first coup enabled a man to trail a coyote tail from one moccasin, or from both if he performed the feat twice. Eagle feathers tied to a man's gun or coup-display stick revealed the number of scalps he had taken. A knotted rope hanging from his horse's neck told of the cutting of an enemy's picketed mount. And the number of horses captured could be read from the stripes of white clay painted under his horse's eyes or on its flanks. From a white clay hand on those flanks one learned that the owner had ridden down an enemy.

Dear Reader,

Like so many of my stories, the initial idea for Pure Sin came to me from a visual image flashing through my mind. I saw a man and a woman standing very close; the atmosphere was palpably sensual. But eventually the man moved slightly away and softly said, "No."

In writing Pure Sin I wanted to explore a variation on the seduction theme—in this case a man being seduced against his better judgment. The choreography of desire intrigued me, and ultimately, of course, it intrigued Adam Serre too.

My heroine, Flora, was inspired by any number of spirited, highly independent female travelers who've left accounts of their journeys around the world. So many wondrously brave women have explored cultures and environments far beyond the boundaries of their normal lives, I recommend reading on the subject. It makes some of our modern lives seem very tame.

Robert Lowie, who spent many years researching the Absarokee people, is the single best source on their culture. But Frank Linderman's oral-history accounts have a wonderful first-hand immediacy as well as a poignant recall of a better, lost time.

I hope Adam and Flora's story has given you pleasure.

Best wishes,

Susan Johnson

P.S. I enjoy hearing from readers.
    13499 400th Street
    North Branch, MN 55056

About the Author

Susan Johnson, award-wining author of nationally bestselling novels, lives in the country near North Branch, Minnesota. A former art historian, she considers the life of a writer the best of all possible worlds.

Researching her novels takes her to past and distant places, and bringing characters to life allows her imagination full rein, while the creative process offers occasional fascinating glimpses into the complicated machinery of the mind.

But perhaps most important . . . writing stories is fun.

The magnificent Braddock dynasty
from the national bestsellers BLAZE
and SILVER FLAME returns in
Susan Johnson's latest spectacular
historical romance.

BRAZEN

Available now from
Bantam Books.